In America, the economy has collapsed. There are mobs in the streets, smoke in the air, and martial law over the nation. Congress hurriedly votes the president extraordinary emergency powers. But President Donnelly is a broken man; he resigns, leaving the office to a vice president selected for him by the chairman of the Joint Chiefs of Staff.

Until Arne Haugen, only one United States president had exercised dictatorial powers: Abraham Lincoln, a great role model. But this is another age, and Haugen a different man.

Besides, Lincoln had been *elected,* while Haugen has been *selected.* The difference could be deadly in the land of the free.

JOHN DALMAS

THE GENERAL'S PRESIDENT

BAEN BOOKS

THE GENERAL'S PRESIDENT

A Baen Books Original

Baen Publishing Enterprises
260 Fifth Avenue
New York, N.Y. 10001

First printing, February 1988

ISBN: 0-671-65384-9

Cover art by Alan Gutierrez

Printed in the United States of America

Distributed by
SIMON & SCHUSTER
1230 Avenue of the Americas
New York, N.Y. 10020

Dedicated to:

WILLIAM BAILIE

U.S. Navy (retired),
devourer of books,
glutton for learning.

ACKNOWLEDGEMENTS

I want to thank the following:

BILL BAILIE for his interest, his comments, and the long-term loan of numerous books, articles and maps on matters military, geographic, geopolitical, and geologic—information sources I found enormously helpful.

JIM BAEN, who, after reading the first draft of early chapters, made a criticism of central importance in developing subsequent chapters and drafts.

EVERETT KYTONEN, for important reference works and for his encouragement when this book was only a concept.

Father JAMES CONNOR and Father RICHARD JUZIX, for helping this non-Catholic keep his fictional priest realistic, and in general for their interest and friendship.

DR. RICHARD HUMPHREYS, M.D., for his advice on story matters medical.

THE REFERENCE PERSONNEL at the Spokane Main Library for their very frequent and unfailingly cheerful help, in person and over the phone. They are real professionals, and I love 'em!

And GAIL, who voluntarily read and commented on each draft, including the roughest, and who never once complained when the reference books overflowed my office to pile up on the kitchen table, occupying it for months and threatening to tip it over backward. I love her too.

Several others, specialists in different fields, critiqued pieces of this and made helpful suggestions and comments, but preferred not to be acknowledged in a book of which they had read only one or two chapters. They know who they are, and have had my personal thanks.

Numerous others provided specific information, most of them in reply to this stranger who called and asked questions over the phone. Their contributions are definitely appreciated.

Excerpt from The unanimous Declaration of the thirteen united States of America, *known as "The Declaration of Independence":*

We hold these truths to be self-evident, that all men are created equal, that they are endowed by their Creator with certain unalienable Rights, that among these are Life, Liberty and the pursuit of Happiness.— That to secure these rights, Governments are instituted among Men, deriving their just powers from the consent of the governed. . . .

Prudence, indeed, will dictate that Governments long established should not be changed for light and transient causes. . . . But when a long train of abuses and usurpations, pursuing invariably the same Object evinces a design to reduce them under absolute Despotism. . . .

Quotation from a letter by John Emerich Dalberg, Lord Acton, written in 1887.

Power tends to corrupt. Absolute power corrupts absolutely.

PROLOGUE

From: *Introduction to* A History of this Planet, *by Mentor Hsu Mei Chun, Ministry of Textbooks, 2034.*

This textbook, which begins with the Shang Dynasty, shows you how the people of the world have created our present reality. For people create reality, create it constantly and mostly unknowingly. This is indisputable.

It is easier to see in the case of a ruler. A ruler creates a broad reality, within which his subjects create their own realities. He creates to whom he will listen, whose advice he will heed, to whom he will give an order, who to praise and who to punish. He even helps to create what other rulers he will challenge, and who will replace him on the seat of government.

Now I just wrote that a ruler creates a broad reality, within which his subjects create their own realities. And it is true. But the subjects also create the ruler, and thus *they* create their entire political reality. This creation by a people of its ruler may not be so apparent to casual observation. But look! The Russian people had repeatedly been invaded and preyed upon by outsiders—Ostrogoths, Huns, Avars, Magyars, Varangians, Cumans, Mongols—until they dreaded foreigners. And in their xenophobia, they created czars who created a strong empire, large and costly to invade. And because the Russian people were disorganized and unruly, it was necessary that

1

they create czars who were domineering and often brutal.

In time, however, the czars were no longer effective enough or ruthless enough. In a word, the people's creations were no longer adequate to their need. Thus the people created an intelligentsia, which they then resented. And the hardest and most intelligent and domineering of this intelligentsia called himself Lenin, a man who had borrowed a socio-economic theory from a German named Karl Marx.

Lenin created a social and governmental system called Marxism-Leninism, with an army and a vast secret police to support it. And from this base, through a series of rulers, the Russians created an even larger empire, and a far greater military force, than any of their czars had done. And this government and army ground the Russian people harshly, which they were used to and which was according to their image of how the world should be.

Now let us consider our own people. Their progress through history has been quite different from that of the Russian people. They created rulers who less ruled them than fed off them. Many of those rulers ruled only enough to keep the people domesticated, so that taxing them would be less strenuous and uncertain than preying on some wild population. And by creating such rulers, our ancestors created national vulnerability as well, vulnerability of the whole nation to warlords and foreigners.

Until finally they tired of vulnerability and the abuse that accompanied it. But they were a people resistive to working together beyond the village level. So they too created a great ruler who was overbearing and hard—Mao Tse-tung. Chairman Mao borrowed Marxism-Leninism from the Russians. But because the Chinese people were different from the Russian, and had created a ruler who was unlike Lenin, and unlike Lenin's successor Stalin, the program and government fashioned by Mao Tse-tung was unlike Russia's. And the successors of Mao Tse-tung were unlike Stalin's successors, because the people created them so, and for a long time had been creating a different stage for them to rule on.

Now in another part of the world dwelt another people, the Americans. And they created themselves as a people from elements of many nations, because mankind's gradual creation of itself toward a space-faring socio-economic body called for such a nation in its evolution.

The Americans too were unruly. And because they had created a very different environment for themselves, one not unduly threatened by invasions, they undertook to create a governing system that allowed them unusual freedom to create their own individual realities. Which they did, in greater diversity than any other people. And they created a series of chiefs of government who did not rule but presided. For the American people did not wish a ruler.

But in conjunction with the other nations, the Americans, who were very powerful creators, gradually created a world which was dangerous to them. And being unruly, and lacking a ruler, they began to feel threatened. . . .

ONE

The burly old man flared his paddle, slowing the expensive kevlar canoe, then pointed. "I worked here one summer," he said.

The younger man, the bow paddler, turned and looked. On the east bank, autumn-bared ash and birch stood pale gray and chalk white, punctuated with dark, spire-like balsam fir and the bleached crumbling bones of blight-killed elm. Among them were the visible remains of an old logging camp, not large. Floors and wooden frames had decayed and disappeared, but he could see moldering floor sills, half covered by the remains of tarpaper nailed half a century past over rough board siding.

An older time, thought Father Stephen Joseph Flynn, S.J. A more careless, less complicated age. A time when the United States was energetic, optimistic, thought well of itself. At least that's what Father Flynn had heard and read. When his friend, Arne Eino Haugen, had worked here in the forest, he himself had not yet been born.

Smooth current took them past, and while Flynn looked back, Haugen did not—not physically. Inwardly perhaps, for he talked about it, smiling.

"During the war, Emile LeBeau and Emil Norrland built a tie mill here, and a camp. I got out of the army in the spring of '46 and went to work for them. There was a good market for sawn hardwood railroad ties, and we cut ash and elm for miles along the river. And any birch that were big enough. Floated them to the mill and held them inside a boom here." He chuckled. "There's hundreds of elm sinkers along the river bottom, unless they've rotted— logs that were too heavy and sank. And we cut all the

4

spruce and fir along the river, that were big enough to make anything—boards, pulp. The pine had been logged out back in the teens. My dad worked on that.

"We called the camp 'the Two Emils,' one French Canuck and one Swede. In the fall I quit to skid pulp for Wiiri Koskinen, and the next spring the mill burned down. So the two Emils went to Littlefork and got drunk, and never really sobered up till they'd gone through about everything they owned. Took them a month."

Haugen stopped talking, to paddle quietly, serenely. The canoe came then to a long rapids, and hurried through clear amber riffles.

"The loss hit them that hard, did it?" said Flynn. "The two Emils?"

"Not really. They just decided it was a good time for a big drunk. Part of logger tradition. Still is, but probably not as much. The days of logging camps are long gone; loggers live in town now, have families. Commute. When the market allows; when there's work. But they still drink a lot."

Perhaps that characterized the country today, thought Flynn. Unemployment and drink. Drink and drugs. Recessions and depressions had been scattered through the history of the country, but this one truly threatened to ruin it. *Or am I being cynical?* he asked himself. *Had they all seemed that way, in their own time?* They'd talked a bit about the new depression, he and Haugen. Haugen seemed to accept it with a degree of equanimity that bothered the Jesuit.

"What would you do," Flynn asked, "if you were president?"

Haugen snorted. "I'd resign. Especially if my name was Kevin J. Donnelly. Not that the collapse is actually his fault, though he may have speeded it up a bit. He's just getting the hog's share of the blame. And he did the obvious salvage actions: closed the stock exchanges, declared a moratorium on mortgages. I'd have done the same.

"What would you do, Steve?"

"First I'd pray for God's guidance and intervention. Then—apply a tourniquet the way Donnelly did. After that I'd give way to some more qualified person."

He'd looked back at Haugen when he'd answered. Haugen grinned. "I thought Jesuits were trained to handle problems like that. Or did that change when Europe stopped being ruled by kings?"

The priest wasn't sure whether Haugen had said it in jest or not. "Times have changed," Flynn answered, "for better and for worse. And Jesuits on the whole weren't involved in court politics. A few were, as the confessors and counselors of kings. Mostly, though, they were the educators of Europe, for generations. Including royalty at times."

Haugen nodded without saying more, and let his eyes roam the banks, the bottomland forest.

Donnelly's closure of the stock exchanges and his moratorium on mortgages had been the big news ten days ago, Flynn recalled, and wondered whether more good had resulted than mischief. The Jesuit had very little knowledge of things like stock markets. For him they were simply parts, presumably critical parts, of the monstrously complex socio-economic machine that western man had built, and now depended on to feed him in his thousands of millions. Mortgages he could understand. Stop mortgage foreclosures and you'd save people's homes. You'd also prevent banks from getting back money they'd loaned, and maybe break them. Too many had gone broke already, and millions of people who'd put their money in them had been wiped out.

To do what, go where, in these times of massive unemployment?

That one was beyond Flynn's ability even to speculate on, and mentally he paused, looking at an earlier thought. *Cynical? Of course I am, in my soul, my heart of hearts. Arne doesn't consider me so, but he doesn't know me as I know me. Cynicism more than anything else stands between the life of Stephen Joseph Flynn and that total compassion, that empathy incarnate, that was the life of Christ on Earth.*

A hiss from Haugen's lips drew him out of himself. *Here I am,* Flynn thought, *riding a forest river through scenic near-wilderness, and forgetting to look around.* His eyes followed Haugen's pointing arm to see a buck gazing at them from the river bank. Its flanks were gray, and it wore a considerable rack of antlers. As it watched them pass, only its head moved.

"Used to be a lot of them around here," Haugen was saying. "The harder winters the last thirty years have set them back. That and fewer fires to open up the timber and grow feed for them. Taking off the wolf bounty probably cut the deer down, too. Although I'm glad they did it. And the moose have made up for the deer decline; they've come back like gangbusters."

A moose, Father Flynn decided, was something he'd definitely like to see. To see a wolf seemed too much to hope for.

"Arne," he said, "why does the water look like this?"

"Like what?"

"It looks like tea."

Haugen chuckled. "It is tea. Tea made with sphagnum moss, leatherleaf, blueberries, and spruce and tamarack needles. It even has Labrador tea in it! The Bigfork drains miles and miles of muskeg swamp between here and Craig."

They rounded a bend, and Father Flynn could see a grassy field that came down to the river. The back end sloped to higher ground, where there was a log house with green asphalt shingles. Outbuildings stood near it, some of them also of logs. "That's it," Haugen said. "That was home for me till I was eighteen."

The old man dug deeply with the paddle, quickening the canoe diagonally toward shore. The Jesuit stroked too, till they were near, then took his paddle dripping from the river. He was not an accomplished paddler; it seemed best to let Haugen beach her by himself. A creosoted log extended down the bank into the river, and as they pulled up to it, he saw that it was anchored to steel fence posts driven deeply into bank and bottom. The older man thrust the canoe gently against the bank, and Father Flynn got out, rope in hand. Haugen followed, crouching, the light ease of his movements belying age and thick body. Taking the nose of the canoe, the old man pulled it well up on the bank, then removed the huge Duluth pack from it while Father Flynn tied the rope to a clump of brush, hoping it was the right thing to do. Growing up in Albany and serving always in cities, he was unsure of himself here,

although in black jeans and checked flannel shirt, he looked
somewhat like a local.

They followed a short steep path up through freeze-
dried grass and sweetclover to the meadow. On their feet,
they looked a mismatched pair, Haugen a bit less than
average height, the priest tall and angular, if a bit thick in
the waist. The meadow grass was waist deep on Haugen.

"Timothy," Haugen said, and for a moment Father Flynn
thought he was saying someone's name. Haugen's right
hand was brushing, almost caressing, the heads of the
grass as they hiked through it toward the log house. As if
sensing the other's confusion, Haugen added, "the grass.
Timothy hay. I rent the field to an old friend. No charge,
actually. He raises a crop of hay or oats every year. If hay,
he only takes one cutting. Leaves the second for the
wildlife.

"Farming it keeps the field from coming in to woods;
keeps it the way it used to be. He maintains the buildings,
too. The house and sauna, mainly, and the *hyysikkä*, the
privy. Every ten years or so, he gets the roofs fixed on
everything."

The log house had four square rooms on the ground
floor, plus a frame kitchen added on the back. Haugen led
through them, looking them over. Someone had been
there before them with broom and mop. And ax, for there
was split firewood beside the living room stove, which was
made of a thirty-gallon oil drum, and more in the big
woodbox near the kitchen range. The kitchen table was
covered with clean oilcloth, red and white-checked. The
only gesture toward modernity was a white refrigerator
powered by propane. Haugen opened it; it held a few
fresh groceries and a bottle of whiskey. In one of the
bedrooms, two single beds had been made up with crisp
sheets and woolen blankets.

What might be upstairs, Father Flynn did not expect to
see. Dust and cobwebs, he suspected. Actually there were
no stairs up, just a ladder spiked against a living room
wall, with a larger trapdoor at the top. Haugen followed
the priest's eyes, and gestured upward with a thumb. "We
boys used to sleep up there." He pointed to a grill in the
ceiling above the barrel stove. "That's all the heat we got;
not much at forty below. Or even twenty below, which we

had a lot of. The frost used to get an inch thick on the window frames, and we had so many covers on the bed, we had to wake up to turn over."

A fire had already been laid in the kitchen range, and Haugen lit it with a match from a box of big kitchen matches. Then he took a blue-enameled pail and they walked out together to the pump just behind the house. There was a private dirt road, somewhat graveled, and tracks that Father Flynn decided were of a pickup—driven by Haugen's friend who had so nicely set things up for them. Another pail, galvanized, sat by the pump, with water in it. Haugen poured a little in the top of the pump, then worked the handle, and in a few seconds a copious flow began to surge out the spout into the blue pail. When the pail was full, he left it there and led the way to the sauna, where he checked the stove reservoir for water, then fired the sauna stove with birchbark and dry wood.

"Swedish kerosene," he called the birchbark.

Before dark they'd eaten a supper of fried potatoes, bacon, eggs; and oven-toasted, buttered white bread strongly enriched with sugar, tasting almost like coffee cake. Afterward they used the sauna, lit by a kerosene lamp, then doused each other with icy water from the well. That done, they dressed, then took coffee, yellow and sweet, into the living room, and sat for a while.

"Is this the way it was when you were a boy?" Flynn asked after a period of silence.

"Nothing's the way it was when I was a boy." Haugen grinned, broad tan face creasing with it. "I'd hate to have to sleep now on the beds we used to have. And these chairs . . ." He patted the one he sat in. "The ones we used to have were homemade. Not bad, but not like these. And the fridge is new, of course. I never saw a refrigerator till I was in high school. Or used a telephone."

He sipped his coffee reminiscently. "We didn't even have a wagon road till I was two years old. The river was the road. It was the main road till I was eleven, when the CCC graded and graveled the wagon road and put culverts in—made an auto road out of it. The country got a lot of good out of those hard-times projects. And when we had a real road, Dad bought an old truck; I learned mechanics on that klunker. Every month or so the whole family'd go in to Littlefork to a movie; it cost a dime each. And we'd eat popcorn! We thought we really had it made."

Haugen laughed and shook his head. "That was a different world."

Father Flynn nodded soberly. That had been "the Great Depression." Now they were in another, in some ways worse.

"We were kind of crowded here," Haugen went on. "There were three of us boys that slept in the loft, and my sister slept in the living room. Mom and dad slept in that room"—he gestured—"and grandma in that one. We had a grandmother in the house till I was grown up and drafted. Sometimes we had two grandmas in the house. Grandma Salminen—we called her 'Mummo'—was with us all my childhood, and Grandma Haugen came to America when I was nine. She was 'Bestemor.' " He chuckled. "Neither one spoke English, and of course, Finnish and Norwegian are completely different. They lived in the same house together for years, sharing a bedroom, but they never had a conversation together. Each learned some words of the other's language and a few words of broken English, but not enough to really talk to each other."

"How did they get along?"

Haugen laughed. "Well, they didn't argue. Actually they were a lot alike. Both were old-country farm women, peasants, and both had a lot of patience. Except for cussedness. Neither had much patience with cussedness."

The two men talked for a while longer, then Haugen took a small, battery-powered alarm clock from the pack, set it, and they got ready for bed. The bedroom was not totally dark; there was faint starlight through the newly washed window. Father Flynn knelt silently beside his army-style bed for a few minutes, then got between the sheets.

"Steve," Haugen said after a minute, "I haven't prayed, actually prayed, since childhood. But while you were kneeling there, I was remembering. When Lois and I were younger, she used to drag me to church now and then. Lutheran. And we'd recite the creed. And there were things I used to wonder about."

Father Flynn lay silent, waiting. After a moment, Haugen continued, reciting from memory.

" 'I believe in God the Father Almighty, Maker of Heaven and Earth.' " He paused. "That part I had no problem with. Understanding it, I mean. But then it went on— 'And in Jesus Christ, his only Son our Lord, *Who was conceived by the Holy Ghost.*' That's where I started to have problems. What does it mean by the Holy Ghost?"

The priest paused only for a moment before answering. "The Holy Trinity," he said, "is important to our understanding of God. First of all, love is essential to God; it is basic to Him; and it's the basis of the Trinity. God the Father knows himself utterly, and his awareness—his image!—of himself is the Son. And the Holy Spirit is the bond of love between Father and Son."

The priest lay silent then, and after a moment, Haugen spoke again. "I once read somewhere in the New Testament where Jesus said 'Ye are all sons of God.' How does that fit in?"

"We are, in a sense, though originally not in the same sense as Jesus. But because Jesus came to us on Earth, he raised us all to his level."

After a few seconds, Haugen continued. "Then it goes on to say: He 'was crucified, dead, and buried. He descended into hell.' Now what was that about? Why did he descend into hell?"

"Well, first of all, hell is for those who are utterly ruined, utterly cut off from God and his redemption. Actually, as the story has it now, it was to purgatory that Jesus went, for three days. Purgatory is where souls go to be purified, souls not eligible for heaven but not beyond redemption. Jesus went there to gather the souls already there."

There was another moment of silence. The Jesuit was a little embarrassed. He always felt that way when trying to explain theological matters to a highly intelligent analytical mind that lacked the background. If you looked at these things superficially, they could sound foolish.

"All right," Haugen said next. "Then it goes on to say, 'I believe in the communion of saints.' What's the communion of saints?"

Father Flynn's voice was quiet, soft. "In this case, 'saints' means all undamned souls, living and dead, and all are in communion with one another. We have a solidarity with the dead and with each other, and they with us. All are one. The living support the dead and vice versa, and we all support each other. For example, the prayers of the living help the dead to rise from purgatory, and the prayers of the dead help the living."

"Hm-m. Interesting. Okay. And it ends up, 'the resurrection of the body; and the life everlasting.' I suppose I know what's meant by life everlasting, but how about the resurrection of the body? It seems to me that God would only need to think it to give you a new body. Why resurrect the old one?"

"It's not the old one he'll resurrect; not in the strict sense. When Jesus comes back, he'll create your body anew, but he'll do it with the material of your old body. It doesn't matter what's become of it. If you are saved, he'll recreate a perfect body for you from the material of the old.

"At the final judgment, Saint Thomas tells us, the world will be recreated. And if you've been good, your body will be recreated in perfection. If you were evil, on the other hand, it will be recreated in corruption."

He paused, then went on. "But a current notion is that you *ensoul* your body. Your soul creates your body and your body creates your soul. And when you die, you ensoul the universe."

He waited then. Haugen asked no further questions. "What do you think of all this?" the priest asked finally. "It's quite a meal for one sitting."

"I don't think of it," Haugen said. "Not now. I'm just letting it percolate. But I'll tell you again, I'm an unlikely candidate for the Church. Even the Lutheran Church." He chuckled, then sobered. "But if there ever was a good time to pray, this feels like it."

Nothing more was said then, and Haugen's breathing quickly took the slow and measured cadence of sleep. Father Flynn lay awake for a bit though, thinking. The year AD 2000 was getting near, the year some claimed would bring the final judgment of man, complete with scourges, plagues, and Armageddon. Times were hard; unemployment was forty percent, and poverty was becoming the mode. More than two million AIDS cases had surfaced, and no one knew how many were latent. The cold war still was cold, but the potential was there for disaster, perhaps holocaust. There'd been a resurgence of religion; his own Church, the Protestant churches, all were finding their pews more and more full, while the apocalyptic sects were doubling and redoubling their membership.

A hooting outside took his attention from his thoughts. An owl; he hadn't heard one since boys' camp twenty-five years earlier. He listened, waiting for it to repeat, until images began drifting across the screen of his consciousness, and shortly became dreams.

Morning dawned with white frost on the grass and a pane of ice on the pail outdoors. Haugen fixed a robust breakfast, and after they'd eaten, took a small shortwave radio from the pack and verified their pickup. Then they walked back to the canoe and set off down the river again. A couple of hours later, Father Flynn could see a steel bridge ahead, and farm fields by the river. Near one end of the bridge, on the road shoulder, a pickup truck was parked. A man stood fishing from the bridge, and when he saw them, waved, then walked with his tackle to the truck. Tall and long-armed, gray-shocked, he was waiting at the water's edge when they got there.

"Hello, Haugen, you old sonofabitch," he said, and the two old men pumped hands vigorously. "*Åssen går de'*?"

Haugen laughed. "*Å, de' henger og slenger.*" He paused, half turning to the priest. "Vern, this is the friend I told you about, Father Steve Flynn. Steve, this is Vern Stenhus. Vern and I went to school together, sixty, sixty-five years ago. He worked for the Two Emils, too."

The tall, still straight Stenhus looked Flynn over quizzically for a long second, as if surprised that the priest was not collared and robed. He put out a large hand, and Stephen Flynn shook it. Then the two older men carried the canoe up the steep path to the road while he struggled behind with the huge pack. Flynn was reasonably strong, but winded quickly. Physical strength persists long after physical endurance has been lost.

After tying the canoe atop the pickup shell and stowing

the pack, they crowded into the pickup cab. Stenhus started the motor and pulled out onto the blacktop.

"I suppose you ain't heard what happened in the news the last couple days," he said as they started down the road. Stenhus's speech had a discernible flavor of Scandinavia which Haugen's did not.

"No," Haugen said. "What?"

"There was some big riots started. Fires and looting. Shootouts with the police—like a regular war you know. In New York first. Then yesterday they broke out in a bunch of other places too. Washington, Detroit, Los Angeles, places like that. I heard this morning that Donnelly sent the army in, and called out the national guard."

Father Flynn felt his chest constrict. Haugen's face seemed to pucker. Outside, the Indian summer sun shone on.

Stenhus turned and spit brownly out the window. "Too bad this country ain't got a president with a teaspoon or two of brains." He looked at Haugen. "You ought to run for president next time, Arne. If there is a next time. You got enough money to get elected, and you're a hell of a lot smarter than that Donnelly." He laughed then, and poked Haugen with an elbow. "Even if you are half Finlander."

Haugen laughed wryly, as much a snort as a laugh. "Me, president?! That'd be the day! I wouldn't have the job if they offered it to me. And the country wouldn't have me if I took it."

TWO

The little OH-6 Cayuse lifted from the Pentagon grounds and swung smoothly north-northeast toward the Potomac. As an observation helicopter, the model had been replaced for more than a decade, but they were an excellent little aircraft, and a few were still used to shuttle brass. This one was the personal shuttle of the chairman of the JCS, the joint chiefs of staff, and just now carried two passengers wearing four stars each.

The Lincoln Memorial and the reflecting pool scarcely registered on General Thomas M. "Jumper" Cromwell as he looked northward past them. He was seeing the bull-dozed remains of street barricades near the State Department Building on 23rd Street, the black scars where cars had burned, and farther north, the blocks of burned-out buildings with smoke still rising from the rubble. The air stunk from it.

He saw an old M-60, probably an A3, roll slowly, ponderously through an intersection, accompanied by three armored personnel carriers. Nothing seemed to be going on with them. Patrolling, keeping military visibility up, that was all. The fighting had dropped way off, to spasmodic sniping, brief infrequent firefights. All but the real hardcases had backed off, gotten lost, at least in Washington. The question was, would they stay backed off or would they go guerrilla?

This was high security airspace. Although the Cayuse emitted a constant identification signal, the pilot had been challenged moments earlier, and responded with the code of the day. Constitution Avenue passed beneath, then 17th Street. The grass was still emerald on the ellipse and the White House lawn, though marred with machine gun emplacements. A few trees were beginning to show autumn colors. Rifle-carrying marines patrolled, in helmets and camouflage fatigues. And there were marines on the White House roof, no doubt with ground-to-air rockets.

But no tourists at all. Of course, there hadn't been many since gas rationing began a year earlier.

Cromwell could see a man in class-A uniform waiting in front of the South Portico, watching them come in. The OH-6 slowed, hovered a moment, oscillating slightly, then settled on the little helipad, a semicircle of marines standing nearby with ready weapons, watching.

When the vanes stopped, the president's military aide strode over to greet Cromwell and Klein. Greetings were minimal. The aide led them briskly across the lawn toward the Executive Wing.

"How's the president doing, Ernie?" Cromwell asked. The question was not a routine courtesy, but a matter of genuine concern.

Brigadier General Ernest Hammaker shook his head. "Not well, sir. Not as well as yesterday. Singleton's with him."

Shit! Cromwell thought, *just what we need at a time like this—the president in the middle of a nervous breakdown.*

They entered the building and walked into the president's office area, Martinelli, the president's secretary, watching bleakly as they passed. Hammaker opened the door to the Oval Office and ushered the two senior generals through.

President Kevin J. Donnelly met them seated. He looked older than his fifty-six years. The skin of his face was slack, as if he'd shrunk inside it these last two weeks, and especially the last three days. The White House chief of staff stood behind his left shoulder, and Colonel Singleton, the White House physician behind his right. *They don't look too damn good either,* Cromwell thought.

"Good morning, Mr. President," he said.

"Good morning, general." The president stopped at that, as if to gather energy, then added, "I'm going to resign."

Cromwell hardly missed a beat. "I understand, sir." He paused. "There's one thing I trust you'll take care of before you do though."

The president simply looked at him.

"There is no vice president, sir. Mr. Strock resigned four days ago, at your insistence. The Twenty-Fifth Amendment requires that you nominate someone for the post. As it stands now, there is no constitutional replacement for you."

The president nodded. "Mr. Milstead pointed that out to me. I am appointing you my vice president."

Cromwell's face suddenly felt as if it was going to shatter and fall off. "Mr. President," he said, "I don't think the Congress would approve that."

Milstead spoke then. "General, we called the attorney general when President Donnelly first brought up his retirement last evening. You're aware, of course, that the Congress passed an Emergency Powers Act on Monday, granting the president extraordinary authority. We reviewed the act together, and it's the attorney general's view that the president can now simply appoint a vice president. During the emergency he doesn't need congressional approval." He went on almost apologetically. "The legislation was rather hurriedly drawn. They may not have envisioned this scenario."

Cromwell's jaw locked with chagrin. Just the idea of being president somehow horrified him. He didn't look for the rationale in the reaction; it was simply emotional. But its roots, whatever they were, went deep.

"General Cromwell?" said Milstead. Cromwell returned to the here and now, and focused on the man. "General," Milstead repeated, "if you accept the post and Mr. Donnelly resigns, you can then appoint a vice president and resign in turn, if you prefer."

"Shit, Charles!" Cromwell snapped, "that's not okay!" He stopped then and looked at Donnelly. "Sorry, Mr. President. Sorry, Charles. But that would be terrible PR! It would look as if nobody wants the job! As if the problems were just too much."

He turned to Donnelly. "Mr. President, would you be willing to stay in office for—two more days? Charles will take care of things for you, and in two days I'll come up with someone who's willing to have the job and able to do it better than I could. If I don't, I'll take it myself."

The president nodded, so doped he looked moribund more than tired. "Two more days?" He looked up at Milstead then. "Two more days, Charles."

"Fine, Mr. President."

Colonel Singleton said nothing, but his tight lips told Cromwell that two days was asking a lot of Kevin Donnelly.

"Thank you, Mr. President," said Cromwell.

"I'll walk General Cromwell to his helicopter, Mr. President," Milstead said. The president nodded slightly, and the three generals left the office with Milstead behind them.

"General Cromwell," said Milstead when they got outside, "I may have to call you. It's not at all sure that the president will be able to function mentally at all in two days. Or even this afternoon; it's a moment to moment thing. And he *has* appointed you; all you'd need to do is accept. You already have, conditionally—if you don't get someone within two days. If the president becomes non-functional before he can appoint someone else, will you take the job?"

He looked intently at Cromwell as they walked along. "Frankly, general," Milstead continued, "I think the president made a good choice. You've demonstrated a large capacity for accepting responsibilities, evaluating situations, making decisions, giving orders . . . Even in declining the president's offer, you noticed a consideration that the rest of us missed."

Cromwell was tempted to tell him to knock off the flattery. But he didn't, because he knew it was true. Instead he nodded curtly, almost angrily. "I'll accept if it comes to that. But don't do it to me, Charles, unless you absolutely have to. My first name is Thomas, for chrissake, not Oliver."

Milstead nodded, and with Ernie Hammaker, stopped somewhat short of the chopper, watching Cromwell and Klein board before turning back to the White House. As the pair of four-star generals took seats and buckled down, Klein said, "Who've you got in mind, Jumper?"

"Christ, Brad, I haven't had time to think yet. But I'll come up with someone."

He looked, when he said it, as if he were facing execution, but by the time they put back down at the Pentagon, he'd thought of someone.

THREE

Excerpt from a sermon by the Reverend Delbert Coombs, of the Stalwart in God Church of the Apocalypse.

There are those who deny God. They will be damned! They are already damned.

And there are those who claim to be Christians but do not believe the Word of God. They are *twice* damned!

And there are those who say they are Christians and claim to believe the Word of God . . . *yet do not believe that the millenium will come!* They deny the Word of God as revealed by John in the book of Revelations!!

Well I'll tell you something, my friend! They too will not enter the Kingdom of God! Unless . . . unless they change their hearts! And they'd better *hurry*, my friends, for the millenium is soon upon us. The years remaining are fewer than the fingers of my hand. And if they do not believe their calendar, and if they do not believe their Bible, *then let them look about them, for the signs are everywhere to be seen!*

There were five joint chiefs. Cromwell was the Chairman; General Fred Hanke was Army Chief of Staff; General Ewell Boyd Trenary was Air Force Chief of Staff; Admiral James L. "Howdy" Dudak was Chief of Naval Operations; and General Francis X. Carmody was Marine Corps Commandant. Bradley Klein made a sixth in the meeting: As commander of the newly reinstituted Continental Command, Klein was in charge of the troops enforcing martial law.

When everyone was seated, Cromwell, as a matter of form, rapped his small gavel on its plate. "All right, gentlemen," he said, "I have some important news for you."

He had their attention. "A little while ago, at 0800, Brad and I went over to the White House. I assumed it was to give the president another rundown, and discuss any ideas he might have before the six of us met.

"He gave us a surprise. A hell of a surprise."

Cromwell paused then, looking around. "I'm telling you this in strictest confidence; it must not be discussed or mentioned to anyone. The president is in very shaky health, and he intends to resign. In fact, he would have resigned when we were there, but I talked him into waiting two days."

Trenary's thin face darkened; he was less surprised than

angry. "Talked him out of it?! Jesus Christ, Jumper! Quitting would be the best thing he's done lately. What in hell did you talk him out of it for?"

"There's no vice president. He needs to appoint one; then he can quit."

"Jumper, he doesn't *appoint* one," Hanke said drily. Fred Hanke was a tall lanky man whose thin hair still showed blond through the gray. "He *nominates* one, and then the Congress has to approve."

"Not now it doesn't," Cromwell answered, then repeated what he'd been told about the emergency powers granted the president.

"Huh!" Hanke grunted. "So he can appoint his own successor! I'll bet that wasn't the intent of Congress."

"Beats me. Anyway that's what Cavanaugh and Milstead came up with. And Cavanaugh practiced before the Supreme Court for years."

"Why didn't he name one last night?" Carmody asked. "Or this morning? Why the two-day wait?" The Marine Corps Commandant was a thick-shouldered, hard-bodied man who, with a sergeant's stripes, could have passed for a drill instructor. Usually he was a quiet, mild-seeming man, but his tongue could take the bark off a tree on occasion, and the whole Corps knew it.

"He did name one, Frank. But the guy didn't want the job."

"Who was it?" asked Dudak.

"I hate to tell you this, Howdy, but it was me. So now I've got the job of finding him one. And I've got two days to do it."

"Wait," Trenary said. "He offered you the job? That's like offering you the presidency! He's got to be off his rocker! That would really heat things up, appointing a president right off the JCS, for chrissake!"

"We don't know that," Hanke commented. "Probably ninety percent of the people in this country want someone to take hold and straighten things out. They might like the idea of a military president, the way things are."

"Or they might not," Dudak put in. "Especially if things didn't work out right away. Which they wouldn't." His features, usually reminiscent of a skeptical cherub, were set now in disapproval.

"Who've you got in mind, Jumper?" Carmody asked. "Someone, I'll bet."

"Yeah, I've thought of someone." Cromwell looked around at the others, then said nothing.

"Goddamn it," said Trenary, "don't be so damn coy, Jumper! Why even bring it up to us, if you already know who you want? You're the one the president told to name one."

"Good question, Ewell. It's someone who's not well known. I felt as if I needed to try him out on you people; see how you react."

He paused thoughtfully. "I'm not sure any of you have even heard of him. He's got a personal track record of successful research and development and skilled management, and he's made a ton of money." His eyes fixed on Trenary. "Unlike a lot of your big money buddies, he inherited nothing but brains; he got rich on new products well designed and well built. No stock manipulations, no mergers, thefts, or public borrow. . . ."

"Spare us the goddamn buildup, Cromwell," Trenary snapped. "What's his name?"

Cromwell said nothing for a long moment, eyeing the Air Force Chief of Staff, and when he spoke, his voice was mild. "Ewell," he said, "I have the floor. And I'm sure they teach military courtesy at the Air Force Academy."

Trenary flushed.

"And if I seemed to insult some of your friends, my honest apologies. There's nothing wrong with being born rich; I wish I'd been. I just wanted to point out that the guy I'm thinking about started from scratch, from a hard-scrabble backwoods background, playing different games with different rules than most rich men. And he's got different qualities. All of which attributes I consider desirable in the president-select.

"At any rate it removes all questions about how generally competent he is." He raised his eyebrows at Trenary, inviting.

"Okay," said Trenary, surly but somewhat appeased. "Is that it for the preliminaries?"

"Not quite. He's not associated in the public eye or the media with politics or party or any particular point of view. And he's highly promotable to the general public."

"You've found a clone of Jesus Christ," Trenary retorted. "What's his name?"

"Arne Haugen. Founder and president of Duluth Technologies."

Trenary stared in angry disbelief. "Ye gods, Jumper! I've never even heard of the sonofabitch! You can't serve up some unknown to the American public and expect them to hold still for it!"

"Okay," said Cromwell. "You've made a point: he's not well-known to the public. That means he doesn't have any broad, ready-made support. Or broad, ready-made enmity either."

"I've heard of him," Hanke put in. "Quite a few people have. He was on the cover of *Tech Times* a couple of years ago—it's got a paid circulation of about two million—for coming out with a lot of significant developments and improvements over the years. In electronics, plastics—I don't remember what all. The father of blow-on instant paint drier and seasoner, for one thing: something the modern painting contractor and body shop wouldn't be without. God knows how many tens of millions he's made on that one alone. Lee Iacocca he's not, but he is promotable."

Dudak looked distinctly interested now. "What are his politics, Jumper?"

"They don't have a brand-name. Believes in basic American values and common sense, like a lot of people. Promotable. And promotable is essential today. No matter how able someone may be, people have to be willing to go along with him if this country is going to get back on its feet.

"He never really belonged to a party, he told me, and today that has real promotional value. He said that given the political system in this country, he could get more accomplished if he didn't get distracted by politics."

Trenary shook his head. "A bird like that wouldn't work as president. Doesn't know enough; too green. In the White House he'd be a babe in the woods, and this is no time for on the job training."

"Okay," Cromwell said. "You've made another point: he's unseasoned. But you're overlooking one thing: He won't have to go through all the usual politics with Congress if he doesn't want to. At least not for the duration of the emergency. He can even name his own vice president."

"Jesus!" Trenary said. "Congress is going to shit when they find out what they did. Or what Milstead and Cavanaugh claim they did."

"Don't be so sure," Carmody put in. "They passed the emergency powers act so the president could take broad steps quickly without 'referring to the legislative process.' I saw Kreiner interviewed on TV the other day, when the bill was before the Senate, and that's the pitch he was using. What it comes down to is, Congress is scared. They're afraid Humpty Dumpty is really broken this time."

May it not be so, Cromwell thought.

"Jumper, how did you get to know Haugen?" Hanke asked.

"I met him at a fishing lodge up in Canada a few years back. I went up there in September after the mosquitoes had frozen out. Then we got a few days of cold rain, and he and I ended up sitting around talking a lot. He was airborne too, back in WW Two. Fought in New Guinea and the Philippines. We started out by comparing wars."

"World War Two? How the hell old is he?" Trenary demanded.

"I don't know. He has to be more than seventy if he was with the 503rd Parachute Infantry in New Guinea. But he could pass for sixty."

"What rank did he hold?" Dudak asked.

"Platoon sergeant. That's a CPO to you naval types."

No one said anything for a moment. Dudak looked disappointed. Carmody's face didn't show it, but he was thinking that a platoon sergeant at least knew how to kick ass, which was more than Donnelly did. Correction: Donnelly had booted Strock when the Qaddir scandal broke; he'd had to.

Then Trenary threw up his hands in disgust. "Jumper, you're going to do what the hell you want to anyway. Why don't you go ahead and do it?"

Cromwell nodded and got up. "Right. Let's take a break; I've got a phone call to make."

They watched him leave. Carmody grinned. "I'd like to listen in on that phone call," he said, then did an impression of Cromwell. " 'Haugen, how'd you like to come to D.C. and be President of the United States for a while?' "

Carmody laughed at his own wit. Hanke smiled. Trenary and Dudak didn't seem to think it was humorous at all.

There'd been more than just conversation between Cromwell and Haugen, that September three years earlier. More than long talks on common interest had impressed the general.

The fishing camp had been some hundred miles north of Sioux Lookout, Ontario. Though the weather had turned bad, the food and company were excellent, and the relaxed atmosphere a welcome change from the Pentagon, where Cromwell had been in charge of the Readiness Command then.

After two days of rain, the radio had predicted a partly sunny day, to be followed by more cold showery weather. He and Haugen had gone out without a guide, so they could talk more comfortably; Carlson, the resort operator, knew Haugen's backwoods background, and allowed him the privilege. They'd motored five or six miles down the large wild lake to a bay Haugen knew, where the pike grew big and had a mean streak. After fishing for a few hours, the wind had freshened and the temperature began to fall. They started back then, and had just cleared the bay when the motor quit.

There was a little tool kit in the boat. They'd paddled to shore, and Haugen had stripped the motor down, using the overturned boat as a workbench. The problem had been a blown gasket. He'd been cutting a replacement out of the top of his boot when the storm hit, hours earlier than predicted. Wind whipped up dangerous waves, and it began to snow. Within minutes they couldn't see a hundred feet through the slanting large white flakes.

Haugen had stashed the stripped down motor under the boat and dispatched Cromwell to cut balsam and cedar branches with his sheath knife. "Get a lot of them," he'd said. But Cromwell wasn't familiar with balsam. "Balsam," Haugen had replied, "is the one with short soft needles. Get a lot of them. The pickery ones are spruce, and they're not good for sleeping on."

Cromwell had walked back into the forest, cutting

branches off balsam saplings with his sheath knife, leaving them where they fell to help guide him back to the boat. When he'd returned, arms full, through the thick-falling whiteness of flakes, Haugen had already broken and cut off saplings and was framing a lean-to with them beneath a big old spruce, tying them together with strings from the big landing net. The snow was beginning to stick on the ground. When Cromwell came back with a second armful, the lean-to was already being roofed with bark from a decayed and fallen birch; the old man worked fast. When Cromwell had come back with a third armful, Haugen was beginning another, smaller steep-roofed lean-to, and the snow was an inch or more deep.

"Go get some dry branches for firewood," Haugen had said. "The biggest ones you can break off." Cromwell had seen just the ideal source, a large fallen spruce a few dozen yards away. When he returned with his first armload of fuel, Haugen was tepeeing punkwood over a little pile of papery outer bark of birch, beneath the smaller lean-to. Minutes later, getting more wood, he'd heard Haugen breaking branches too.

When they had a large pile of broken-up branchwood, Haugen had baked pike in the foil from their lunch wrappers. They'd eaten supper beneath their lean-to then, while dusk darkened the forest, and the snow deepened inch by inch.

They spent the night there, a damp, cold, smoky night huddled together on the fir boughs, dozing and waking, the smaller lean-to reflecting heat toward them from the fire. Every now and then, one of them would put more branchwood on. The snow had slowed, and sometime in the night it stopped.

When daylight came, they'd tipped the boat, dumping off most of the six inches of wet snow. Then they'd brushed it clean, more or less, and Haugen finished his repairs, fingers red and clumsy with cold, while Cromwell watched, feeling useless. Then, together they'd launched the boat, and with a little persistence, gotten the motor started.

They'd gone about a mile when they'd sighted the launch out hunting them, Carlson at the wheel. He hadn't been worried, Carlson told Cromwell later. If he'd had any doubt that Haugen could handle whatever came up, he'd never have let them go out without a guide.

A president select! And himself responsible for the selection! Apparently it was constitutional; it was if the Emergency Powers Act was. It felt un-American though. But then, so did the troubles.

Cromwell shrugged off the strangeness in the situation, buzzed his secretary, and told her to get Arne Haugen on the phone, at Duluth Technologies in Duluth, Minnesota.

FOUR

Arne and Lois Haugen deliberately avoided watching the news at breakfast. She considered it a poor way to start a day, and he tended to agree. And he didn't often turn on the set in his office at all. But things now seemed so damned critical that, when he arrived at work that morning, he turned on CNN. A commercial was showing, and while waiting through it, he got a cup of black coffee from the coffee station beside his drafting table.

With the cup in his hand, he paused to look out the window. The main management-manufacturing complex of Duluth Technologies stood near the brink of the Superior Plateau, and his large thermal window looked northeastward across the north end of the city. Beyond lay Lake Superior, ice-blue in the sunlight, stretching to a distant horizon and disappearing. A single freighter steamed outbound, a bulk carrier. From its small size and its black smoke plume, it was one of the ancient coal burners renovated when Persian Gulf oil had stopped flowing a year ago.

Carrying wheat, probably, he thought. Other shipping

was way down. Fewer and fewer ships had been in and out of the harbor in recent months.

Times were very bad in Duluth. They'd been bad for decades as the iron mines played out, then had gradually improved. More recently they'd crashed, and hard times had taken on new meaning. But there'd been no riots here, and hardly any demonstrations.

Ordinarily he took the TV news with more than a grain of salt; if ten homes were lost to a forest fire somewhere, they'd give the impression that a town had burned up. But last night they'd shown aerial views of fires and fighting in half a dozen cities, and mentioned a dozen others; it had been a sobering, even a frightening thing to watch. For the first time in his life, it was really real to Arne Haugen that the United States of America could go down the tubes.

Now, from his chair, he watched film of a small battle in the Sierra Nevada of California. Troops against a paramilitary outfit. The newscaster called them "survivalists," but survivalists weren't likely to be challenging the army. Whatever they were, they'd been surrounded on the crest of a forested ridge by elements of the 7th Light Infantry Division, late the day before. The firefight wasn't intense, as firefights went, but Haugen could recognize bursts of automatic rifle fire, the staccato racketing of occasional machine guns, the thump of mortars, now and then the slam of rockets. From both adversaries; the paras had a lot more than deer rifles up there.

It occurred to Haugen that, while much of the video photography was seemingly from a helicopter, apparently using zoom lenses from a distance, the sound pickup was on the ground, with the infantry.

Then there was another sound, the growing sound of helicopters. Their threat, their promise, drew his attention from the gunfire. Then a camera showed them coming, a flight of five, lean and not very large. As they approached the ridge, four of them veered and began to circle it at a little distance. The fifth moved nearer, and he could hear a bull horn of some kind calling on the paras to lay down their weapons, and file down the ridge with their hands on their heads.

It had only begun to repeat the message when a rocket

struck its lightly armored side. The craft staggered, then
veered away, still flying. The others didn't hesitate; they
came in shooting, releasing searing flights of antipersonnel
rockets, while their chain guns ripped the fabric of morning. The rockets tattooed the forest then, the upper ridge
slopes, throwing debris. The attack continued for perhaps
half a terrible minute before the choppers withdrew.

The cameras didn't show the result—limp bodies,
wounded prisoners. The photography, Haugen thought,
must be military; the intent was not to shock but to sober,
and to demonstrate that the government was in full control. He felt effectively sobered indeed. The network commentary was brief; there'd been several significant fights
between military units and backcountry paras.

There'd also been a siege, of "La Raza" paras who'd
captured and fortified a country jail in rural New Mexico.
There was no footage of the firefight, but a silent camera,
after the fact, showed the heavily pockmarked building,
and inside, rooms shattered by rockets and grenades, large
bloodstains on the floor. Most of the seventeen paras there
had died. The military force had been a national guard
company whose troops were also from northern New
Mexico.

Interesting, Haugen thought. It was as if people were
reacting against the destructive violence of the few, even
when the few were their own. Perhaps most of them were
ready to try keeping the machinery going, trying to survive.

Coverage had shifted to central L.A. when the phone
buzzed. Haugen touched a key to cut the sound volume
from the TV, then answered the phone. His secretary's
voice issued from the speaker.

"Mr. Haugen, there's a General Cromwell for you on line
one."

A puzzled frown touched Haugen's face. "Thanks, John,
I'll take it." He hadn't seen Jumper Cromwell for—it had
been three years in September. He touched the blinking
key, and the general's face appeared on the phone screen.
"Good morning, Jumper. What can I do for you?"

At his end, Cromwell was renewing his image of Haugen's
face: broad, with high strong cheekbones, a wide mouth with
the thin lips of age. The nose was somewhat flattened and
slightly crooked, probably a souvenir of some long-ago brawl.

"It is a pretty good morning here at that," Cromwell answered, "compared to the last couple. Arne, can you fly to Washington today? If I send a plane for you."

"Fly to Washington? What for, Jumper?"

"It's confidential. I can't tell you over the phone."

"Umh! How long would I be there?" Haugen's mind was reviewing his plans for the week as he asked.

"Maybe a day, maybe longer. Depends on what you decide to do after we've talked."

He wouldn't be asking me if it wasn't damned important —to him anyway, Haugen told himself. *And for a day or two . . .*

"Sure. I can do that. I suppose that'll be from Duluth International?"

"Right. I'll have you picked up at the Air National Guard Office. Just make yourself known to whoever's in charge. Or if there's any problem about getting there, I can have you picked up at home or your office."

"No. I'll have someone take me."

"Good. It's—what? Eight twenty-five there now?"

Haugen glanced at the clock. "Right."

"It's about a two-and-a-half-hour flight for the plane I'm sending, and it'll leave here in about an hour. Then say a half-hour layover at your end for refueling and whatever else the pilot has to do. You'll take off in about four or five hours from now."

Haugen's expression turned quizzical. "Five hours? Make it 5 P.M. instead." He was testing: The general seemed to be pushing for time; how urgent was this, really?

Cromwell's expression didn't change, but his mind raced. He wanted Haugen there while Donnelly was still rational. But if he pushed too hard, Haugen was likely to insist on knowing what it was about, and if he told him over the phone, five would get you ten he'd shy off.

"Okay, 5 P.M. will be fine," Cromwell said. "I'll see you tonight."

"I'll bring clothes for two days."

"Make it three days?"

"Three then." It made no difference. Arne Haugen always kept a bag packed and ready.

When they'd disconnected, the general realized his forehead was dewed with sweat. *What're the odds he'll tell you to go to hell, Cromwell?* he asked himself. He really really didn't want to accept the presidency himself. Because if he did, and couldn't make it work . . . He veered away from the thought.

Haugen sat back in his chair and watched a few more minutes of news—up till the weather forecast. The president was rumored to be ill. The latest unemployment figure was forty percent, but that was the week before the blowup; it might easily be fifty or sixty by now. The final games of the baseball season, plus the league playoffs and world series had all been cancelled, and Baltimore declared champion on the basis of the best record—101 wins. And the Iranian army had finally taken Baghdad; at least the Ayatollah Jalal had something to cheer about.

Then, after turning off the set, Arne Haugen reached and dialed his home. His wife answered. They hadn't had a maid recently; Lois had decided to try a twice-a-week cleaning service for the privacy it gave.

"Hey, Babe," he said, "I've got to fly out of town about four-thirty or five this afternoon. How about I take the rest of the day off? We can drive up the North Shore and enjoy the color, stop at Bjerke's for a late lunch, and come back."

"Oh?" Her brows had risen. "Well, I like the driving and eating part. Where are you flying to?"

"D.C."

"Hmh! Okay. Shall we drive the Elf? It doesn't ride like the Caddy, but I've hoarded enough gas coupons for a tank and a half."

"The Elf it is then. I'll be there in ten minutes."

They disconnected. He took his jacket and safety helmet off their hooks and started for the lot where his little Yamaha 250 was parked. He wasn't speculating on what the trip was about; he'd find out when he got there.

FIVE

As his wife drove him to the airport, Arne Haugen couldn't help wondering again what this was all about. Could Cromwell want him to take on some electronic project? He had no experience in weapons development, had never done anything for the Pentagon except pay taxes.

Maybe they'd gotten wind of the GPC.

When the DOD's executive jet arrived to pick him up—a beautiful little Rockwell T-39 without military markings—he found it was being flown by a bird colonel, and that really piqued Haugen's curiosity. A bird colonel detailed to shuttle a private businessman!

A brain-picking session maybe? Or did they want him as a technical advisor? But surely he didn't have that kind of reputation; he didn't even have a master's degree. And besides, this would be a strange time for Washington to have much attention on anything other than the domestic emergency. Except maybe Iran.

Maybe they *had* learned about the GPC. He'd just have to wait and see.

And why the secrecy?

After they'd taken off, he turned on his seat light and took Spider Robinson's latest novel from his small bag. He was a rapid reader; it would just about last him to Washington.

In Duluth, the October evening had been clear, with the promise of a hard freeze. Washington, by contrast, was under a miles-thick blanket of soggy cloud, and when they broke through the ceiling at Washington National Airport, it was raining hard.

31

The plane didn't taxi to the terminal; it stopped at the edge of a taxi strip. The copilot, a captain, came aft, picked up Haugen's larger suitcase, and carried it to the door, which he opened. Damnedest redcap he'd ever seen, Haugen decided. On the streaming concrete outside, a young man in civvies was waiting with a large umbrella. He took the suitcase from the captain, then promptly held the umbrella over the disembarking Haugen, in the process exposing himself to the rain.

They walked rapidly to a service entrance of the terminal. Inside the building, there were remarkably few people except for employees mostly standing around looking worried, as if they thought they might all be laid off. Haugen supposed they knew plenty who had been. The young man took him to a plain gray government sedan parked in a no-standing zone, and drove him through the downpour to the Airport Hilton. There he led him past registration without registering him.

Curiouser and curiouser, Haugen thought. They got off the elevator on the fifth floor and went to a room. By that time, Haugen wouldn't have been surprised at anything. The young man brought forth a key and opened the door.

Actually it was a suite. Jumper Cromwell, wearing civvies, was standing inside, waiting.

"Good evening, Arne. Using the expression loosely. Have a chair, it's your room."

"Don't mind if I do. Jumper, what the hell is this all about?"

The general looked at the young man who'd just put down Haugen's large suitcase. "Thanks, Steinhorn," Cromwell said. "Wait in the lobby. I may be here awhile."

Steinhorn saluted, about faced, and left.

"Arne," Cromwell said when the door had closed, "how's your health these days? I should have asked you when I had you on the phone earlier, but I was just assuming you were as healthy as when I'd last seen you."

"My health? Fine. Jumper, you didn't answer my question. What is this?"

Cromwell took a deep breath. "I guess the best way to tell you is to start at the beginning."

He took a few minutes to get to the big question,

describing and explaining his way there and rationalizing his evaluation of the kind of person needed, under the circumstances. All he left out was that he, Cromwell, would probably end up with the job if Haugen refused it. He didn't want to indicate any options at all. When he finally asked the question, he did so in an indirect way, hopeful of forestalling a quick negative. "You're the one I decided on, Arne. To be appointed vice president. I'll need your answer no later than tomorrow afternoon."

Haugen simply stared at him, unable at the moment to deal with it.

"Here's a copy of the enabling legislation," Cromwell added, handing him an envelope. "It's surprisingly short and concise. It'll give you an idea of the powers and potential you'd have in the job."

Haugen looked at the envelope in Cromwell's hand as if it might hold scorpions, then took it anyway, drew the two sheets of paper from it and began to read. Jumper Cromwell realized he'd been holding his breath, and exhaled covertly. *He may do it,* Cromwell thought. *He's considering it. Otherwise he wouldn't be reading the Emergency Powers Act.*

Haugen skimmed it once, then read it more carefully. The powers were granted until Congress repealed them, but for no longer than one year unless extended by the Congress.

When he'd finished, Haugen put the sheets back in the envelope and looked at the general.

"This is for real, isn't it?" He shook his head slowly, not in the negative, but in amazement. "My god, Jumper, it's hard to believe this is happening to me. Or to anyone!"

"You don't need to answer now," Cromwell said. "Sleep on it if you'd like. And keep the envelope, in case you want to look at it again."

Haugen nodded slowly. "I will. Sleep on it. But one thing more: Why me?"

Cromwell smiled slightly. "First of all, Arne, there's the matter of time. I was only given two days; that's not time enough to do a big search. And beyond that, it seems to me you're as good a choice as any."

Haugen frowned. "Jumper, supposing I say no. You've sure as hell got an alternative in mind. Who is it?"

Cromwell exhaled gustily. "The option is . . . The option is *me*. Donnelly named me as vice president. I asked him for two days to find someone else. I don't think the people would go for me as president; not with this kind of power. People would be remembering every damn military dictator they'd ever heard of, most of them bad.

"Besides, the idea of it scares me silly. I wasn't that scared jumping behind Communist lines in Laos, twenty-five years ago."

Subliminally, Haugen's mind was sorting factors; he could feel it working. "And you actually think I can handle it?"

The general nodded soberly. "I really think you can."

"I've got no experience in government. Or politics."

"You're going to find government a lot less complicated to work with, with these emergency powers. And I'll get Donnelly's staff and cabinet to stay on long enough to brief you and teach you the ropes. Then you can bring in your own people if you want. Besides, like I said earlier, not having been involved in politics should be an advantage with the public. You can make it one, anyway.

"But you don't have to decide tonight. Sleep on it. I'll get your answer in the morning."

Cromwell had remained standing. Now he turned and disappeared into a dressing room. Haugen heard a refrigerator door close, and the general reappeared with a pint of Cutty Sark on a tray, along with two glasses and ice. "I remember you liked Scotch," he said, then put the tray down and poured two short drinks.

Silently they sipped. Then Cromwell got up again and gestured toward a closed door. "That's your bedroom in there." He stepped over to it, opened it, and spoke. "Sergeant Kearney, come out here."

Haugen stared, puzzled. A man emerged, of rather ordinary size and wearing civilian clothes, but Haugen knew at once this was no one to pick a fight with. Even in his youth, he told himself, he'd hardly have had a prayer, fighting Kearney.

"Yes sir, general," Kearney said.

"Meet an old friend of mine, sergeant. Arne Haugen. Arne, this is Sergeant First Class James Kearney."

Haugen took the proferred hand and shook it. "Glad to meet you, Jim," he said.

"Glad to meet you, sir." Haugen doubted the man's words meant anything beyond military courtesy.

"Sergeant Kearney will be your bodyguard tonight," Cromwell went on. "I'll come by at 0700. If it's a yes, we'll go to the Pentagon for breakfast; it's only about a mile from here. After we've eaten, we can go see the president from there."

Cromwell shook Haugen's hand and left, Haugen staring at the door as it closed behind him. Then, saying nothing more, he picked up the tray and went into the bedroom, coming back a minute later for his suitcases.

"Have a good night, sergeant," he said, and disappeared into the bedroom again.

Arne Haugen didn't go straight to bed however. Or have another drink right away. Instead he dialed long distance. Lois answered.

"Babe," he said, "they've offered me a job here. . . . That's right, in Washington. A house goes with it, and it won't last longer than a year, maybe less. . . . I can't tell you on the phone, honey; it's top secret. But it's important, and I have to say yes or no in the morning, so I need to know if you'd be willing to live here for a while. . . .

"Well, I'm not sure. I think I might. It sounds really interesting. . . . Good. Thanks, Babe. I'll call you sometime tomorrow and tell you what I've decided.

"And Babe, I love you. . . . You do, eh? I kind of thought so. Talk to you tomorrow."

He hung up then, poured another drink, and leaned back thoughtfully in the chair. Controlling the violence, he thought, would be the easy part. If he took the job. It seemed to be pretty much controlled already. The hard part would be getting things running right again. If he couldn't do that, nothing else he might accomplish would matter.

SIX

The next morning at almost precisely 0700, Cromwell, in civvies again, knocked at Haugen's door, to be let in by Sergeant Kearney. Haugen had just finished knotting his tie—something he seldom wore.

"How'd you sleep last night?" Cromwell asked.

"Pretty well, actually."

They looked at one another for several seconds. "Well?" Cromwell said at last.

Haugen grinned. "The answer is yes; why the hell not? I'm bound to do as well as a lot of possible selectees would, and better than some. Present company excepted."

He laughed then, and Cromwell's eyebrows raised. "I'm remembering a conversation a few days ago," Haugen said. "An old friend of mine said I ought to run for president next time, 'if there is a next time.' He was joking, of course. I told him, 'No way. And if I did, people wouldn't have me.' I'm half a liar already, it looks like. We'll have to see about the other half."

Cromwell grunted. He wasn't up to having humor this morning. He felt like a man reprieved, but there was no joy in it; merely relief. The country was still in deep shit. Kearney picked up Haugen's larger bag, and in a few minutes they were in another plain gray GSA sedan, this one larger and better appointed than last night's. Haugen asked himself, not seriously, if Cromwell would have brought a limousine if he'd said yes the evening before.

There was more traffic than Haugen had expected—government employees going to work, he presumed—but far far less than there'd have been a year earlier. And no traces of past street fighting along the short route between airport and Pentagon; apparently neither mobs nor urban paras had reached this part of the city.

It was his first look at the Pentagon, a vast building reminding him of some mesa in New Mexico. They got out in front of a broad, colonnaded entrance and went in. An elevator and corridor took them to an outer office, where a female master sergeant with caramel complexion had them wait for a moment while she buzzed her boss.

"General Cromwell is here, with a gentleman," she said. She nodded at Cromwell then. "General Hanke says to go right in."

They did. Hanke was on his feet, waiting for them.

"General," said Cromwell, "I'd like you to meet Arne Haugen, of Duluth Technologies. Arne, this is General Fred Hanke, Army Chief of Staff." As the tall general shook hands with the broad older man, Hanke's pale blue eyes examined Haugen openly.

When they'd finished the courtesies, Cromwell said, "Hanke, Arne has given me a yes on my proposition. Now I'm taking him to see the president. If I'm not back in time, I'd like you to chair this morning's meeting."

"Fine. Anything you want me to tell them?"

"Tell them I got a 'yes' from Arne."

When they'd left, they paused at Cromwell's office for just a moment while Cromwell called the White House and spoke to someone named Charles; they'd be there in ten minutes, he told him.

In the corridor again, Cromwell said, "I wanted Hanke to meet you. It's good PR, and Hank's a hell of a good man. Best man on the JCS, in most ways; better than me, better than Carmody."

Which left two chiefs of staff unmentioned, Haugen noted. A small helicopter waited for them on a helipad outside; Cromwell had arranged for it in advance, he supposed. From the air, he saw what had not been apparent while driving to the Pentagon—the widespread damage and destruction north of the river. There was no smoke though; the evening's heavy rain had seen to that. Trucks were out, along with front-end loaders, clearing away the remains of dozed out barricades. That suggested that the sniping had ended, or nearly enough for whoever had made the decision.

Haugen had visited the White House once, nearly forty years earlier, as a tourist. Now there were no tourists, only marines, and he was met on the lawn by the president's military aide, General Hammaker, and Charles Milstead, chief of the White House staff. Cromwell made the introductions; then they walked together to the Oval Office, where President Kevin J. Donnelly met them seated, a full colonel standing behind him with a Medical Corps caduceus on his shirt collar.

The president looked terrible, like a long-term invalid, his flesh and complexion like bread dough. *Not drawn like yesterday,* Cromwell thought. *Puffy.* The result of some drug, he supposed. Some medicine, and perhaps no sleep or too much sleep . . . *But he straightened when we came in; he's that much in control.*

Haugen wondered if Donnelly was dying.

Cromwell made the introduction, and the president stared at Haugen without extending his hand. Then, without preamble, Donnelly asked: "Mr. Haugen, are you willing to be vice president?"

Haugen's voice was unexpectedly husky. "Yes, Mr. President, I am."

Donnelly sat briefly silent, as if gathering himself. "Good. You are now the vice president of the United States of America."

Then he turned his eyes to Milstead, questioningly. "Is that it?" he asked.

"Yes, Mr. President, that's it."

Again a lag. "Then I resign," he murmured.

Milstead started to speak. His voice broke, and Haugen looked at him; tears had overbrimmed the man's eyes, and it seemed to Haugen that this man and Donnelly had had dreams together. Milstead gathered his control, sucked in his cheeks and started again.

"Yes Mr. President. We are witness to your appointment of Vice President Haugen, and of your resignation." He looked at Colonel Singleton; Singleton nodded.

"Gentlemen," Singleton said, "if you please." Milstead led the others out of the office. Donnelly's secretary turned away from the door as they came out, but a box of Kleenex was open on her desk. She knew. Haugen felt like an inheritance tax collector at a funeral. Milstead took them into his own office, next to the president's. They could have entered it directly from the Oval Office, but apparently, under the circumstances, Milstead thought their manner of departure was more appropriate.

"Mr. President," Milstead said to Haugen, "we've arranged to have President Donnelly taken at once to Bethesda Naval Hospital. An aerial ambulance should be arriving very shortly."

Milstead paused, seeking mentally for a moment, then took a notebook from his desk, seeming to gain poise and strength as he scanned it. "The first lady and I," he said, "organized the evacuation of the Donnelly's personal and household effects last night. I'll have the household staff notified next. Actual removal should begin tomorrow, and the White House will be yours by the end of the week, or sooner if necessary. Between now and then, a guest room has been prepared for your occupation."

Arne Haugen, President of the United States of America, began to feel a heavy mass settling on him.

"I appreciate that you've had no briefings, nor time to arrange for your own staff," Milstead went on. "I'm available to continue as White House chief of staff until you've selected a replacement, and I believe we can assume the same of most of the appointive staff, including the cabinet. Many of them, I'm sure, have anticipated something like this."

He turned a page in the notebook. "With your approval, sir, I'll call your press secretary, Mr. Okada, now. The nation needs to be informed . . ."

Abruptly a shock hit Haugen, and he interrupted. "Mr. Milstead," he said, "I have to make a phone call. Right now!"

The man looked startled. "Of course, Mr. President."

"How do I get long distance on your phone?"

"Dial nine."

Haugen leaned over the desk, picked up the privacy receiver, and rapped out his home phone number on the keypad. While he waited, he said, "I can't have my wife learn about this on television!"

The ringing at the other end stopped, and Lois Haugen answered.

"Hi, Babe," Haugen said. "I took the job. It starts today.

. . . Well, it's kind of hard to tell you, but—I'm the President of the United States. . . . I know that's not funny; it's true though. I was just appointed vice president a few minutes ago and then President Donnelly resigned. . . . No I'm not crazy either. It'll be on the news later today; I'm calling from the White House right now. . . . Lois? Are you there? . . ."

He turned his face to Cromwell and rolled his eyes.

"Yeah, that's right. I'll have someone on the staff call later today and talk with you about what stuff we ought to ship out here. . . . I know. That's how it feels to me too." He smiled slightly. "It's like the old saying: It's dirty work, but somebody's got to do it.

"Look, I'll call again later. Right now I've got a ton of stuff to do. Okay? . . . Right. . . . If you watch the twelve o'clock news, you'll probably know more about it than I know now. . . . Thanks, sweetheart. You too."

He disconnected and turned to the others. The call seemed to have raised his spirits considerably. "Okay," he said, "let's call Okada in."

The penthouse office of Paul Willard Randolph Massey measured twenty-five by thirty feet, and the suite it was part of occupied the entire fifty-eighth floor penthouse of the Randolph Building in lower Manhattan. There was plenty of room on the adjacent landscaped roof for the private helipad. Massey had been informed that Manhattan was now safe, and he'd had himself flown down after breakfast.

The office furnishings could be described as expensively tasteful or quietly ostentatious, if you were connoisseur enough to realize how much they cost. The whole southwest wall of the office was a polarized thermal window. The drapes were drawn back, exposing a view across Upper Bay toward the Statue of Liberty, and in the farther distance, Staten Island.

The aesthetics of it didn't mean much to Massey, only the convenience. He was a gamesman, the game was power, and only some of the markers were money.

The late morning sun was angling in; it was just past noon, Eastern Daylight Time. His phone buzzed discreetly. A code flashed on its screen, telling him it was a direct line, scrambled, bypassing his receptionist. He touched a key, and a familiar face appeared on the screen. He touched another, activating a recording device that had no telltale. And a third, completing the connection.

Massey hadn't activated the camera at his end. He usually didn't; even in phone conversations with an employee, he liked to operate unseen. Instead he identified himself by his preferred name. "Willard," he said.

"Sir, this is Barron. There is something on the television news you should see. I have it on CBS."

Massey touched keys on a remote, and a picture, with sound, popped into being on his wall set.

"I have it, Barron," he said drily, then neither said anything more as they listened to Lester Okada, the White House press secretary.

". . . per the Emergency Powers Act," Okada was saying. "President Donnelly therefore appointed a vice president and resigned. We now have a new president." Okada paused; the screen cut to a face-on close-up. "The new president's name is Arne Eino Haugen. President Haugen will be formally sworn in this afternoon at 2 P.M., before the cabinet, the Supreme Court, and leading members of the Congress."

After a moment of reportorial silence, Okada proceeded to choose individuals out of the clamor that arose, and answered about ten minutes of questions about Donnelly and Haugen and the legality of the process. When he was done and the network cut away to its commentators in New York, Massey lowered the volume nearly to nil and turned back to Barron Tallmon on the phone.

"Barron," he said, "contact Jaubert. Have him see what he can learn about this Haugen—his finances, his interests, his personal habits and idiosyncracies. Anything discreditable will be particularly appreciated."

He cut Tallmon off and sat quietly thinking for a few moments, then gave his attention to the report he'd been dictating.

SEVEN

Transcript from the evening news, NBC-TV, October 10. Read by Elliot Blanchard.

"Washington was startled, earlier today, by White House press secretary Lester Okada's announcement that President Donnelly had named a new vice president and then resigned. Our new president is Arne Eino Haugen of Duluth, Minnesota.

"The most common response has been 'Arne Who?'

"We have put together the following information about Arne Eino Haugen, and it provides a very unusual and interesting picture.

"Arne Haugen was born on April 3, 1924, reportedly in a log cabin, on a backwoods homestead in Koochiching County, Minnesota, only a few miles from the Canadian border. He was the third of four children, three boys and a girl. His parents were Karl Oskar Haugen, a Norwegian immigrant, and Eila Salminen, a Finnish immigrant, and the children grew up speaking both Norwegian and Finnish. The family had very little money.

"Arne Haugen grew up working for his father on the farm and in the forest, and a few days after his eighteenth birthday, entered the army in April 1942. There, following infantry training, he volunteered for the parachute infantry and was assigned to the Eleventh Airborne Division.

"On completion of parachute training, he went with his division to Australia for jungle training, later participating in the liberation of New Guinea from

42

Japanese occupation. Later, as a platoon sergeant, he took part in the liberation of the Philippines, including the capture of the Los Baños prisoner of war camp on Luzon, behind the collapsing Japanese lines, rescuing the hundreds of American prisoners there before they could be removed or possibly killed by their Japanese guards.

"Both of Haugen's brothers, Kaarlo and Martin, were killed in World War Two, Kaarlo with the 101st Airborne in Normandy, and Martin with the marines on Okinawa, in the last great battle of the war.

"After the war, Haugen worked for a time at logging. Then, on the G.I. Bill, he attended the University of Minnesota, where he studied electrical engineering, participated in intramural wrestling, married Lois Hedstrom of Thief River Falls, Minnesota, and graduated *summa cum laude*—with high honors —in 1952.

"After graduating, Haugen was employed briefly with the Koochiching County, Minnesota, Electric Co-op, which supplied electricity to farm settlements. In 1954 he opened a television repair shop in Duluth, Minnesota, and began spare-time research that, by 1957, had led to several profitable patents in electronics.

"In 1957 he founded Haugen Electronics, Inc., to manufacture and market products based on his patents. He, a cousin, and his father-in-law were reportedly the sole shareholders. By 1961, when he changed the firm's name to Duluth Technologies, Inc., it was reputedly worth two million dollars. It has grown vastly since then, with factories in several locations, and is said to remain family owned.

"The Haugens have two grown children—a son Karl and a daughter Liisa—and seven grandchildren.

"Reportedly, Arne Haugen is a voracious and rapid reader who is respectably informed on a wide variety of subjects. Apparently he will be by far the best linguist ever to occupy the White House. Both he and Mrs. Haugen are said to have studied one language after another for years, and to be at least modestly proficient in about a dozen of them, including Russian, Spanish, Japanese, German, French, Swedish, Tagalog and, not surprisingly, Norwegian and Finnish. Spoken Chinese is reportedly a recent project. Nothing was said about Arabic and Hebrew.

"The president is said to be very healthy, still strong and active, and to have a good sense of humor. All of which he will need. He is also said to be nonpolitical, which will certainly be unusual in a president.

"In a time of domestic troubles unequalled since the War Between the States, the nation will watch this new leader with what undoubtedly will be unprecedented interest and attention, and the interest of the rest of the world will hardly be less."

Party Secretary Boris Alexeevich Kulish sat presiding over the morning meeting of the Politburo. Copies of the previous day's intelligence summary, printed late the night before, were routinely set at each man's place before the members arrived. Normally its review was the first piece of business. This morning though, it lay so far unexamined, except for what it had to say about the new American president.

In the Soviet hierarchy, listening to the BBC, the Voice of America, and Deutsche Welle, are regular, albeit illegal, practices. The night previous, the Politburo members had listened with particular interest for what they could learn about Arne Eino Haugen.

Not that they believed what they heard. In a subculture where lies in politics are essential not only to success but survival, under a philosophy which states unequivocally, that lying is an important tool to be used without hesitation, it is assumed that anything is likely to be a lie.

GRU agents in America would even now be gathering more details on Arne Eino Haugen. Meanwhile, all that the Politburo knew with any confidence was that Haugen was a capitalist-industrialist and a technologist. Obviously his reported background as a poor country boy and laborer had to be false—an artifact manufactured by publicists for public consumption. Very probably, claims of his skill as a technologist, and his youthful experience as a parachute trooper in the Great Patriotic War, were also lies.

And most important, his inexperience in government, at any executive level, was proof that he was a Pentagon puppet.

So now the American president not only had dictatorial authority; America also had a president who might prove effective in using that authority.

It was not at all clear what would ensue, but it could hardly be favorable to Soviet interests. Heretofore, their own greatest advantage over the Americans had been the sometimes unbelievable discoordination and incredible security weaknesses of American government; but now, under Pentagon control, presumably these would be much reduced. The GRU would have to intensify its efforts to monitor and analyze the activities of the American government.

Meanwhile, just now the Politburo had a war and its own serious internal problems to see to, and it was no time to generate unpredictable major complications. Thus it would be well not to move, just then, to capitalize on American social unrest; that could spark unpredictable responses.

Of course, if the new government in Washington should begin a serious anti-Soviet program, perhaps to divert the American people's attention from their troubles at home, that would be something else.

Dave Fiori touched a key, and the flashing light on his phone turned steady white, the beeper stilling. "What is it, Millie?"

"It's Mr. Haugen for you on line three."

"Thanks."

The chief. Everybody's chief now! Fiori touched the button marked 3, and his phone screen lit up. Haugen's face looked through at him, Haugen's voice talking to him from the speaker.

"Dave, I guess you know what's happened back here."

"Right, Mr. President." He grinned. "I'm not sure whether it calls for congratulations or condolences though."

"I'm not either. But it changes some things. I want you to get together with Laura and Morrie and make the final

selection of GPC target communities, and then activate
the release program, but only for the U.S. Same basic
timetable as the original, but set to start tomorrow."

Fiori nodded. It had first been scheduled to start four
days ago, then postponed until the civil scene got sorted
out.

"Any questions?" Haugen asked.

"Nope. I'm glad it's on again."

"Me too. Have fun with it. I've got a ton of stuff to do
here, and I've never given a state-of-the-nation address
before. Gotta get at it. So long."

The screen went blank, and the light on the key pad
blinked out. Fiori unfolded from the chair and left his
office, long legs scissoring down the hall and across a
heatable skywalk that led to the new assembly plant.

There was no need to go there. He just wanted to look
once more before calling Laura and Morrie. He liked looking at it. Simply, it excited him.

In the plant, from a catwalk, he peered out across the
assembly line. It was cleaner than it needed to be; the
manufacturing conditions necessary for the GPC were not
especially demanding. Men and women there wore white
coveralls; the place was nearly spotless, and thoroughly
and softly lit without noticeable shadows. Silent circulators
cycled the air, removing dust electrically.

The activity here was not intense; the chief wasn't big
on intensity, just on production and quality. He preferred
things calm and businesslike. Thick ceramic housings—head-
high cylinders with one end open—lay on low electric jack
trucks along one side, then ranged truckless down an assembly
line on the other side in a sequence of increasing met-
amorphosis. They looked like maroon culvert sections with
bases. On feeder lines that ribbed the space, workers assembled modules which other workers installed in the housings.

None of them knew what they were making, though
they thought they did. Not even the U.S. Patent Office
knew what they really were. The designs and models had
them in miniature as part of something else entirely.

A nearby warehouse stood half full of the devices, ready
for freight cars. And assembly lines were being installed in
new buildings at International Falls, and at Fort Frances,
Ontario.

Phase Two, to be financed by Phase One, would produce small, lightweight units in several sizes.

As he turned and started back for his office, Dave Fiori had both a sense of exhilaration and a nervous stomach. *This time,* he told himself, *it's really on. This time we're going to do it.*

EIGHT

The Chamber of the House of Representatives contained almost a hundred senators and more than four hundred representatives, plus media people and guests— all the room would hold. One of them was Senator Robert Morrows, and for the moment he was hardly aware of the crowd around him. His attention had turned inward, and backward in time.

It had been hard to do anything the last week and a half. The word of the week was *futility.* For a couple of days it had seemed that the country was starting its death throes, and government had been frantic. But since Donnelly's resignation, it was as if everything in Washington had gone suddenly on *hold*—everything but the media and hopefully the Pentagon. And even the media were notably less frenetic than usual. Except in the area of emergency relief—especially food distribution—almost no one in civilian government was doing more than the absolute minimum, if that. A sort of lethargy—a waiting to see what would happen next—hung over everything. Congress was getting very little input from the agencies, and none at all from the White House. But then, Congress wasn't doing much with what it did get.

It had been a time for talking in corridors in small groups, mostly talk with little heat or any other energy.

What heat there'd been was over Donnelly's use of the Emergency Powers Act to appoint his successor without congressional approval, but it was a heat that hadn't spread. Donnelly was under psychiatric care at Bethesda, and somebody had been needed fast. And as Grosberg and Kreiner had pointed out, under the circumstances they'd undoubtedly have approved the appointment without debate. This was no time for campaigning for favorite candidates, and according to Blake, the White House legislative affairs assistant, the option had been Cromwell. In fact, Blake admitted, Cromwell had recommended Haugen.

They'd find out soon enough whether the goddess Serendipity was with them, or whether Murphy's law applied.

The rumor was that Chief Justice Fechner had been so angry with the whole situation that he'd refused to swear the new president in, or attend the swearing in. So Justice Killian had done the honors. Who swore a president in was a matter of tradition, not law.

Months before the violence began, Morrows had had this recurring sinking feeling that the country was going to founder and fail. The exchange of all-out bombing raids between Iran and Iraq, that had resulted in crude oil prices of $67 a barrel, had been the trigger. Followed by wage and price controls, rationing of gasoline and fuel oil, demonstrations when work was accelerated on nuclear power plants, and violent counter-demonstrations against the antinukes . . .

Most of the Congress, on both sides of the aisle, had felt as he did—that the country was going down. That's why, with the collapse of Wall Street and the banks, it had been possible to so quickly ram the Emergency Powers Act through the resistive minority in each house. Just hours ahead of the first major street fighting. Some said it had triggered the fighting, but hardly anyone in Congress really believed that. There'd been some ugly riots before that.

Meanwhile here he was, Robert Jesse Morrows, Bachelor of Political Science *magna cum laude* from Cal State Northridge, junior United States senator from California, ex-state senator, ex-state assemblyman, attending a state-of-the-nation address by a president who'd never been elected to anything and apparently had no training in government or politics.

He was probably a Pentagon front, a false face for military dictatorship. Which might be what was needed. If it hadn't been for martial law, this building would be a looted, burnt-out shell right now. But sooner or later, if the country was to mean anything, if democracy and freedoms were to persist here—maybe if they were to persist anywhere—the United States would have to return to representative democracy.

Benjamin Franklin had said it after the Constitutional Convention, and Lincoln, generations later: Democracy was an experiment; there'd been no assurance it would persist, or any real instruction manual on how to keep it running decently. But what a damned shame if it should end.

Two men walked out onto the dais. The bald-headed one was Kenneth Lynch, Irish-born Speaker of the House. The bandylegged Jewish leprechaun was Senate president pro tem Louis Grosberg. Grosberg was eighty-one, but he'd aged well, standing straight and moving briskly, his shock of white hair semi-erect above bushy black brows.

Then Haugen walked out. From his seat close to the dais, Morrows examined him. The President of the United States was heavy-set, and looked solid and strong in his precisely fitted dark blue suit. He stood perhaps five feet eight. His hair had long since thinned, but there was enough of it, showing enough yellow amid the white, to mark him as a genetic blond. The skin beneath it was tanned. His mouth was wide, the broad face square rather than round, the cheekbones prominent. Thin-rimmed glasses perched on a blunt nose. Haugen had never been close to handsome, Morrows decided, but he emanated a sense of power that grew only partly from thick shoulders, chest, and neck. And a sense of relaxed self-control that aligned well with the impression of physical strength.

If people wanted a strong man with an aura of stability and judgment, the senator told himself, Haugen might be the one. Morrows glanced at his watch: 6:30 P.M. and thirteen seconds. Apparently the new president was also punctual.

He was looking down at the lectern, arranging cards or

papers there. Morrows caught himself wishing this Arne
Haugen well, at least for the time being. His arranging
finished, the president scanned the audience, then seemed
to choose someone among them to direct himself to.

"My name," he began, "is Arne Haugen. And to my
surprise, as much as yours, I find myself President of the
United States. I want to thank Congress for letting me
speak here. This talk, however, is to the whole nation, and
not to the Congress alone.

"This will not be the usual kind of inaugural address.
Because while ordinarily a president takes office well-
known to the people, in this case you do not know me. So
while I'll be telling you how I intend to operate as president, I'll also use part of our time together to let you know
something about me.

"I won't cover everything you might like me to tonight,
but I promise to speak to you frequently as things develop. More frequently than has been usual for presidents.

"To begin with, let me point out that the emergency is
not an emergency of violence. We were in a crashing
emergency, in serious danger as a country, before the
recent violence broke out. The violence was simply an
offshoot of what came before, a sign of how bad things had
gotten. And of course, as is commonly the case, violence
made them worse.

"The violence is over now, at least for the present, but
the country remains in serious, perhaps even critical, condition. We have a lot to do to get it running decently, and
to reform certain institutions so that it doesn't go off the
tracks again. The financial system is in collapse. The production and distribution of goods, including the orderly
distribution of food and fuel, has been seriously disrupted,
as most of you know all too well.

"Things have continued as well as they have, only because many people have been willing to keep working
with no assurance that they'd see a paycheck. Those people are part of the solution. Some others have been part of
the problem.

"Many businesses have closed, folded, due to the un-
wise practices of government, banks, corporations, specu-
lators, and the businessmen themselves. Apparently few of
these practices were criminal in a legal sense, but many

were irresponsible. More commonly they were the actions of people following more or less established ways, which we now see were destructive."

Haugen paused to scan the audience in the chamber.

"Obviously we need to change some things," he went on. "And we will.

"It is appropriate to be critical, and to start criminal proceedings where called for. But almost all of us share responsibility for the catastrophe. We all saw the direction in which things were going, have been going for years. Yet political parties, candidates, office holders, weren't willing to bite the bullet and make the changes necessary. And why not? Because we the people of the United States of America didn't tell them to. We didn't insist on it. Many of us didn't even want them to.

"We *gimme'd* our way into this mess. Now we need to create and work our way out of it. And my job is skipper, captain, the person at the wheel."

It occurred to Morrows that the president didn't seem to be reading, only glancing down now and then as if at notes. He'd heard of people like that, who could look at a page, then look up and recite a paragraph or two verbatim. It made them seem to be delivering extemporaneously. And when Haugen looked up from his speech, it was at someone, apparently a different someone each time. Morrows wondered how much of that was deliberate and how much unconscious.

"To begin with," the president was saying, "I'll continue to take stopgap emergency steps, as President Donnelly did, while putting together a broad rebuilding program, using the best data I can get. Meanwhile I'll update you from time to time, telling you what we're doing, what we plan to do, and what we need you to do if we're going to salvage and rebuild this country.

"I'll talk about specifics later, as we work them out. I'll be discussing economics, health care, the legal system, the environment, and anything else that seems necessary."

He paused as if to emphasize what came next, scanning the audience again. "This isn't going to be your standard democratic process, you know. When a ship is in danger of foundering, of sinking with all hands, that's no time to sit around and play tug-of-war, or argue, or protect cherished prerogatives. The government, with me at the wheel, will continue to operate under emergency powers and martial law.

"Incidentally, President Donnelly first offered the vice presidency to General Cromwell, the chairman of the Joint Chiefs of Staff. He felt that strongly that a firm hand was needed. But General Cromwell declined; he felt that the country might not accept a general as president, and that at any rate a civilian viewpoint was preferable."

He leaned forward now, forearms on the lectern, peering at the audience as if in confidence. "So now you have Arne Haugen as president," he continued. "Why me? Why was I asked to serve? I don't know all the thinking on that, but I can tell you a little about myself that may have influenced the decision.

"I'm an electrical engineer, which reflects enough personal discipline and enough organized intelligence to get through a tough, not much nonsense set of university courses. I'm also a highly successful inventor, which reflects a considerable ability to apply what I know to the solution of previously unsolved problems."

Haugen paused and straightened. "And to ignore standard ways of doing things, when they aren't working. That's been important in the way I work. It may prove important on this job too.

"I'm a self-made multi-millionaire who started out with very little. Which does *not* make me holier than thou. But I did it by manufacturing useful things that I, and people who work with me, invented or improved. And not by the greed-oriented financial gamesmanship that many others have gotten rich by.

"I also did it by living frugally, with minimal borrowing, and working lots of hours, in order to get started and establish a well-developed operation."

He paused again, then grinned unexpectedly. "Incidentally, I'm the first president in more than a century to have been born and raised in a log house. People can use that information someday in playing Trivial Pursuit. And I personally know something about poverty. Though in important respects, farm poverty during the 1920s and 30s was a much less demoralizing experience than urban poverty in the 80s and 90s. Perhaps nothing helps morale more than production does, and we did a lot of that. As a matter of fact, I didn't know we were poor, and I doubt that my parents thought of us that way. We just had very little money. And there was no television, no full-color commercials, to show or tell the Haugen family what it didn't have, what it wasn't able to buy. As far as that's concerned, there wasn't even electricity in our part of the country. And our neighbors were hardscrabble backwoods settlers just as we were.

"I'm also the first American president ever who grew up in a foreign language household—three foreign languages, actually. My mother knew almost no English when I was small; her native language was Finnish, but she could also speak, somewhat, a Swedish dialect. Which was close enough to my father's Norwegian that they could converse effectively. Also each of my grandmothers, one Finnish and one Norwegian, lived with us much of the time, neither speaking English. So I grew up speaking Finnish and a sort of Swedified Norwegian.

"Finnish, incidentally, is utterly different from Norwegian, and learning both at once, I developed a very flexible subconscious program for learning languages. Since then I've found languages both interesting, and easy to learn, and I speak and read a number of them. Which should prove useful in foreign relations."

The president looked up at the video cameras. "And as far as war is concerned," he went on, "I have firsthand experience. Incidentally, the information that found its way to the media was not entirely correct. I trained with the independent 503rd Parachute Infantry Regiment and fought with it in New Guinea and on Noemfoor Island where I was wounded. After rehabilitation, I was *then* assigned to the Eleventh Airborne's 511th Parachute Infantry Regiment, and later wounded on Leyte. After that I fought in southern Luzon and took part in the Los Baños drop. I lost both my brothers to combat, one in Normandy and the other on Peliliu, not Okinawa as reported.

"I do not look on war as something desirable."

He scanned the chamber then, the congressmen. "And now for some things I am not: I am neither politician nor lawyer. There is nothing wrong with being a politician or a lawyer; Lincoln was both. But because I am neither of them, I look at government and many other things from a different viewpoint, a different tradition, than lawyers and politicians do.

"Also, I am not, and never have been, a military supplier. I say that not from any sense of superiority; I'm not putting down the arms industry. I'm simply saying that I have no vested interests in weapons production. If it was not for the arms industry, however, we'd be in a lot worse trouble than we are."

He paused again, brows drawn down for a moment in a severe line, but when he spoke, it was casually.

"And I don't particularly care whether people like me or not. I'd prefer they do, but it isn't important to me. The compulsion to be liked is a trap. I'm going to do what seems to me most likely to salvage the situation and leave the United States of America stronger and more effective, and a better place to live, than ever before.

"Let me restate that, because it needs to be understood. I'm going to do—or try to do—what seems to me most likely to salvage the situation *and to leave the United States stronger, more effective, and a better place to live than ever before.*"

Once more he paused, and when he spoke again, his words were slow and measured. "And to do that—to leave it stronger and better—we'll need to change how we do some pretty basic things in this country. Which I'll talk about later when I've sorted them out more fully.

"And while it's now my responsibility to plot a course and see that the ship's officers steer that course . . . *the rest of you have responsibilities too.* This is not a luxury ship; it's not even a passenger ship. You're not passengers, you're the crew.

"But on the other hand, this is not a slave galley, and I will not make it one.

"There are others who'd like to run this government. Some would like to run it from outside, through puppets. To some of them, even the idea of democracy, of a people free to run their own lives and their government, is utterly unreal. And if those others ever take over, forget freedom for a long time. For lifetimes.

"On the other hand, I am committed to the principle that people should run their own lives. You'll see my dedication to that very soon. I also believe they should run their own government, and I intend to move us further in that direction than this country has been for a while.

"Not that I'm guaranteeing we'll make it. This nation has gone a long way down the road to hell, and it didn't happen in just the last few months or years. It took a long time to slide this far. Also, I can't promise you that I'm wise enough to plan a workable course back out.

"Nor— Nor that you've got the guts and self-discipline to travel such a course. I'm sure that some of you do—that many of you do. The question is, do enough of you?

"But—" He looked the audience over, his expression blunt; then he eased and smiled. "But it's the most interesting, and challenging, and potentially rewarding task that any nation, by which I mean any people, has taken on for a long time. Or any president. And if we pull it off, we'll be a greater nation than ever. I do not exaggerate. If we pull it off, we'll be the greatest nation in history. Young again. Energetic. And more able than ever. Because we'll have learned a lot, and had the experience of overcoming as a people. And we'll have gained a viewpoint that the founding fathers, with all their genuine wisdom, didn't have, couldn't have had back then."

Jesus! thought Morrows. *This man can be inspirational! Now if he's only competent—competent enough.*

The president seemed now to be ignoring his notes. For a moment he contemplated the center camera, his left forearm resting on his abdomen, right elbow propped on left hand, chin cupped thoughtfully for a moment between thumb and forefinger. Morrows watched, intrigued; the man was an even better, a more varied stage performer than Reagan had been.

"For now though," Haugen said, "I'm the boss. Someone has to be. The situation demands it, to reduce the time needed to make decisions and start actions.

"Not that I intend to try running everything. I intend to let people and cities and states solve their own specific problems *so far as they can*. Or to keep their problems if they want to, so long as those problems do not seriously impede national recovery. The main federal function, as I see it, is to create a situation where people *can* solve their own problems, with a little intelligence and guts. But creating such a situation is going to take some doing, take some time, take some changes. Because in recent decades, despite important progress in certain areas, government has, by and large, inhibited real solutions, imposing its own prescriptions and programs and creating a large array of new problems.

"Don't misunderstand me. This will not be a simplistic, hands-off government. Just now, things are in serious shape, and we'll do what is necessary to get them back on track again.

"Some of the things this government will do may prove not to work. When that happens, I will not keep failure alive by refusing to admit that government was wrong. Or that I've been wrong. If I establish some program or executive order and it clearly isn't working, isn't working in spite of having had reasonable time and resources to work, I'll change it or throw it out.

"But I do not intend a society and economy planned and controlled by government. We are not the Soviet Union. We will try not to repeat our own mistakes and we will certainly not repeat theirs. We will give private individuals as much freedom and opportunity as circumstances permit.

"And mentioning the Soviet Union brings up another matter: foreign affairs." The president paused and scanned around. "So what I have to say now, I am directing not only to you, but to other nations, other governments.

"As of now, it cannot be taken for granted that any of yesterday's foreign policies will necessarily be in force next month. Consistency in policy is a virtue only so far as that policy works. Our foreign relations with all countries will be reviewed, with the help of the Foreign Relations Committee of the Senate and the Foreign Affairs Committee of the House of Representatives. And of course with the policy level of the State Department and informed persons outside government.

"These informed persons outside government will include foreign ambassadors and, when it seems useful, the heads of foreign governments. I suspect that some of them will be interested in learning firsthand what this new, little-known American president is like."

The president stood for a moment with lips pursed, as if

considering something, then looked the audience over. "And that, my friends, is all I have to say tonight," he finished. "I've got a lot of work waiting for me. Wish me luck with it, as I wish you luck with yours. Thank you for listening, and I'll talk to you again soon."

He raised his hand in a half wave, half salute, then turned and left the dais, accompanied by Grosberg and Lynch. Secret Service men, who'd been standing quietly at the sides of the dais, preceded and followed them. In the audience, a few people were getting to their feet, but most still sat, sorting out what they'd heard. There was a growing buzz of quiet voices.

Morrows looked around, then within. *Well*, he thought, *I don't know how I'll feel about this tomorrow, but right now I feel better than I did when I got here.*

NINE

Excerpt from a sermon by Reverend Delbert Coombs, of the Stalwart in God Church of the Apocalypse.

Do you believe, do you really believe, that you can fend off the wrath of God at this late day by changing your earthly ruler? No way! Man has been too long on the road to hell! It started with Eve accepting the forbidden fruit from the serpent in the Garden of Eden. But that was just the first step.

In *Revelations*, Jesus showed his beloved John how the world would end and be renewed. And in Chapter Six of Revelations, John tells us: "And behold, a white horse, and its rider had a bow; and a crown was given to him, and he went out aconquering and to conquer." My friends, that showed John how man started out to rule other men. Man went out aconquering, and that was a long step on the road to eternal damnation.

Then Chapter Six goes on to say: "And out came another horse, bright red; its rider was permitted to take peace from the earth, so that men should slay one another; and he was given a great sword." My friends, that was when men began to kill each other, especially in wars. We were really on our way to hell then!

And then John was shown a third horse, and he described it like this: "And behold, a black horse, and its rider had a balance in his hand; and I heard what seemed to be a voice saying, 'A quart of wheat for a denarius, and three quarts of barley for a denarius.'" A denarius was worth about twenty cents. And the balance the third rider carried wasn't the scale of justice, my friends, it was a scale of *injustice*. It was a scale used for selling things. *That's* when people had to start *paying* for their food, and if there'd been any hope before, that finished it off.

And there was a fourth horse shown to John. For John wrote: "And behold, a pale horse, and its rider's name was Death, and Hades followed him; and they were given power over a fourth of the earth, to kill with sword and with famine and with pestilence and by wild beasts of the earth."

Now friends, we all know who Death is, but you might ask who is Hades? Hades is the ruler of the grave, and he is also the ruler of wealth, the king of riches! Though people don't generally realize it, it's Hades they are bargaining with when they undertake to become wealthy!

And *Revelations* says that Death and Hades were given power to kill with the sword, and with famine and pestilence, *and by wild beasts!* Now what do you suppose those wild beasts will be, that will descend upon us in our time? In just a few years from now?

Friends, John was a simple man who lived nearly two thousand years ago. He'd never seen machinery.

What the angel of God showed to John were *tanks!*
Army tanks! And John saw them and figured they
had to be some kind of wild beast. Just like you or I
would have figured in that time, if we'd been with
John and saw what he saw.

So you can see there's no use trying to change
what's going to happen to the world. It's too late
for that now. It's been too late for a long long time.
Your only hope—YOUR ONLY HOPE—is to be
washed in the blood of the lamb! Confess God and
repent of your sins, and thou shalt spend eternity
with the angels!

Or don't, and spend eternity in hell, being tor-
tured by the devil forever.

In the early morning of his fifth day in office, Arne
Haugen awoke with a sense of urgency and a muffled cry,
wakening Lois.

"Is anything the matter?" she asked.

"Not as far as I know; nothing that wasn't the matter
yesterday."

It still wasn't daylight out; the bedroom was lit as much
by the small night light low on one wall as by the faint
dawn filtering through curtains. He peered at his bedside
clock: 0553; the alarm had been set for 0700. "Go back to
sleep if you'd like," he suggested. "It's not six yet."

She responded by turning on her other side. She'd
spent a long day supervising the unpacking and placement
of household and personal things flown from Duluth, while
establishing a working relationship with the huge household staff. Her husband got out of bed and padded to his
bathroom in jockey shorts; he'd never worn pajamas one
night in his life.

He went through his morning toilet routine more or less
on automatic. His mind was buzzing. Something was wrong,
all right: So damn much to do was what was wrong. He
was off his own turf, outside his own area of expertise, and
the machinery was unfamiliar.

On the first day he'd given Milstead his first order: For
the time being, keep operating as if the president was out
of the country somewhere.

His second order had been to remove the handsome,

tradition-rich *Resolute* desk into storage and fit the Oval
Office with a desk designed to accommodate a computer
and accessories. And to move in a file cabinet of his own.
And a coffee station.

Meanwhile he'd worked in a small adjacent room. He'd
spent much of two days preparing his inaugural speech;
nothing was more important at that time than saying the
right things to the nation and the Congress, as best he
could define the right things. And it helped him sort
things out.

He'd also nominated Cromwell his vice president. Cromwell had been more than unhappy about that, but Haugen
had promised to find someone else as soon as he had a
chance to. Then, he said, Cromwell would be welcome to
resign as V.P. He'd had Milstead send Cromwell's nomination to Congress for approval. There wasn't the kind of
urgency that called for bypassing them, and it was politic
to refer it to them.

After his speech, Haugen had spent the rest of the day
getting oriented on White House staff operations, as they'd
been handled under Donnelly. He'd willingly accepted
Milstead's offer to remain; in fact he'd asked all of Donnelly's
staff to stay on awhile. He himself had no political staff,
nor any friends with operating experience at anything
approaching this level of government. No people of his
own had spent the usual months getting informed on how
things were done in the Office of the President, developing their own concepts on it, in preparation for taking
over. Nor was he willing to strip his Duluth offices of
people he relied upon there, bringing them to Washington
for training.

When he began to make changes in operating procedures, and he could already see things he'd probably
change, Donnelly's people would have to adjust. No doubt
he'd end up replacing some of them. But for now their
experience was essential, and he'd let them operate pretty
much as they were used to.

The day after that he'd spent from 0900 till 1700, including a working lunch, getting briefed by six of his
cabinet secretaries or acting secretaries—State, Treasury,
Defense, Justice, Interior, and Agriculture. They were
holdovers too. They'd given him written summaries of

their departmental operations, and after supper he'd read until midnight. Today he was scheduled for a National Security Council meeting at 1000. Then, after lunch, more cabinet secretaries.

While dressing, he played with possible strategies for keeping things manageable and him on top of them. At 0614 he left his bedroom, wearing slacks, shirt, and loafers, and started for his office. Two waiting Secret Service men got up from their chairs when he entered the Stair Hall, replied to his brisk "Good morning," and fell in beside him.

The corridor to the Executive Wing took him past the White House press area. When the shooting began and martial law was declared, it had been vacated on the stated basis that the fewer extraneous people there were in the White House, the less confusion and distractions there would be, and security would be easier to maintain. At this gray and silent hour, the sense of vacancy in the corridor was profound.

The Oval Office, by contrast, seemed friendly. He left the ceiling light dark, turning on only his desk lamp. Somehow the room seemed more intimate that way. Then he began quietly to dictate tentative operating policies and guidelines, the Haugen version, for the Office of the President. When his secretary came in at eight, he'd give her the tape to type. He'd have her give the written version to Milstead, with a request for his comments.

And he'd ask for her comments too; a secretary is likely to know things about an operation that the boss might never notice.

He worked fast. By 0640 he'd done as much on that as he was prepared to, and started diagraming cabinet departments as he remembered them from his briefings. At 0700 the black pencil flow chart of existing State Department operations, as he understood them, was taking on a scattering of red lines—changes were beginning to grow out of the president's creative mind. And on a ruled yellow pad, a list of questions was taking form.

Then the First Serving Man came in. Apparently, Haugen decided, the domestic staff had a system for knowing when the president was up and about.

"Sir?"

"What is it, Jerry?"

"Yesterday the First Lady said to ask you where you'd like breakfast served. President and Mrs. Donnelly usually took breakfast in the family sitting room to the morning news, but you can have it served anywhere you'd like."

"For today, right here will be fine. Mrs. Haugen is sleeping in this morning. I'd like a two egg omelet, with mushrooms, ripe olives, and Mozzarella. And two slices of diet whole wheat toast, well buttered. No potatoes for breakfast. Orange juice and a battery of vitamins. Any problems with that?"

"I'm sure there won't be, sir. Would eight o'clock be about right? I can have it here by seven-thirty if you'd like."

"Eight o'clock is fine today; I don't have any appointments till ten. But as a general rule— Hm-m. I'd better talk with Mrs. Haugen about that. She's my head of household."

"Yes sir." Jerry left, and Haugen continued to modify, on paper and conditionally, the Departments of State and Treasury. He didn't take what he was doing very seriously at this point. As much as anything it was to exercise the knowledge he'd gotten in yesterday's briefings, make it really his, and identify gaps in his understanding.

His secretary arrived at almost the same time as the omelet, and so did the daily intelligence summary from the CIA. It shared his attention with breakfast. Some of the information wasn't too meaningful to him yet; he lacked contexts for it. As he chewed and read, he promised himself more relaxed breakfasts, once he got his feet more firmly on the ground.

When he'd finished eating, he buzzed his secretary, who came in while he stacked his dishes on the tray. "Ms. Martinelli," he said, "I'd like an appointment with Senator Harley Borden for seven this evening, if possible. And one with Senator Kanazawa for tomorrow morning at 11 A.M. And phone Professor Dell Krzinsky"—he spelled the name for her—"of Penn State University; ask him to call me at nine this evening. If any of them ask what it's about, tell them I'm looking for advice."

She left, and he continued reading the summary, scarcely noticing when Jerry took away the dishes. It wasn't as long as he'd half expected, and he absorbed it rapidly. The Iranian army had executed some of the top people in the Iraqi government and military, but beyond that, the feared post-conquest bloodbath wasn't taking place, at least not by the Iranian military. Some militant Iraqi Shiites had killed some government officials, but that seemed to be an evening of old scores, not the beginning of any wide-scale sectarian massacre.

Haugen shook his head. The Iranians had been nothing if not persistent. The war had been going on since— when?—about 1980, with occasional periods of vigorous activity and longer spells of logistical regrouping. At times it had seemed it would peter out and die. Then, under the leadership of the Ayatollah Jalal, Iran had reorganized both its government and its military. And when they'd struck again, their manpower predominance had been decisive.

More worrisome, a Soviet army group was on manuevers in the Caucausus. Another had moved into the Afghan SSR—what had earlier been known as Afghanistan—and encamped between Herat and Tir Pol, which the map showed within one hundred miles of the Iranian border. It was believed—or hoped—that these were only posturings to intimidate Iran, in case the victorious Ayatollah had designs on Kuwait. The Soviets had condemned Iran as "anti-revolutionary"—certainly a weird view of Iran—and considered it an enemy of the USSR.

He'd nearly finished the intelligence report when his phone buzzed. He touched the blinking key. "What is it, Ms. Martinelli?"

"Father Schwanze is here, Mr. President. He was President Donnelly's White House chaplain, and he'd like to see you if you have a moment."

Haugen wondered what that was about; the White House organization chart showed no chaplain.

"Send him in," he said.

The man who entered was perhaps a decade younger than Haugen, but frail, and wore clerical garb—a suit not quite black and certainly not new, with clerical collar.

"Good morning, Mr. President," he said. His voice was more robust than his body. "I'm Father Albert Schwanze. President Donnelly felt a need for a White House chaplain. I'd been his parish priest back in Colorado, and he arranged for me to be assigned here. I was away on sick leave when he resigned, and I've come to get my things. Unless of course you'd like me to stay."

His gaze was direct, his manner confident, and despite the name, the man seemed somehow Irish to Haugen.

"Although, from your origins," Schwanze continued, "I imagine you're Lutheran."

"Thank you, Father," Haugen said. "I hadn't thought about a chaplain; hadn't realized that was part of the establishment here."

"It hasn't been; President Donnelly was an exception."

"Hmm. Thank you for bringing the subject up. I have a friend . . ."

He didn't finish, changed directions. "I suppose you have friends here among the staff."

"Mainly the domestic staff." Schwanze chuckled. "They work hard, but they're not as absorbed by their work as the executive staff."

"Right. Let's see now." Glancing at the household directory beneath the glass top of his desk, Haugen found the chief usher's number and touched keys on his phone. "Mr. Lavender, this is the president. Father Schwanze came to get his things. Have someone help him. And have the chief housekeeper arrange a farewell luncheon for him if he'd like one. Let the household staff know, so they can attend."

He stood then, in unspoken dismissal, and shook hands with the priest. "Thank you for the offer, Father Schwanze. I trust your next assignment is as interesting as this one must have been." His grinned flashed. "Or less interesting, if you'd prefer."

Schwanze laughed. "They're all interesting, Mr. President. Different but interesting." He sobered then, but just a little, retaining a certain lightness. "Though perhaps not as interesting as the one you've taken on. You have my best wishes, Mr. President, and my prayers." He laughed again. "I'm quite willing to pray for a Protestant, you know."

With that, the priest left, and when Haugen finished reading the intelligence summary, he returned to his diagrams. After a bit he looked at the wall clock: 0934. Again he buzzed his secretary. "Ms. Martinelli, I'd like you to call a Duluth, Minnesota number for me: Regis High School. That's area code 218, and the number is 723-5110. Tell the receptionist it's the President of the United States calling Father Stephen Flynn."

He grinned again as he turned his attention once more to a diagram. He'd finished before Martinelli buzzed back. "Father Flynn is on line one," she said.

He touched the blinking key, and Flynn's face appeared on the CRT. "Hello, Steve. Glad you could call back."

"Oh my! No problem. A secretary came and got me out of class." He laughed, not a frequent event for the usually serious Flynn. "You should have seen the faces in my class when she said the President of the United States wanted to speak to me. You've made my reputation, Mr. President."

"Glad to help keep life interesting. And between you and me, I'm still Arne. Look. Do you think your superior would approve your coming to Washington as the White House chaplain?"

The silence at the other end stretched on for five seconds or more. Haugen's grin grew.

"Are you okay Steve?"

"Yes." Flynn grinned briefly back. "And I have little doubt that he would. But— Why is it you've chosen me?"

"I haven't really rationalized that." Haugen laughed. "Shouldn't every ruler have a Jesuit behind him?" He turned thoughtful then. "I suppose I want an auxiliary conscience, in case my own fails me. Someone in addition to Lois that I can talk freely to and trust—and with a non-government viewpoint. And we're friends, and you're a trained listener."

Again there was brief silence, this one shorter. "Arne," said Flynn, "I'd be happy to. To be of any help I can. How soon must I be there?"

"There's no urgency about it, but there's no reason at this end to delay, either. Let's say in ten days, if that's all right with you and the school. But you'll be welcome sooner if it's convenient. Why don't you take it up with your superior and let me know. My secretary is Ms. Martinelli; she'll make sure I get your message, or your call if it's practical for me at the time."

Haugen paused. "This *is* all right with you, isn't it? It

occurs to me that you might miss the classroom, and the associations."

"Don't worry about that, Mr. President. This is something I'll be very happy to do. But a warning: If I'm to be your chaplain, I'll be speaking my mind on things."

"Fine. I'll want you to.

"I'll let you go now though. I've got a National Security Council meeting in a few minutes. My first. I'll look forward to hearing when you'll arrive. Meanwhile have a good one."

"Thank you, Mr. President."

The line went dead, and Haugen looked again at the clock, wondering really why he'd done what he'd just done.

TEN

The emergency phone beside the presidential bed ruptured Haugen's sleep with shrill urgency. He groped for it, nerves vibrating. "This is the president."

"This is General Hammaker, Mr. President. I have something very important to tell you."

His military aide. Haugen squinted, reading the luminous dial of his bedside clock: 1138. He'd been in bed less than half an hour.

"All right. Let's have it."

"The Soviet Union has invaded Iran, about an hour ago. An army group, part of the Trans-Caucasus Command, moved south across the border, out of the Nakhichevan SSR. Another army group started across the eastern border from the Afghan SSR at about the same time."

"When did you find this out?"

"Intelligence picked it up monitoring Iranian and Soviet military radio less than an hour ago. We have satellite verification now."

The president was aware of his wife sitting up, looking at him. He covered the mouthpiece with a hand. "Russia's invaded Iran," he murmured to her. Then, into the phone:

"What's the action situation?"

"We don't have much on that, but they're moving pretty rapidly."

"All right. Have a communication center set up here in the White House by 0700. With computer equipment that can generate large-scale maps and receive and process satellite images. Can that be done?"

"I'm sure it can, Mr. President."

"Fine. Do the media have this yet?"

"Not that I know of. But if they don't, they will soon. They're sure to know about it in Ankara by now, and probably Amman and Jerusalem. Uh— Regarding the media, is there something you want stated or withheld?"

"No." Haugen sat silent for a moment. "I'm going back to sleep now. Call me again at five and update me."

"Yes sir, Mr. President."

Haugen hung up, then switched on his bedside lamp and sat staring at nothing. Lois got out of bed.

"I don't know about you," she said, "but I'm wide awake. Would you like a midnight glass of wine with me?"

He grunted. "Just what I had in mind." Insomnia was something neither of them had trouble with, but he'd need to settle down for a few minutes before he'd be ready to sleep again.

Paul Willard Randolph Massey slept alone; at age sixty-four, he was long a widower and disinterested in sex. This morning he too was awakened by phone, its ring less strident than the president's. The basic message was much like that received by Arne Haugen, but eight hours later; it was already daylight.

The official throne of the Massey financial empire was in the Randolph Building on Manhattan, but it was so tightly organized and run that most often its master stayed at home in the forested hills of Connecticut's Litchfield County.

To those who have always had a great deal of money, other interests tend to be paramount. And as often as not, what Paul Massey worked on had nothing to do with business, or was peripheral to it.

In the last decade of the twentieth century, the electronic communication net allowed a new mode of operation. And when electronic communication wouldn't do—if he was needed in Manhattan or preferred to be there— there was always the helicopter.

Of course, electronic communication is not as secure as face to face communication in a safe place. And in some enterprises, security is important. But electronic safeguards—scramblers and other countermeasures—had become extremely sophisticated; while with ultra-miniaturized bugs, and other even more advanced listening devices, even face to face communication involved a degree of security risk.

After eating, Massey called Barron Tallmon, his chief of staff for Holist operations. From another apartment in the Massey compound, Tallmon's long horsey face appeared on the screen.

"This is Barron."

"Phone up Jaubert for me."

"Mr. Massey, Jaubert is here. At the compound. He arrived last evening about nine. We have just eaten breakfast and were talking."

"Put him on please, Barron."

Another face replaced Tallmon's, rounder, and fine-boned beneath a mostly bald head. The mustache, thin and black as a mascara brush, seemed a relict from the 1920s or 30s.

"Yes, Mr. Massey?"

"What have you been able to obtain on Haugen?"

"Nothing of conspicuous value. Actually he did belong to a political party in the 1970s—the Libertarian Party. But he did not participate beyond attending some meetings, and he left it in 1978, reportedly with the comment that its overall philosophy was impractical of implementation. Or words to that effect.

"So far, my people have uncovered no indication of scandal or criminality in either his personal or business life."

"Hm-m." Massey looked unconvinced. "Keep looking, Jaubert, keep looking. And remember, it is not essential that we find anything factually disgraceful. Although that would be best. Something that can be interpreted . . . D'you know what I mean? If it *suggests* something reprehensible . . . If we can't have an exposé, then a whispering campaign will do, especially if it is rooted in some actual association. Yes." Massey's mind raced. "Check his close associates, from boyhood on. For, say, neo-Nazi associations, the Ku Klux Klan, homosexuality . . . You see what I mean. After all, we will not be connected to any accusations. We'll leave that to the media. The tabloids if necessary; they're widely read, even if most people don't take them seriously."

"Of course, Mr. Massey."

Paul Massey was beginning to feel a certain exhilaration. Yes, this Haugen would be handled. "Put Barron back on please."

Barron Tallmon had, of course, heard all of it. They were not using a privacy receiver; output at either end was normally through a desk speaker. Massey somehow seemed to overlook that, perpetually. Tallmon simply moved in front of the miniature video pickup.

"Yes, Mr. Massey."

"I am encouraged by Mr. Haugen's background in the Libertarian Party. Even given his rejection of it as a political organization, to the extent that it reflects his philosophic tendencies, he will botch his presidency."

He paused as if pulling on some thread of thought.

"And while you're at it, Barron, please have Mr. Jaubert investigate General Cromwell. As vice president, it would be helpful if we could find some latent scandal fermenting in his past.

"Oh, and one thing further. In contracting with Mr. Jaubert, please do not be prodigal with my money. I realize that Jaubert's is a very valuable, a very resourceful, a very *circumspect* agency, to be treated with a certain generosity. And that you two are—close friends. But after all, Barron, you are responsible for the judicious management of project funds.

"Do you see my position on this?"

"Of course, Mr. Massey. I understand fully."

"Good. I was sure you would. I'll be in the steam room and then with the masseur for a while. After that I expect to spend most of the day with Barnes at the computer. As soon as you and Mr. Jaubert have completed your busi-

ness, I'll want to talk with you personally. Do not hesitate
to interrupt me then.

"Meanwhile please give Mr. Jaubert my best regards."

"Yes Mr. Massey." *As if,* thought Tallmon, *Alain wasn't
right here listening.*

When Massey broke the connection, he sat contemplating the carpet for a minute. Scandal didn't have the impact
it used to, unless it was flagrant. And anything flagrant
would bring investigation, which could prove dangerous if
the scandal was bogus.

I suppose, he thought, *it would be well to have Barron
prepare contingency plans for the demise of this Haugen.*

But it wouldn't do to bring the subject up in the presence of an extraneous third party, and murder was not
Alain Jaubert's kind of business.

ELEVEN

As General Hammaker had promised, the communications center with the Pentagon had been set up in
Hammaker's office when Haugen arrived at 0700. Hammaker
didn't say much, just let a summary scroll slowly up the
large screen, interrupted by occasional maps and recon-
naisance overflight pictures.

There were photos from a recon satellite—photos whose
detail astonished Haugen. Even more detailed were photos shot from seventeen miles up by Lockheed's latest
version of the SR-71. And as always, Iranian and Soviet
radio traffic had been recorded.

Neither combatant was issuing combat communiques.
So far, in fact, the Soviets had said only that they had
"sent military forces into Iran to end its barbaric genocide
of the Iraqi people." Whether that meant that the Russians planned to take over both countries was not clear.

There had been fighting in Teheran itself hundreds of miles in advance of Soviet ground forces. The Russians had dropped *spetsnaz* commandos—suicide companies—into the capital to kill key government figures, destroy key government and utility installations, and sow general confusion. The Iranians claimed that all Soviet commando units had been eradicated, but overflights and radio monitoring indicated that some still held out under heavy pressure. They'd done a lot of damage, but the Iranians insisted that the Ayatollah Jalal had escaped "the godless terrorists" and was leading the Iranian people in their holy fight against the Great Russian Satan.

In the northeast, in the angle formed by boundaries with the Turkmen and Afghan SSRs, the terrain was not as ill-suited to rapid movement by ground forces, especially now that the desert's summer heat had passed. And particularly since the Iranian army had pulled its better-trained, better-equipped units out of the region for use in the conquest of Iraq. Soviet "motor-rifle divisions"—mechanized infantry—preceded by strong aerial ground support and heavy mortar and rocket bombardment, had broken through Iranian defense positions, and Soviet tank divisions had poured through. Already these had collapsed the entire Iranian defense zone there. Soviet second-level mechanized infantry divisions—units superior to the first level shock units—were now moving briskly down the road toward Teheran some six hundred miles west. Also, airborne forces were being used to take and control occasional difficult terrain.

In the northwest too, road access was limited to a single highway, and in addition the terrain was rugged. It was very difficult country to invade through; the Pentagon wasn't fully agreed on why the Russians were even bothering. One suggestion was that they were using it as a sort of training and shakedown mission. Whatever their primary purpose, they were proceeding methodically, according to the Soviet textbook, and it was providing an excellent test of invasion procedures for mountainous country.

Here the Iranian army had set up a defense zone in depth, suited to the circumstances, but apparently it too was manned mostly by second-class troops. Reportedly and apparently, when the Soviets had begun their threatening military demonstrations north of the border, the Iranians had hurried demolition squads to bridges along the sole highway, to blow them if and when the Russians invaded. Numerous other small units had already been located close below strategic ridge crests and in side valleys, from which they could either shell bridges, and the road itself where it traversed steep sideslopes, or make coordinated strikes against Soviet military columns on the highway.

However, there was no indication of major fighting. Apparently and predictably, the Soviets had dropped *spetsnaz* forces at numerous points to take bridges before they could be blown, and to destroy hardened artillery and rocket emplacements. Also, after sharp air attacks, airborne assault battalions, elites of the Red Army, had been landed to destroy or disperse Iranian counter-strike forces which the Soviet command considered important enough.

Nonetheless, the Iranians had destroyed several bridges, and the highway had been severely damaged in a number of awkward-to-repair places. Soviet engineering units, equipped with motorized, prefabricated bridge sections, giant Mi-6 and Mi-10 transport helicopters, heavy construction equipment, and specially trained and equipped demolition specialists, had moved quickly to span ravines and in general clear the highway of obstructions as the army came to them.

Despite Russian dawn airstrikes on Iranian airfields, the Iranian Air Force had managed to fly sorties on both fronts, but both their electronic countermeasures and their surviving numbers were inadequate in the face of the world's best mobile surface-to-air defenses. USAF radio monitors in Turkey reported fights between Iranian and Soviet planes, and losses by both sides.

That was the status of the Soviet-Iranian war eight hours after it began. Haugen frowned thoughtfully, reached for a house phone, then changed his mind.

"Thank you, Ernie," he said, and left the room. Walking briskly to his office suite, he paused at Martinelli's desk.

"Ms. Martinelli," he said as she looked up, "what is your first name?"

"Why, Jeanne, Mr. President."

"Good. I noticed that first day that Milstead and others called you Ms. Martinelli, so I've been following their example. But as frequently as I speak to you, I'd rather call you 'Jeanne.' If that's all right with you."

"That's fine, sir. You can call me Jeanne if you prefer. I suppose the others call me 'Ms. Martinelli' because President Donnelly did."

"Good. Jeanne, get General Cromwell on the phone for me."

"Certainly, sir. And sir, Mr. Okada asked to talk to you as soon as practical."

"Okay, I'll take him first."

He went into his office wondering what she'd say if he invited her to call him Arne. No point in breaking needlessly with tradition though. He hadn't sat down yet when she buzzed him. "Mr. Okada was across the street, sir. At the Executive Office Building. He should be here in three or four minutes."

"Thanks." Haugen's eyes moved to the clock and he sat back to wait. There was a moving-belt underground walkway from the Executive Office Building; three or four minutes was a reasonable prediction.

Actually it took three minutes and twenty seconds for his press secretary to arrive.

"Good morning, Mr. President."

"Good morning, Lester. What is it you want?"

"The White House press corps is pretty eager to find out what you've been doing; they've been after me about it, actually. And it occurred to me that it might be good public relations if I could schedule a press conference for you."

Haugen frowned. "What do you mean, they've been after you?"

"Their spokesman, their pipeline to me, is Frederick Rohmer of the AP. He called me at seven this morning and said they want to hear your reaction to the Soviet invasion of Iran."

"What did you tell him?"

"I told him I hadn't had a chance to talk to you about it yet." Okada paused, clearly not done yet. "You could brief me, of course, or have Mr. Milstead brief me . . ."

The president was frowning: The Secret Service would

shit a brick if he let the press back into the White House. "Where would a press conference be held?"

"I've arranged for a room across the street to be available for presidential press conferences. When I talk to them, I go to the temporary press area in the Quaker Hotel."

"Okay. Tell them I'll talk to them across the street at—" Haugen looked at the clock. "At eight-thirty."

"This morning?" Okada was clearly startled.

"Why not?"

"Well, it's already five after eight."

"They'll just have to hustle around and get there. It's feasible for them, isn't it?"

"It would be calling it pretty closely sir, for the television coverage. But what I meant, sir, is— That doesn't give you any time to prepare. Briefings and so forth."

"Lester, I've been getting briefed for the last several days. I'll tell you something. I'm going to be communicating with the public more than any president in history, and if I have to spend a lot of time getting ready, each time I decide to talk, I'll never get anything else done.

"Tell them ten o'clock then. That'll give me time to look at the daily intelligence summary. That'll have to be preparation enough." He grinned. "If they try to eat me alive, it may get pretty interesting."

Okada nodded, clearly worried. "Yes sir." It seemed as if he was going to say something further, then decided to let it go at that.

"Is that all, Lester?"

"Yes, Mr. President."

"Fine. Let 'em know. Now I've got things to do."

He reached to his phone as Okada left, and buzzed Martinelli. "Jeanne, call General Cromwell for me now."

He waited. After a few moments, Cromwell's face appeared on the screen. "Jumper," Haugen said, "I want a briefing on the Kremlin. I've already read a written brief provided by State, but I'd like an outside viewpoint. And I remember hearing about some deputy Soviet ambassador who defected about three years ago. You mentioned him when we were in Canada—said he was the most interesting source you ever heard. How do I get in touch with him? Without going through State?"

"Mr. President, if we're going to talk about that, let's run this conversation through a scrambler. Have you been shown how?"

"Hammaker showed me."

"Good. And it's probably best if you take it on your privacy receiver. Okay?"

"Be my guest."

The line and screen both cleared. Haugen rapped keys and picked up the old-style receiver from its cradle. After about ten seconds, Cromwell's voice spoke to him from it. "His name is Nikita Bulavin, sir. Naturally he's been sentenced to death by the Kremlin, for treason, and the KGB would love to assassinate him. So he's under careful security. Even the CIA doesn't know where he is; I can practically guarantee it. And not more than three people in the FBI. State doesn't have the foggiest where he is.

"But it so happens that I can get in touch with him personally. When would you like to see him?"

"Is this afternoon feasible?"

"I'm pretty sure it is. How about 1400 hours? If he can't make it then, I'll let you know."

"Good. Where?"

"How about your office?" Cromwell asked.

"That's fine with me. Give me a rundown on him."

"He's ex-GRU—Soviet Military Intelligence—a major general. But earlier he was what the Sovs call an illegal—that is, he ran a GRU spy ring in California. He's about as experienced and cool as anyone you'll ever meet. His English is excellent and we've had his face altered. Even his mannerisms are American. He'll walk in there as if he paid taxes. Which he does these days."

"At 1400 hours, you say?"

"If that's all right with you, Mr. President. He'll arrive there as military—a bird colonel. Colonel Schubert."

"Huh! I look forward to it."

"One thing more sir. Have you decided about the Saudi request yet? For fighter squadrons?"

The president frowned. "What's that about?"

There was a lag in Cromwell's response, as if in reaction to the president's not having heard. "We got it by the grapevine that the Saudi ambassador got in touch with

State last night. They've asked for a couple of USAF fighter squadrons; they're worried about the Soviets."

"What time did he call?"

"About 3 A.M. our time. About 10 A.M. there."

"I may have something about it on my desk. What problems would that make for the Air Force?"

"Trenary says none. He says we could have them there in thirty-six hours. Their support unit would take a little longer, but they could use Saudi support people to begin with."

"I'll let you know," Haugen said. "And thanks for bringing it up.

"I'm going to hang up now, Jumper. I've having a press conference across the street at 1000 hours, my first. I don't know when they'll telecast it. Maybe live. Watch if you have a chance. You can critique my performance."

As usual at a presidential press conference, the room was filled. Haugen stepped up and looked around.

"Ladies, gentlemen, I don't know the protocol here, but I'm going to set my own ground rules. When you've been picked to ask a question, give your name and affiliation before you ask it. I like to know who I'm talking to, and TV viewers may also want to know.

"All right, let's start." He pointed. "Yes."

"Betsy Mitchum, *Omaha World Herald*. What is the government's formal position on the Soviet invasion of Iran?"

"Our position is that it's a criminal invasion of a sovereign nation. The Kremlin's claim that it attacked to save Iraq from genocide is not believable. First, the Iranians were not carrying out genocide; genocide has become a buzz word. What Hitler carried out against European Jews and Gypsies was genocide. Secondly, in the past, the Kremlin didn't hesitate to kill large numbers of people, millions of them, within its own boundaries. And even given that Stalin is long dead, it's hard to credit the Kremlin with that much concern over human rights and lives. I think we can say they have other purposes that we haven't identified yet.

"Next." He pointed. "The slender man in the plaid jacket. Yes."

"Have you divested yourself of your financial holdings in Duluth Technologies, and if not, why not?" The words per se were not offensive, but the tone they were delivered in was accusatory, hostile.

The room became abruptly still, almost breathless. This president operated under extraordinary powers, and the country was under martial law.

"I'm sorry," said Haugen, "but you didn't identify yourself. Start over again."

"I don't see why I should identify myself!" The voice was defiant now. "You're just trying to intimidate us! If we announce our names, you can put anyone on your hit list if you don't like their question."

Haugen looked quizzically at the man. "You're right," he said, "I could. But I wouldn't." He scanned around. "Next?"

The reporters didn't react with their usual alacrity. Then one hand went up, another, and another.

"The tall man in the blue shirt. Yes."

"I'm Roger Brent. *U.S.A. Today*. I found the last question interesting. *Have* you divested yourself of your Duluth Technologies stocks? And if not, why not?"

"No, Roger, I haven't. For one thing, I don't consider them an investment; they constitute control, of a company I've spent most of my life developing. It's my creation—the child of my mind, you might say. And I don't know how long I'll hold the presidency, but presumably not long. Hopefully not more than two years and very possibly not even one. Duluth Technologies is where I'll return when I'm done in Washington.

"And beyond that, there's a technical reason. It's not an open corporation, it's a family corporation. I can't offer the stock on the market; in fact, I'm closely limited in who I can sell it to. But the main reason is the one I gave before.

"Next. The lady in the russet suit. Yes."

"Elaine Guttierez, *L.A. Times*. Mr. President, I realize you've only been in office for a few days, but when can we expect to see some further economic measures to improve the condition of the public?"

"Most of my time in office has been spent in briefings, finding out what goes on behind the scenes and how the machinery works. President Donnelly took the immediate, and most obvious, coping-type steps. The necessary first aid measures. The military has authorization to follow up with other measures of the same general kind, as needed. They're the people with organization, who are out there on a day after day basis, seeing what's happening. The next stage, the stage that's just getting started, is a diagnosis of what the root problems are. Treatments will follow that. Expect to hear some specifics in under three weeks."

Once more he looked and pointed. "The man in the plaid jacket again."

This time he identified himself. "Robert Mantes, the *American Daily Flag*." The man's eyes were bright. "Are you not, in fact, a dictator instead of a president?"

Haugen didn't blink. "First of all, *president* is a term applied to someone who presides. Right now I'm presiding over the government of the United States, so the title fits. As for dictator, in the sense of the authority I hold, I suppose that fits too. But for obvious reasons, the word carries a lot of heavy emotional luggage, dating from the days of Adolf Hitler and Joseph Stalin, to name familiar examples. Or Papa Doc Duvalier. So I would hope people will think of me as the president and not as a dictator.

"Meanwhile I understand your concern, which I'm sure that more than a few people share. But I haven't exactly been throwing my weight around. I will throw it around later, to a degree, as I decide on what changes need to be made. I'll have to, to make things move. But I don't expect to throw it around against the public. I'll be throwing it against parts of the system, as lightly as feasible, as heavily as necessary, in order to get the system moving. Like pushing a car stuck in the snow.

"This government will be installing some rather basic changes, in the direction of making the entire country more effective while protecting individual liberties. And things won't always run smoothly. But then, when have they? Read the history of the 1780s and 90s to get a picture of a nation adjusting, and at times flapping around.

"First aid won't keep the patient alive for long, let alone get him healthy again. So we'll complete our diagnosis and apply some systemic prescriptions.

"Let me talk more about that for a minute. Some of the more basic problems of this country carry a lot of agitated emotion—resentment, bitterness, distrust, anger. You know about those, Robert. Emotion generated by old injustices, old disappointments, broken expectations, broken promises.

"Not all those broken expectations were reasonable or even possible, but that doesn't lessen the emotion.

"And a lot of those basic problems are held in place by vested interests.

"Those are the major reasons I'll be talking to the people as much as I will: to defuse emotions, and for public support against vested interests. Those are the reasons I'm here talking to you less than two hours after Mr. Okada brought up the matter of a press conference.

"Next. The man with the salt and pepper beard."

"Alfred Johnson with the *Atlanta Constitution*. Mr. President, are you or are you not under the control of the Pentagon?"

Haugen's eyebrows rose. "Why do you ask that?"

"It's been speculated that General Cromwell declined the presidency because he thought he could run things more effectively behind a civilian front man."

"Sorry to ruin such a juicy rumor, but it's not true. Feel free to be skeptical, but when you've gotten to know me better, I think you'll accept that I'm nobody's puppet.

"Next."

The president answered three more questioners, then ended the session.

The president's phone buzzed. He answered it.

"Mr. President, I've got Secretary Coulter for you now, on line one."

"Thank you, Jeanne." A thick forefinger jabbed. The handsome features and thick white hair of the Secretary of State appeared on the phone screen. "Good morning, Mr. Coulter." The president's words were cordial enough, but the tone was crisply neutral.

"Good morning, Mr. President. I'm sorry I was out of the office when your secretary tried to get me before. How can I help you?"

"What have you heard from the Saudis since the Soviets invaded Iran?"

"Well, their principal communication was a request to have American fighter squadrons posted in their country."

"I see. Did you suppose I wouldn't be interested in knowing about that?"

"Not at all, sir. I intended to bring it up before the National Security Council tomorrow morning. And frankly, Mr. President, I'm rather surprised you didn't call a council meeting for this morning."

The president looked intently at the face on the screen. Coulter didn't seem to notice. "I considered it," Haugen replied, "and decided to allow the military situation there to develop further before we met. I saw nothing in either the intelligence summary or the military briefing that called for an immediate meeting. Now about the Saudi request: What do you recommend and why?"

"Sir, we have provided the Saudi Air Force with three wings of F-16Ds, two of F-111Gs, and a squadron of F-21Bs. I considered their request for Air Force squadrons an unjustified, knee-jerk response to the Soviet action."

"Mr. Coulter, that sounds to me like a military evaluation. That bailiwick belongs to Campbell and the Pentagon. Do you have any *diplomatic* reasons to send or not to send American squadrons to Saudi Arabia?"

Coulter's reply was slow, measured. "President Donnelly's diplomatic policy has been to avoid any further military buildup in the Middle East. The Iranian military machine was already inferior in equipment to the Saudis; they have mostly older, export models of Soviet equipment, and American equipment dating back to the Shah. The Syrians have been too concerned with the Israelis to worry the Saudis, and they've been on good terms with the Iraqis, as of course the Jordanians have been, and also with the Saudis.

"As regards the Soviet invasion of Iran, it is doubtful that they will go farther than to capture Teheran."

Haugen didn't answer at once, merely looked at Coulter's image thoughtfully. Was the bastard trying to confuse him? "Thank you, Mr. Coulter. I'll let you know my decision when I've made it. Meanwhile, for your future reference, I like to know promptly about things like the Saudi request."

Another key was already flashing when he disconnected.

He touched it, and Martinelli's voice spoke to him. "General Cromwell is holding on line two for you, Mr. President. Can you talk to him now?"

"Sure." He touched a key, and the general's face appeared on the screen. "Good morning, Jumper," Haugen said.

"You asked for my comments on your press conference, Mr. President. I'm pretty good at keeping my temper, but I could hardly believe how cool you stayed, handling that turkey from the *Flag*. I'd have blown my stack at the sonofabitch."

"Thanks." Haugen smiled. "He was pretty hostile, wasn't he? And apparently a little crazy. But he did me a favor; he made me look good."

The answer threw Cromwell for just a moment before he went on. "And the question about whether or not you were a front man for me—you defused that nicely too."

"Thanks. Listen, Jumper, while I've got you on the line, Emerson has asked to be replaced as National Security Advisor. Who would you suggest I name for the job?"

"May I think about that, Sir? Frankly, I'd like it myself, but as vice president I won't be eligible."

"Okay, I'll ask you again tomorrow. Jumper, my intercom's flashing; Martinelli's trying to tell me Ed Wachsman's here for our lunch meeting. He's head of the Bureau of Economic Analysis."

"Right. Good luck on understanding him."

The president smiled. "Wish *him* luck. I'm going to make him justify everything he says."

TWELVE

The president's phone buzzed, and as he reached for it, his eyes moved to the clock: 1402:21. Bulavin was reasonably prompt, if that's who it was.

"What is it, Jeanne?"

"Colonel Schubert is here for his appointment."

"Send him in."

The man who entered looked like a career army officer. Seeming about fifty, he appeared lean and fit. About five-feet ten, his weight might have been 160. His face was lined and hard-looking, but humor lurked in the eyes and around the mouth. His cropped hair was in the zone between blond and brown.

He stopped in front of the president's desk and saluted. "Mr. President, General Cromwell tells me you'd like a briefing on the Soviet government."

Haugen answered in Russian. "That's right. Best you give it in English though." He grinned. "My Russian vocabulary may not be up to the subject."

The Russian nodded.

"I'll be recording this briefing," Haugen went on. "So if you need to say anything that might compromise your cover, let me know. I'll turn off the recorder. The tape will be for my use only, but we might as well be careful."

Bulavin/Schubert's smile was rueful. "I'm used to being careful. It's been necessary most of my life."

"I can believe it." Haugen reached to his computer console and touched a short sequence of keys. "All right, we're recording. This is a briefing by an intelligence specialist on the subject of the Soviet government." He looked up at the Russian. "Start."

Bulavin contemplated for a moment, then began. "What I'm going to do, Mr. President, is give you a brief sketch of the recent history of the Politburo, to give you an idea of how it functions, and of the men and the situation there. Mainly I'll deal with the period since Mikhail Sergeyvich Gorbachev became General Secretary of the Communist Party of the Soviet Union. Party Chairman for short.

"But now and then I'll look back before that, for perspective. And I'll leave a much broader written review with you, with maps, statistical tables, and a glossary."

Nikita Bulavin sat back in his chair and stared unseeingly above and past Haugen's head.

"Comrade Gorbachev took over the chairmanship in much less then a position of full power. Symbolic of this, he was given neither the office of premier nor that of president, although Nikolai Tikhonov, who held the premiership, was unquestionably and notoriously senile, while the presidency was vacant! In the Soviet Union, the post of president is ornamental, of course, honorary, and the functional importance of the premiership is not great. But both had symbolic meaning: It had been the stamp of true power when a chairman attached the premiership to himself, and to also hold the presidency signified that power was complete."

Bulavin's eyes focused again, and for a moment met Haugen's. "Actually, when Gorbachev first became Party Chairman, the heart of power still lay with the KGB, as it had since the death of Yuri Andropov. And indeed since Andropov had become chairman. For Andropov had commanded the KGB prior to becoming chairman—had used the KGB to make himself chairman—and in a sense, when he ruled, the KGB ruled.

"You may recall that it was during Andropov's tenure as chairman that international terrorism so greatly expanded. That was no coincidence. Some western so-called experts talked about Andropov as, hopefully, a liberal. With experts like those . . ." Bulavin shrugged, smiling wryly.

"At any rate, by appointing other top KGB men to the Politburo, Andropov put the KGB in a position to continue its rule after his death, at least during Konstantin Chernenko's brief tenure as Party Chairman.

"For Chernenko was never more than a figurehead. He was appointed because there were two strong contenders for the position, Grigori Romanov as well as Mikhail Gorbachev. And someone was needed to occupy the throne without controlling power, until one of the two vanquished the other. The world is fortunate that Romanov did not win."

Bulavin looked intently at the president. "There is a key relationship that is important to know, for anyone who wants to understand Soviet politics. During the sixty years of Soviet rule prior to Andropov's chairmanship, the power structure had been three-cornered, the corners being the Party, the army, and under one name or another the KGB. The army had much the greatest sheer power, enough to destroy either of the others. To prevent this, the Party had early installed a system of political officers within the army, to indoctrinate the troops. There was a political officer in every unit, down to company level.

"Meanwhile the Party had also created the KGB, and one of its major functions was to help keep the army from taking over the government. The KGB did this by having literally thousands of spies within the army, monitoring personal associations and political conformity; by openly investigating and passing on the political attitudes of all army candidates for promotion; and by assuring the removal of any senior officers, or anyone else the Party decided might be dangerous in some way to the Politburo.

"For the Politburo was the Party's ruling organ. And it was also the top level of the vast bureaucracy which controls the Soviet Union to a far greater degree than your government controls here. The bureaucracy that the Politburo controlled was very much larger than the army, although unarmed and far less disciplined.

"The Politburo's main *source* of control in this three-cornered power structure has been the power of patronage, of appointment—that and its position as the source of political ideology. Its main *tools* of control were the army and the KGB. It used the KGB to control the army, and at times it used the army to control the KGB. And of course, the cadre section of the Party secretariat researched and appointed KGB officers.

"At times the Politburo had been controlled by a single man—its chairman; most notably for almost thirty years by Joseph Stalin. At other times its leader had often been constrained to some extent, sometimes to a rather large extent, by other members of the Politburo. But with the sole exception of Chernenko, the chairman was the most powerful Politburo member. Chernenko had too little force, personally, to use the reins when they were handed to him."

Bulavin paused to evaluate his listener. Haugen seemed to be absorbing the information without difficulty; he nodded to the Russian to continue.

"The Politburo had created the KGB to curb the people and the army, and so this serpent, the KGB, also had to be powerful. Nothing less than powerful, ruthlessly powerful, could have controlled the army and the ethnic/national mix of the empire with its many languages and affinities. So in the tradition of Russian security police, it had been brutal as well as powerful, more brutal than any Czarist predecessor.

"Now this brutal creation of the Party was quite willing to eat bureaucrats. The Politburo had used it repeatedly to purge the government, the army, and the Party itself. By Stalin in particular, but later also by Andropov, it was used even to purge the Politburo. Thus the government cadres had a fear and horror of the KGB."

Haugen listened engrossed. *I wonder,* he thought, *if Bulavin realizes that, as he talks about this, he begins to sound Russian?* It wasn't a matter of accent but of diction—of word selection and sentence structure.

"When Gorbachev took power," Bulavin went on, "Gromyko was more than foreign minister; he wielded important political power within the Party apparatus, which is to say, the bureaucracy. As did several other Politburo geriatrics to lesser degrees.

"But time had weakened their ranks, and the KGB had decided they must go. Thus less than five months after Gorbachev became chairman, he 'promoted' his sponsor, Gromyko, into the vacant presidency. Which in fact meant he retired him. And replaced him as foreign minister with KGB General Eduard Shevardnadze. This, in fact, had been one of the conditions the KGB had exacted before agreeing to Gorbachev as Party Chairman.

"The KGB also began, bit by bit, to replace the GRU—Soviet military intelligence—in all of its peacetime foreign roles except that of espionage. Which of course was its major peacetime role anyway, outside the Soviet Union."

"Just a minute," Haugen interrupted. "Isn't the KGB the Soviet espionage organization?"

"Not primarily. The GRU, military intelligence, has always held the foreign espionage role. But it maintains a very low profile. Some experts have even assumed that the GRU is a branch of the KGB, but nothing could be further from the truth. Each has been used to purge the other, and they have a long tradition of mutual hatred, a tradition carefully nurtured by the Politburo."

"Well then," Haugen said, "if foreign espionage is the function of the GRU, what's the KGB's function outside the Soviet Union?"

"The KGB spies upon, and otherwise monitors, Soviet citizens not only inside but outside the USSR. And frequently also non-Soviet Communists. It is especially active in monitoring the views, loyalty, and activities of embassy and consular officials and employees. And it is the KGB which is primarily interested in locating defectors, in some cases to get them to renounce the West and return home. Or in cases like my own, to arrange disappearances or fatal accidents.

"It is also responsible for the encouragement and subversion of indigenous revolutionary movements in foreign countries, and since Andropov, the major development of international terrorism.

"And with its new predominance, the KGB carried out the arrest and imprisonment of several key GRU officers on political charges or charges of corruption. A number of others were demoted from positions of power and influence to routine positions, for example in information processing. In a few cases, GRU officers with unusually influential connections were transferred to consular positions outside the USSR. Such positions have always been considered highly attractive, but they are outside the circles of power."

Again Bulavin smiled his wry smile. "GRU officers become quite sophisticated. You might not believe how much they value assignments outside the Soviet Union.

"Meanwhile, Gorbachev replaced the remaining Politburo geriatrics with people of his own, people whom the KGB would find acceptable. Including Nikolai Ryzhkov, another of Andropov's people, who replaced the confused and useless Tikhonov as premier.

"Gorbachev made no attempt to preempt the position for himself. Which strengthened the KGB's attitude that he was controllable. For after all, Gorbachev had not risen to high position by force of character or single-minded ambition, nor on the basis of executive or technical competency. Not that he lacked intelligence and strength, but he had risen to the Central Committee and then to the Politburo by being in the right places at the right times.

And by being a loyal and competent lieutenant to two men who would later sponsor him—Fyodor Kulakov and especially Yuri Andropov. And finally to Andrei Gromyko, turned power broker in his old age, who sponsored him because Gromyko feared and detested Grigori Romanov, Gorbachev's rival for the post.

"In fact, it seems that, of the three, Kulakov had been the most influential of them all on Gorbachev, though that was not at once apparent. Kulakov was unquestionably the most able man in the Brezhnev Politburo, and he combined pragmatism with principles. In fact, he reputedly said that in the infinitely improbable event that one actually gained the chairmanship, one should, when he had entrenched his position, do all he could to 'turn things around'—make the Soviet Union an effective nation. Otherwise one's life would have been meaningless.

"But Kulakov had died under extremely suspicious circumstances during Andropov's ascension to power, and Andropov's principles were quite different from Kulakov's.

"At any rate, to have the KGB in the primary position was a worrisome thing for the Party, including Mikhail Gorbachev; it could gobble up any one of them in a moment and spit out his bones. While the army had always hated the KGB, and deeply resented the reduction of its own covert action arm, the GRU.

"So Gorbachev quietly built his own personal mafia. As had every Party Chairman before him except the decrepit, emphysemic Konstantin Chernenko. And in building up his own mafia, Gorbachev took a lesson from the book of Yuri Andropov: Although at the start he chose several men from his home district, a tradition among Party chairmen, mostly he selected men with some special qualification, regardless of their origin. Except, of course, they were all ethnically Russian. In fact, most of them had been Andropov's own people, as Gorbachev himself had been. Men whose loyalty he then proceeded to cultivate by giving them favorable positions, the power of which depended on Gorbachev and his continued dominance."

As Bulavin talked, Haugen had noticed the man's muscles begin to twitch, to flutter, although his face remained stoic. Now the Russian picked up on Haugen's awareness. "Excuse me, Mr. President," he said. "It is a nervous automaticity that sometimes turns on when I speak of these matters.

"I was describing how Mikhail Sergeyvich—Gorbachev— built up his power. As Party Chairman, he also continued quietly to cultivate the loyalty of key members of the Party apparatus. Especially some who had shown willingness to propose, and even to install, different ways of doing things which it might be hoped would prove more effective.

"And even before his first appointment to the Central Committee, Gorbachev's success had been due in no small part to his personality, which in America we might describe as laid back and courteous. Genuine courtesy is very unusual in the Kremlin. More common are obsequiousness, coldness, and arrogance. When ruthlessness seemed called for, Mikhail Gorbachev was ruthless, but he was not gratuitously unpleasant."

Along with his twitching, Bulavin's voice was becoming noticeably monotone now. Haugen interrupted, at the same time turning off his recorder. "Let's take a break, Colonel. Walk around the office if you'd like. Would you like tea, or have you developed a preference for coffee? I can also offer you hot chocolate if you'd like, or bouillon."

The Russian emerged from his recollections and stood up, rotating his shoulders to loosen them. "Thank you, Mr. President. I've become quite a coffee drinker in America." A smile played at the corners of his mouth. "Even Mikhail Sergeyvich could have taken lessons in courtesy from American presidents."

Haugen didn't respond to the comment. "This is decaffeinated, by the way," he said. "Cream and sugar?"

"If you please."

The president poured. His own coffee he took black; for decades he'd carried on a low intensity campaign to control his weight. After a few minutes of small talk, Bulavin seemed relaxed again. Haugen turned the recorder back on and picked up the line of the briefing. "You were telling me about Gorbachev building his power relative to the KGB."

"Yes. It later became apparent that he also cultivated key army personnel, without being obvious about it. Including Colonel General Serafim Petrovich Gurenko, commander of the GRU. Previously, a commander of the GRU would ordinarily hold the rank of full army general. That Gurenko did not was a symptom of the GRU's reduced status and power, for by the Soviet system, he was eligible not only for the position but for the rank as well.

"And while building his power, Gorbachev remained always very cooperative with the KGB. As a matter of fact, at that time his major problem with them was not their activities but their power, which was dangerous to him. And the KGB, in their turn, was less interested in his orthodoxy than his cooperation."

Bulavin's voice was normal now. Pausing, he sipped his coffee, seeming to savor its sweetness. "As you perhaps know," he went on, "Gorbachev's economic and social reforms caused much more unhappiness within the bureaucracy than within the KGB. This was partly because some of his reforms failed, and partly because some of them succeeded, but mostly because they required that the apparatchiks be accountable. Then two successive years of very poor crops, of continuing industrial shortages and unfulfilled expectations, brought about sporadic outbreaks of strikes and even riots.

"Which made Gorbachev susceptible to being ousted, and perhaps caused him to move more drastically than he otherwise would have.

"At any rate, more than three years ago, after KGB troops had brutally put down unusually severe disorders in the Uzbek SSR, Gorbachev shifted production allocations further toward relieving the more drastic civilian shortages. He then began new negotiations with the USA, Canada, Australia, and Argentina for wheat, and with India, Iran, and Iraq to sell them more export-level weapons as a means of getting foreign currency for wheat purchases.

"But for negotiations to be productive, it was necessary that the KGB curtail its program of terrorism. Which it was not willing to do.

"The commander of the KGB was General Kir Nikolaevich Turolenko, and Gorbachev had asked him to discuss certain matters with the Politburo. He had also arranged for six *spetsnaz* officers to be present in a small chamber off the conference room. When he'd begun the meeting, the six officers came into the room. Then Gorbachev read a list of crimes of which he accused Turolenko. In several of these, a member of the Politburo, Alexis Semyonovich Pokrovsky, was also accused as an accomplice. Both were arrested on the spot, and taken from the chamber.

"But they were not handcuffed, as one might have expected them to be.

"Then, in the corridor outside, there was a burst of gunfire. Both Turolenko and Pokrovsky were shot dead, supposedly in a scuffle for one of the officer's guns.

"The arrest was a signal for GRU commander Gurenko to purge the KGB of roughly fifty key officers—a purge carried out by teams of *spetsnaz*, which are, you understand, a branch of the GRU.

"And the way the *spetsnaz* carried out this assignment foreshadowed things to come. Because they murdered a considerably greater number than the fifty or so whom rumor said Gorbachev wanted removed. This was followed by a large-scale purge of KGB agents within the army, a purge carried out entirely on the army's initiative. Of these, while many were shot, most, presumably thousands, were put into army penal battalions in the Transbaykal and Far East Military Districts. They could not safely be put into Siberian prison camps because the camps are run by MVD battalions, and the MVD, which you might think of as the non-secret police, are in fact dominated by the KGB.

"This purge of the KGB involved more murders than had been seen in upper echelons since Stalin died—far more even than when Andropov was taking power, and more blatant. And while they might be ascribed to the long enmity between KGB and GRU, they certainly had the effect of increasing the army's power, relative not only to the KGB but to the Party. It could correctly be said that the army crocodile was shaking off its leashes."

Bulavin stopped talking to sip coffee, and for a long minute, neither man said anything. Some twitching had begun again, but Bulavin's voice remained normal.

"While these events were transpiring," he went on, "Gorbachev removed the KGB's Shevardnadze as foreign minister, accusing him of incompetence and replacing him with one of his own mafia.

"Now it was necessary that Gorbachev move quickly to rehabilitate the KGB at a safe level and rebalance the power triangle as it had been before Andropov's time. Before the army could take broad advantage of its new predominance, yet without gaining its serious enmity. So he appointed one of his own mafia, Semyon Grigorovich Dolin, as head of the now demoralized and fearful KGB. Dolin, who was from Stavropol, Gorbachev's home district, had been a KGB colonel on Andropov's staff, but he had no particular reputation to attract the army's ire. Dolin then set about rebuilding the KGB command structure with people of his own selection who were approved by Gorbachev.

"Meanwhile Gorbachev also retired Gromyko, who suffered from heart failure and was on continuous medication, and quickly appointed Marshal Fedor Petrovich Durukan as president. No army man had been made president before, so some western experts interpreted this to mean that the army's position was being still further strengthened. That was not so, and everyone in the Kremlin and the army understood that. Durukan had been a very strong, very bold Minister of Defense, very active and strong-willed—very adamant about getting the army the weapons and research it wanted, despite the severe economic problems of the state. Now, for all practical purposes, he was retired.

"In Durukan's place, Gorbachev quickly appointed Marshal Oleg Stepanovich Pavlenko as the new Minister of Defense. This placated the generals somewhat, as Pavlenko would probably have been their own choice if they could not have Durukan. But meanwhile Gorbachev had demonstrated that he controlled.

"Not long afterward, during a Politburo meeting, Premier Ryzhkov suffered a severe stroke. This allowed Gorbachev to remove him gracefully from office and have himself elected to the premiership by the Politburo. He seemed not to have coveted it, but holding it made it clear to all that he ruled virtually beyond argument.

"And so far as I know, there is no evidence that Gorbachev's subsequent death in a plane crash was anything more than an accident. Though naturally there were suspicions and accusations. Some probably remembered the fate of Chief of the General Staff S.S. Biriuzov in the 1960s. The KGB pointed out that the aircraft was operated by the GRU, but that is true of all Aeroflot aircraft, including those that fly regular commercial schedules to this country. While the army suggested that the KGB had arranged the crash to get rid of the man who had had it purged.

"The best evidence that Gorbachev's death was truly accidental was that a power vacuum resulted. No plotters moved to take command. The Politburo consisted mainly of Gorbachev appointees not experienced in power changes at the Politburo level. And he—Gorbachev—had been healthy and vigorous. Thus there had been no 'crown prince,' or even any candidates with an eye on the throne and their own machinery of supporters prepared to lever them into office. Nor was there any longer a Suslov or Gromyko at hand as an experienced power broker. No one was prepared, and loyalties were uncertain.

"For more than a week, no one held the reins, while unprepared candidates sought supporters. And during this hiatus of leadership, the army began to purge its political officers, starting in the important Moscow and Kiev military districts.

"The Politburo, seeing this as a major army move for power, finally went into an all-night session and appointed Boris Alexeevich Kulish as Party Chairman. Kulish was an apparatchik, as Gorbachev had been; a bureaucrat you would say, one appointed to the Politburo by Gorbachev. But like Gorbachev, Kulish was not without steel; he too had been one of Andropov's people. The first thing he did as Party Chairman was to call in Marshal Pavlenko and threaten to turn the now considerably rehabilitated KGB loose on the army unless the Main Political Directorate— the Party's political-ideological network in the army—was fully reinstalled.

"The army acquiesced, but unhappily. It wanted more than ever to hold power itself, and hated the KGB even more than before, fearing it would take power again. But the leading officers had to ask themselves who around them might be, in fact, an undetected KGB spy, waiting to pull the trigger. What entrance guard? What chauffeur? What member of his own staff?"

Bulavin sat forward in his chair, sighed and raised his

arms, rotating them to loosen tight shoulders again. "The recorder, Mr. President?"

Haugen turned it off.

"At any rate," Bulavin continued, "shortly after the army was brought to heel, I was appointed deputy ambassador here—First Secretary is the actual title. It is not uncommon for a GRU general to hold that position in an embassy. I defected within days of my arrival. And of course, I have not been personally close to events in Russia since then. However, as would be expected, Kulish quickly developed his own mafia, drawn mostly from the Leningrad District, and soon was displaying considerable leverage. But both agriculture and industry continue in serious trouble, thus Kulish's tenure is at risk. And his response has been the conservative one; he has in part repealed Gorbachev's reforms, which has placated the bureaucracy.

"That is how things stand at present—or how they stagger at present. The internal problems undoubtedly account for the invasion of Iran."

"Oh?"

"You see, on the whole, the Russian people are only superficially ideological, but they are very patriotic and nationalistic. And it is an old Russian tradition to distrust foreigners. Thus very many Russian people see domination of all the surrounding lands, in these days including the western hemisphere, as their best national safeguard."

Haugen frowned. "What about the hundreds of thousands who went over to the Germans in the first year of the Nazi invasion?"

"Millions are more like it. Mostly though, they were Ukrainians. Many Ukrainians still consider the Ukraine an occupied nation, occupied by the Russians. Many Ukrainians but not many Russians went over to the Germans."

"Hm-m. I knew that about the Ukrainians and other ethnic minorities. But I hadn't realized that the Russian people were especially patriotic."

"They are, Mr. President, they are. And as a culture they are also xenophobic and more than a little apathetic. They feel that, as a people, they cannot solve their own problems. Thus they hope always for a strong leader to tell them what to do. That was as true in czarist times as now.

The Bolsheviks won the civil war not so much because of their ideology as because they offered a strong man, V.I. Lenin, as ruler. The Mensheviks, on the other hand, offered freedom, social democracy, which to most Russians equates dangerously with anarchy, with chaos.

"The Russian people, I regret to tell you, are more willing to start a war with the West than their rulers are. Their rulers better understand what war would do to the Soviet Union. It is not that the Russian people *like* war, but most of them believe that the rest of the world is waiting its chance to attack Mother Russia. As historically it has. Repeatedly. And a preemptive war seems acceptable to many of them, particularly if it does not bring nuclear devastation on the Motherland.

"Traditionally the Russian people have transposed 'defense' and 'offense,' and the Western concept of defensive war is meaningless to them."

Bulavin laughed silently, sardonically. "And now, particularly with the old butcher dead, they love Stalin! That was how Andropov won them over: He was brutal and overbearing, much like Stalin, and there was no nonsense about him. Tough! During his short rule, Andropov actually became loved. When Khruschev died, and Brezhnev, the Russian people shed no tears, but many wept at Andropov's death. We are all of us very fortunate that he had only fifteen months as Party Chairman. He would have tested your presidents severely, and there might well have been war.

"About Stalin— The feeling in his lifetime was not so much love as fear, but it was a fear that contained a sort of adoration that an American cannot understand. I remember; I was eleven years old already when he died. In the Russian culture, fear of a cruel strong ruler has an element of love in it. You should read the life of Peter the Great."

Haugen had, and he thought he knew what Bulavin was talking about.

That night, in the privacy of their bedroom, Haugen listened again to Bulavin's briefing, this time with his wife. Haugen didn't think Bulavin would mind. And Lois was his confidante and sounding board, and ex officio advisor when she chose to be, or when he asked. As such, she needed to know.

When it was over, she looked thoughtfully at him. "How different is this from what you were told in your State Department briefings?" she asked.

"Quite a bit. I thought it might be. It's interesting that Bulavin didn't try to feed me policy or even try to evaluate policy for me. Mostly he gave me information and insights that presumably he felt were valid. State, on the other hand, did about the opposite. They've got an institutional viewpoint to support, and I suppose they'd prefer I have their opinions, rather than facts to draw my own. And they have a track record, plus current programs and procedures, that they feel they have to defend. Consciously or unconsciously."

He sipped the expensive port they allowed themselves as a nightcap. "After hearing Bulavin, it was hard to sit and relisten to my briefing from Wachsman."

"Is that the economic analysis you were scheduled for?"

"Right."

"How was it?"

"That's a good question. I really gave him a hard time; I think he's used to snowing people. Every time he used a word I didn't understand, I'd pin him down for a clear definition. And every time I didn't follow an argument he gave, I wouldn't let him go on until he made it understandable. A couple of times he got confused and finally admitted he didn't understand either. He'd been reciting, not explaining, and hadn't even realized he didn't know what he was talking about."

Haugen snorted, a sort of half chuckle. "Part of the time he was thinking in slogans, in a kind of rote. A common enough failing. I don't know if an actual understanding of economics is possible today. I suspect they only understand their computer models, not their actual subject.

"Anyway I'm getting a briefing tomorrow from Roy Jones of the Federal Reserve Board. I've made up a list of questions I'll ask him, partly from what Wachsman told me. And day after tomorrow, in the morning, a Dr. Bill Finnegan will be here from Purdue, and in the afternoon a Dr. Murchison from Harvard Business College, to give me the really real scoop." He grinned. "None of them will know I've talked to the others, and I won't be telling them.

"When I've finished hearing all of them, and getting my questions answered, I'll let things ferment for a couple of days and start writing up the economics policies of the Haugen administration. If I'm going to keep whatever public confidence I've got, I'll have to get moving on the economic problems pretty damned soon."

THIRTEEN

Paul Massey faltered, stopped, looked back at the mansion he'd just walked out of. *Damn!* He'd forgotten something.

Without speaking to the bodyguard preceding him, Massey turned toward the wing of the house that held the servants' quarters. Where it joined the building proper were Barron Tallmon's office and apartment.

The door through which Massey entered opened into a short cross-corridor; he strode the few yards down it to Tallmon's office door.

It was locked. "Barron!" he called, and knocked firmly. "Barron, I need the summary report on Sumitomo Trust."

For a few seconds there was no response. Then, as he fumbled out a key chain, a voice came, muffled by the solid teak door. "Just a minute, Mr. Massey. I'll bring it."

Massey frowned, then pulled out the keys anyway and unlocked the door. Pushing it open, he found Tallmon fastening his belt.

"I was about to bring it, sir," Tallmon said.

Massey's eyes fixed on him. "Who is in here with you?"

"No one sir."

The older man turned and looked back down the hall;

his bodyguard was just entering from outside. "Wait for me in the yard, Mr. Mueller," he called. "I'll be along directly."

He watched the large, neatly-suited man leave. Then he closed the office door behind him.

"Who?"

Tallmon only shook his head, his face flushed now.

Massey scanned the office, then looked at the door to Tallmon's private restroom. Closed. He went to it and turned the knob. Locked.

"Open it!" No response. He rapped loudly. "Open this door!" Still nothing. Looking back over his shoulder, Massey saw Tallmon standing motionless. Once more he knocked. "If you do not open, I'll have my bodyguard force the door. You will then be in serious trouble."

He waited. After three or four seconds he heard the lock slip; the door opened. Inside was a boy of about fifteen, Hispanic, from Waterbury probably, who Massey had seen working for the groundskeeper on weekends. His jeans were on, but his undershorts lay over the rim of the washbowl. Massey looked him over; the boy's cheeks darkened.

"It's Wednesday, isn't it?" Massey said to him.

Surprised at this seeming non sequitur, the boy nodded. "Yessir."

Massey's voice was curious, rather than angry. "How did you get out here today?"

"I caught a ride with the grocery truck, sir. That's how I always come out." The boy was looking past him through the door now; at Tallmon, Massey realized. "I tol' them I was suppose' to work today," the boy added. His nerve was already coming back.

"Ingenious." Massey was aware of Tallmon's approach. "Aren't you supposed to be in school today?"

"They don' do nothin' to you for not goin' to school, Mr. Massey. I skip lots of times; I tell them I was sick. My mother don' speak English, so they don' bother her about it."

"I see. What's your name again? I may have heard, but I don't remember it."

"Joey, Mr. Massey. Joey Jerez." He pronounced it in the Anglo manner—Juh*rehz*.

"All right, Joey." Massey stepped back out of the bathroom. "I want you to go— Let's see. Just wait outside.
And don't worry. You're not in trouble."

Joey started for the bathroom door.

"Oh, and don't forget your underwear."

Turning, the boy looked around, confused for a moment, then saw the shorts, grabbed them and stuffed them
in a pocket. Massey watched him almost to the hall door.

"Joey!"

Reluctantly the boy stopped and turned.

"How much was Mr. Tallmon going to pay you?"

The answer was little more than a mumble. "Thirty
dollars, sir."

Massey turned to Tallmon, impressed; these were hard
times. "Is that right, Barron? Thirty dollars?"

Wordlessly Tallmon nodded.

"Then you should pay the boy before he goes. We can't
have him come all the way out here and send him off
without paying him."

Tallmon's cheeks flamed at this. He dug his wallet from
a pocket and drew forth three bills. The boy was standing
straight when Tallmon handed him the money, pleased at
how things had developed but being careful not to smile.

"Now wait outside, Joey. In the yard. Mr. Tallmon has
some things to do for me in town. He'll be out in a few
minutes and take you in with him."

Massey followed Joey Jerez to the door, watched him
down the hall and out, then closed the door and turned to
Tallmon.

"Barron, I'm disappointed in you. I have never objected
seriously to your liaisons with mature and competent adults
like Jaubert, but really, this is not all right. How old is this
Joey Jerez?"

"Sixteen." Tallmon's voice was as expressionless now as
his face.

"Indeed? I'd have thought fifteen at most. Ah well, I
suppose these adolescent latinos look younger than they
are."

Massey looked thoughtfully at the carpet. "I presume
you've worked out how you'd handle things if the boy
talked to the authorities. Or if his parents found out and
called the police."

"He wouldn't talk." Tallmon's voice was husky now. "He's Puerto Rican or Mexican. His father would kill him if he found out. And besides, the boy wouldn't jeopardize his source of money."

"You've done this before?"

Another nod. "Once. Last Saturday."

"Hm-m." Massey's voice became curious. "Tell me, who plays which role?"

"We take turns."

"Ah. Oral or anal?"

It took a moment for Tallmon to answer. "Anal."

Massey's eyes examined Tallmon's face. Tallmon's eyes slid away. "Barron, I'm afraid you've overlooked some serious risks here. A boy like that will flaunt his money. Some bigger, rougher boy may make him tell where he got it. The story could spread. Or he could spend it on drugs, and babble. And I cannot risk the scandal." Massey shook his head. "No, we'll have to make sure that nothing like that happens."

His lips tightened. "Take him to town. Waterbury?"

Tallmon nodded.

"But don't take him home. Drop him off outside his neighborhood. I suppose we have his address?"

"Edwards will have it in the employee files."

"Good. When you get back, call one of the New York fatality contractors and arrange to have the boy disappear. Or die in some apparent mugging—whatever the contractor feels will work best. Just make sure it can't be traced to us. Do you understand?"

Again the nod.

"And Barron, something like this must not happen again." He looked hard at Tallmon, who in spite of himself allowed a meeting of eyes. "You do see my position, don't you?"

"Yes, Mr. Massey."

"Good. And Barron." He paused, shook his head. "You are very valuable to me; you are my right hand. We'll talk about this when I get back. There are physicians, you know, who can relieve you of these compulsions."

"Yes, Mr. Massey." The voice was thick with emotion.

Massey looked at him for another moment, then nodded and left. When he settled himself in the helicopter, Tallmon had not yet come out of the building. *Poor bugger,* Massey said to himself, then grimaced at the unvoiced, inadvertent pun. The man was losing his grip.

He'd talk to Dr. Merriman about him. Maybe Tallmon could still be salvaged; he'd seen Merriman do remarkable things with PDH—pain-drugs-hypnosis treatment. Otherwise, well—Disposing of Tallmon should be no problem, but replacing him would be a real nuisance.

FOURTEEN

The president had drawn the heavy drapes back, and the dawnlight was stormy gray through curtains. Separating them, he peered out across sodden lawn. A blustery wind swirled the first falling leaves, and flung irregular flurries of raindrops sharply against the window. "Don't let me talk you into anything, Babe," he said.

"No, it's a good idea," she answered. "I like this weather too, and I haven't had much exercise since we left home." She pulled running pants onto legs that were longer than her husband's. She was tall, and still fine looking. "I'm going to take it easy though."

He shrugged into his warmup jacket, then sat down and put on jogging shoes. "Me too. But I really need it; all I've done lately is move papers. I'm going to start either jogging or swimming every day." Another spatter of rain rattled against glass, and Haugen grinned as he got up. "You don't suppose our guardians will try to protect us from the rain, do you?"

She laughed at an image: two Secret Service men jogging beside them, umbrellas bobbing up and down as they ran. "They take their work so seriously! All of them do. We shouldn't laugh, even privately between us."

Moments later, four sober-faced Secret Service agents met them in the Stair Hall. Warned, they'd donned raincoats. No umbrellas were evident, but two of them held each a short jacket. The president hadn't seen one before, but he realized what they had to be: flakjackets.

"We're supposed to wear those to jog in the yard?" Haugen asked.

"Yes sir, Mr. President. Actually, Mr. Ashley would prefer that you stay indoors except when necessary."

The president's expression became curious. "Is this standard, or what? What's the story?"

"Well, sir, there've been threatening letters. Quite a few; more than usual. And while most of that sort of thing is just some nut blowing off steam with his pen, you can figure there'll be those few who'll try to follow through. And the FBI's reported more than the usual number of threats, too."

The president nodded, thoughtful now. It made sense that this would happen with a president who'd entered office as he had, and with dictatorial powers, at that. Pulling off his warmup jacket, he put out his right arm and Wayne helped him into the flakjacket. It was moderately heavy, but not unreasonably so, considering its function. Haugen looked at his wife. She was doing the same. "Are you sure you still want to come along?" he asked. "You could be sitting in front of a log fire in the library, working on your book."

She shook her head. "I have lots of time for that." She touched his arm, smiling. "Whither thou goest . . ."

Protected now against worse than chill, they went out a south, ground-floor door and began to jog easily on the close-trimmed grass, the rain cold on their faces. It brought a scene back to the president's mind, of walking through autumn forest, a four-foot long, one-man crosscut saw over a shoulder, axe and pickaroon gripped in his other hand, handmade birch felling wedges tightening a hip pocket. The rain and the air had felt much like today's, but then he'd worn a lined denim barn jacket—of cotton, not some military high-tech material—and physically he'd felt *strong*, beyond challenge. And the smells had been different—wet balsam fir, balm of Gilead olive-barked and pungent, the thick layer of sodden leaves underfoot.

A grouse had clucked at him from the ground a few yards away, not smart enough to fly at his approach. He'd killed it with a throw of his pickaroon, opened and cleaned out its abdominal cavity with a thrust and flick of hard fingers, and eaten it later for supper.

He'd been . . . twenty-three then, had cut and piled 276 sticks of popple pulpwood that day; close to two semi loads. It had been good cutting, with virtually no cull, the timber too dense for much underbrush or many limbs, the trunks slender enough that he could saw and manhandle the hundred-inch-long sticks freely and rapidly, but stout enough that the piles grew quickly into sleighloads waiting for winter's snow.

He chuckled inwardly. *Oldtimers' disease,* he told himself. *The symptom is perfect recall of anything twenty or more years ago.* But he'd always had that kind of memory—detailed, visual, ready when wanted. It had been useful; still was.

And in a year, what would he remember of today? Today would be the day he'd first worn a flakjacket, first met with the leaders of the Joint Senate and House Committee on Taxation. He'd be asking them to draw up a model tax bill—one they'd like to see if they had full authority to start from scratch without pressure from anyone. Because they wouldn't have to push it through Congress, through a snowstorm of lobbyists.

Make it simple and rational, he'd tell them. And do it inside of six weeks. He wondered what they'd come up with. Or whether they'd tell him to go jump.

They were about as knowledgeable as you could hope to find, but how creative? How free thinking?

A gust threw rain against his face, bringing him into the here and now. He laughed silently at himself and began to look about him at the beauty of the moment. Beside him, Lois's cheeks were pink from cold rain.

He jogged on, giving no thought at all to any hidden gunman.

The president finished scanning a report that Milstead had hand-carried in, then took a drink of half warm coffee. "Charles," he said, "this morning one of my keepers told me there'd been an unusual number of threats against the president's life. How many more? Double? Triple?"

Milstead looked sharply at him. "Who told you that? That sort of thing's supposed to come only from your security chief."

Haugen's eyes were mild but unyielding. "I'll answer your question after you've answered mine."

Milstead wasn't easily flustered. "Sorry, Mr. President. There've been roughly four or five times as many—still not an awful lot. Not as many as we might have anticipated; it certainly hasn't become an emergency situation. Most of them are from parlor psychotics who sit and fantasize but never move. But we need to remember that there'll always be that one or two percent, most of them fortunately incompetent."

Haugen nodded. "Fine. That's about what I'd expect, and about what I was told. I'm not going to tell you which of them told me, because he was answering my direct question. When I ask someone a question, I expect them to answer it. Besides which, I'm even less enthused about betraying a confidence than I am about withholding something from someone I depend on, like you."

He grinned then, grimness gone. "How does that sit with you, Charles?"

Milstead had gotten used to his mercurial chief; he smiled back, though not broadly. "If you say so, Mr. President." Then, carefully casual, "President Donnelly didn't want to hear about threats. They upset him."

"I don't upset easily, Charles, but I don't believe in wallowing in bad news either. So about threats—no point in distracting me with them needlessly. Just tell me what I need to know, and what I ask for."

The president smiled ruefully as Milstead left. At least there should be a vice president by evening. Both houses of Congress were to vote today, and while there'd been some debate, Cromwell was supposed to be a shoo-in.

It was already nearly dark—daylight savings had just given way to standard time—when the small pickup truck drove up the graveled, puddled, woods-lined driveway and stopped in front of the old farmhouse. The headlights switched off. Both cab doors opened, then slammed shut behind a woman and man who hurried around through the rain to take a box each of groceries from the camper shell in back.

On the porch, the man found the tattered screendoor hooked, and kicked its frame impatiently, then stood muttering until a man came and opened it. They went in. "Sorry, Mark," the man said. "Tris just sort of hooks it automatically."

Two others, a woman and man, were sitting at the large kitchen table, beers open in front of them. The woman got up and helped stow the groceries; the man watched. When everything was put away, Mark opened the refrigerator again and took out two bottles of beer, uncapping them with an opener mounted on the counter. He handed one to the woman he'd arrived with. They too sat down then, Mark's face surly.

"Tris," he said, "don't hook the fucking screendoor, okay? It doesn't do any good anyway; hell, even the cats go in and out through the rips. And I don't like to come home from work and find myself locked out of my own house."

"Sorry," she said.

He turned to the third man. "So what'd you hear from Mr. Mystery?"

The man smirked his customary smirk. "No sweat. The deal is wrapped. He's got it guaranteed; it's just not delivered. It's coming from someone big, not some two-bit speculator."

"And we can definitely haul it in the pickup?"

"No problem. It ain't Fat Man, you know. It'll be in, like a big suitcase, and the bomb itself only weighs forty kilos. A pickup like ours could haul a dozen of them."

Again Mark scowled. *Ours.* The asshole. *Yours* was the word; the pickup was his, Mark's, just like the house. Just like the groceries and beer. He considered for a moment saying something about it, but didn't, because Rafe was the man with the contact. You had to be willing to put up with certain things for a contact like that. And he had a source for gas, too, all they needed.

"Rafe," said Mark's girl, "how dangerous is it, hauling it around like that?"

"It's not dangerous. Just don't sit on it very long." He

laughed. "You'd really have hot pants if you sat on it too long. We get it, load it in the Cessna, and Phil and Tris fly down to Calvert Cliffs and drop it down a stack."

Phil looked alarmed at that. "You mean I've got to drop it down a *stack?!* Shit, man, the odds of . . ."

Rafe laughed. "It's a figure of speech. Don't be so literal. You don't have to drop it down a fucking stack, for chrissake. Like I said before: All we want to do is hit the building if we can—the roof. Those places are really built heavy; lots and lots of thick concrete. But if we hit the building, we've maybe got a chance to blow the piles. What a bang that'd make! Make old Chernobyl look like nothing, and wipe out all those millionaire summer homes along the bay."

His tone turned patient. "We know you're not flying a B1 bomber with a computerized bombsight. You yell when you've lined it up, Tris releases the latch that lets the bomb slide out, and you fly the hell out of there while it floats down under the parachute. Shouldn't be any more trouble than when you practiced dropping the dummies on that sandspit. And if you miss, you miss; our part of the bargain's been fulfilled. It's twenty kilotons, you know? So if it doesn't blow the piles, it'll still blow the place to hell, and scare shit out of the whole country, especially the atomic energy pushers and the government."

He laughed. "And the goddamn dictator of the United States. If the wind's right . . . It's only fifty miles from Washington, and maybe he sleeps with his window open." He laughed again, perhaps at the idea that a window would make any difference.

Mark had registered the pronouns Rafe used: it was *we* hit, and *we'll* wreck the place; but *you* have to, and if *you* miss. Nor had he missed the comments on Mary's having hot pants. *Bastard.*

"How long before we can actually pick up the stuff?" Tris asked.

"He said three weeks at the most. Maybe no more than a week."

Mark scowled. "And he's just *giving* this to us? It costs nothing?"

Rafe smirked, but his eyes were hard. Mark always backed down before those eyes; he'd seen eyes like those when he'd been in San Quentin, and nowhere else. "That's not quite right, Marky baby," Rafe answered. "It only costs *us* nothing. Somebody paid through the nose for it. *His* contact has the stuff, and contracted with him to get it delivered on the plant. Bet your ass he's getting paid for arranging it with us; probably a lot. And as the delivery people, we get the bomb for nothing, and get to blow up a nuclear power plant."

Mark subsided. But he couldn't help wondering where the stuff was coming from. From the commies maybe; Rafe could be KGB. Or maybe from the Arabs. They wouldn't like nuclear power; it was competition; and they loved to stick it to the United States, too. Well, whoever. Once they'd turned the stuff over, whoever it was could go to hell. The main thing was to stop nuclear power in America.

FIFTEEN

"Thank you, gentlemen. That will be all." The president got up, and the others followed suit: Greg Lambert and the Secretaries of the Treasury, Commerce, and Labor. Commerce and Labor rose tiredly; this man in the White House was damned difficult.

By contrast, Lambert, the White House Assistant for Policy Development, was cheerful. Though under Haugen he was only an advisor, editor, and source of information, he enjoyed watching the president's mind at work, charging ahead, questioning and absorbing data on the run, seeming rarely to doubt his own judgment.

And Lambert found a certain perverse pleasure in the president's independent toughness. Sandforth and Komisky—Commerce and Labor—had requested this meeting to make one last try at changing the old man's mind. Because once tonight's speech was made, he and they were committed. He'd listened patiently at first to the same arguments in new clothes. Then his jaw had begun to clench, to jut. Still, he'd heard them out; they'd have to give him that.

To Haugen, cabinet secretaries were not makers of government policy. They were administrators of major executive departments. Because they were knowledgeable, their input was to be sought and listened to, but he felt no need to be guided by them or swayed by them. He could get input from any number of experts—had and would—and made his own decisions.

They filed from the room, the president last. General Hammaker was waiting for him outside the door. While Lambert and the secretaries went down the hall to the elevator, Haugen stopped.

"What have you got Ernie?"

"The Soviets have reached Teheran from the east. They rolled into the city and basically leveled the government district."

"And the Ayatollah?"

"He got out, apparently yesterday, and surfaced in Islamabad an hour ago."

"Good."

"He made a speech there, in Arabic. I left a videotape of it with Martinelli; it has an English translation. It'll probably be all over the world on the evening news. He really laid it on the Kremlin; called for an Islamic jihad against the Great Russian Satan."

Haugen, tired, grunted, and started for his office with Hammaker beside him. A Farsi-speaking Persian, Haugen mused, addressing in Arabic an audience whose native tongue was Urdu. Arabic was, in its way, as big an international language as English, but the nations who shared it as their first or second language managed to fight each other as much as any other group of countries in the world. So much for the concept that having a single planetary language would engender world peace.

"D'you think anything will come of it?" he asked. "Jalal's speech, that is?"

"Not any declarations of war, that's for sure. There'll probably be some verbal artillery aimed at the Soviets. Chances are some KGB and GRU people will get picked up and disappear, and it's barely possible we might run into a little more friendliness. It might even reduce the terrorism frequency a bit, or redirect it at the Soviets, especially in their Moslem regions. Time will tell.

"This is probably the biggest PR goof the Kremlin ever made; worse than Hungary." Hammaker fell silent then, caught again in the question of why the Soviets would do something so stupid. But then, why did nations, rulers, people in general, do some of the stupid things they did?

They arrived outside Martinelli's office. "I'll look at the tape now," Haugen told him. "It'll give me a change of pace before I put together this evening's speech. And thanks."

Hammaker saluted and left. As he headed for his office, he thought about what the president had just said. Change of pace before he put together this evening's speech! Judas Priest! The old sonofabitch certainly didn't require a lot of lead time.

Jumper Cromwell had been sworn in as vice president, and introduced to his new office and secretary down the hall from the president's; *and* his new office and secretary in the old Executive Office Building; *and* his new office and secretary in the Capitol Building just off the Senate floor; *and* his whole damn suite of vice-presidential offices and staff in the Dirksen Office Building.

He wasn't going to get involved in any of it, more than he absolutely had to. Which was very damned little. Haugen agreed, he was the president's backup and unofficial national security advisor, and that was it. He'd had to leave active military service, and of course his chairmanship, before swearing in—a constitutional requirement. But he'd arranged for a small office in the Pentagon, and to stay on all the routing lists he'd been on before. To keep up with things.

The phone buzzed on his Pentagon desk. He reached; tapped keys. "Cromwell," he said.

"General, this is Major Chilberg. It's about our project. I have something to give you."

Jesus, Cromwell thought, *what a tangled web we weave. Or try to unravel.* "Good. I'll meet you here in my office. Right away."

"Yes sir."

Cromwell tapped another key and returned to the contents of his IN basket. The paper kept flowing, regardless of the real world. The country was still wobbly after taking a standing eight-count; there was war in Iran; and the Readiness Command wasn't ready, although it soon would be again, with the National Guard taking over the entire internal peace-keeping job. Even if the Red Fleet was sailing up the Potomac, paper would flow in the Pentagon. It was part of an insatiable information hunger.

He scanned another memo, initialed it, and tossed it in his OUT basket. Chilberg was in charge of his unofficial research on the Holist Council; there was no guessing what he'd gotten hold of.

The president's communicator buzzed. "Yes Jeanne?"

"I found Father Flynn. He's here now."

"Good. Send him in."

A moment later the priest entered. "Sit down, Steve," said the president. "Coffee?"

"No thanks."

"I've been ignoring you. My apologies. I'm still at that stage where I'm running and don't dare slow down. Actually I've gotten on top of things somewhat: I'm through the worst of the briefing phase—the urgent, four-alarm part. I've worked out and issued operating procedures and delegations of authority that save me a fair amount of time and trouble, and I've gotten the feel of the people who work for me. Canned a couple of them, and in general gotten the machinery somewhat tuned up and oiled.

"I'll tell you what," he added, "Donnelly had some good people with him, especially Milstead and Martinelli. They've gotten to be like my right and left arms."

Flynn nodded. "For me, being in the White House has been more like a vacation than a job. I'm enjoying more time for study and reading than I've had since seminary." He cocked his head and looked Haugen over. "You've developed little satchels under your eyes, Arne—not enough sleep or too much reading—but other than that you look well."

Haugen grinned. "I keep making resolutions to sleep more and exercise, but other things keep getting in the way. My health is not top priority; the business of living outranks it."

The Jesuit's eyebrows raised. "And what is the business of living?"

Haugen's eyes held energies. Father Flynn marveled that this man could have so much life at his age. As if he wasn't using it up; as if he created it as he went.

"The business of life? It's whatever you make it," Haugen replied. "Man wasn't born to take care of himself, he was born to do things."

He chuckled. "My first week here, with everything that was happening, Singleton tells me to come in for a physical. I told him I'd had one in August and I was too damn busy now. When he started to argue, I told him to back off, that I'd call him, he wasn't to call me.

"A person does need to keep the machinery functional, but there are times when maintenance and repairs have to be postponed, backlogged, to get more important things done when they need to be."

The priest nodded. "I have no argument with that. But I hope you don't postpone too long. You're remarkably fit and strong for a man your age. Or a man of fifty, as far as that's concerned. Just don't squander yourself."

The president raised his right hand. "I promise," he said. "Matter of fact, I'm flying John Zale in from Duluth. You've met John; he was my executive secretary there. He's going to be my personal expeditor here. I've worked out his job description with Milstead so they won't step on each other's toes. It'll give me more time and take some pressures off Charles; he's too valuable to use up."

Haugen's face went serious then. "This is the night I give the speech on the economic measures we talked about, and right now I've got a case of nervous stomach.

"Will you be watching?"

"By all means, Mr. President."

"Good. You know, I've seldom operated rushed like this before. I'll tell you a secret though: It's exciting as hell. Using the term 'hell' figuratively.

"Meanwhile if there's anything I do that bothers you, that seems unethical or otherwise wrong, I hope you'll let me know. I'm depending on you to."

The Jesuit's blue-gray eyes were steady on the president. "I will, Mr. President," he said. "I will."

*   *   *

The White House broadcast room required little preparation for a telecast; little more than lighting a fire in the fireplace. After a late supper with his wife, the president took the stairs down from the presidential apartment, was made up for the cameras, and went in. At 9 P.M. eastern time, 6 P.M. Pacific, he was on his feet beside the fireplace, and the telecast began.

"Good evening," he said. "I'm speaking to you tonight from the broadcast room in the White House." His voice was mild, quiet but easily heard, the words distinct but casual.

"I'm not going to talk just now about the war in Iran, other than to mention that the Soviet invaders captured Teheran today. Many of you have already heard that. We're not ignoring what's happening there; the Pentagon is following events closely. But just now my attention is on problems at home. And what I'm going to talk to you about this evening is the economy. Or actually, certain important aspects of it."

He strolled to a desk and sat down. "This desk isn't mine, incidentally. Mine has a computer terminal on it, and it isn't usually this tidy.

"First I want to commend the army, and more especially the national guard, for their vital work in seeing that the distribution of food and fuel have continued and been improved. Without their work and your cooperation, this country would go down the tubes regardless of anything I could do.

"Also at this time I'd like to commend President Donnelly and his advisors, operating under martial law, for their emergency slashing of federal salaries and wages, tying them to week by week economic indicators. And I'd like to commend state, county, and municipal governments for their similar actions. With the crash of wages and prices generally, the gross reduction of tax income has meant much less money to pay public employees with.

"The alternative approach, which President Donnelly wisely rejected, was to print and distribute large quantities of money backed by neither goods nor public credit. In other words, worthless money. If he'd done that, we'd have had several hundred percent inflation by now, or worse. And planning, and the recovery steps I'm going to outline for you here, would be much more difficult.

"I'd also like to commend the American people for their wide acceptance of emergency wage slashing and rent slashing in the private sector. It kept a lot of businesses going, and a lot of people employed. And it kept vital goods flowing.

"Incidentally, our latest figures show unemployment at fifty-eight percent. So you can see why the president's been given emergency powers."

He paused, pursed his lips slightly, then continued. "With regard to federal taxes, I have personally talked with the new Commissioner of the Internal Revenue Service, Mr. Fred Buhler. The recent flurry of IRS property seizures has been halted, with property being returned to the people it was taken from. If any more such seizures occur without proper court action, let your nearest FBI office know. They have orders from me, through Director Dirksma, to handle whoever is responsible. Meanwhile, twenty-three IRS personnel have been reprimanded and reduced in grade. Nineteen others, including ex-commissioner Edwin Balthazar, have been fired, and the FBI is looking into possible malfeasance charges against them, which could mean criminal proceedings and jail sentences. I'm sure that no one will be happier to know this than the large majority of IRS employees who've done the best they could and have tried to operate in a sane and ethical manner."

The president's eyes were direct, as if he were looking at his audience through the camera. "None of this means that tax cheating is all right. What it does mean is that the IRS is not above the law. And that its authorizations do not include arrogant, arbitrary, or vindictive behavior. Also, it means that the IRS, like the rest of us, *needs to adjust its operations ethically and responsibly to the emergency situation*. Right now, top priority goes to salvaging this nation.

"Regarding jobs: The Federal Highway Administration, the Office of Community Planning and Development, and the Labor Department have been putting together a program of public works which will employ several million people within the next couple of weeks. Some of you have seen the first of these public works projects starting up in your communities. To give credit where credit is due, these agencies had begun the planning before I took office, assuming that such programs would be wanted.

"The wages will be low, because the United States Treasury is very low, and because government incomes from taxes have been enormously reduced. But these projects will give a lot of families a wage earner, and the opportunity to buy things they need. And the convenience and dietary variety of getting their food in a local store, instead of having to go, usually on foot, to an emergency food distribution center and stand in line. This program will also provide road and park improvement and new construction that will be greatly appreciated in the future.

"There are several reasons we've been able to actually get these projects underway so quickly. But the central reasons have been martial law and the Emergency Powers Act. These allowed the suspension of a lot of barriers and delays, the slashing of government wages and of payments to government contractors, and the suspension of bond payments, leaving us with something for project funds. These cuts and suspensions have been hard on certain people, but they were necessary adjustments to a critically dangerous situation.

"And that's all I have to say for now about what we might call relief measures. Important as they are, and they are *very* important—vital—much of my attention is on rebuilding the economy on a solid base.

"Basically, the crash has slammed us back to economic square one. Suspension of contract strictures on wages, prices, interests, etcetera, have allowed the country to make the adjustment without going back even further, to square zero. So the question I've been working on is how do we get up to square two and above.

"I've been given a lot of different advice on the economy in the short time I've been in office. You might not believe how different some of it has been. And almost all of it supported by what sounds like convincing data and logic. But very little of the advice was the kind I could put into action for quick, broad, positive results that were consistent with a return to democracy.

"So I decided that if experts had such different ideas about what was best to do, I was justified in starting from scratch to see where logic would take *me*.

"Which I did. I wrote it up and gave it to five economists of generally different views. And got it back with their independent critiques."

From one side of his desk, he took a neat stack of paper and held it up before the cameras. On the topmost, penned jottings were conspicuous in the margins and between the double-spaced lines.

"And I've paid attention to them. Because although the study of economics might still be in its adolescence, economists *have* studied the known phenomena of economics and the theories about them. And the economists I've talked to are very intelligent people, among the best, at the forefront of their still rather crude specialty. Just as some of the doctors of a hundred and fifty years ago were highly intelligent people, who had studied all the medical knowledge of the time and were limited by it.

"The upshot is that I've prepared some new law based on ideas that didn't offend most of those five economists too terribly. It deals with fair wages and salaries. Right now, wages and salaries are whatever an employer can afford. Or what he claims he can afford. This has kept the ship afloat, barely, but it has inevitably resulted in considerable suspicion and resentment, and a certain amount of gouging.

"So we need to establish ground rules on wages and jobs, which will be followed by rules allowing the 'desuspension' of mortgage payments and the reopening of stock markets.

"What we're going to do next—what I am going to tell you about now—will upset some people. It has already upset some of my cabinet, who have the responsibility of seeing that laws, orders, and programs are carried out.

"Because it's different than the way things have been done, and because it'll have to be debugged in use. But you and I know, and they know, what grew out of the way things used to be done. And I'm not changing what doesn't need to be changed.

"What I'm going to outline for you now applies to any and all businesses that do business across state lines or with the federal government, or have done during this calendar year. And it will be in effect until the first of next October, unless Congress or myself sees fit to cancel it."

The president looked around, scanning the panoply of cameras as if looking at the audience of viewers.

"By a week from next Monday morning at eight o'clock"—
He paused for emphasis and repeated deliberately. "By
a week from next Monday morning, every such employer,
except for governments, every such employer with more
than three people working for him, outside his own family
or household, *is to make the financial records of his business available to his employees*. Or to employee representatives. In a form readily understood. And management
and employees are to negotiate new wage and salary agreements based on"—he paused for emphasis—"on *a sharing
of income*. Management's share will not come off the top,
nor will labor's. They will come after other operating
expenses are paid. Expenses such as rent, material, debt
payments—things like that. Labor's wages, as always, will
come out of the same pot that profits and management's
salaries do. *But now labor will know what's in that pot*.
And the negotiations are to determine the proportions—
who gets what percentage."

The president cocked his head, hand cupped behind an
ear. "I can hear the screaming from here. But let me
comment that Duluth Technologies is an employer. Even
now it has something like seventy-two hundred employees
including sales representatives. So this new law impacts
the firm I built, and that I will return to from here. For
that reason, if for no other, you might expect me to be fair
toward management.

"Meanwhile, all old wage scales and salary contracts, for
everyone from sweepers to corporation presidents, are
cancelled. Not just suspended, as they have been lately,
but cancelled. And this includes those of government
employees.

"By the first Sunday in January, each of those employers, and his or her employees or employee-elected representatives, must have negotiated a new agreement, to take
effect on that date."

The president steepled his fingers, and his eyes focused
elsewhere, as if in thought. When he spoke again, it was
more slowly, as if choosing his words carefully.

"So what we're talking about here is what you might call
floating salaries and floating wages. When company income goes up, everyone's share goes up. When company
income goes down, everyone's share goes down. The sweep-

er's and the chairman of the board's. Labor will have something to say about management salaries, as well as management having something to say about labor's wages."

His brows drew down slightly now, less in a frown than in serious emphasis. "But labor had better recognize the value of good management," he went on, "and the need for profits as a reward for investment and a necessary means for expansion. Labor should not get carried away by their new position and try to cut their own throats.

"I want to stress here that top management carries more responsibility than anyone else for company income, which means everyone's income, and it needs to be rewarded accordingly. But on the other hand, being top management does not justify an unreasonable share of company income.

"One of the reasons that our economy foundered—*one* of the reasons—was the desire of both management and labor, both of them, to have everything they wanted, and right now. Or as close to everything and as close to right now as possible. This was a desire rooted in good old human ambition, and force-fed by advertising.

"Now as far as I can see, there is nothing wrong with wanting to have a lot—or in having it. But first you have to create it." The president's voice rose in emphasis. "Prosperity is not a matter of 'gimme,' of wanting and demanding. It's a matter of production and distribution and sales. Each of us, and that includes *you*, has to create, has to produce, our own prosperity. We, you, have to produce goods and services, and exchange them with others."

He paused. "And that's an important part of what this new law is about: Seeing that production, and the exchange between supplier and purchasers, comes before salaries and wages. It's fine for the businessman or manager to want a big boat, a diamond bracelet for his wife, a summer home in the mountains, a condo in Florida. And the employee can't be faulted for wanting a second car, a Hawaiian vacation, weekends on the ski slopes or in Las Vegas, and a stock portfolio. Those are all justifiable desires." Once more the president slowed for emphasis. "But the money has to come from somewhere, and if it doesn't come from production and sales, at prices that don't feed inflation, then the ship will finish sinking, and we'll end up with something more or less like the Soviet people struggle with.

"Basically that's the choice. And you're the only ones who can make it.

"And something I almost forgot to mention, related to wages— Both sides should consider bonuses for outstanding individual contributions to company income. That's not part of the new law, but it's a part of good sense."

Haugen leaned forward, both elbows on his desk now, crossing his forearms on it. "And there's more to this law. As of the first Sunday in January—" He enunciated the words almost one by one: "Starting in January, job security is tied to job performance. I'll repeat that: *Job security will be tied to job performance*. Allowing for sickness and other special circumstances to be worked out between management and labor. For example, if you're an assembly line worker whose production frequently fails to meet agreed upon—*agreed upon*—quality and quantity standards, management must have the right to fire you. Fair standards and fair procedures for this are something that management and labor need to work out together as part of the labor-management agreement.

"At the same time, if you are a hired corporate executive whose decisions have been harmful to the company's economy, you can and should be fired. Labor and the stockholders should insist on it, because the inept manager hurts their earnings. The new law gives labor the leverage to get it done. I'll leave the evaluation and firing procedures to be worked out between management and labor.

"Of course, if the manager also owns the business, he can't be fired. But he can go down with the ship."

The president's voice, which had been business-like, changed, taking on a pleasant, genial tone. "Now there may be, out there, an occasional executive who is thinking, *I don't need to worry about this new law. We'll find loopholes, or otherwise work our way around this. That's what we hire expensive law firms for.*"

His eyes hardened, and his voice took an edge. "To this individual I say, don't challenge me on this. You could find yourself working for room and board, making canvas products for Federal Prison Industries. And all the lawyers in New York, not to mention Philadelphia, won't be enough to save your butt."

He paused again, took a breath, and continued. "Now, if management and labor can't get together on what the income shares should be, and the working conditions, and job evaluation and discharge procedures, before the second Sunday in December, they'd better agree on and bring in an arbitrator for binding arbitration. Otherwise the federal government will provide the arbitrator. And we'll charge outrageously for it, which will cost both management and labor dearly until they've finally finished paying. Because we don't want the arbitration job; we want management and labor to take responsibility themselves.

"And all of this holds for nonprofit organizations as well as for those that hope to make a profit. Except that it does not hold for the majority of churches—those that have non-profit status."

The president sat back then. "This is all being published in detail. It will be available in stores within a week. There are people in government who are sweating blood to see that deadlines are met on this; my thanks to them.

"And that's all I have to say for now. Before too long, I expect to report to you on energy, the environment, and taxes. I believe you'll like what I have to say about each of them."

He got up from his chair. "Thank you all for listening. God bless you and good night."

When the cameras ceased recording and the microphones were off, Arne Haugen walked slowly into the center hall to an elevator, and rode up to the presidential apartment, where his wife waited. Enroute, he seemed to shrink two inches and age ten years. When he entered the living room, she got up and embraced him.

"You were very good," she said quietly. "I was proud of you."

He smiled ruefully. "Thank you, my most impartial friend. I feel as if I'd been hammered through a knothole."

She nodded. "I can understand that. But you *did* do well. Very well."

"The next question," he said, "is what the other 260 million think of it. Will they really try? And if they do, will it work or won't it? If they won't, or if it doesn't, you can forget democracy in America, and probably in the rest of the world."

He sank down in his favorite chair and this time let Lois pour a glass of wine for him; usually he did the pouring. "I think I'll go to bed early tonight," he said, then grinned. "Anyway I've still got my ace in the hole. I know damn well it'll work."

SIXTEEN

Arne Haugen left the presidential apartment after breakfast with his mouth tingling from toothpaste. He was a resilient man; he'd recovered nicely from the previous evening's emotional exhaustion. The two Secret Service agents answered his cheery "good morning, Will; good morning, Frank," with identical replies—"good morning, Mr. President" —and accompanied him as unobtrusively as practical, one to his left, the other behind, as he walked to the head of the grand staircase. He seldom used the elevator, down or up; the physical activity was welcome.

It occurred to him that, except for the Secret Service men and the doormen, he hardly ever saw any of the household staff unless their presence was requested. There were supposed to be sixty of them. Occasionally he'd glimpse one—maybe once or twice a day—but that was all. In his preoccupation, he'd given it no thought.

He thought he knew why this gentile near-invisibility; he'd once asked Gil why the Secret Service men so seldom spoke in his presence, and why they answered so briefly when he spoke to them. "A president's a busy man, sir, with a lot on his mind," Gil had answered. "He needs as much privacy as he can get." Then, opening up a bit: "This is your *home*, sir," he'd added, stressing the word.

The day before, Haugen had seen a vagrant spray bottle beside a potted plant, its user out of sight somewhere. Perhaps waiting in the nearest unoccupied room, dust cloth in hand, till the President was past.

Presumably most Presidents were more or less thoroughly oriented on household operations by their predecessors, but Donnelly had been in no condition to, and Haugen hadn't wanted to impose on Mrs. Donnelly. So he'd gotten by with a mini-briefing from Jackson Lavender, the chief usher—equivalent to the steward in a British mansion.

Haugen's eyes roved, probed. It wasn't as if the help weren't busy. Big as the place was, it was clean—dusted, mopped, the banisters polished . . . He'd have noticed if it weren't. Haugen paused on the first-floor landing to examine a rubber plant; even the leaves were dusted. The world economy was in collapse, the Russians had invaded Iran, there were religio-political guerrilla wars in Malaysia and on Mindanao, and the threat of final solution in southern Africa. Hell, according to the apocalyptic sects with their estimated eight million American members and growing, God was about to shut the world down! But there was no dust in the White House.

Be grateful for things done well, he told himself.

The corridor past the press area was quiet too; he was willing to bet that when the press was allowed back in, their level of courtesy and consideration would be a lot lower than that of the Secret Service or the household staff. But then, he reminded himself, their job was different, and different personalities gravitate to different activities.

Martinelli was already busy at her desk when he arrived, typing his evening dictation into her computer. She was fast, fast; her keyboard sounded like a muffled popping of popcorn.

"Good morning, Jeanne. Get hold of Lavender and ask him to come see me."

Then he was past, her "yes Mr. President" almost cut off by the closing door. *Jesus,* he thought, *speaking of courtesy! Maybe they do try to talk to you, and you just don't notice.* He about-faced and opened the door again; she was in the process of keying her in-house phone.

"And one thing more, Jeanne," he told her.

She half turned, questioningly, and he grinned at her. "Sorry I hustled through so brusquely. Goes with the territory, I suppose. You do a helluva job, Martinelli, and I appreciate hell out of you. Just in case you were wondering."

For an instant she looked uncertain, then abruptly smiled back at him. "Why, thank you, Mr. President." Another hesitation, then, "You do too, sir." She blushed. "Do a helluva job, I mean."

Having said it, she looked away, and Haugen, laughing with pleasure, turned back into his office.

Three minutes later, Lavender, the chief usher, arrived. He was the majordomo of the household staff, and looked the part, a tall man, straight, seeming naturally dignified, his complexion almost Caucasian light, his cap-like, tightly kinked hair graying. "Yes, Mr. President?" he said.

The president gestured at a chair. "Sit down, Lavender, I've got some questions for you." He waited till the man was seated. "How does the staff know I'm coming? They seem to get out of my way."

"There are bells, sir, on each floor. Three bells means the President is coming, two the First Lady. Everyone gets out of sight then."

"Hmh! Has it always been like that?"

"Mostly, sir. A few Presidents changed it when they were in, but mostly that's the way it's been. To give the First Family more privacy."

"Hmm. I can see why that would be. What're the hours for the cleaning staff, the gardeners, people like those?"

"Mostly six to three, sir."

"Okay. Tell you what, Lavender. Let's dispense with all that ducking out of sight. It's got to be a nuisance to people, and for Mrs. Haugen and me it's not necessary."

"Yes sir."

For the life of him, the president couldn't tell, by looking at the man, how he was receiving this. "How does that seem to you, Lavender?"

"Fine, Mr. President. It *will* make things a little easier."

Haugen looked at him thoughtfully. "I want you to speak frankly with me. How is morale in the staff?"

There was a very brief lag before Lavender answered.

"Pretty good, sir. They've got jobs, and that's a big blessing in these times."

" 'Pretty good.' " Haugen's eyes never left the man's face. "What's in the way of it being very good?"

The lag was longer this time. "Mr. President," Lavender said at last, "they're worried. There are no tourists, no guests, no banquets or receptions, and the government's short on money. President Donnelly let some people go—fifteen or so that were young and pretty new, or eligible for early retirement. So people are worried that there'll be some more let go. And they've got nothing to fall back on, hardly any of them. What they had in the banks, they lost in the crash. So they're worried."

The President looked thoughtful. "I see." *Worried,* he thought, *like the rest of the country.* He straightened. "Lavender, I want you to tell them something for me. This emergency isn't going to last forever, and when it's over, or maybe before, things'll get back more or less to normal around here. Then whoever's president will need a full staff, experienced and ready. The household budget's been cut all right. But with no costs for banquets or house guests, no more tour guides—things like that—we should be able to keep within the budget without discharging anyone. We may have to cut a few more corners here and there, but I intend to keep the household staff intact."

"Yes sir."

"And Lavender, tell them that Mrs. Haugen and I appreciate them and the good work they do." He rolled his chair belly-up to his desk, eyes still on the chief usher. "That's all for now; I've got to get to work. Thanks."

"Thank *you,* Mr. President."

Haugen watched the man's straight back out the door. *It's remarkable how much quality you run into around here,* he told himself. *People are an education.*

The absence of tourists, and his policy of not having house guests, receptions and the like, not only allowed the president to work with minimal distractions and interruptions. It also allowed him more time with his wife than some presidents had had, especially with the arrival of John Zale on his office staff.

Nonetheless, Haugen had stopped trying to reserve lunch

as family time; only breakfast and usually supper were with Lois. The TV was kept off at breakfast, though supper was likely to be eaten to football, hockey, or basketball.

He'd begun eating lunch with Steve Flynn, with the top-rated TV midday news as background. They'd talk, and sometimes watch something on the screen.

They were discussing the Papal attitude toward birth control when a news item caught their attention. A considerable crowd of demonstrators was shown near the vast CIA building, waving signs and chanting. Brief interviews indicated they were demonstrating against CIA university scholarships, which, as the commentator pointed out, were largely in foreign languages, computer sciences, mathematics, and electronics.

Some of the demonstrators were waving placards, while others were haranguing, reviling, and shoving cameras at the faces of CIA employees walking to the entrances. Still others roamed the executive and employee parking lots with small videocameras, photographing cars, people, and license plates. Cameras; a fear technique, the president decided, that they'd copied from some police forces. But there was no indication of serious trouble; employees were not being interfered with physically. Squads of gas-masked troops stood in quiet, separated rows, preventing the demonstrators from approaching the building closely. But not even the gas masks suggested impending trouble; they'd become familiar—standard military garb during the recent troubles.

When the flow of employees had ended, the demonstrators began to move down access roads as if returning to their transportation. Apparently the show was over. That's when the tear gas grenades were fired, and in an instant the view was shattered with screaming people running, stumbling down the road. Then a truck-mounted water cannon appeared from somewhere, and with its powerful jet, sent demonstrators sprawling, washing them physically along the pavement.

It was over inside a minute. When Father Flynn's eyes left the set to find the president, Haugen's face was dark with repressed anger.

He got up from his chair. "Excuse me, Stephen," he muttered. He almost never said "Stephen"—"Steve" was nearly invariable. He went to his desk and keyed the intercom. "Jeanne, get me General Hammaker. At once. If he's not at his desk, have someone find him."

He waited then; they both did, priest and president, Haugen's blunt fingers drumming. In the background the TV jabbered on, ignored. During eight months of friendship, Flynn had never seen Arne Haugen angry before, or even notably irritated. He wasn't sure how much of it was due to the abusive actions of the demonstrators and how much to the attack on them. To Flynn, the attack seemed unjustified. A more understandable time for the troops to have acted was when the demonstrators were harassing the employees.

Three or four minutes passed; the general's face appeared on the small screen. "Yes Mr. President. What can I do for you?"

"General Hammaker, are you aware of the fiasco outside the CIA building this morning?"

General Hammaker, not "Ernie." From Hammaker's facial response, it seemed clear to Father Flynn that the general had *not* heard what had happened. But he'd definitely picked up on the president's anger; he looked uncertain and concerned. "No sir, Mr. President. What happened?"

Haugen described it, his words clipped, his consonants sharp and hard, and for the first time, Flynn discerned an accent, essentially Finnish, as the president spoke. But by the time he was done, the edge of anger was gone from his voice. "Do you see what this does?" he finished.

"I believe I do, sir. It was gratuitous violence by a military unit. It will make a lot of people angry, and make the army look bad."

The President nodded. "That's right, as far as it goes. Now that civil violence has stopped and civilian attitudes are constructive . . ." He paused, then enunciated— "Some goddamn nitwit in uniform decides to act like a commissar! This government can't afford to appear oppressive."

He paused again, and when he continued talking, it was quietly. "Find out for me who was responsible, Ernie, who set this up. If it was a CIA request, I want to know who made it. And who in the army agreed to it. And if you have trouble getting the information, remind them of martial law. Tell them I won't hesitate to run someone's ass publicly up the flagpole if they try to cover on this.

"Find out by evening—by 2000 hours—and let me know. The sooner the better. Because I'm calling a press conference for 2100. If I don't smooth this out, people and the Congress are going to wonder what kind of government this is. And it'll smooth a lot better if I've got someone by the short and curlies."

Once more he paused, thoughtful now, lips pursed. "And Ernie, there was something peculiar about the whole event. As hard as it is to get gas these days, and considering that the CIA Building is out of town, that was a lot of demonstrators. Especially considering what they were demonstrating about. If they drove, did someone provide gas? And if they rode buses, who provided the buses? I'm going to get the FBI onto that as soon as I've finished talking with you."

He grinned then, surprising both Hammaker and Flynn. "Actually I've already finished, but you've hardly had a chance. Anything you want to tell me while we're on the line?"

Hammaker shook his head, his expression still serious. "No, Mr. President. I'll get on that right away and get back to you as soon as I learn anything. It shouldn't take long to find out who in the army gave the orders. What the CIA involvement was, if any, might take a little longer."

"Thanks, Ernie. I apologize for being testy, but I was really pissed off. You'd have to see the thing on TV to appreciate how it looked to viewers.

"So I look forward to hearing what you find out."

He disconnected, turned to Flynn, and smiled sheepishly. "And so much for my Christian charity." He laughed again. "But then, I'm not a Christian."

He didn't realize how much that troubled the priest.

Hammaker sat back in his chair. He'd ordered his own aide, Captain Robertson, to find out who'd been the officer in charge out there. Fast. Hammaker himself would question whoever that might be about any CIA instigation.

Then he'd called the CIA Director's office. Blackburn had been out, supposedly, but his deputy had promised to find out who in their shop, "if anyone," had been involved. The promise didn't mean much, Hammaker told himself: They'd do whatever they wanted that they thought they could get away with. If Blackburn's office seemed to be covering up, he'd get in touch with Cromwell; Cromwell had told him to call anytime the president was having trouble with the military. And Cromwell had people everywhere, or so the rumor went: army intelligence or simply friends.

It would be interesting to see how the president handled this, he told himself.

The press had been notified in advance: President Haugen wasn't taking questions tonight. He walked out in front of the cameras, looked around, nodded and began, his voice mild, his words measured.

"Good evening. I called this conference to talk about the CIA. And the violence outside the CIA Building this morning and what I'm doing about it.

"First of all, Captain Edwin Rantelle was the officer in charge of the army guard unit there. Captain Rantelle ordered the gas grenades fired—in fact he fired the first of them himself—and had also given the order that the water cannon was to go into action as soon as the gas grenades exploded.

"He has admitted that there was nothing in the behavior of the demonstrators which called for such drastic action at that time. Indeed, the demonstration was over and the demonstrators were in the process of leaving.

"Captain Rantelle has heretofore had a good service record. I have reprimanded him in writing, and the reprimand, of course, goes on his service record. Any of you who are or have been military officers know that a formal reprimand in one's record is a significant hurdle to overcome when being evaluated for promotions and assignment."

The president's voice continued patient. "The responsibility was not Captain Rantelle's alone, however. Mr. Carl Anderson, the CIA's officer in charge of building and grounds security, had requested that Captain Rantelle do this. Mr. Anderson has stated that he was tired of the verbal abuse which CIA employees, most of them secretaries, computer technicians, maintenance people and so forth, have to put up with periodically when people decide to demonstrate there.

"He's not the only one who's tired of that.

"Mr. Anderson has also been reprimanded. And it has been made clear to both the army and the CIA that any repetition of needless violence there will result in a court martial in the case of the responsible army officer, and in suspension or firing of the responsible CIA official."

He paused, looking over the attending journalists, letting his audience wait for five long seconds.

"Now," he said, "I have something to say about demonstrations like that one. There are people watching now who feel indignant that these two men were only reprimanded. But Mr. Anderson had a valid point, though it did not justify the action taken. If you watched the TV coverage of the demonstration, you heard the insulting language shouted at the CIA employees as they walked from the parking lots to their work. No one should have to put up with people running alongside them shouting insults and obscenities at them.

"So I have ordered the guard detail to prevent that in the future. Demonstrators will be kept well away from employees, and any who break the law while demonstrating will be arrested.

"Of course, that's part of what such demonstrators want—to be arrested. Because until very recently, arrests at demonstrations for trespassing or disorderly conduct usually meant little. The arrested were booked, paid a modest bail, and were released. Our overcrowded prisons usually lacked room to hold them longer.

"Now, as you know, we have prisons of tents and barbed wire, with ample space, and quite comparable in livability to the army camps of early World War Two. So such an arrest will lead to a more extended and impactful experience, and if you demonstrate, you might want to consider doing it in a lawful way."

Again the long pause while the president's calm eyes scanned the room.

"I also appreciate that the CIA tends to be poorly regarded in this country. To some extent this has resulted from actions of its own, and to some extent from a planned program of disinformation by agents of foreign powers:

lies, exaggerations, distortions, and truths told out of context, that have been passed along by our own media and accepted as true by many Americans.

"But easily the CIA's biggest image problem has grown out of an ill-advised organizational situation dating way back to 1948. The same cause which, for nearly fifty years, has significantly impaired our gathering of needed information about our enemies.

"And believe me, regardless of what some may tell you, we have enemies.

"In 1947, the Congress established the CIA, the Central Intelligence Agency, to help keep the executive branch of our government informed on foreign activities, especially Communist Bloc activities. It spies in the traditional sense, but even more, it collects and winnows through masses of information, including huge amounts of publications from both sides of the iron curtain. It monitors radio broadcasts; it examines in minute detail, satellite and aerial overflight photography. And it has other kinds of spy devices. Then it evaluates and organizes the relevent material from all this daily, and gets it to those who need to know. And does all this with remarkable skill.

"Just as Congress intended it should.

"As set up by Congress, the CIA was to be *purely* an intelligence operation. That was the intention. So-called 'covert operations'—dirty tricks, the covert support of foreign military and paramilitary activities, that sort of thing— were not a part of its charter.

"Now, looking back a few years earlier, to World War Two, our government had set up what was called the OSS—the Office of Strategic Services—which was responsible for covert operations behind German and Japanese lines. And as the Cold War developed, it was decided that a covert operations organization was needed again. So without going through Congress, in 1948 the old OSS was reinstituted as the Directorate of Operations and put into the Central Intelligence Agency. It is *not* the main part of the CIA; it is relatively the lesser part. But it's the part that gets the publicity."

Haugen was winging his talk now without glancing at notes. "Yet it is covert operations," he went on, "that has gotten all the press. It is covert operations that has made the CIA so susceptible to campaigns of disinformation, and brought it a bad reputation with many people abroad and at home.

"And to make things worse, almost every CIA director has come out of Operations. Covert operations people seem to have had an advantage in in-house politics. At times the intelligence branch has even been pressured or ordered by CIA directors to slant or edit their intelligence findings to support covert operations proposals and programs.

"So—" He paused, then went on. "Let's drop back a step now, and ask why covert operations has such a bad image. Aside from disinformation campaigns by its enemies abroad and at home. First of all, at times they have broken American law, sometimes flagrantly. When this has been exposed, the excuse has sometimes been made, at least within the government, that it was necessary. You're well aware of that.

"Also, there is a personality type which seems to gravitate to covert operations, a personality type which doesn't necessarily have criminal impulses but seems to enjoy being illegal. So we have some of those involved. And besides that, covert operations are something carried out in foreign countries, and their actions are seldom legal by the laws of those countries. In that sense, any covert action field personnel almost always have to act illegally to accomplish their ends. They get used to that; it becomes a part of life for them.

"Now, their actions in foreign countries are also restricted by our own laws and regulations, and sometimes they don't feel as constrained as they should by these either."

The president paused for emphasis. "Particularly since *they are the individuals at risk of death or capture. They are the individuals trying to accomplish the often very difficult. They are the ones who know what the local conditions are.*"

The president's voice eased, became casual again.

"They are the ones who work intimately with the local people, who tend to develop affinity with the locals and with their cause, and become frustrated by red tape and restrictions from Washington, even though much of that red tape, and many of those restrictions, are necessary.

"Thus as long as we have a covert operations organization, and we definitely seem to need one, we will have problems with regulations and laws being broken by some agents. Of course, even if it was squeaky clean, we'd still have problems with foreign and domestic disinformation programs."

The newsmen were quiet. Tape recorders and video cameras turned silently. "Which means," Haugen went on, "that we can expect some continued antagonism here at home toward our covert operations.

"So I am taking covert operations out of the CIA, and putting it into a separate organization, to be called by its old name, the Office of Strategic Services, OSS. I haven't decided yet what branch of government it will be part of—that is, who it will answer to—but it will be outside the CIA, and closely monitored by the National Security Council.

"This should allow CIA recruitment and training to go ahead unharassed. It will also very largely free its intended and vital intelligence-gathering function from pressuring by covert operations.

"The divorce will take place no later than a month from now."

Haugen rested his elbows on the lectern and leaned forward, scanning the press. His smile became almost predatory.

"And now, speaking of dirty tricks—covert operations—I'm going to tell you about one carried out by one of your own media organizations. We have unequivocal, first-hand evidence—submitted affidavits and his own statement—that Arlen Baines of Foremost Cable News rented eight buses to take demonstrators to the CIA Building this morning, using money from what he termed 'the special operations fund.' He has implicated others. Mr. Baines was arrested earlier this evening at his apartment, and just moments before I began talking with you, the FBI impounded the records of that fund."

Haugen stood regarding the utterly silent room for several seconds before continuing.

"You may cover demonstrations, certainly. But news organizations have no business inciting or supporting demonstrations. The government is initiating legal action that will quite likely result in Foremost Cable News losing its broadcasting license.

"Which will be no loss to the country. There are far more reputable channels, cable and otherwise."

He scanned the room again. "Now one more thing. I realize that papers have to be sold. And that ratings are important to the sale of commercial time on TV and radio. And that reporters and editors and producers and anchor people have their ratings evaluated by higher ups. But ethics and integrity should not be cancelled by expediency, in the media any more than in government. The media and its people still have a responsibility to be honest.

"Some news organizations do pretty well on this, while some show as little respect for honesty as the law and clever legal staffs allow. More than a little of what the media peddles as news is colorful rumor, unsubstantiated accusations, or simply misleading headlines, printed or broadcast to sell, with little responsibility shown for reputations damaged.

"Too many of the rumors and accusations that turn out to be untrue are destructive to society and individuals. Too often the misleading headline is all that gets read. Even in more normal times, this degrades our society and our nation."

The room was intensely quiet. The assembled journalists waited for the ax to drop, the announcement of censorship. Then the president continued.

"So I'm having federal libel laws reviewed, to better protect people from libelous media actions. Undoubtedly this will severely affect the tabloids.

"But repeatedly the media, especially the newspapers, have uncovered serious frauds, crimes, bureaucratic abuses, and other skullduggeries, in government and elsewhere. And the media cannot be bridled and fulfill their function of national watchdog. We cannot expect them to be perfect, and we cannot legislate perfection. We have to let them function.

"So as an American citizen, you still need to view critically and read critically what the media tell you. What is the evidence? Who's saying it? And why? What ideological fish is this editor or that commentator trying to fry? Is he exercising some prejudice he has? Ask yourself whether you're willing to believe what you're being told."

He paused. "By them and by me."

The president straightened then. "I believe I've talked enough for now; we've covered a lot of ground this evening. I thank you all for listening, both citizens and press, and no doubt I'll be talking to you again soon."

Paul Massey stared unseeingly at the newly blanked TV screen in his living room/office. This Haugen was a dangerous demagogue! And the White House press corps had sat on their hands while the man had intimidated them with his attack! What had become of the spirit of American journalism?

Any kind of investigation of Foremost Cable News would show who held controlling interest in it: Connecticut Investments. And a little further looking would turn up who owned controlling interest in Connecticut Investments: Paul Massey.

FCN was one of his favorite tools, and now he'd almost surely lose it, while attention would be drawn to himself.

He reached for his phone. It was time to call Tallmon and have him take action to terminate this president.

SEVENTEEN

Howard Kreiner and Louis Grosberg walked across the Senate dining room and took seats next to a window. Two days of showery weather had passed, and hazy autumn sunshine lit the capital grounds.

On the table, the flowers of the day were something blue. Neither man paid attention to them. Grosberg, as president pro tem of the Senate, and Kreiner, as minority leader, both had their attention very much on something else.

A waiter had started toward them with coffee pot and menus before they'd even sat down. "The usual, Marty," Grosberg said, as the waiter poured. Kreiner matched

Grosberg's order, and the waiter left with the menus still under an arm.

Grosberg shook his head. "Werling's the biggest problem on my side of the aisle. And he has more favors owed him than almost anyone in the Senate." He flashed a grin. "Except for you and me. His pitch is that Haugen's using his powers a lot more broadly than intended."

Kreiner grunted. "What makes that sonofabitch the authority on what was intended?"

Grosberg nodded agreeably. "But that's how he's pitching it. Surely you're getting some of that too?"

"Not much. Probably because I was on the committee that brought the bill out in the first place. And of course, we're not in the same situation on my side that you folks are. We're not in the position of seeing a term as majority party being diluted by a president who can decree his own laws."

He sipped his scalding coffee carefully. "If it comes down to it and the bill gets out of committee, how do you read the votes on your side?"

"Not serious yet," Grosberg replied. "As of yesterday, only maybe twenty-two to forty for repeal. But tomorrow— Who knows? There's an awful lot of pressure on them, from just about every business lobby in the capital. The kind of thing that can convince people, some of them, that black is white—or at least light gray."

Kreiner grunted. "I read it about ten to twenty-eight on mine. What I'm hearing mostly is that the emergency is actually over because there hasn't been any shooting for a few weeks."

He grinned then, and took a stout envelope from the attaché case he'd brought in with him. "Seen this morning's *Times* yet?" He pulled a photocopied article from the envelope. "It's probably in just about every other paper, too."

"What is it?"

Kreiner handed it to him. "Food for thought, Louie, food for thought. A survey by Morrisey and Spencer on what people think of Haugen's performance so far. Marquez saw it this morning and had copies made; brought 'em to me."

Grosberg adjusted his glasses and read. It was from a

"stratified systematic sample" numbering 2,874 respondents in seventeen states, questioned at food lines, bus stops, and by telephone. And made since the speech on labor and management. There'd been two questions. The first was, "Would you say the president is doing a good job or a poor job?" The answers were: good, 73%; poor, 12%; neither or undecided, 10%; refused to answer, 5%. *Six to one liked Haugen,* Grosberg said to himself. It was very rare for a president to get that kind of public approval. And only 15% were undecided or wouldn't answer. Allowing for some people's automatic refusal to answer questions, that was pretty unusual too.

The second question was, "Do you consider that the future looks hopeful or not hopeful?" The answers were: hopeful, 64%; not hopeful, 13%; undecided, 18%; refused to answer, 5%.

The standard error of the estimate was supposed to be 7% for both questions. Grosberg snorted. You couldn't calculate a standard error for that kind of sample; not unless probability theory had changed since he'd gone to college. For this survey, you couldn't even define the population you'd sampled, for chrissake. But they were probably decent estimates. He scanned on.

Those who felt that Haugen was doing a good job fell almost entirely in the hopeful and undecided categories, the surveyors said. Those who felt he was doing a poor job fell almost entirely into the "not hopeful" group. And almost all who were undecided about Haugen were undecided or "not hopeful" about how the future looked.

He looked up at Kreiner. "Interesting. You know what this looks like to me?"

Kreiner nodded. "Most people like Haugen, and most of them are hopeful or not hopeful according to whether they like him or not."

"And," Grosberg added, "it's a little like Franklin Roosevelt said in 1932 or three: 'All we have to fear is fear itself.' That's not true of course, but with hope, the country's got a chance. Otherwise . . ." He made a thumbs down sign across the table, then held up the Xeroxed sheet. "I'll get copies made of this. Most of my people will see it today anyway, but I'll give them copies, just to make a point."

"Yeah," said Kreiner. "Maybe it'll cool things for a while."

Raphael Dietrich came abruptly awake in the dark room and spotted the vague grayness of the door opening.

"Rafe!" It was a whisper.

"Come in and shut the door," he murmured.

Mary Vizzini stepped in and pulled the door closed behind her. He could hear the bolt click shut, saw her dim form cross the bedroom toward him. "Mark called, collect," she murmured. "From Dover." She lifted the quilt and crawled under it. "He won't be back till two or three o'clock—maybe even till tomorrow afternoon. The computer there was really fucked up and he's still working on it. Making overtime."

"Good." He pulled her to him and bit her ear. His hands found only a long shirt covering her, and stroked the curve of her back.

"Rafe?"

"Yeah?"

"How long is it going to be before your contact gets the hot stuff?"

"Baby, the only hot stuff I'm interested in now is you."

"Um . . . But Rafe, it's really on my mind. Getting the stuff."

"Hell, baby! I told you guys at supper yesterday: I don't know. *He* doesn't know. All he knows is that his source has put it off for now. Without telling him why." Rafe's hand caressed the back of her legs. "He says not to worry; he'll get it. That kind of thing is tricky, for chrissake."

"I was thinking," she said. "Maybe we could blow it off in D.C. Take out the White House."

The thought alarmed him. "No way, baby. For two reasons. First we don't want the army running the country. Plus our source is giving this to us for one reason: to blow a nuke plant. He doesn't want the army running the country either, and I don't want the goddamn mafia or something looking for me for crossing him up."

"And you really don't have any idea who the source is?"

"My contact does. But me? I don't give a shit. Why should I?"

"I'll bet it's an Arab."

He chuckled, his hand beneath her shirttail now. "You'd like to be in bed with an Arab I'll bet," he said. "A rich one."

"Uh-uh. Not an Arab, rich or otherwise. I like being in bed with you."

"How about Mark?"

"Mark's okay. Is it a Russian?"

"It's an American. With a big dick."

She giggled, then sobered. "Rafe?"

"Yeah?" His fingers fumbled with shirt buttons.

"When you leave here, can I go with you? I like you a lot better than Mark."

"Don't tell him that, for chrissake! It could screw the whole project."

"I wouldn't tell him. I'm not that dumb." She paused and, half sitting up, shrugged out of the shirt. "I don't suppose your contact would tell you anyway."

"He told me, all right. We've done stuff before, different times; he knows me. We got stoned together and he told me."

"Is it really an American?"

"Yeah. Unless he was shitting me, it's really an American. But I don't know if his dick is big or not. He's too old for it to make any difference anyway."

She giggled. "Old? I'll bet it's the president then."

He almost laughed out loud. "Then you'd lose your bet. Now cut the goddamn questions. I've had enough of them."

"Just one more, Rafe. You didn't answer me. When you leave here, can I go with you?"

"If you promise to quit the goddamn questions, yeah. You can go with me."

EIGHTEEN

This time the president was at breakfast when the phone interrupted. If the operator passed it through this early, it was probably important. Haugen picked it up.

"This is the president."

"Mr. President, this is General Hammaker."

"I'm eating breakfast with my wife, Ernie. What have you got for me?"

"The Soviet army in the Teheran district is moving again. Apparently an entire army group—three armies. They're headed south. It could be they simply want to take and secure the towns of Qom and Hamadan. But on the other hand, it's possible they plan to head west from there, through the Zagros Gate and down into Iraq."

Haugen recalled being shown pictures of the Zagros Mountains, big, barren-looking, *rugged*. "The Zagros Gate. Is that the pass through the mountains?"

"Yes sir."

A move west toward Iraq was at odds with the Joint Staff's evaluation of the situation and the available intelligence on Soviet thinking. The Soviet army that had come down through the northern Zagros had just that week finally arrived at Teheran, days after the city had been taken by the Soviet army from Afghanistan. They'd had a long tough trip of it, and both the CIA and the Joint Staff deemed it highly unlikely that they'd get themselves involved with more of the Zagros very soon. Especially now that winter was settling in at higher elevations and much of the Iranian army had returned from Iraq.

That had been the expert evaluation, and it made sense. "Any reason to think they *might* move west?"

"Nothing compelling, sir. But there's the size of the

force they're moving with; they shouldn't need a force anywhere near that large to take and hold Qom and Hamadan. And they're moving more troops into Iran from both the northwest and the northeast."

"What does the CIA think the Soviets are up to? Geopolitically that is. Or the Pentagon?"

"If they have an opinion, sir, they haven't expressed it. But offhand— The oil from the gulf's been cut off for more than a year now, and a lot of countries are suffering for it. Worse than we are. It's conceivable that the Soviets want to set up as the big oil broker of the world—rebuild the pipelines and refineries and docking facilities there. But that's a long, hard, hostile way from Russia for a project like that, and the Sov economy's in real trouble. It's questionable whether they have the resources to pull it off with."

Haugen examined the oil broker idea and smiled inwardly; if that was true, it was going to be a big disappointment to them. "Um-m. Okay Ernie, thanks. Let me know if anything further develops." He paused. "But Ernie, not at breakfast or supper unless it's urgent. And important doesn't necessarily equate with urgent; this could have waited a half-hour. Okay?"

"Yes sir. I'll keep that in mind, Mr. President. And I'll keep you informed."

"Thanks, Ernie." Haugen broke the connection, then résuméd the call for Lois. "And I've got a premonition," he finished. "For what it's worth. The Soviets *are* going to move down into Iraq."

A phone call from Cromwell had driven the new Soviet move to the back of the president's mind. The general wanted to bring someone over. To give another briefing, this one on an NSA project. Haugen had told him okay, come on over. Cromwell said it would be forty or fifty minutes; he had to fly the guy in from Fort Meade.

The president finished scanning another report, initialed it, then another, and six more, putting them in his OUT basket. He looked at his watch; forty-five minutes had passed. Getting up, he walked to the big window and parted the curtains. The day was cloudy. Breezes vagrant and unruly chased occasional leaves; the last to fall. The grounds staff had harvested the main crop. In Duluth the earth would be snow-covered by now.

The National Security Agency. The name itself had a certain built-in camouflage, Haugen thought. A lot of people thought it meant the National Security Council, the NSC, the group everyone knew about that set defense policy. He'd thought so himself till he'd been briefed, early on.

The NSC consisted of himself, the Secretaries of State and Defense, and Cromwell in his unwanted role as vice president. There was also a slot on the NSC for a national security advisor, but Haugen hadn't appointed one, felt no need for one.

But the National Security Agency, the NSA, presumably was functioning with the same people as before. After having been briefed on it, his first week in office, the president had assumed he knew what he needed to about the NSA: It was the most secret of secret agencies, non-political, totally technical, in charge of cryptography, of intelligence gathering by satellites, and the safeguarding of armed forces communication. And like several other agencies, it monitored foreign communications for intelligence purposes. Now Cromwell, on a security line from his Pentagon office, had told him there was more, had admitted it was something he hadn't wanted to talk about until the president had gotten well grooved in on the job.

Haugen's gaze out the window had gone unfocused, opaqued by thought. Flynn, he decided, shouldn't attend this one. He'd had Stephen sit in with him on quite a few meetings and interviews, which had made some people nervous, even though the priest sat quietly out of the way. Or was it *because* he sat quietly out of the way? Haugen mused. Or did they think of the priest as a shaman of some sort, sorting out their inner thoughts, their motives? It wasn't that he was a Jesuit—a lot of people had a weird idea of Jesuits—because almost none of them knew the order Flynn belonged to.

Maybe they simply felt ill at ease that a president, a non-Catholic president at that, chose to have a priest close at hand, Haugen thought. Today, parts of intellectual society had become so utterly secular that the very existence of religion seemed to make them uncomfortable. Apparently it wasn't churches that troubled them—churches were organizations, something they could understand—but *religion* for chrissake!

Not that he himself was religious, even privately. Haugen hadn't felt any urge in that direction as far back as he could remember, which was as far back as had any meaning to the subject. But he did have a notion, however nonrational and ill-defined, that Flynn was a valuable adjunct conscience. That just the priest's being there had an effect, without anything being said between them. And Haugen was not a man to argue with impulses that felt right to him. He'd gotten rich off impulses like that.

Still, Flynn's presence at this NSA briefing didn't quite seem appropriate. Partly because when he'd asked Cromwell if Campbell, the Secretary of Defense, would be sitting in, Cromwell had said no, and asked him not to mention it to Campbell or anyone else. As if something about it was too secret for even the Secretary of Defense to know about.

Yet the NSA was *under* Campbell, and supposedly reported to him. Weird!

His intercom buzzed, and he went to it. "Yes Jeanne?"

"General Cromwell is here, Mr. President, with another gentleman."

"Send 'em in."

The man who entered with Cromwell appeared to be Hindu—tallish, slim, still young. "Mr. President," Cromwell said, "this is Dr. Mahendra J. Gupta of NSA."

They shook hands—Gupta's, fine-boned, engulfed in the beefy Haugen fist that seemed altogether too large for a man his height. The Hindu grinned nonetheless, seeming entirely at ease, and when he spoke, there was no trace of accent. "You might prefer to call me James, Mr. President," he said. "Or Jim. Mahendra's a little awkward if you're not used to it."

The president's brows arched. "All right. Jim it is. American born and named?"

"Southern California."

"Well, I guess that qualifies. Sit." Haugen gestured. They took seats, each visitor setting a briefcase by his feet. "What's this about?"

"Probably the most confidential piece of business in the

government," Cromwell said. Then he pointed at his brief-case. "What I've got in there is a sort of ECM. To scram-ble certain electronics, in case someone's managed to bug the place."

Haugen fixed him with his eyes. "D'you think they have?"

"No sir. I doubt hell out of it. I just don't want to take chances on this."

"Hmh! In that case—" Haugen went to his office door, opened it and looked out. "Jeanne," he told her quietly, "no interruptions please." Then he closed the door and locked it.

"All right," he said when he was seated again. "Let's have it. What is it that's so confidential that apparently even the Secretary of Defense can't know about it?"

Cromwell looked at Gupta. "You might as well do the talking, Jim," he said.

"Right." The black eyes found Haugen's. "It's about little green men, Mr. President." Cromwell winced. "Not literally," Gupta continued, "but we do have compelling, if circumstantial evidence of extraterrestrial visitations."

"Visitations? That's plural. When?"

"On a number of occasions, especially during the de-cades of the fifties and sixties and into the early seventies."

"Circumstantial? Then what's so confidential about it? Probably half the people in the United States believe in flying saucers."

"There are some puzzling aspects to the observations, sir. That's part of it. But mainly it's the work that's re-sulted that's gotten the heavy security lock."

"What work?"

"Research and development."

Haugen gazed without speaking, eyes intent.

"Let me start from the beginning," Gupta said. "The Soviets have similar evidence for ETs, but tending to be more xenophobic than we are, it worried them a lot more. The subject came up at a summit conference back in the seventies, and it was decided that the two governments should collaborate in the development of high-tech weap-onry. The United States' role in this is under the aegis of the NSA. Perhaps not the logical place for it, except for the secrecy aspect, but that helps in the cover. Currently I'm in charge of our work on the project."

"Interesting," Haugen said. "How old are you?"

The grin flashed again. "Thirty-four, Mr. President. They decided, on the basis of my doctoral dissertation, that I was coming so close to confidential work from outside the security wall that they'd better get me inside, so they hired me. Since then I seem to have risen through the system."

"I wouldn't be surprised. So if we're collaborating with the Soviets, why the secrecy? I presume they know what we're doing."

"Not all of it," Gupta answered. "Usually both sides hide what they're doing. Then, after a couple of years—three or four—there's an exchange of information. Usually when both sides have run into problems that seem to require it, or get worried about what the other may have come up with that they haven't. Each side's afraid of falling behind. Actually, some of the scientists, on both sides apparently, would like the work to be totally open—two countries, one project—but policy doesn't allow it. So we settle for trading periodically, neither side giving up anything without getting something of similar magnitude. You should be at one of those sessions; they reek with distrust!

"Finally one side tightens up and everyone goes home suspicious, to play with what they learned."

Again Gupta's grin flashed, lopsidedly this time, as if the whole affair held a certain ironic humor. *And if you really look at it, it does*, Haugen thought.

"So the secrecy grows out of two things," Gupta went on. "First, if Side A can know what Side B is doing without exchanging what it's doing itself, then Side A will certainly withhold, and thereby gain an advantage.

"But at least equal in importance, neither side wants the public to hear about it. The rationale is that, if they knew, a lot of people would be scared and panic. Supposedly. And a lot of others would more or less give up on solving human problems, waiting for imagined saviors from space to solve them for us."

As he'd talked, Gupta had watched Haugen alertly, for indicators of the president's attitude. He decided now to take a chance. "Actually there's a bigger reason than either of those." He paused. "It's the importance of the work.

Security freeze-up tends to increase as the square of project importance, regardless of actual security need."

The president's only response was a nod. "So what's the nature of this work?" he asked.

"It has to do with extremely large-scale energy transfers, and some pretty remarkable things that can be done with them."

"Large-scale energy transfers," the president echoed, and looked thoughtfully at him. "Okay, let's see how far I can take it from there, speculating. Correct me when I go astray. The Soviets got hold of Nikola Tesla's notes, or copies of them, from the Tesla Museum in Yugoslavia, and eventually got to playing with scalar resonance on a large scale."

Cromwell stared, thunderstruck. Haugen continued.

"And for some of the same reasons that had stopped Tesla, the Soviets had gotten stalled on it. But they'd gotten far enough that we'd begun to realize what they were doing. Right?"

Cromwell continued to stare. Gupta's face had slipped a couple of inches; he nodded.

"Meanwhile," Haugen continued, "the ETs were letting themselves be seen, or letting their ships be seen, or whatever it was that some people were seeing, and the evidence was becoming pretty indisputable. So the government began to suppress information and spread disinformation. And finally the Kremlin and the White House got together on what was perceived as the ET danger."

"Mr. President!" Cromwell broke in. "Is it that damned obvious? Or has someone leaked? You couldn't have known about the scalar resonance work without a leak!"

Haugen shifted his gaze to the general. "No leak; not that I know of anyway. But there's a lot of evidence, if you look around enough. I've been wondering about it for years.

"Let me run it down for you, from my personal viewpoint. First of all, electrical engineers learn a lot about Tesla's work; or my class did anyway. I mean, this was the man who invented the transformer, right? The man who made large-scale commercial electrical development practical, and long distance, high-voltage power transmission possible, who invented the radio . . . Inventively inclined people like me can get pretty interested in Tesla."

"The radio?" Cromwell said. "I thought Marconi invented the radio."

"Marconi got the credit; still does, I guess, despite the court decision. But decades later, in the 1930s I think it was, the courts reviewed the evidence and declared that Tesla had beaten Marconi to it; there were more than enough witnesses and written reports of his early demonstrations. So legally at least, Tesla's the inventor of the radio. Whatever; the man was an intuitive electrical genius.

"With strong emphasis on intuitive.

"The thing is that when you look over his record, his big successes came early, in the late 1800s. Later he kept on claiming big new developments soon to be released, but never delivered on them. It's as if he kept having these big—cognitions let's call them, strokes of intuitive genius, but couldn't explain them successfully. Nor develop working models. He'd talk about plans, and give apparent explanations, but generally his explanations seemed to have basic scientific flaws.

"So people started thinking of him as a crackpot. And of course, we can't examine his notes to see his experimental evidence, if any, because after he died—at the end of the war, actually—the Yugoslav government got custody of them. And I suppose the Soviets got copies before Tito broke with them.

"Over here, different people tried to follow up on his claims and invent things Tesla talked about, but these didn't pay off. Which tended to discredit them."

He looked the other two over. Cromwell looked impressed. Gupta's grin was back; he looked like a man enjoying himself.

"But the suspicion persisted among a few of us that his *intuitions* were correct—that he just didn't have the theory to explain them convincingly, nor the technical support structure or financing to work them through.

"Anyway, I suppose the Soviets made some progress on scalar resonance but lacked some of the support technology to get any further. So we traded them some of the technology they needed for reports on what they'd done. On the common ground of advancing human science and technology in case the ETs got acquisitive."

Neither of his visitors seemed inclined to correct him.

Haugen's face went thoughtful. "Which means," he added slowly, "that we've got scalar resonance transmitters too. Otherwise we'd be in deeper trouble than we are."

"Right, Mr. President," said Gupta. "We've got three of them. One each on the Hanford Nuclear Reservation, the Nevada Test Area, and in Australia."

"In Australia! Hmh! That makes sense."

"Wait a minute, Mr. President," Cromwell said. "Did you figure all that out here today, just on the basis of your interest in Tesla and what Jim said?"

Haugen shook his head, grinning. "Nope. I like to think I'm smart, but I'm not that smart. But large-scale work on scalar resonance, with the scale of physical effects produced, and with all the meteorological, geophysical, and radio research and monitoring going on on this planet . . . There've been observations and speculation about those effects for twenty years. Enough that some people have gotten interested and asked questions, and a few very bright people have done a damned good job of figuring out what had to be causing them. You must know about Paul Fairbairn's book, at least."

Cromwell nodded. It was coming together for him now.

"I read it a dozen years ago," Haugen went on. "And I read some of the pamphlets that were published before and after that. In some ways they made a lot of sense, but in other ways they didn't. Like, if the Soviets were able to do some of the things they were supposed to be doing, why hadn't they extorted us into rolling over and playing dead for them? That kind of constraint from them just didn't make sense. So not many people took the claims seriously.

"Some of the pamphlets even claimed we were working with the Soviets, but they never made a convincing case for that either. The whole thing sounded paranoid; even Fairbairn's book did, good as it was. What was missing, what was necessary to make it make sense, was the ET angle."

The president turned to Gupta then. "Show me this compelling circumstantial evidence for ETs."

"It's in there," said Gupta, indicating his briefcase. "In a report. I'll leave it with you. And I should point out—I'm *required* to point out—that it's classified Top Secret."

"Right. What can you tell me about the actual technology?"

"That's in there too, sir. If you have any questions and need to get in touch with me, the general can tell you how to handle that."

Haugen turned to Cromwell.

"No problem," Cromwell said. "The connection is programmed into your phone. I'll show you how to access it before we leave."

The president nodded. "Another question: Why have the rumors on this dried up? I haven't read any for, hmm, half a dozen years or longer."

This time Cromwell answered. "Because large-scale testing stopped. Partly due to apparent environmental side-effects, and partly to a political agreement. There was an unpredicted minute slowing of the Earth's rotation, enough to cause detectable aberrations in atmospheric circulation, for one thing. And the only halfway convincing explanation our computer models came up with was that large scalar resonance tests were having effects on the molten outer core." He turned to Gupta. "Is that about it, Jim?"

"Close enough," Gupta said.

"And shutting down the Soviet use of scalar resonance to manipulate global atmospheric circulation was part of Wheeler's trade-off with Gorbachev at Brussels," the general continued. "Along with stopping the electronic and laser sniping at each others' rocket launches and satellites that went on for a while there.

"Wheeler's line on that was, they'd either stop kicking up seismic activity and messing around with our weather, or we'd go beyond token reprisals. Of course, except for the one at Hanford, our installations weren't as powerful then as theirs—they take a hell of a lot of electric power, and at that time we didn't have practical high temperature superconductors. But we had the advantage that we could focus ours more precisely, and with no need for preliminary registration to get on target."

For a moment, Cromwell's mouth was a tight line. "And Wheeler stated flat out to Gorbachev that if a major attack took place with resonance weapons while he was president, he'd use nuclear retaliation. Wheeler was a damned good man, Mr. President. Too bad he had that lousy coronary."

Haugen nodded idly, gazing blankly at the carpet, and

when he spoke again, it was as if he hadn't heard. "So," he said slowly, "the transmitters take a lot of power. That figures." He looked up at Gupta then. "Why wasn't that as big a factor for the Soviets as it is for us?"

Gupta frowned. "I suppose they have nuclear generators at theirs," he said. "Only one of ours has, at Hanford."

"Interesting," said Haugen, again after a pause. "Jim, I want you to find out definitely for me whether the Soviets have nuclear generators at their scalar resonance installations or not."

Gupta nodded. "Yes sir, Mr. President."

"Are we done with the briefing now?" Haugen asked.

"Unless you have more," said Cromwell to Gupta.

"I'm done," Gupta answered, and looked quizzically at Haugen. "This was a lot easier than briefing President Donnelly. You did most of the work." He took two thick reports from his briefcase and handed them to the president. "There's an abstract in the front of them and a summary at the end, along with a video tape in a rear pocket. And they're thoroughly indexed, tabbed, and highlighted; not as hard to get through as they look at a glance. You won't have any trouble with them."

There wasn't really anything more to say then, and in two or three minutes, the president's two guests left; he didn't offer them coffee. He intended to read the reports right away. It promised to be one of the more interesting things he'd done in quite awhile.

And a plan was beginning to stir in his creative mind.

Haugen took only one real break in his reading: He buzzed John Zale.

"Hello, John," he said. "How'd you like to start drilling me in Polish? I sort of remember what you taught me before, but I never really mastered it. When I try to speak Polish, it tends to come out half Russian."

Zale laughed. "I've noticed. Sure, Mr. President, I'd be glad to. I'll soon have you speaking Polish well enough to run for Pope."

NINETEEN

The president could have had someone find Father Flynn for him, but he went himself. It wasn't really a hunt; the priest was right where the president expected: in the White House library.

As Haugen went over to him, the Jesuit looked up.

"Good book?" Haugen asked as he lowered himself into a chair.

The Jesuit closed the book on a bookmark and showed it to the president. Gilt letters on the cover read *The Story of the Constitution*. "Excellent book. Were you looking for me?"

"To invite you to supper with Lois and me. Will you?"

Flynn nodded. "I'd be delighted." He smiled. "Lois just walked out of here. That's an interesting project she's got, you know. Until I came here, I'd never even thought about the White House having a domestic staff, although obviously it would. As for what it would have been like under Jefferson, or Jackson . . . Has she ever written a book before?"

"No, but she carries on great correspondence: writes ten and fifteen-page letters, the best I've ever read." He looked out the window. "The sun's out a bit. I'd been thinking about inviting you for a walk, but somehow it feels like too much trouble. I'm not feeling up to snuff today."

"How *do* you feel?"

"Listless. Not much energy. Nothing physical; it's what Lois calls the glums."

"I know the symptoms. Why don't we take that walk?"

Haugen smiled. "That's what I needed: a push. Shall we

go out in our shirt sleeves? I don't feel like rounding up a jacket." He got up, gesturing at Gil and Wayne who'd come in with him. "And the Service has decided the marines keep the area safe enough that I don't need a flakjacket in the yard after all."

Flynn nodded, answering with a smile of his own. "Shirt sleeves? Why not! After all, we are transplanted Minnesotans."

The breeze had faded, and it wasn't that chilly if you walked briskly. Wayne and Gil kept pace in their suit jackets, at Haugen's request staying far enough away to leave the president and priest their privacy.

"How was your day before the glums hit?" Flynn asked. "Or did it start with them?"

"No, it started out fine—about as interesting as any I've had here. I was going to talk about some of it after supper." He looked back through his day. "Everything was fine until a while ago. I was reading a report and got this feeling of futility."

They walked on in silence for a minute or so while Haugen reexamined the moment.

"I see my problem, Steve," the president said at last. "It goes with being president."

That, thought Flynn, *I can believe*. "Tell me about it."

"There's a lot I'd like to accomplish in this job—or at least start—but it takes so damn much time to work out the operating details. The 'how to's.' Time I just don't have. There are too many things to deal with—coping kinds of things."

"Can others work out the details for you?"

"The fine details, yes. In fact, that's generally the way I operate in product development. The problem is working things out to the point where others can take over. And this time the product is so damn important!"

They continued walking, along a wrought iron fence now. In better times there'd have been tourists on the other side, or local people out for a walk of their own. Now there was no one except armed marines in scattered threes around the neighboring grounds, watching the surroundings and occasionally stealing a look at the president.

"You get as much done in a day as anyone I know," Flynn said. "Can you delegate more of what you're doing?"

Haugen grunted. "I already delegate as much as I feel good about. If I delegated any more, I'd get too out of touch to do the job. Being captain isn't the same in a dangerous storm as in fair weather."

"Suppose you could somehow arrange or make the time. What then?"

Again the president didn't answer at once, and finally Flynn tried another tack.

"What sort of thing is it you want to do? Can you give me an example?"

"Hm-m. What I'm actually doing now is trying to get things up toward a new normal."

He turned to look at the priest. "We can't survive old normal. Not for long. We'd hit the skids again. There are areas in government and economics and society that have been on long downtrends, and we're wasting our time trying to salvage the country if we don't handle them. Not just haywire them together and patch them up. Handle them. Make basic corrective changes.

"And I don't have all the time in the world. Congress is already getting restless about a president having emergency powers."

Haugen turned inward again, his eyes on the ground ahead of him. The Jesuit frowned thoughtfully. The era of kings who ruled, or even of real dictators, seemed to be past at least in modern nations. Now it was democracy or rule by committee. And in America, one could wonder if enough people were willing to do what was necessary for democracy. If too many wanted quick satisfaction and no responsibility, then salvage was impossible.

But he would not say these things to Arne. To discourage him would be an act of spiritual violence. And it also seemed to Stephen Joseph Flynn that, as things stood, if some strong man didn't face the job and grapple with it, someone who people might follow, there was no hope at all.

"Well, if you had the time," Flynn replied, "how would you go about it?"

Once more Haugen lagged in answering. Finally he said, "Okay. Thanks. I've got it now."

"What's that?"

A break in the clouds had uncurtained the sun again,

and it shone slanting down on them walking among the naked trees. The Secret Service men were twitchy; they didn't like the president so exposed, nor as far from them as he was. They'd edged a little closer, to twenty feet or so. Haugen noticed neither sun nor guards; his attention was on what he'd discovered.

"Time's not the big problem; that's a cop-out. My real problem's a lack of confidence, a fear of failing. I'm afraid the country won't go along with me. And if they don't go along willingly, actively, we'll end up with Communism or a military dictatorship." He turned his face to Flynn's. "The end of a dream. A good dream."

"The country seems to have responded pretty well to you so far," Flynn pointed out. "Look at the public opinion surveys. Morale is surprisingly good."

"Yeah, they have at that. But we need to show some solid results; they've seen too many promises fail."

"You haven't told them about the GPC yet."

Haugen brightened. "That's right, I haven't. That could make a heck of a difference to them."

The president looked at Flynn again. Like his long legs, the priest's soul marched to a different cadence than his own, but it seemed to have the same goal. "And suppose they tell me to go to hell," Haugen said. "We won't be any worse off than if I don't try. So I've got nothing to lose and everything to gain."

He laughed then. "You know what? I hadn't even thought about the GPC today; it's as if it didn't exist. I'd gotten too deeply into 'problems' to remember the ace in my sleeve."

The president angled toward the White House now, legs moving briskly, strongly. "It's time for me to get back to work, Steve. I've got a few things to do before supper. Don't forget you're eating with us." He grinned at the long-striding Jesuit beside him. "And thanks for the help."

There was dinnerware enough in the family dining room to feed a convention, and Lois Haugen had familiarized herself with all of it. She'd been having dinner served on a different set each day, on the basis of "why not?". This evening they were eating from plates of a beautiful gold-leafed porcelain.

She'd pointed it out to her husband when he failed to

comment. *He has a good sense of aesthetics,* she told herself, *but he hardly notices these days.*

"Stephen," she said when they were nearly finished eating, "Arne and I don't often take seconds. But if you'd like, the cook has another filet ready. I specifically told him to."

"Thank you, Lois, but I'd best leave well enough alone."

"Dessert then?"

"No thank you. I'll settle for conversation."

She laughed. "Conversation? I don't know." She looked at her husband, and her still warm alto voice became suddenly old and accusatory. *"Haugen! Ska' vi ha samtal eller föredra'?"* She turned back to Flynn. "It's a little game we play—have for years. We assume the roles of old people we once knew. I was wondering whether we were going to have conversation or a lecture tonight—whether to wear my wife and buddy hat or my official sounding board hat."

Her husband grinned sheepishly. "Wear them both, but the sounding board hat goes on top."

They left the table to the dirty dishes—someone would pick them up—and went into the sitting room, where the president poured an after-dinner wine.

"Steve," he said, "you may have thought it overdone a bit when you were interviewed here for security clearance. That was so I could legally talk to you about anything. But I'd never expected anything quite as confidential as I'm going to talk about this evening.

"And I don't want to lay something on you that may be more than you want to hear. Are you willing to hear it?"

Flynn's usually sober countenance was more sober still. "I am," he said.

The president nodded. "And at the same time, to fulfill my responsibility for official secrets, I need to emphasize the confidentiality of what I want to talk about. From what you told me once about the Seal of Confession, no priest, except I suppose an utter renegade, would violate it. Is that right?"

"That's right, Mr. President."

"Does that hold for something a Protestant or non-Christian might tell you under the Seal?"

"It would, but Arne, the Seal of Confession applies only

to Sacramental Confession, not to other confidences. Not even the most important."

"I see." Haugen shrugged thick shoulders. "Well, I've made my point: This belongs in the most rarefied stratum of Top Secret. And I'm telling it to you on the basis that you're both close personal advisors of the President of the United States, and need to know what's going on with him."

Haugen got up then, and pacing slowly about, summarized his session with Cromwell and Gupta. When he was done, the others looked both stunned and mystified, their wine untouched since he'd begun.

"Arne," Flynn said, "what is scalar resonance?"

"Without getting into the physics of it, let's say—let's just say there is now a means of setting up a standing wave . . . No, let's just say that—for one thing, we can establish and maintain high or low pressure cells in the atmosphere that can shunt a jet stream around. And both we and the Soviets can use these to manipulate the weather to a very considerable degree. Anywhere on the planet. For example, the Soviets have played around with making Siberia warmer. Unfortunately for them, this caused a series of droughts farther south in their Central Asian provinces, hurting their wheat crops there.

"And we know pretty conclusively that some of the weird North American weather in the seventies and eighties resulted from Soviet tests.

"A more straightforward aspect of the work involves the ability to set up and manipulate local resonances anywhere in the Earth's crust. Within close limits of accuracy.

"What you're actually doing when you do that, is transferring energy. If you do it in one abrupt, concentrated dump, the effect is explosive. Do it in a fault zone where there's enough existing stress, and you'll generate an earthquake. There's pretty conclusive evidence that the Mexico City quake in 1985 was a Soviet test."

Flynn's face had been solemn; now it looked shocked.

"Is that the electrical energy you talked about?" Lois asked.

"No no. The electrical energy simply powers the condenser and transmitter. You extract ambient energy from—the environment. What I think of as matric energy. You can do this from a fairly large volume of the environment, and it can be at a distance. Then you transfer it to where you want to release it; not through real space, distance, but through what I think of as the Tesla Matrix.

"Do you remember the case of the mysterious giant mushroom cloud witnessed by pilots of at least five airliners over the western Pacific in 1984?"

Lois nodded; Flynn shook his head.

"It was a mushroom cloud that would have done credit to a nuclear bomb, but without an initial flash and with no radioactivity at all. It came from 'dumping' an immense quantity of heat at an underwater coordinate, dumping at a distance by an installation in the USSR. The mushroom clouds in the southwestern Indian Ocean recorded from orbit in 1979 and 80—the ones that had the media speculating about South African nuclear tests—those were the same kind of phenomenon, but they were ours."

Smiling grimly, he looked at his wife and the priest. "Heavy duty, eh? That sort of thermal release in a metropolitan area would leave nothing but the nonflammable rubble. Or by releasing it more slowly and diffusely, you could heat the atmosphere and form a low pressure cell."

He chuckled without humor. "Potentially the balance of terror can cover more than nuclear and biological weapons. Publicize this with the millenium so close at hand, and the apocalyptic churches would really pull in converts."

Lois Haugen looked as sober as Stephen Flynn just then. "At least it wouldn't poison the atmosphere and crops," she said. "And the soil."

"True. And by the nature of the equipment, you couldn't use it to cover an entire continent with quick destruction. But it's another tool for international extortion, and the Soviets have a much larger network of generators than we do. So since Wheeler's Brussels Conference, we've relied partly on the threat of nuclear retaliation to help discourage the Soviets from using them.

"But that's not as effective now as it was. The Soviet ABM network provides them with a degree of protection against nuclear attack even greater than the media have been suggesting."

"Is there nothing you can do about this?" Flynn asked.

"Beyond the threat of retaliation? If there is, I haven't

found it yet. Right now the only thing I can think of is to hang tough, rebuild the country, and play with the possibilities."

Flynn looked thoughtful. "And when will you tell the nation about the GPC?"

"The GPC? Within three weeks, probably. As soon as we have the stage set for it."

Arne Haugen's body was not unaesthetic, Lois told herself as she watched him disappear into the bathroom in his shorts. Not if you found aesthetic compatible with sturdy. She didn't know exactly how much he weighed these days; somewhere around two hundred and ten on his five-foot-eight frame. If not aesthetic, he was at least strong, definitely strong. And durable.

Now if he'd let her shave the patches of hair on his back . . . She chuckled. Actually he probably *would* let her; he was probably the most amiable person she knew. But she preferred him as he was, tufts and all.

She heard the sound of tooth brushing. He'd always taken care of himself. He was only getting about six hours sleep a night lately, getting up earlier than usual, but it didn't seem to be harming him.

Her mood slumped a bit then. She thought about "scalar resonance" weapons, and nuclear weapons, and all that Arne had to worry about. Everyone else was in the same danger of course, but Arne was president. It had become his job to worry about it. Although with him, worry might not be the right word. "Take responsibility for" was more like it.

And somehow it didn't seem right that he should have to carry so much of it at his age.

Not that he'd agree with her on that. She'd mentioned taking it easier, a year or so earlier. "At your age," she suggested, "maybe you shouldn't work so hard."

He'd snorted. "Age! Bodies wear out eventually, and a lot of the time they take the mind with them. But they're to use, and as long as mine works reasonably well, I'm not going to baby it." And his did work well. He didn't hear as well as he had, but it wasn't a problem yet. And he still got by without bifocals, which amazed her, considering the way he went through books. He even had all thirty-two teeth, albeit most of his molars had fillings.

She was glad she was healthy too. Given a little luck they might have twenty good years or more yet.

"What're you thinking about, Babe?"

She'd been so occupied with her thoughts, she hadn't noticed him come back in. He was standing by the foot of the bed, eyeing her quizzically.

"Nothing much. I guess I'm a little depressed by what you were talking about after supper. About weapons." She smiled then, and assumed an aged voice, querulous and accusatory, using the Minnesota bondspråk—the Swenglish patois—of her girlhood. *"Gubbe! Ja' vill inte bli änka! Vem ska' göra alla barnkjårsena?"* [Old man, I don't want to lose you! Who would do the barn chores?]

He grinned at her and answered in accented English. "Ol' voman, I ain't goin' to go vit'out you. You'll have to tell me v'en you're ready." He shifted into Norwegian then. *"Du er jente me', og min beste venn, som jeg elske for alltid."* [Thou art my girl, and my best friend, whom I will love forever.]

Her eyes blurred, and she answered in her own voice. "Haugen," she said, "I love you too, and you are *my* best friend. You make me a very happy woman."

"Good," he answered simply, and sat down beside her, taking her hand. "Then I'm a success."

His phone jerked the president from sleep. He was wide awake as he picked up the receiver; at this hour, it wouldn't have rung if it wasn't something drastic.

"This is the president," he said.

The voice was Hammaker's. "Mr. President, there's been a coup in the Kremlin. An army coup. A Marshal Pavlenko is in charge there now."

The president looked the statement over and saw nothing there but the bare, unadorned fact. "What do you know about him?"

"He's the Minister of Defense. Or was. That's all."

Now the name came back to Haugen from his briefing by Nikita Bulavin. Kulish had appointed Pavlenko; now Pavlenko had ousted Kulish.

"Anything else on that?"

"I got a call about an hour ago from White House liaison at the CIA; they'd just gotten report of a big firefight in and around the Kremlin, and artillery fire from one of the suburbs; from the direction of KGB headquarters. That was all; our source hasn't checked in since then, and the CIA is starting to worry about her. Moscow radio announced the new regime a few minutes ago, and I was just notified."

"Umh. Okay. I suppose I'll have an update when I get to my office."

"Of course, Mr. President."

"Good. And thanks. Anything more now?"

"No sir."

"I'll see you in the morning then, Ernie." He hung up.

"What is it, Arne?" his wife asked; she sounded wide awake.

He looked at the clock: 0133. "Get up and have a drink with me, and I'll tell you," he said.

The Soviet army in power there! He wondered what that would mean a week from now, and next month.

The next time he awoke was to a burst of automatic rifle fire, followed by more from two weapons. Then nothing. It had sounded nearby, but distant enough not to alarm, not to set his system racing. The marines, he thought. He wondered what they'd shot at, and whether they'd hit it, and also whether he'd be able to go back to sleep. That was the last thing he remembered thinking before his clock woke him again to get up.

TWENTY

The morning's intelligence summary told him nothing more about the coup, nor was the brief biographical sketch on Pavlenko particularly enlightening. The president decided that, with no more information than this, a special NSC meeting wasn't worth the time, and notified Milstead.

Then he keyed up Cromwell on his security phone.

"Jumper, this is the president. Why has Campbell been kept ignorant of the scalar resonance work? Why didn't Donnelly have him informed?"

"Secrecy and the need-to-know principle, Mr. President. The joint chiefs aren't told, either, except the chairman. Wheeler didn't tell Allison or LaForge, and that established a precedent that Donnelly followed."

"Hm-m. LaForge either? I suppose Coulter doesn't know then."

"That's right, sir."

Haugen thought for a moment. "What would you think about my replacing Campbell as secretary of defense?"

"Well, sir, I'm sure you could find a better one. Campbell's an . . . He can be arbitrary, sir, not to mention obtuse at times. I guess he runs his department well enough. Or lets his deputy run it, actually; Campbell's more a policy maker. And as far as I'm concerned, his policies generally become problems."

"All right. This is confidential, Jumper: I want you to give me the names of three people, civilians, that you think would make good defense secretaries. Have them on my desk tomorrow morning, with your thinking on them.

"And that's all I've got for you now. Anything you need to tell me? Or ask me?"

"Not really, sir. I'm curious about what you think of the Kremlin coup though."

"I don't know enough about it to have an opinion. Anything else?"

"No sir."

"Okay. Thanks, Jumper." He disconnected. He'd check out Cromwell's candidates with Burke, chairman of the House Armed Services Committee, and Rietveld of the Senate's. Then he'd ask for Campbell's resignation and go through the standard congressional approval procedure for his replacement.

He'd barely begun to read his daily news clippings when the security phone interrupted.

"Good morning, Mr. President." It was Gupta. "I have the information you asked for. Not one of the Soviet scalar resonance transmitters has a nuclear reactor on site or close by; that I can say for sure. Nor any other major power source that we can see. To seven of them, there isn't even an aboveground, high-voltage transmission line!

"And if there are buried transmission lines, we can't see any sign of them either. And we should be able to pick up signs of any excavations for at least a decade back; longer in the arctic. It's an absolute mystery, and an embarrassment. No one ever wondered about the power source before. My people here are freaked about it."

"Right. Thanks, Jim," the president replied. "I'll explain when the time is right. Anything else?"

Gupta hesitated. "No sir," he said.

"Fine. Thanks again."

Haugen chuckled as he disconnected. He'd felt the unasked question in Gupta's mind: The man was squirming to know what Haugen was withholding. He'd just have to stay curious for a while.

Meanwhile, the NSA physicist had confirmed a suspicion for the president, and made a decision easier. Now if Monsignor Koenig could pull off a minor miracle . . .

It was a weekday—gray, blustery, and below freezing. Not a day to inspire an outdoor walk. But the still great number of unemployed had time on their hands when they weren't waiting in line somewhere. And a few had the urge to move around despite the weather, perhaps to commune with themselves or get out of the house. Thus the parks of the capital were not entirely abandoned.

John Richey only appeared to be one of those people. Actually he had a job; he was a subcontractor on his way to work. Hunched in a too-large government surplus greatcoat—a navy bridgecoat, actually—he looked as if he wore beneath it everything he owned. Walking up to the Washington Monument, he went in. A uniformed woman, a Park Service attendant, got on the elevator with him. The male operator scarcely looked at them; he had worries on his mind.

When they arrived at the observation level, there was no one else there. After the operator had started back down with the elevator, Richey shot the female attendant twice in the chest and once in the head, with the muffler-equipped 7.62 mm automatic pistol he carried.

Having done this upset Richey a bit in spite of himself, and left him a little disoriented. Although he'd been there before, the first window he went to faced the wrong direction, and he had to go to a second to get a view of the White House. It was 960 meters away, as estimated by scaling the distance on a city map. From within his greatcoat and sweaters, he then took an export model M82 light antitank weapon and extended it to its firing length: 107 cm. He carried only one rocket for it; there was a limit to what the greatcoat could conceal.

Nine hundred and sixty meters was beyond the designed range for the weapon, but the window was nearly 500 feet higher than the target. The contractor had had someone compute the ballistics and jury-rig a combination telescopic sight and level for the weapon, reading in degrees of elevation. It had proven easy to use, after a few dry runs: Set the correct angle on the little mirror, then while keeping the vertical hair aligned on the target, center the bubble and *squeeze* the trigger.

It was more awkward than the standard electronic sight, but it allowed for the extra distance.

After emptying his muffled pistol into the window's heavy glass, and replacing the clip, he made himself go through the pre-firing sequence twice, settling his nerves. His target was the center window of the Oval Office. Then once again he aimed, inhaled, held his breath for a moment, and fired. The rocket launched with a slam, and he never did catch sight of it. Not that it mattered; it was beyond his control then.

Presumably the Monument personnel, 500 feet below, were unaware of what had happened.

He lay the launcher on the floor where it couldn't be seen from the elevator, then dragged the dead woman out of sight too. Finally, back at the elevator door, he took a capsule from a pocket, swallowed it, and pushed the call button. He also put a hand on the reassuring hardness of the pistol in his pocket, in case the operator noticed the blood on the floor to one side, or asked where the attendant was.

Richey'd been told that the capsule he'd taken contained a secret drug, developed by the CIA. And that it would improve his reflexes and speed considerably for fifteen or twenty minutes, greatly improving his chance of escape. He could expect a bad headache later, but it would be worth it.

The elevator hadn't yet arrived when Richey's knees gave way. As he lay on his side, watching the closed door turn blurry, he realized he'd been suckered.

The rocket hit on line but a few feet low, slightly damaging the White House lawn. One of the basement offices built beneath the lawn was substantially damaged. Because the rocket exploded well beneath the surface, none of the White House's tempered glass windows were broken.

The president was in the Oval Office at the time, talking with his press secretary, Lester Okada. After viewing the damage together, the president instructed Okada to set up a presidential press conference to be televised that evening at nine, Eastern Time—six, Pacific Time.

Paul Massey learned of the rocket attack on the six o'clock news. One of Barron's contractors, he supposed. Of course the White House would be well-guarded, but still it seemed to him to have been a low percentage kind of attempt.

At least it would upset White House activities, and might inspire free lances to try their luck. And Barron had undoubtedly arranged for multiple efforts.

Fortunately, Barron was functioning quite satisfactorily these days—actually he seemed more efficient than ever—without having been sent to Merriman and his PDH facility. It was just as well; pain-drug-hypnosis treatments sometimes had troublesome side effects, and he'd really come to rely on Barron.

Meanwhile though, he'd let Barron worry about Merriman. It was good for him.

Massey knew it wasn't wise to depend on anyone to the degree that he depended on Barron Tallmon; he told himself, not for the first time, to see about breaking in a backup man. He would have already, but he'd have to arrange it himself. A nuisance! He was used to simply giving orders; actually doing things was tiresome and unfamiliar for him.

Perhaps he should bring it up with Merriman, he thought. He might be able to provide someone. But Massey was hesitant: Merriman seemed unpredictable, unreliable.

As usual, when the time came, the press room was packed. The president walked in looking assured and alert. "Good evening," he said, and the cameras and microphones sent the sight and sound around the world. "We'll operate by the same ground rules as before: When I recognize you, give your name and affiliation before asking your question.

"I'll take a few questions and then make a prepared statement." He looked around at the upthrust hands, and pointed at the dean of the corps. "Mr. Rohmer."

"Frederick Rohmer, Associated Press. What is the government's reaction to this morning's coup in the Kremlin?"

"Our reaction is interest. So far we don't have enough information to react beyond that."

He looked over the room. "Next? The lady in the pink knit beret; yes."

"Valerie Szigety, the *Cleveland Plain Dealer*. How does Marshal Pavlenko compare with Chairman Kulish in regard to their positions on world peace?"

"Valerie, we'll have to wait and see. Party chairmen in the USSR have been known to change their stripes on taking office." He scanned the room. "Sorry, but I won't take any more questions today, related to the coup.

"Next? Mr. . . . ." The president snapped his fingers as if trying to conjure back the man's name. "Mr. Brent."

"Roger Brent, *U.S.A. Today*. Mr. President, where were you when the rocket struck the White House lawn, and what effect will this attack have on White House routine?"

"I was in my office, talking to Mr. Okada about setting up a press conference. As far as White House routine is concerned, it won't be much changed." He grinned. "I'm told that routine at the Washington Monument will change though."

"Next?" He pointed. "The lady in black."

"Bernice Deering, *Rocky Mountain News*. What does the first lady think about this attack?"

Haugen looked quizzically at her. "She doesn't approve." When the brief laughter had died, he continued. "Her main reaction was concern for my life. I reminded her that I've already lived most of it."

He looked the room over. "Mr. Mantes?"

"Robert Mantes, *American Daily Flag*. There have been no significant civil disorders now for more than a month. When do you expect to return government to regular constitutional procedures?"

"If you're referring to my using the Emergency Powers Act, I'll keep using it until the economic emergency is over or until Congress repeals those powers. Right now they're needed. I assume this will be discussed when I meet with the Joint Congressional Committee on the Emergency. I presume that meeting will be televised.

"And regarding martial law: It's still in force because of the 2,300 internees being held for their part in the insurrection.

"Next? The tall man in the light green shirt and bolo tie."

"Ray Zelenski, the *Tulsa World*. Entirely apart from the new Kremlin situation, the country's been told very little about your foreign policy. When are you going to discuss that for us?"

"Ray, I appreciate that you people have been left in the dark on that. And frankly, I'd expected to get to it before now." The president paused, seemingly considering how to proceed with the subject. "Like most of you people, I've always had opinions on foreign policy. But I didn't have to function in the area, and my opinion was just an opinion. Suddenly I found myself in the position of 'put up or shut up,' and I decided to shut up until I got better informed. I've been leaving day-to-day operations almost entirely to the discretion of the State Department; and leaving policy to the National Security Council, of which I've been the mostly quiet chairman. Not that that's unusual in a new president.

"So far I've been giving most of my attention to domestic problems and the machinery of government, which had to have priority. But now, after receiving numerous reports and briefings, and reading a month's worth of daily intelligence summaries, I'm beginning to feel some confidence in foreign affairs. And I can tell you that I'm working on an agenda for a foreign trip, during which I'll talk with the heads of government of several countries. So far we've drawn up only a tentative list of those, so I'm not willing to name them."

Again he scanned the room. "I'll take one more question. Mr. Carnes."

"Greg Carnes, *New York Times*. Mr. President, I have it from someone who should know, that you plan to remove all restrictions on the construction of nuclear power plants. Will you comment on this for us?"

The president looked long at him, then smiled ruefully. "Mr. Carnes," he said, "if someone really told you that, someone who's supposed to know, I'm embarrassed for him. Anyone who should know, should know better than that. Or maybe they said something else and it's been misinterpreted that way. Or maybe you made it up, to see how I'd respond. Whatever. I assure you, I have no intention of making any changes at all in the legal requirements for building nuclear power plants or putting them in operation. Now or later.

"I can appreciate that you might ask, particularly with the painful price of fuel oil. But I'll tell you what: I'll be very surprised if such a statement would be taken seriously a month from now."

He paused; hands waved eagerly for attention, but he ignored them. "And now for my prepared statement. First about NASA. The National Aeronautics and Space Administration became almost moribund under the Donnelly Administration because of severe federal budget problems. At the same time, more than a quarter century has passed since the first moon landing, and we still haven't allowed more than a token development of private enterprise in space. Private French and Japanese companies have successful and expanding commercial space activities, and the Chinese government has gotten active in the business recently. But here? Here we still have legal restrictions to protect NASA's virtual monopoly.

"So I'm taking NASA completely out of the *business* of space and giving them a specific non-military project. NASA long ago proved its ability to carry out such projects, and I am directing it to build an orbiting space station for launching manned and unmanned probes to other planets. It won't have much of a budget at first, but it now has a goal.

"When their first-order plans have been fully developed, we'll sell the copyright to a commercial publisher for broad public sale. We can expect the advance on royalties to help cover the cost of planning, and the technical information will help the development of commercial space ventures.

"The business of space will go to business. NASA *could* do it, with appropriate reorganization and direction, but we will all benefit from competition between space corporations, here and abroad. We can expect to see different approaches to hardware and to management, and a lot of cross-pollination of ideas. Which will lead to more rapid technical advancement.

"Meanwhile the Department of Defense will get two of the existing NASA shuttles."

Haugen paused to look over the media people, some holding up directional recorders toward him, some taking notes. The TV camera people were intent on their instruments.

"Now for more domestic matters," he went on. "A president gets a lot of mail. All kinds of mail. And an awful lot of it asks me to do this or that. Prohibit this; require that; stop the other thing. All to solve problems, or what are thought of as problems.

"Tonight I'm going to give you, and the American people, my positions on a few of these things. These positions have just been written into law. They will become effective as of next Monday, or more exactly, as of midnight Sunday.

"First, abortion. I will not legislate barriers to abortion, but the states may prohibit it within their boundaries if they want to. *However, if a state prohibits abortion, that state must ensure adequate care for the child and for the pregnant mother, including a medically adequate delivery.* And if they have much sense, I don't think they'll want to get into a program like that one.

"Next, the increase in venereal disease, especially the very large number of AIDS cases that have surfaced, has caused considerable pressure recently for laws prohibiting extramarital sex. There used to be such laws, years ago. Some of them may still be on the books. We know how ineffective they were and are. A government that tries to actually enforce sexual morality intrudes heavily into the private lives of individuals, and deserves all the trouble and expense it gets.

"However, to legislate against harming others is another matter. Therefore, as of next Sunday midnight it will be a felony for a person to infect someone with a venereal disease, after symptoms of their own infection can be presumed to have been evident.

"It will be a felony, not just a misdemeanor. And anyone found guilty of this felony will be held accountable for one-half of the reasonable costs of the disease in the person they infected, whether those costs initially are born by a private individual or by some public or private agency.

"Again, you will note that this is not legislation of morals. It is a correct allocation of accountability for harm to others.

"Another sex-related matter is the number of rapes in America. Courts often seem to have difficulty in deciding what constitutes rape and how to deal with rape charges. So I'm helping them out. As of Sunday midnight, rape includes any forced sexual intercourse, intercourse with any person against their expressed unwillingness. And that unwillingness can be expressed by verbal objection; it does not need to be by physical resistance, which can be dangerous. Rape includes forced intercourse with anyone—a prostitute, a man, anyone including one's own wife. Rape is always a felony. And rape charges may be accompanied by other, related charges such as assault with a deadly weapon, and battery.

"Of course, the case has to be proven in court. But this clarifies and simplifies deciding what the charge should be."

While the president talked, Lester Okada watched from his position ten feet to the president's right. And it seemed to Okada that this press audience was more intent than any he'd seen before. It should be, he told himself. They were witnessing a basically un-American phenomenon: law by presidential edict.

"Now for another matter," Haugen was saying. "In recent years, some progress has been made on getting child support payments actually paid by a parent in another state. We're taking it the rest of the way. Per a new law, failure to make such payments is a felony. If you are supposed to be making child support payments across a state line, you'd better make them, or you will be subject to arrest. If you receive federal money, part of it can be withheld and sent to help support your child. If you are employed, you have the choice of making payments willingly, or having your wages garnisheed. And if your income now seems too low to make the payments set in the past by a court, you can seek arbitration for a payment level you feel you *can* afford. But understand that the arbitrator may not even leave you beer money, because the child comes ahead of most other things.

"Finally, if all else fails, you can be put in jail for your felony, and your prison wage sent to help support your child. I'm not talking about imprisonment for debt. Realistic and feasible payments can always be arranged short of prison. I'm talking about imprisonment for the felony of refusing to help support your child.

"And let me add that if the child becomes a ward of the state, the state can sue either or both parents for child support."

The president looked intently into the cameras and rapped the lectern with a thick forefinger. "This is not a matter of punishment. There may be a few people who can't see that, but it is *not* a matter of punishment. I'm not much into punishment. This is simply a matter of requiring that people take responsibility for their actions. To father a child, or to bear one, even unintentionally, is not a trivial matter.

"And that's all I have to say about that, except to point out that these laws were not etched into stone on top of Mt. Sinai. Nor did they come from the Congress. But they are certainly susceptible to being changed by Congress.

"On the other hand, it may be that the American people will like them well enough to insist that they be continued. For now, they are law. Full written versions have been drafted and reviewed by competent legal experts, and will be available to you when you leave. They will also be mailed to legal jurisdictions tomorrow. I trust that they'll be in your newspapers tomorrow, also."

He looked his press audience over. "And ladies and gentlemen, that's it for this evening. Have a good night."

As he rode the underground walkway to the White House, the president wondered what Judge Liederman would say about these laws when he met with him the next evening. And Senator Lawes and Professor MacLieth next week. Perhaps he should have held off till the legal reform package was ready. But this would serve to prepare people, and give him some feel for public acceptance.

TWENTY-ONE

A plane carrying a President of the United States is ordinarily recognizable. In this instance however, it was a very ordinary-looking Air Force C-17B cargo transport, with temporary facilities that allowed its several passengers to work and sleep. And to clean up properly for a secret meeting, for there would be no layovers enroute.

The transport flew seemingly unaccompanied, but half a

hundred miles to both north and south, sea-rescue aircraft flew parallel courses while tracking her by radar. Arne Haugen wasn't aware of them. There was no particular reason that he should be; the risk was slight.

It had been early afternoon when they'd taken off from Andrews Air Force Base, flying toward westward-creeping night. Their destination was six time zones east, and the prospect of jet lag suggested going early to bed, but meanwhile this was an opportunity to read something the president had been putting off as of relatively low priority. He opened the report that Cromwell had given him more than a week earlier, on the executive boards, past and present, of the Holist Council. It was in a post-binder, thick, with a detailed table of contents, an index, and protruding tabs to help access it.

He forgot about bed until he'd finished it; his fellow passengers were already asleep. He had a drink then and stripped to his shorts, while an Air Force corporal prepared his bunk. Afterward he lay awake for a time, thinking about what he'd just read. Although it was a listing of open activities lacking any direct information on motives or conspiracy, it had given him a different perspective on the problems of his country, and by extension the world.

It would take awhile to digest it properly, to integrate it sufficiently within his subconscious database that he would compute with it automatically, subliminally. But the world, and especially America, would never look quite the same to Arne Haugen again.

At the same time, it did not alarm him. There was nothing urgent about it; it required no immediate action. He would put it out of his attention and free his mind for more immediate things, matters to which the new information was operationally irrelevant.

The unmarked Bell Mescalero SOC helicopter lifted from the joint German-U.S. air base at Leipheim and headed south over the black forests of the Schwäbische Alb in bright early sunshine. Here and there, snow powdered the firtops on higher ridges, and before long the little aircraft had crossed the dark green water of Lake Constance into Switzerland. The Swiss air defense network monitored its passage, but it had clearance; the symbol crawling across their CRTs was watched for routine air safety rather than military security. High rugged snowscapes loomed ahead on the splendid Glarner Alpen, then passed below, making the entire world seem white beneath blue. The chopper, with a performance ceiling of 6,500 meters, lifted lightly over knife-edged arretes and toothed tors, where snow plumes curled coldly in a northwest wind.

The high ridges and peaks became the Alpi Lepontine, and crossing the last major crest, the pilots and their passengers looked south down a long valley, blue with lake, dark with forest and drab with autumn meadow, separating two snowy ridges of the Italian forealps.

On a broadly rounded side ridge, newly snow-covered, stood the villa of an Italian industrialist who found pleasure in privately hosting the eminent; a man who kept secrets well. The Mescalero swung low. Its pilot noted the groups of armed and uniformed men below, all watching, ready, and there were sure to be others he couldn't see. Their weapons included what had to be SA rocket launchers. He'd been told there'd be heavy security—heavy and *very* touchy.

For a moment he hovered, then landed in a gritty swirl of white. When the vanes had stopped, three men strode toward her, one an African robed in black.

Arne Eino Haugen climbed out, with Father Stephen Joseph Flynn, John Zale (acting now as Haugen's travel secretary), and Papal Nuncio Msgr Robert Alfred Koenig. They met the greeting party halfway, and greeters and greeted went into the villa together, talking as they walked, while the Mescalero lifted and left for a prearranged refueling at an Italian army base.

It was back in little more than an hour, and waited, leaving with its passengers early enough to return to Leipheim before the early nightfall. The C-17B was waiting, ready to fly. Arne Haugen would eat breakfast in his own apartment the next morning, having been away less than forty hours on "a visit to the Nevada test site." He was returning well-briefed on the character of General Wojciech Jaruzelski, the Premier of Poland, and on the somewhat precarious semi-autonomy his country maintained, close against the armor-plated breast of the Russian bear.

His Holiness the Pope knew Jaruzelski, and was always very well informed and up to date on things in his homeland.

Cromwell tapped a key on his phone, accepting the call. "Good morning, Mr. President," he said with a smile. "I hope they were good to you in Nevada."

"Very good, Jumper. The flight was fine, and the people I talked with were very helpful. On the way there, I read Chilberg's report. Interesting as hell. Do you have any more on that?"

"No sir. But we recently acquired an inside contact we're working with now." Cromwell hesitated, then decided to say no more about it just then. They'd managed to install a spy device in Massey's Connecticut residence, an opportunity of the moment that could hardly have been foregone. He'd write up a request for authorization for the president's signature and give it to him later today.

TWENTY-TWO

The hearing chamber was full, with media people occupying more than half the gallery seats. The committee was large: seven senators and seven representatives. Senator Tim Brosnan was the chairman, Congresswoman Margaret Bushnell the vice-chairman.

The president sat alone at a table, facing the committee. To emphasize that this was not an interrogation, he'd brought no aides or counsel.

Senator Brosnan rapped his gavel. The buzz of voices fell off abruptly, then died beneath the senator's scanning, bristly-browed eyes. "All right, I guess everyone's here that's supposed to be. Let's get started.

"Mr. President, I'd like to thank you for agreeing to come here this afternoon. If you've been reading the wrong newspapers, you may have gotten the impression that this committee is hostile toward you. I believe you'll find we're not.

"As you certainly know, there are members of both houses, in both parties, who feel it is time to repeal the Emergency Powers Act. And a bill authored by Senators Harmer and Van Dorn has been submitted to this committee, proposing the repeal of that act. The committee is considering the bill, and you are the first person we've called on to talk to us about it."

Brosnan looked toward the Congressman farthest to his left. "We'll start the questions with Congressman Huan of Hawaii."

Huan stood, a book open in his large hands. "Mr. President, I would like to read, from the *American Heritage Dictionary of the English Language*, the definition of *emergency*." He looked at a page and read: " 'Emergency. A situation of a serious nature, developing suddenly and unexpectedly, and demanding immediate action.' " He put the book down. "Considering that definition, would you say that a state of emergency now exists in the United States?"

Haugen considered for a moment. "Let's look at that definition," he answered. "It says that an emergency develops unexpectedly. The recent collapse of the economy, and of public confidence, and of law and order, was *not* unexpected. Various observors and commentators had been predicting it for years.

"But the Congress obviously considered it an emergency when it passed the Emergency Powers Act. And while it wasn't passed until serious rioting began, this special committee had been seated and was considering emergency powers legislation for more than a week before that. So in deciding whether a state of emergency now exists in the United States, I consider that far more relevant than the definition you just read. We had, and we still have, a national state of emergency.

"This state of emergency is analogous to the medical conditions 'critical' and 'serious.' We are now through the critical stage; the patient is no longer in momentary danger of dying. But its condition is still serious, requiring special treatment. We need to build its health sufficiently that it can function without the danger of another quick collapse. And that recovery is by no means a simple matter."

He paused. "I believe that answers your question, congressman, but I'd like to say a little more about the subject if I may."

Huan nodded. "By all means."

"As of last Saturday, the patient, the United States of America, still had 42% of its work force unemployed. *Forty-two percent!* That's a substantial improvement, but it's very far from being something the country can live with for long. Numerous businesses have reopened, but far more have not.

"And beyond that, many millions of people have lost their savings, their investments, their pension funds—whatever security they had for their old age. Millions of elderly people are destitute; many have been found dead of exposure and illness, compounded by malnutrition. Many insurance companies have gone bankrupt, leaving families without death protection, health protection—any protection at all.

"And with these losses, people also lost their confidence in government as it was—government which allowed, and even led, the economy step by step to ruin. Not deliberately, but through error and doggedly persistent short-sightedness.

"I can only hope, you can only hope, *the people* can only hope, that over the next year or so we will hammer out workable procedures that will provide and maintain an operational economy and a just and intelligent, functioning democratic government." He paused again. "While at the same time reestablishing the level of personal liberty intended by the founding fathers. And gradually eroded by government, the professions, special interest lobbies—let's say by 'the establishment.'

"If the emergency government fails to provide those procedures, there is little chance that the people will look to government as it was. They will look elsewhere. Fortunately, right now the American people are willing to let the emergency government, and myself, lead them through a reconstruction. It seems to me to be a good idea for the Congress to let us continue."

The president sat back. A brief spatter of applause sounded from the gallery, to die of embarrassment and Senator Brosnan's frown.

"Senator Cerotti of New Jersey is recognized," Brosnan said.

"Mr. President," Cerotti said, "recently you took it upon yourself to restructure a very large segment of the national economy, when you decreed law regulating the interactions of business and labor. Would you say that you acted beyond the intent of Congress in doing that?"

"Presumably," Haugen replied, "Congress passed the Emergency Powers Act to empower the president to handle the emergency. And ending the emergency can't be done simply with bread lines and cheese lines and potato lines, as I'm sure you agree; or by food lines and emergency work projects combined. Those are vital short-term actions, like administering oxygen and plasma. But to end the emergency, we have to correct the things that caused the emergency, and the things that hold it in place.

"I consider that my principal responsibility."

The president sat back, and Brosnan looked to his left again. There were eleven more to ask questions, not including himself. There'd probably be time for a second round by most of them. "The chair," he said, "recognizes Congressman Washington of Georgia."

In his living room, General Cromwell watched and listened, sipping absently at whiskey and water. His daughter sat near. He was a widower, she a senior at George Washington University, majoring in mathematics.

"What do you think of him, Julie?" he asked.

"The president? He's either very good or very dangerous, or both. I think I like him though; at least he's not more of the same old stuff, and he's got class. I'm willing to let him continue awhile."

Cromwell nodded, wondering how representative her view was among students.

During the single break, Brosnan and Kreiner talked together over coffee.

"What do you think?" Kreiner asked.

"It's going good. We'll see how Bender behaves."

Kreiner nodded. "Bender thinks of himself as the reincarnation of Thomas E. Dewey. The great prosecutor. But he only gets one question at a time; no chance to confuse and hammer on the witness. Or in this case the guest. That's an advantage of this format."

"We're going to have to send the bill to the floor, you know," Brosnan said, "regardless of what we think of it. The subject's too loaded, too hot to kill in committee. And by the nature of the beast, there's no reasonable way we can send it up altered or amended."

"I suppose you've been reading your mail?"

"I've been reading the tally sheets. Since the Harmer-Van Dorn bill hit the news, the volume's been way up, with about six to one for leaving the emergency powers in place. But there's a hell of a lot of lobbyist pressure; the heaviest I've seen in my twenty years here. I've even heard a few voices say they're afraid the IRS will lay a punitive audit on them if they don't vote to repeal."

"The IRS!" Kreiner's voice rose an octave. "Who the hell started that bullshit? Haugen handled the IRS; the psychotic faction over there is on the street now. The IRS is walking the straight and narrow these days, what with four criminal indictments filed and more expected."

Brosnan shrugged. "Let's face it, Howard. A few of our colleagues aren't B-R-I-G-H-T. Start a rumor like that and you can scare some of them. And a month ago, the threat would have been real, as witness Wilheit and Cameron. And Cade."

The look he fixed on Kreiner was serious. "I can count all right, and I'm not concerned about how the vote would go if it came up tomorrow. But the way it looks to me, Arne Haugen doesn't have a lot of room for mistakes."

Lois Haugen turned from the television to Stephen Flynn. She looked calm, even serene. *But then, perhaps I do too,* Flynn thought. Inside he was not. Inside he felt an ill-defined uneasiness, a nervousness, a low-intensity, formless fear. He could not have said more than that about it; its roots were beneath his reach.

"He's doing well," she said with utter certainty.

It was that appearance of certainty which had always struck Flynn as her most intriguing attribute—as if she knew what she knew, right or wrong. It seemed incredible that someone could live for more than sixty years with that attitude intact.

Or maybe, he thought, *she hasn't had it through all those years. Maybe she'd gained it late in life*. Perhaps someday he could know that certainty, he who had more need of it than most, and perhaps less of it than many.

"Yes he has," Flynn replied. "He's done marvelously well." *But where would it lead?* "Power tends to corrupt," Lord Acton had written. Not the usual misquote that "power corrupts." Power *tends* to corrupt. How susceptible was Arne Haugen to that tendency? That, Flynn knew, was why his friend had invited him to the White House. The "auxiliary conscience" he wanted was to help him guard against just that.

Conscience, that "still small voice," was the Holy Spirit, God in man. But man had the option of ignoring conscience; many seemed totally deaf to it in the face of temptation. Arne Haugen wasn't deaf to it, but he might be cozened by a swell of public approval, or by what he perceived as one.

Flynn wondered how useful Lois Haugen would be as an auxiliary conscience. Was she the "all-accepting, all-supportive wife," or did she call her husband on significant points of difference? With a man like Arne, a man fair-minded and so often right, an attitude of "all-accepting, all-supportive" might be easy to fall into. Perhaps that was the source of her certainty, her serenity.

"Excuse me for a few minutes," Lois said, getting up. "If you'd like, you might want to rummage through the refrigerator while you wait."

She left, probably for her bathroom, and he went to the birch-veneered refrigerator that stood like a cabinet near one wall. He could have used a drink of the scotch he found there, but he settled for 7-Up.

Even Bender had not proven particularly antagonistic. As if he'd been defused by the president's earlier statements. And the president had not seemed to tire during the nearly two hours of questioning. Now Brosnan fixed his gaze on the last questioner there'd be time for.

"The Chair recognizes Senator Morrows of California," he said.

"Mr. President," Morrows began, "you've spoken to us here of hammering out a viable system. You've indicated that you'll be decreeing further laws. And you've apportioned blame—or responsibility rather; I appreciate the difference. You've apportioned responsibility for what happened not only on the Congress but on the Judicial and the Executive branches. And finally on the people and on special interests.

"And it seems to me, Mr. President, that to work out that viable system you spoke of would be very difficult without changing the Constitution. What are your views on that? And if you envision a need for a new Constitution, from whom would that Constitution come?"

Haugen didn't hesitate. "I see no need for a new Constitution. I do see a need for amendments. But my view from here is that *most* of the needed changes can be made within the framework of the Constitution as it is, without amendment. Certainly the original document, including the Bill of Rights, should stand.

"Nor should any amendments infringe upon the basic principles it contains. They should support those principles and perhaps elaborate them. The purpose of any amendments should be to elaborate those principles explicitly for today's world, and for what we can foresee of tomorrow's. While making full use of more than two centuries of American experience with representative democracy."

He paused for emphasis. "And I personally would like to see an amendment allowing federal legislation by popular referendum; let the people vote on key issues. It would stimulate public interest and discussion in issues, and reduce the power of special interest lobbies."

He paused. "And full use should be made of the experience we will have had under this emergency government. I'll be installing more new ways of doing certain things, and if they work—if the people like them—I'd expect them to be continued.

"As for who should draw up any constitutional amendments: The Constitution defines that. The Congress proposes, and the state legislatures approve or disapprove.

"Although when the time comes, I'd like to see a nation-wide referendum on the proposed amendments, so the American people can express themselves on them as guidance for the legislatures.

"And that," he said to Morrows, "is all I have to say about that."

Senator Brosnan leaned elbows on his desk. "Thank you for your time and frankness, Mr. President. You've answered a lot of questions, and I'm sure you've set to rest some misgivings and concerns, as well as providing food for thought." He looked around at the committee. "That ends the session for today. This committee will meet again tomorrow morning at nine-thirty."

Julie Cromwell looked at her father, and he at her. "Daddy," she said, "I don't know how this is going to turn out. But right now I'd have to say you did a damned good job of picking your man."

TWENTY-THREE

For more than a year, Barron Tallmon had coveted access to a particular concealed safe; coveted it since he'd first known of it. Not to rob it; his idiosyncracies did not include any particular desire to steal. But to know what was in it; he was a snoop.

More recently he'd become a snoop with an intent to injure. Maximally. Also recently, by means of an audio-visual bug he'd gotten hold of, he'd watched Massey dial the safe.

He had free access to Massey's office of course, and occasionally entered it legitimately. This time he entered it with treachery in mind.

Aided in the gray dawn by a small, tightly focused flashlight, he opened the safe. Inside, it was larger and deeper than he'd thought, containing two metal boxes, some large envelopes, and a book. His hands, unexpectedly shaking, withdrew one of the boxes at random. Finding the lid unlocked, he knelt with it on the carpet.

It held photographs and papers. He looked through them, careful not to disturb their order. All were old, perhaps kept for their blackmail potential. He filed in his memory the principal surname involved—it might prove useful—put the items back into the metal box, and returned it to the safe.

The book, richly bound, took his attention again. After a moment's hesitation, he removed it, and in the growing dawnlight scanned the large type of its first vellum page, its second, then beyond. His fingers and eyes moved quickly, then putting it back, he closed and locked the safe and slipped quickly from the room.

The next time Mr. Massey went to New York and left him here, Tallmon told himself, he'd photocopy the book.

On the second day after his congressional appearance, the president convened the National Security Council to hear Norman Godfrey, the CIA's chief specialist on the situation in the USSR. The CIA felt it had a reasonably complete and accurate picture now of the current situation there. Besides Godfrey and the Council—the president, vice president Cromwell, Secretary of State Coulter, and Secretary of Defense Campbell—several others were present around the large table: Milstead, as usual, and the directors of the CIA, the Defense Intelligence Agency, and the State Department's Bureau of Intelligence and Research. In addition, Father Flynn sat out of the way in the background.

After introducing Godfrey, the president turned to the CIA director. "Dr. Blackburn," he said, "is there anything you'd care to fill us in on before Mr. Godfrey begins the briefing?"

The CIA director stood up. "One thing, Mr. President—a matter of security; the gentleman in the clerical collar, whom you neglected to introduce. I believe his name is Stephen Joseph Flynn. He has no function here, and I recommend you send him out. We can anticipate some sensitive information being discussed."

The president didn't answer at once, but his face darkened visibly, and all eyes drew to him as if to a funnel cloud. The silence was electric, and after a very long fifteen seconds, the president spoke, his words measured.

"Dr. Blackburn, I do not invite security risks to NSC meetings, nor do I need you to approve whom I invite. And if you ever again imply that the President of the United States is a fool, be very very careful that it's not to his face."

The tone of voice was dead calm, deadly calm, and the director's face reddened while Haugen spoke. At the end, the president's eyes locked with his, and the pink paled to an astonishing whiteness. For a moment it looked as if Blackburn might faint from lack of blood to the brain, and some of the others wondered what he'd seen in those blue eyes.

There was another long moment of silence, which Blackburn broke. "My apologies, sir," he said.

The eyes did not at once let him go, but when Haugen spoke again, his tone was casual, if more metallic than usual. "Sit, Dr. Blackburn."

The man sat, still pale, and the president turned his gaze to the specialist. "Further introduction shouldn't be necessary, Mr. Godfrey. We know your post, and we can assume you're qualified, so go ahead and start. We may interrupt from time to time, but mostly we'll try to let you talk, and save any questions till after you're done."

"Fine, sir." Godfrey seemed perhaps the least affected of them all by the president's unexpected anger, and it occurred to Haugen that Godfrey was probably the one here who knew Blackburn best. Perhaps he'd been pleased at what had happened; that could explain his calm.

"I was told you wanted this to start with the Kremlin coup," Godfrey said, "but I'd like to begin a few steps earlier, with the events just before the invasion of Iran. They seem definitely to be related."

Haugen nodded. "Fine. Go ahead."

Godfrey's focus withdrew inward to his subject. "The worsening worldwide economic decline of the past few years hit the Soviet Union too," he began. "Their perennial agricultural problems had eased somewhat with Gorbachev's reforms, but two successive drought years presented the Soviets with really serious food shortages. And the depression made the effects a lot worse than before, by seriously hurting their dollar inflow from exports: minerals, arms—even natural gas sales from their new pipeline to Europe. Which severely restricted their ability to import food, notably grain, because their credit wasn't worth much." He smiled ruefully. "There's been a lot of that going around lately.

"So there'd been some big demonstrations in the Soviet Union—even in the Russian Federated Republic, where that sort of thing had been almost unheard of. Less visible but more to the point, worker morale and discipline had slumped everywhere, and that includes Siberia, where the population has more freedom and privileges than elsewhere. And of course, industrial production slumped when discipline and morale slumped, which we can assume led to a further reduction in discipline and morale."

He paused and looked around at the others. "Those are things we have information on. Now we get into speculation. Our assumption is that the Kremlin decided to use their big military resource to develop some trade leverage, through a small, relatively safe war that could also be used to drum up the patriotism of the Russian people. Those, of course, are both ploys that other governments have used from time to time.

"And Iran was a likely target: Most of its army was in Iraq, and a puppet government in Teheran would give the Soviets trade leverage. We know now that the possibility was at least brought up in the Kremlin that with a puppet government in place, a Soviet-Iranian syndicate might be formed—a Soviet operation, actually; the Iranians would be window-dressing—to rehabilitate the gulf oilfields and refineries in return for long-term credits from Japan, western Europe, and others.

"The proposal may not look very promising, considering the Iranian topography, present Soviet resources, and the general hostility of Iranians to foreign influence, let alone foreign control. But sense or not, the fact is that the Soviets invaded. Really, the economic situation in the USSR is probably as bad as ours, overall—worse in some respects, not as bad in others—and there was undoubtedly a strong element of desperation in the situation." Godfrey shrugged. "And desperation can easily result in poor decisions.

"We're pretty much satisfied," he went on, "that Kulish and the Politburo never intended to take and control the entire country of Iran. Capture Teheran and establish a puppet regime; that was the rumor in the Party Central Committee. And of course, the Central Committee has its pipelines into the Politburo and the Military Council.

"Subsequent events indicate there was also a predictable side project of setting up an Iranian extension of the Afghan semi-autonomous Soviet Baluchistan, just to keep things upset and violent; if Iran ever became an independent nation again, a separate Baluchistan would ensure perennial trouble for it in the south.

"And if the Soviets decided later to pull out—even if a Shiite theocracy took over again there—the Soviets could always say they'd accomplished what they'd purportedly invaded for: to get the Iranians out of Iraq."

He spread his hands. "So trade leverage and a spur to patriotism seem to have been the Kremlin's rationale for the invasion. Which brings us to the coup.

"We definitely know that the Soviet army was very unhappy with Kulish's continuing rehabilitation of the KGB. And that it had been unhappy for years with Kremlin management of the economy. They considered, and correctly, that the Central Committee did a lot poorer job of running the civilian bureaucracy than the Military Council did with the military bureaucracy. But of course, they were overlooking the difference in scope and circumstance."

Godfrey had shifted into a lecture mode. But he was a good lecturer, Haugen decided, and the subject was interesting.

"Meanwhile," Godfrey was saying, "things at home hadn't improved with the invasion. Civilian morale in Russia itself may or may not have risen a bit, but in the rest of the Soviet Union it definitely got worse. You know about the strikes and riots and sabotage in the Moslem SSRs.

"And then of course there was the truck-bomb explosion in Tashkent, in the Uzbek SSR. That shook a lot more than buildings; it shook the entire upper strata of government to realize that such a thing could happen in the Soviet Union. It was a trauma that went far beyond the physical damage; that we know as fact.

"So our conjecture is that Pavlenko and his immediate group in the Ministry of Defense decided to take over. And they needed—let's call it covering fire. We definitely know that Pavlenko's aide, Colonel Ivan Milukov, had flown to Teheran the day after it was captured, and talked to Army General Zotov there. We believe he carried a secret order from Pavlenko to attack into Iraq.

"An order not from the Politburo, but from the Ministry of Defense.

"Of course, they'd already have had a contingency plan for that. General staffs make plans for almost everything." Godfrey's eyes moved to Cromwell. "As the vice president can tell you, that's part of the job. The purpose of Milukov's trip would have been to activate it."

Haugen stopped him with a gesture. "Back up a step, Norman. You said Pavlenko's people needed covering fire to take over. What do you mean, 'covering fire?' And how does that tie in with ordering the invasion of Iraq?"

"Basically, sir, an expansion of the war would hold a considerable amount of national attention. The people wouldn't have their attention just on the coup; it wouldn't seem like quite such an enormity to the Russian people. And it's the *Russian* people we're talking about, not all the Soviet people.

"Also, an attack southwest toward Iraq *without Politburo orders* would absolutely have to draw severe disciplinary action against army high command. In Soviet politics, anything less would be taken as a fatal sign of weakness. And in the face of severe disciplinary action, a coup could be explained as the patriotic army defending itself against the corrupt Party. As it was, in a sense of the word.

"And with the military controlling the government, if for some reason they decided to pull out of Iraq, they could always say it was the old regime that had ordered them in. Who would there be to call them liars?

"Anyway, we have firm information that the Kremlin called Zotov to Moscow for disciplinary action. And he obeyed, to the extent that, that night, he got on a plane and started back. But *obeyed* doesn't seem to be quite the word for it. He probably went because flying back to Moscow would help the army cover its intention. His seeming to obey would make it look as if the army wasn't ready for a showdown.

"But his plane stopped at Vnukovo Airfield, some twenty miles southwest of Moscow, to avoid his arrest by KGB troops we know were waiting for him at Sheremetyevo Airfield.

"And at 0915 the next day, two companies of *spetsnaz* made a low-altitude daylight drop inside the Kremlin walls. That's about 230 men, all topflight killers. There was a firefight with the elite KGB troops inside that must have been a doozy. But when an airborne assault brigade began landing from Mi-6 helicopters, minutes later, in and around Red Square, the *spetsnaz* had the Kremlin gates open for them.

"At the same time, 0915 hours, a parachute division, replete with light tanks, armored rocket launchers, and armored automatic mortars, began dropping near KGB headquarters, outside the ring road, and enveloped it. Then they proceeded to more or less blow it apart, with everyone in it. There was quite a firefight there, too. By attacking in the daytime, they caught and destroyed probably seventy-five or eighty percent of the KGB headquarters staff. And with the certain exception of the *spetsnaz*, it's very doubtful that anyone below the level of regimental commander knew where they were going when they took off, or what they intended to do; so that hopefully no KGB spies would find out. They probably got their orders in flight.

"The entire operation was successful, except for one major failure: Party Secretary Kulish; his first deputy, P.S. Shafirov; and General Dolin, head of the KGB, somehow escaped the Kremlin. We don't have an inkling of how they pulled it off. The rest of the Politburo were arrested. Several were executed later that day, while three others condemned Kulish, Shafirov, and Dolin as traitors to the State. All civilian telephone service was discontinued, of course. And all nonmilitary air traffic was suspended, 'to prevent the criminals from escaping to the Americans.' "

Again the president gestured, and Godfrey stopped. "How did the Russian people react to all this?" Haugen asked.

"About the way we thought they would: They sat back to wait and watch. They don't seem to care much which way it goes.

"Incidentally, it's interesting that the army initially accused Kulish and company of being 'traitors to the State' instead of 'traitors to the Party.' But apparently they rethought things afterward, because since then they've called them both, in a sort of package curse: 'Traitors to the State and Party.' And meanwhile they've been wiping out all the KGB they can get their hands on.

"Of course, most of the KGB went underground, those who weren't underground already. Or dead. We know they're behind at least some of the demonstrations and outbreaks of sabotage in the Moslem SSRs. And even the Ukraine. If you'll recall, it was on Kiev television that Kulish and Shafirov appeared the day after the coup to denounce 'the counter-revolutionary czarist usurper, Pavlenko,' and call for the army to revolt and return to 'the principles of Marxism-Leninism.' "

"I wondered about that," Cromwell said. "How did they manage to pull off that TV appearance? And how has Kulish stayed free so long?"

"Basically," Godfrey answered, "the army's done a lousy job of police work. They're not set up for it. The MVD is in charge of ordinary police work in the USSR, and they're mostly staying pretty much neutral, keeping their options open. Also, the central police files were stored in the KGB master computer in Moscow, and these were destroyed when the army shelled the place.

"There are thousands, probably tens of thousands of mimeograph machines cranking out pamphlets and underground newssheets attacking the Pavlenko government, and we can assume that the KGB is behind most of them. Or at least many of them. Opposing them are the army-controlled media: radio, television, and the press.

"So what they have going on there is a sort of semi-war between the military on the one hand and the KGB on the other. In a sense, the Party is actually more or less outside of it. It's semi-disowned the old leadership, to the extent of not mentioning it, and survives in the form of the bureaucracy, as a sort of apathetic political organism. The army needs the bureaucracy to keep the machinery of government and industry more or less running, and it's simply taken over without providing ideological leadership.

"Meanwhile the Russian people are more or less nonpartisan spectators, doing less work than ever, pilfering more than ever, and waiting to see who comes out on top. While ethnic non-Russians, mainly the Moslems, are exercising their decades of resentment by committing lots of minor and some major sabotage. And assassinations of local Party bigwigs with KGB help. Even though nominally the KGB is on the Party's side; anything to sow confusion and disorder until they get rid of the Pavlenko government and take over themselves.

"Actually, the Balts and most of the ethnically non-Russian Slavs have stayed relatively quiet, what with all the troops on hand. But they're surly, disobedient, and uncooperative."

The president interrupted. "Where do the Poles stand in this?" he asked.

"They're waiting too, but it's a different waiting. They're waiting for things to get worse. There are only two Soviet divisions in Poland itself, but there are twenty in East Germany and about fifteen in Byelorussia, on either side of Poland. Along with five more in Czechoslovakia to the south.

"If Soviet army morale begins to unravel badly—say there are mutinies in the Soviet divisions in the west—the Poles may very well revolt, and that could begin a more general revolt by the Czechs, East Germans, and Hungarians. They've all revolted before, of course, in the fifties and sixties. The danger, and it's a real one, is that the Poles may act too soon. It's the sort of thing that could pull the Russians together, and we'd rather see things reach a nice deep level of chaos before that happens."

Godfrey looked around the table then. "And that's about it. Are there any questions?"

While Godfrey waited, the president looked him over. "Mr. Godfrey," he said, "whose would you judge is the Soviet faction we'd have the best chance of negotiating some sort of accord with? A reasonably functional accord—functional enough that we wouldn't be living under the sword of Damocles."

Godfrey pursed his lips in thought. "Kulish's, I suspect. If there is a Kulish faction. Outside the government, there's too little visible organization to know. We can evaluate Pavlenko for you pretty well right now, but beyond that, there's no faction we can identify. Unless it's the fugitive KGB, and we have no idea of who's in charge. Probably no one, really."

Haugen nodded. "Play with it," he said. "See what you can come up with." He turned to the Secretary of State. "Any objection to Godfrey doing it instead of some of your people?"

Coulter looked as if something tasted bad. "No. If you want him to do it, that's all right with me."

Haugen's eyes lingered on Coulter for just a second before he turned back to Godfrey. "It's yours then. Do the best you can for me."

The president got up from his chair more slowly than usual. "Unless someone has something they have to say to the council as a whole, this meeting is adjourned. As far as I know now, we won't get together again until our next regularly scheduled meeting."

He stood by the door shaking hands with the others as they left. Including Blackburn. Flynn was last. "Steve," Haugen said, "let's go to my office. Okay?"

"Certainly, Mr. President. Arne."

Together they walked to the Oval Office, where Haugen poured coffee for them both before he sat down.

"What did you think of the NSC meeting?" he asked.

Flynn looked soberly at him. "I—felt out of place."

"I'm not surprised. That was Blackburn's intention."

"Maybe he was simply worried about security, as he said."

The president looked reflective. "No," he said slowly, "I'm pretty sure we can rule that out."

"Why do you think so?"

"When we clashed, our eyes met. And from what I saw there, I'd say that Dr. Blackburn is psychotic."

Flynn stared.

"That's a subjective evaluation of course," the president went on. "But meanwhile, I don't want a psychotic heading up the CIA. Or the OSS; he's slated to go to it when it's born next week."

"Maybe what you saw was fear," Flynn said. "You looked

truly angry, you know. If I'd been Dr. Blackburn and you'd looked at me like that, I'd have been frightened."

"Ah-h," Haugen said, "I'm a pussycat." He grinned then, surprising the Jesuit. "I used to love a fight when I was a kid, did you know that? Not that I fought a lot, probably not more than once a month, but I loved it when I did. I hardly ever fought mad; that may have been part of why I enjoyed it. Usually I fought someone else that liked to fight. Someone would challenge, or some other guys would set it up, maybe with a prize, and we'd go at it."

He fingered his long-ago broken nose. "I kind of out-grew it, I guess. When I went to college, I sort of got out of the habit. It just wasn't done there, not like up home in Koochiching County, or in bars in the airborne. And I never got back into it again." He cocked an eye at Flynn. "Did you fight as a schoolboy?"

Flynn smiled ruefully. "I've probably had five fights in my whole life. Fights just seldom came my way." He grinned then. "I won one of them, though. My last one, with a boy named Emilio Peccioli. We were in the tenth grade. Sister Mary Theresa was really disillusioned with me."

"So you know how much fun it can be." The grin teased. Then, suddenly businesslike, the president buzzed Martinelli. "Jeanne, get me the FBI—Director Dirksma. Have him call me back on a security line."

Flynn's eyebrows rose. Haugen disconnected.

"I'm going to have Dirksma investigate Blackburn," Haugen said. "If I'm right, and I'm sure I am, we need him put away."

It seemed unreal to Flynn. There'd been no evidence; only something Arne thought he'd seen in the man's eyes. "And if you're not right?"

"I'll be very surprised."

"Well," Flynn said, "the investigation should settle the matter, shouldn't it?"

"It certainly seems like it." The president sipped his coffee. "Want to bet?"

"Bet? About Blackburn?" The priest looked quizzically at the septuagenarian president. Arne Haugen could be whimsical, almost boyish, despite his age and situation. "How much?" Flynn asked.

"Pushups. I'll bet you—" He eyed the priest. "You're pretty tall; it's a long way from your feet to your shoulders. Ten should be enough. I'll bet you ten pushups."

"You're on! Ten pushups!"

That night, before his shower, Father Stephen Joseph Flynn lay down on his stomach and did pushups. To his surprise, he actually did ten, though only by resting for a moment on his stomach after each one.

Ah well, he thought, *Arne won't give you a bad time about it. He's not the type.*

TWENTY-FOUR

The president was eating lunch with Father Flynn when the security phone buzzed. This time the CRT was in split-screen format, showing two faces: FBI Director Peter Dirksma, and another man.

"Mr. President," Dirksma said, "this is Agent Aaron Gonzalves. He has some preliminary information for you on Director Blackburn. Incidentally, your call to the National Security Agency was very helpful; it got us covert access to CIA's central computer. Without that, we wouldn't have been able to get some of this without making ourselves known. Which might have enabled a coverup."

"Right," the president said. "What did you learn, Aaron?"

"In Dr. Blackburn's earlier commands," Gonzalves said, "there was a history of personnel breakdowns and losses. However, in eight years of project commands, he had three major, or at least substantial, covert operations victories to his credit, depending on how you define major. Apparently three is considered good performance in that time frame.

"He was promoted from project leader to chief of Covert Operations in the Southeast Asia Division. After two years on that, he was promoted to deputy director of the CIA. Two years later, when Director Grasso died, President Donnelly designated Blackburn as the new director, and the Senate approved. That was eight months ago.

"I've looked through Dr. Blackburn's personnel files, and there are a couple of reprimands there for mistreatment of foreign personnel while visiting Bangkok. Pretty unpleasant stuff. I'm amazed he got promoted over them; in the Bureau he'd have been fired."

Haugen blew silently through pursed lips. "Who sponsored Blackburn with President Donnelly?"

"Secretary of State Coulter, sir."

"Oh hoh! Okay, what else did you find out?"

"Well sir, his doctorate isn't a Ph.D. as I'd thought it would be. He's got an M.D., from Johns Hopkins; he's a licensed psychiatrist."

"Huh! That's interesting." The president paused as if thinking. "Anything else on him?"

"Not yet, sir."

"Tell you what: I want you to find out for me if he has a personal laboratory or clinical facility in the CIA Building. Do you have someone inside over there that can check that out for us?"

"Yessir."

"Good. If he does . . ." The president paused, thought of using martial law, then decided not to. "Tell you what, Peter. I'm going to suspend Blackburn on the basis of the reprimands in his file. Then I want you to arrest him; hold him under the Official Secrets Act. We can do that legally, can't we?"

"Yes sir, for up to ninety-six hours."

"Okay. Wait an hour and then arrest him. His suspension will be finalized by then. I want all the information necessary to either charge him or clear him, inside of ninety-six hours.

"He may try to get away from you, so be on your toes. He's likely to be pretty competent at things like that.

"Oh, and one more thing. Find out who wrote the reprimands on him. And what they're doing now."

When he'd disconnected, the president looked at Flynn

with grim satisfaction. "Steve," he said, "it's time to start practicing your pushups." Then he buzzed Milstead and initiated the suspension of Blackburn.

When they finished eating, Father Flynn excused himself, and Haugen called Godfrey at the CIA. "Norman," he said, "I have some more questions for you. How long will it take you to get to the White House from Langley?"

"At this time of the afternoon? I can probably drive it in half an hour."

"When can you start?"

Godfrey looked a trifle pained, as if he was in the middle of something. "I'll dump what I have in memory and be on my way inside five minutes, if that's all right with you, sir."

"That's fine. Do it. I'll see you in thirty-five or forty minutes."

The president broke the connection and started to read a report he'd asked for, on the current status of Russo-Finnish relations. He did not find it enjoyable. He'd finished it and was reading one on Russo-Turkish relations when Godfrey arrived.

"Norman," the president said, "I may have called you over here for something you could tell me over the phone. If I did, I'm sorry. But it occurred to me that your calls over there might be monitored, or that you might feel uncomfortable about talking freely from there.

"Anything you want to say about that?"

"Only that I have no reason to think my calls are monitored."

"Okay. What I want to know is, what does CIA staff think of Blackburn."

After a moment's pause, Godfrey answered. "Well, sir, they're mainly of two schools: his buddies, and those who don't like him. No, make that three schools: There are those who are scared of him."

"Interesting. Which do you fit in?"

Again a pause. "Well, sir, I'm not in Covert Operations, so I don't ordinarily have much contact with him. But I'm one of the 'don't likes.' Basically he's a mind-fucker. And when he became director, several agency people who'd had run-ins with him before, got transferred to field projects and supposedly dropped out of sight."

"Dropped out of sight? What does that mean?"

"Supposedly no one hears about them anymore. It could just mean they're in a project somewhere that's so highly secret, it's as if they don't exist."

"What do you think?"

"I don't know enough about Covert Operations to have an informed opinion."

Haugen's eyes seemed to probe, as if looking inside Godfrey's head. It might have been offensive, had the gaze not been so neutral. "You said *supposedly* a couple of times. What does that mean?"

"It means that what I know about it is rumor. You might not expect there'd be rumors in a close-mouthed outfit like the CIA. And mostly there aren't. But now and then you hear one, almost always about Covert Operations. I've always suspected that someone starts them deliberately."

The president sat contemplatively for a moment, fingers drumming on his desk. "Can you give me the names of the people you mentioned, who're supposed to have dropped out of sight?"

"Sure." Godfrey named three.

"And was there anyone in Covert Operations that hadn't gotten along with Blackburn but who's still around there?"

"Yes sir. One that I know of. His name is Thompson or Thomson, first name Bill. He held some major post; I think it was chief debriefing officer. A lot of people were pretty loyal to him: he's a good guy. I suppose he had too many friends and he was too visible to just ship him out. He's black, for one thing. And very outgoing, which is kind of unusual around the shop. After Blackburn took over, Thompson got a lateral transfer to Personnel—away from the action."

When Godfrey had left, the president got on the phone and talked to Dirksma. Gonzalves had already left for CIA headquarters. Haugen played back his conversation with Godfrey. "I consider that Godfrey is probably reliable," he said. "Get those names checked out, and have Gonzalves talk privately with this Bill Thompson.

"And have someone find out what the routing-out procedures are for people who leave Covert Operations for civilian life. Not just the standard, but procedures for special cases, too. Thompson may be helpful on that.

"And Peter, I've got too damn much attention on what may be a situation there. That's *Situation* with a capital *S*. I need to get it sorted out enough to take my mind off it; enough that I can let others handle it without worrying about it anymore.

"So I want you to update me no later than nine o'clock this evening, even if you haven't learned a damned thing more. I want communication. And if you find out something at midnight that you think I should know about right away, call me then."

Dirksma called back a lot sooner than 9 P.M. Blackburn had suicided. The arresting agents had allowed him to take a little travel kit with him after searching it. Later, in the cell they put him in, they found him dead of cyanide poisoning. The shaft of his manual razor had been hollow. Inside it were two more cyanide capsules.

The Bureau's investigation had thereby gained another facet: Why had he suicided? The possibility that had occurred at once to Dirksma was that Blackburn had been a double agent. But that was sheer speculation; there was no evidence for it, and only the poisoning even to suggest it.

The president didn't give his opinion—that Blackburn had been psychotic. There'd been something in the man's eyes, when they'd met the president's, like a flash of sheer terror, as if he'd thought the president, looking into them, had somehow found him out. Even guilt of treason, it seemed to Haugen, wouldn't account for terror in a sane man. Not under this morning's circumstances.

TWENTY-FIVE

Wojciech Jaruzelski's grandfather was killed in 1920 fighting the Red Army, and his father died in a Soviet prison camp during the Second World War. Wojciech himself, a student at the elite Jesuit lycée in Warsaw, was arrested by the Soviets at age sixteen and imprisoned in labour camps, first in Kazakhstan where he worked as a coal miner, then in Siberia where he laboured cutting trees. In Siberia he was afflicted by snowblindness which permanently damaged his vision. . . .

From: *"Wojciech Jaruzelski,"* pp 235-241, IN Heads of Government of the Twentieth Century, *Ploughshare Books, London, AD 2001*

On Air Force One, crossing to Norway, the president spent much of the time practicing his Polish with John Zale. Especially reading it aloud, getting more thoroughly at home with the Polish orthography. He'd played at learning the language since first he'd known that Zale was fluent in it, but had never before taken it on as a project. Its many cognates with Russian made it far easier for Haugen than it would otherwise have been, the grammars were very similar, and his pronunciations had become quite good, quite Polish, with not much trace of American or Russian influence. But his conversational ability—particularly his recognition vocabulary—didn't extend much beyond small talk.

Their first day in Europe, Arne and Lois Haugen spent in Norway. It was an official state visit, a "working" visit, not a sentimental trip to the parish where his father had grown up. They'd visited there several times before, had met his old-country relatives while Arne was still a young man, hiked the mountain ridge where his father had raced slalom as a teenager, when *slalom* meant skiing down a winding trail through the forest, dodging trees. *Real slalom*, Arne thought of it.

Haugen's talks with the king, the prime minister, and the minister of foreign affairs, were formalities. His short, televised speech before the *storting* was memorable in only two respects: It was only the second ever delivered in Norwegian by the head of a non-Scandinavian state, the first having been by Willi Brandt, years before; and it was widely approved by the people of Norway, watching in their living rooms.

By agreement, it was not telecast outside Norway. The president had insisted on that. It was a later speech that he wanted to receive international media attention, though of course he didn't say so.

The second day was spent in Helsinki, where he spoke with the President of Finland, his prime minister and foreign minister. As in Norway, Haugen was already familiar with his ancestral district, Pori, and his short televised speech in Finnish to the *Eduskunta*, was the major event of his visit.

His third day, in Sweden, differed mainly in that the Swedish minister of defense sat in secretly on Haugen's talk with the foreign minister and prime minister. It was deemed appropriate that he address the *Riksdag* briefly, as he had the Norwegian and Finnish parliaments. This time his wife stood beside him and also spoke, both in Swedish.

When Arne Haugen went to bed that third night, it was with relief; the preliminary stops were over. There was a lot to do back in Washington. But the Scandinavian visits had been vital stage setting. Tomorrow he'd accomplish more; hopefully a lot more.

The next morning before dawn, the presidential party flew out of Stockholm's Bromma Airfield in a thin, dry snowfall, in a chartered SAS 727. An hour later they landed at Warsaw, 470 miles south.

*   *   *

They emerged from the armored limousines before an imposing stone building. The late autumn sunshine was thin and weak, the wintry breeze out of the east. *Out of Russia*, thought the president, then inwardly grinned at himself. *Haugen, that's pretty dramatic for an old cedar savage.*

The honor guard, in heavy green greatcoats, stood at present arms, forming a precise human corridor bastioned with rifles. Among the party climbing the entrance steps were the American president, his ambassador to Poland, the ambassador's interpreter, and John Zale.

Of the Poles who'd met them at the airport, three had introduced themselves as Foreign Ministry officials. They had been friendly but nervous—concerned, Haugen supposed, for his safety. The KGB and the GRU would both have agents in Poland, and just now the Russians seemed highly unpredictable. The Secret Service had argued strenuously against his coming, fearing that the KGB might try to kill him to embarrass the Kremlin, or that the Kremlin might try to kill him to embarrass the Poles.

The CIA had been considerably less concerned. They had a lot of respect for the Polish secret police, who made life highly uncertain for Soviet agents. When they caught one, he was more likely never to be seen again than be deported, and Warsaw, they said, would be no more dangerous for the president than any other European capital.

What had *really* upset the Secret Service was the president's decision to leave his agents on the plane in Warsaw. He would let the Poles protect him. Gil Rogers, special agent in charge of this trip, had been grim to the verge of rudeness. Haugen let him be; he'd come more and more to admire his single-minded "keepers."

Besides the Foreign Ministry officials who'd met them, there were ten Poles who had not been introduced; they didn't have to be. Despite the cold, they wore jackets instead of coats, open jackets, and they looked about continually. The president suspected that, despite their considerable size, their agility and reflexes would be excellent. And there were no crowds to hide a gunman, either at the airport or at the government square, only men armed and uniformed, in little groups at a distance.

Inside the massive building, two other men, deputy ministers, met the presidential party. After introductions, they marched through a rotunda, immaculate and impressive but rather cheerless, and down a wide hall to an office. A working office, large, and with broad windows facing south. Presumably, Haugen thought, for the winter sun.

Two men stood waiting. The older man with the thick glasses was the premier himself, General Wojciech Witold Jaruzelski. He was about Haugen's age, and when they shook hands, his grip was hard. The younger man, his age perhaps thirty, would be the premier's interpreter.

"Mr. President, we are honored to have you." Jaruzelski said it in accented English, perhaps learned for the occasion.

Haugen answered in Polish. "General, I am honored to be your guest."

The premier's eyes, small behind thick lenses, examined Arne Haugen. "I have been told you speak our language, Mr. President." Jaruzelski said this in Polish, and the ambassador's interpreter, forewarned of the president's limitations, translated for him.

"A little," Haugen replied, again in Polish. "Mostly I must depend on Ambassador Tyler's interpreter, Mr. Marovich. I speak rather much Russian, but have only recently begun to learn Polish." He indicated John Zale. "My secretary, Mr. Zale, has been teaching me. We have looked forward to being here."

Jaruzelski's voice was dry. "I will try to be a better host to you than your President Reagan was to me. He refused to see or speak with me when I visited your country. Some of the time he did not even honor us with an ambassador. He made my position more difficult here in dealing with elements who wished to Sovietize us."

As the interpreter repeated the premier's words in English, Ambassador Tyler's expression turned disapproving.

"I am not Ronald Reagan," Haugen replied, in English now. "And while I do not apologize for him, he was poorly advised."

He undertook Polish again: "It is easy to be poorly advised in foreign affairs. So while I always listen to my foreign ministry, I also went secretly for advice to one of your own countrymen. You know him: Karol Wojtyla."

The ambassador's interpreter was startled at the reference to Karol Wojtyla. *The president had talked with the Pope?* He was sure the State Department didn't know about that. Certainly the ambassador didn't.

Ambassador Tyler knew too little Polish to have followed Haugen's words, and sat waiting for someone to speak English.

Haugen's Polish had already included several words that were properly Russian, though they'd been delivered with the Polish stress and accent. He continued now in English.

"Wojtyla appreciates the severe difficulties you contend with, here against the belly of the bear. And also your accomplishments in civil liberties, the further decentralization of government, the continued freedom of farmers from collectivization . . . All of it. I share his respect for you."

The premier's eyebrows had lifted slightly at the name. "Ah yes," he said. "Karol Wojtyla. He did not trust me at first, and even now I am no favorite of his. But he recognizes our circumstances here, and gives me my due." He smiled a slight wry smile. "And we must understand his problems. It has to be burdensome, being infallible."

Only now did Tyler show dawning awareness that they were talking about the Pope.

Jaruzelski gestured at a chair. "Let us sit. At our ages, standing is harder than walking, and sitting is better than either.

"You are a wonder to the world, you know," Jaruzelski added when they had settled into chairs. "An American dictator!" He watched closely for Haugen's reaction to the word; there was none. "Yet apparently the most democratic of dictators. And the story of your youth spent in the forest: It seems not to be propaganda after all. When I shook your hand I knew it; such a hand could only come from a boyhood with the ax or plow. Early, when the bones are still growing."

The Pope had not prepared the president for this exposure of personality by Jaruzelski; he was reputedly a cold man. Haugen grinned at him. "It's impossible for a political figure in America to sustain a false history," he said. "The newspapers and television would display its falsity for everyone to see. More than two hundred journalists with cameras descended on my home district within two days of my being named president. The cafe keeper in my village made his fortune from them. So many drove through the forest to visit my home farm that the moose and wolves fled into Canada."

Jaruzelski laughed, taking his own interpreter by surprise, and a frown of annoyance crossed the ambassador's face. The president noticed.

"Tell me, General Jaruzelski," Haugen went on, "how do you get along with Ambassador Tyler?"

For a moment, Tyler's mouth fell open. He flushed. The general too was clearly taken by surprise. "Ambassador Tyler? I hardly know him; we have little contact. It would be helpful though if he spoke Polish.

"I believe your State Department did not consider it important to have an ambassador here," he continued. "I believe Ambassador Tyler, through no fault of his own, is intended as a token—a symbol, rather than as an executor, of foreign policy." Jaruzelski eyed Haugen thoughtfully.

"Hm-m." The president pursed his wide mouth. "Perhaps that foreign policy has changed.

"General," he went on, shifting gears, "you agreed to let me address the Polish people on television, on the condition that my speech was not dangerous to the welfare of your country. I have it here to show you." Zale opened an attaché case and took out two thin sheaves of papers, handing one to the president and one to the premier. "It is in Polish," Haugen continued. "Mr. Zale assures me that I read it convincingly. Perhaps you and I can go over it together and determine whether changes need to be made."

He turned to the ambassador. "Mr. Tyler, you might as well leave. This will take some time, and the speech is in Polish. Take Mr. Marovich if you'd like, to see you back to the embassy."

Tyler flushed again, got up with a curt nod, and beckoning Marovich to follow, left the room.

Once more Jaruzelski's eyebrows had raised a few millimeters. Now he leaned over the large print and began silently to read.

The Sejm, the Polish parliament, was not in session, but

a number of its members were in the chamber. The rest of the seats had been taken by the Polish and foreign press, representatives of labor and the Party, their wives, and the foreign diplomatic corps. There were no permanent facilities for televising, and cables snaked across the floor. Lights glared hotly at the rostrum, and dollies with camera booms stood strategically. The speech would be beamed not only over all of Poland, but upward to a satellite that would send it to most of the world.

A world that was very interested in this unusual American president. A world hopeful and afraid, hopeful of someone who might make progress toward peace, afraid that Haugen instead simply marked the end of democracy or perhaps a policy of truculence.

Jaruzelski introduced the president and first lady. Then the president stepped to the lectern, seated reading glasses on his broken nose, and looked out at the audience.

"I am glad," he said in Polish, "to be in Poland, and to speak to the Polish people. A people I have long respected and admired."

That was as far as he was willing to go in speaking Polish off the cuff. He looked down at his speech and began to read, hesitating occasionally at a pronunciation.

"I especially respect your unusual accomplishment in retaining such a large degree of independence from foreign rule. You have faced severe problems, and your success is a result both of your great courage as a nation and the skill and patience of your government in dealing with foreign powers."

No one in the audience failed to know who in particular the American president meant by "foreign powers." Not even Tyler, who was watching in his embassy office, with Marovich interpreting.

"And in this world of ours," Haugen continued, "skill and patience are as important as courage. Courage without skill and patience can lead to destruction. Skill and patience without courage are fruitless.

"One of the central realities that we must face, both Poles and Americans, is the Soviet Union. We must face it with courage, but we must also face it with patience, with wisdom and watchfulness."

He glanced up at his audience, then back to his speech.

"My own patience and desire for peace have been shown by American forebearance with Russian imperialism in southern Asia. For that matter, it seems that the Russians have greatly harmed their own cause by their imperialist assault on Iran. It is proving a pit of trouble for them, far worse than Afghanistan.

"And their problems in Afghanistan were not truly solved by declaring it to be the Afghan SSR. Nor did the rest of the world consider it a Soviet domestic matter when the Red Army used poison gas against the mountain peoples there. It is especially interesting that they did this on the largest scale *after* they'd declared the Afghan people to be citizens of the Soviet Union.

"We should not doubt for one minute that the Russian Empire is powerful and dangerous. But at the same time, the Kremlin is aware that America and its allies are also powerful."

He let his gaze rest on his audience again before looking back at his speech. "Yet in this time of Soviet troubles at home and abroad, I have not considered an attack on the Soviet Union. Nor will I, even if the Soviet government collapses. Certainly not then.

"Nor do we expect the Soviet Union to attack the West. Russia's ability to expand its empire is weakening under Kremlin mismanagement, and under the continuing resentment and lack of cooperation of the subject peoples it has conquered. And also under the cynicism and apathy of so many of the Russian people themselves.

"Of course, America has troubles of its own. But the American people and the American government are moving effectively to correct our problems. While the Kremlin seems to have given up on correcting theirs, and is trying unsuccessfully to draw their people's attention away from those problems by making war in the Middle East.

"Russia is a nation of large resources and notable qualities. It is interesting to speculate on what the Kremlin might accomplish at home if it discarded its mental fixation on world domination—that old Russian imperialism which it tries now to disguise as 'world revolution.'

"It will be fascinating to see how the Soviet factions resolve their present difficulties. Perhaps the result will be a government clear-sighted enough to recognize that every nation should be allowed to work out its own destinies free of dictation by some great power.

"The United States is perfectly willing that Russia—*or any other nation*—be a marxist state, *if that is what that nation, that people, truly wishes*. But we insist upon our right to be a nation free from Russian dictation. On our right to evolve politically, technically, and economically in our own directions. We also support the right of our allies to do the same. And fortunately we are in a position to defend that right. And we *will* defend it if it comes to that."

The president scanned the room. "But enough talk of fighting. I doubt very much that the United States and Russia will ever go to war against each other. We don't want to and they don't want to, and I would much prefer to be a friend to Russia than an enemy.

"It is time to build, not destroy. It is time to create, to allow each other to build futures instead of armies. In the United States we are renewing not only our economy but our spirit of democracy and personal liberty. And we are creating new technology, much of which is not the technology of war. A generation from now, we may reasonably hope to have entered a truly golden age.

"That golden age, of course, is still speculation. But what I will tell you next is fact. Within the next few weeks you can expect to see the release of a major new technology. A new, peaceful technology, the result of a basic scientific breakthrough that will change the welfare of mankind for the better, both economically and in our understanding of the universe.

"That will not mean the end of problems. But along with recent and future developments in computer technology, super conductors, genetics and other fields, it will move this planet to a new level of accomplishment and human opportunity.

"And the United States will not hide this technology. It will send it promptly to many nations. Before the end of winter, it will go to Mexico and Australia, Britain and West Germany, Scandinavia and Japan and China. And to Poland. I have agreed to that today with General Jaruzelski."

Again he looked at his audience and then at the center camera. "Thank you for listening to me, people of Poland," he said. "Once again your premier has demonstrated his courage, by letting me speak to you like this. I value your friendship, and I want to close by wishing you happiness and prosperity."

He looked up at his audience then. "Long live Poland!" he cried. "Long live the Polish people!"

He stepped back from the lectern, and the Polish audience, silent till then, began to applaud. Not wildly, not enthusiastically, but strongly, until, after standing there for twenty seconds, the president bowed and left.

The premier's escorted limousine took Arne and Lois Haugen and John Zale to the American embassy, where they were to spend the night. After they arrived, Lois went to their suite and Zale to his room. No ambassador had met them, no deputy ambassador, only marine guards, so the president asked a marine to take him to the ambassador's office. No one was there, so he looked over the in-house directory beneath the glass top of the ambassador's desk. Then he dialed the ambassador's apartment and told him he wanted to speak with him personally, in his office.

Tyler kept him waiting a quarter hour, but when he arrived, Haugen didn't comment on it. "Mr. Tyler," he said, "we have things to talk about. And apparently there's something you'd like to tell me. I'd like to hear it."

"Mr. President," Tyler said, and his voice was husky with emotion, "you have humiliated me in front of the premier. I can no longer serve here effectively."

The president bit back the impulse to tell him he never had served effectively. Instead he said, "All right, I got that. You shouldn't have been sent here anyway. There's got to be hundreds of persons who could serve here who speak Polish, and . . ."

Tyler interrupted angrily. "I'm learning Polish! I get an hour of lessons daily."

"For how long? When did you start?"

"Two weeks ago."

"When did you get here?"

Tyler reddened. "May fifteenth."

Gentle Jesus, Haugen said to himself. *He's been here more than six months. What the hell is this? Our ambassadors in Scandinavia seemed competent enough.*

"Well, you've started anyway. What are your qualifications for the job?"

"I have a degree in International Affairs from Harvard, and I worked in the State Department for six years before being posted here."

"For six years? In Washington, or abroad?"

"In Washington."

Well, Haugen thought, *they knew what they were sending anyway. They can't claim ignorance; not of this.* He was beginning to see an explanation. This embassy was a listening post inside the Iron Curtain; its main function was intelligence gathering. The ambassador was window dressing. But even window dressing should be good.

"All right, William. Now let me point out something. First of all, an ambassador is supposed to be a diplomat. I suggest you look up the word. An American diplomat does not behave arrogantly, not in this era. Certainly not to the point of keeping his own chief of state waiting without telling him he'll be delayed, or even explaining afterward. Certainly not to the point of waiting six months to begin learning the language.

"And secondly, a diplomat should not display petulance toward a head of state as you did this morning toward the premier. That was totally unacceptable behavior."

While Haugen had spoken, his tone had shifted from mild and patient to sharp and metallic. Now he changed tone again, speaking more mildly.

"Who recommended you?" he asked. "I suppose President Donnelly must have appointed you, and the Senate confirmed it, but who sponsored you?"

"Secretary Coulter."

"I see. And who recommended you to Secretary Coulter?"

"I have no idea. Probably no one. He'd probably noticed me."

"Did it seem to you today that General Jaruzelski lacked respect for you as ambassador?"

"Jaruzelski is a Soviet stooge! It doesn't make a damn bit of difference whether he likes me or not!"

Abruptly the president stood. "Tyler," he said, and his voice was suddenly intense, almost menacing, "You are done here. Get your stuff packed and be on a plane out by

Tuesday. You are no longer ambassador, as of this moment. You will no longer give orders here."

He turned and strode out of the room, then hunted up the aide in charge for the night. The place seemed dead. He found the man reading a recent issue of *Newsweek*.

"Who's second in command here?" Haugen snapped.

The man looked up, then jumped to his feet. "Mr. Bennett, sir."

The president took the edge off his voice. "Get him for me, please."

"Yes Mr. President." The man hesitated. "I believe he's in the radio room, sending the daily intelligence report."

"Thank you. Get him for me now." Haugen watched while the man sat back down and dialed. *So the second in command is BIR*, he thought—the State Department's Bureau of Intelligence and Research. And maybe CIA too. It occurred to him that he wasn't really clear on the lines of responsibility in intelligence; perhaps they weren't distinct.

He was willing to bet though that this second in command was a lot sharper than Tyler.

Suddenly weary, the president took a deep breath and asked himself again how something like this could have happened.

TWENTY-SIX

Almost daily, Jumper Cromwell could be found in the vice president's West Wing office at the White House for an hour or two in the afternoon, but the rest of the day he usually spent in a small office at the Pentagon. Of course, he had no authority there now, but a vice president didn't have much authority anywhere, normally.

With the president out of the country, the routine had been different. Cromwell had been "camping out" in a White House guest room, and spending his workdays in his White House office handling paperwork and being available.

After four days he needed a break, so early the fifth morning he left the White House, Secret Service men in tow, and took a helicopter to the Pentagon to catch up on his IN basket there.

During the brief flight, he was thinking about the president's Warsaw speech of the afternoon before, and feeling mostly good about it. Although he was curious, and a little edgy, about the technological breakthrough the president had mentioned. The TV news the evening before had referred to it as "the president's Christmas surprise," seeming not to know quite how to treat it.

The only thing Cromwell could think of was that the NSA had something going he didn't know about. Which was hard to imagine. But in World War Two the Manhattan Project had been so secret, President Truman hadn't known about it till after the first successful test in New Mexico.

He hoped it was good, whatever it was.

In a Pentagon corridor, on his way to his office, he ran into a grim and harried-looking Trenary. "Good morning, Ewell," Cromwell said.

The Air Force Chief of Staff stopped so abruptly that Cromwell stopped too. "How'd you like to attend a Joint Chiefs meeting this morning?" Trenary asked. The way he said it was more a challenge than a question or invitation.

It took Cromwell by surprise. "It's not okay for the vice president to meddle in the affairs of the Joint Chiefs."

"Meddle shit! I've got some questions I want to ask you." The tone was accusatory now. "And the others are going to want to hear what you've got to say!" He started to leave.

"Just a second. Aren't you going to clear this with Pelham?"

"Pelham's home with the flu. Come on!"

Trenary started off again, and Cromwell, shrugging, followed. His good mood of a minute earlier was gone; Trenary could do that to him. *When something's bothering the Air Force Chief of Staff,* Cromwell told himself, *it's got to bother everybody.* Only Carmody seemed immune to the man. Despite Trenary's acknowledged talent for making good decisions, Cromwell wondered, not for the first time, how the abrasive little sonofabitch had made it up the chain of command.

Carmody was in the conference room ahead of them, reading, and glancing up, eyed Cromwell quizzically as he entered. Cromwell went to his old seat, Admiral Pelham's now, and sitting, began to read through the daily defense intelligence summary. Two minutes later, Hanke and Dudak walked in, paused when they saw who was in the chairman's place, then took their own. Something was bothering them, too; Cromwell recognized the signs. Chances were it was the same thing that was bothering Trenary; or Trenary himself.

When he'd finished reading through the intelligence summary, Cromwell looked up. Trenary was already done, looking impatient. Then Hanke looked up, and Dudak. *What the hell,* thought Cromwell, *why not?* He picked up the gavel and rapped the plate with it.

"All right, gentlemen. Ewell invited me here. He said he has some questions you'd want to hear the answers to. Ewell, let's have 'em."

Trenary glowered. "I presume you listened to the president's speech yesterday."

"That's right. I don't suppose there were too many people who didn't."

"And you didn't see anything wrong with it."

Cromwell knew what this had to be about, but he'd let Trenary get it off. "What did you see wrong with it?" he countered.

"Jesus Christ, Jumper! He can't get away with throwing out stuff about major new technological developments! To be released within the next few weeks, for chrissake! No one can get away with saying something like that unless they're able to produce it."

Dudak entered in. "You don't know of any secret new development, do you Jumper?"

"No, Howdy, I don't. But he's gotten pretty thick with the chief of research over at NSA."

"Shit, Jumper!" Trenary spat it out. "The NSA doesn't

have anything like that going. We'd have gotten wind of it if they did."

"Not necessarily."

"Something else, Jumper," Dudak put in. "Assume that NSA does have something going, some new development that somehow we haven't heard about. There's a matter of tool-up time, the time it takes to build plants, get into production, things like that. He made it sound like it's going to make an immediate difference. He can't get up in a couple of months and say, 'All right, we've got a workable system to generate clean, cheap nuclear power without radioactive waste. In three or four years we'll open our first fusion power plant.' Or whatever. It just won't wash."

As soon as Dudak had finished, Trenary jumped in. "And he's got the State Department completely demoralized. Do you know he fired the Ambassador to Poland yesterday? Gave him till Tuesday to get out of the country! And had Jaruzelski critique and approve his speech in advance! Jaruzelski! A goddamn Kremlin stooge! And he said he'd had a private audience with the Pope about Jaruzelski. Now when the hell could he have done that? You know damn well he hadn't been out of the country till this trip. He's hardly been out of the White House, for chrissake!"

Trenary glared at Cromwell. "And the way he's stirred things up over at CIA headquarters! Blackburn committed fucking suicide! Did you know that? Jesus Christ, Jumper! The man is turning into a disaster!"

"Okay, Ewell," Cromwell said patiently. "Let's look at some of that garbage. Jaruzelski's no Kremlin stooge; a Kremlin stooge would never have let the president read that speech on television. Something would have gone wrong—a technical failure of some kind." He paused. "How do you know the State Department is all that demoralized?"

"I was talking to Coulter yesterday, at supper."

Of course, Cromwell thought. The two of them lived in the same posh apartment building, probably ate together in the restaurant there.

"And I'll tell you something else," Cromwell said. "He did see the Pope. Two weeks ago, when he supposedly went to Nevada. I helped him set it up. He was out of town less than forty hours. He wanted to check out Jaruzelski and get a papal briefing on Poland."

Trenary's mouth opened and closed, then opened again. *"The Pope! What in hell does the Pope have to do with the United States government?! That goddamn pompous . . ."*

Carmody's voice snapped like high voltage arcing. "Ewell, shut up!" Trenary stopped in mid-sentence, staring at the normally cheerful marine commandant, and Carmody's voice quieted. "I've had about enough of you. Let somebody sane talk for a while."

Cromwell smiled grimly. Carmody probably didn't go to church except at Easter—well, maybe Christmas—but apparently he felt some loyalty to it. "That's right, Ewell," he said, "let someone else have the floor. You're overwrought.

"Hank, you haven't said anything yet."

General Hanke spoke mildly. "What bothers me has already been brought up: the president's promise of a new technology in the immediate future. I honestly can't envision what that could be, and frankly I find it very hard to believe. The morning papers featured it, and they're skeptical too."

Cromwell hadn't read a paper, nor the clipping sheets yet. The television commentators hadn't sounded skeptical yesterday though. Interested, puzzled, but not skeptical.

"Thanks, Hank," Cromwell said. "Ewell, I need to point something out to you. This is a meeting of the Joint Chiefs of Staff, not an encounter session for somebody who can't control his emotions. If you need professional help, get it."

His eyes sought for Trenary's and failed to reach them. Trenary seemed to have gone blank, deflated.

"Now, is there anything else you guys need to talk about here this morning?"

Their business took only thirty minutes more this day, and as they dispersed to their individual offices, Cromwell looked at the situation that had come up. He felt ill at ease about Trenary—about the man's fitness for command. He'd have to talk with the surgeon general about him.

Meanwhile he wished he'd thought to ask Trenary where he'd gotten his information about the CIA and Blackburn.

But Trenary, in his overreactive way, had made valid points. While as for himself—perhaps he'd underreacted.

No, he said inwardly, *don't go into that self-questioning bullshit. You'd noticed it and you'd filed it; that's all you can do. That and ask the president about it when he gets back.*

Cromwell sat down at his desk. He'd just reached for his IN basket when it hit him, the point that somehow he'd overlooked before. The others had too, perhaps because they hadn't looked beyond the seeming unlikelihood that there'd really been a big breakthrough. *If the United States, say the NSA, had some revolutionary new technology in the wings, ready for release—if there really was such a thing . . . The president had said he was going to release it all over the world! China, Japan, Poland! The Soviets would have it inside of a month—hell, inside a week—if he did that!*

And the media were sure to pick up on it. Someone there would.

Senator Brosnan had hardly ever seen things come apart quite so swiftly. This was the group that had drafted and unanimously backed the Emergency Powers Bill. Two days ago, ten of the fourteen on the committee had been in favor of leaving the emergency powers in place. One had been undecided. Of the other three, none had been anti-Haugen; more than anything else, they'd been influenced—worn down—by the arguing of lobbyists.

Then, early yesterday afternoon, the president had talked to the Polish parliament, and the world had watched and listened. The lobbyists, seeing an opening, had begun screaming before the afternoon was over, and by supper, the State Department had been leaking complaints like a sieve. It could almost have been scripted.

What the new status was in committee remained to be seen; its members still were straggling in. Those already there were discussing the matter.

"So you're unhappy with the speech," said Kreiner. "I don't mind telling you, Morrie, I wasn't overjoyed by it. But that doesn't change the continuing need for emergency powers."

"It's not as simple as that," Bender retorted. "We don't

have the powers by themselves. We have the combination of the powers and the man—Haugen. They're starting to look like a deadly combination. I wouldn't be surprised if the president's getting senile."

Margaret Bushnell's red eyebrows arched. "Bullshit," she said. "Delusions of grandeur maybe, but no way is that man senile. Look at the way he's operated until yesterday! Morrie, he can whip you in memory, mental computations, or rassling." She grinned at his facial response. "And that's pretty damn good," she added, "because you're not half bad yourself—at the first two anyway."

Brosnan grinned. She'd known how to defuse the congressman from Illinois. Self-conscious at being five-foot three and 110 pounds, he compensated by being cocky and aggressive. And when, on occasion, someone put him down, he either got truculent or very quiet. But Margaret's added sentence took the sting out of it and made truculence too awkward.

"It looks to me," Morrows was saying, "as if the president's hit a slump. He's been batting .400; then yesterday he went one for five and dropped a fly ball. That's not too bad, as long as he breaks out of it."

"Spare us the sports analogies," said Cerotti. "How the hell is he going to pull a technological breakthrough out of his hat? Who the hell writes his . . ."

Keith Huan of Hawaii was three-quarters Polynesian, a large brown man with a short thick neck and enormous chest. Almost without raising his voice, he stopped Cerotti in mid-sentence. "Has it occurred to you," he said reasonably, "that he may have one? A breakthrough? And that when he gets back, he may show it to us? Wouldn't you feel a little foolish then if we'd hurried Harmer-Van Dorn out of committee and it got rammed through a floor vote?"

Brosnan looked at the clock. Almost time to call the meeting to order. He could already see the direction things would go: No action today, and hopefully no action until they could question the president.

The biggest trouble spot just now was the business lobbies. The Warsaw speech was just a stick for them to wave, or maybe poke at the president's face with. As for Foggy Bottom, let them be upset over there. Coulter was arrogant and had long since used up the congressional good will he'd started with. He suspected Coulter was seeing his last days as Secretary of State.

Being a senator had never been easy, and sometimes it was more interesting than he liked. Actually, there'd been a lot more agreement during the emergency than he'd ever seen here before; probably the most since World War Two.

TWENTY-SEVEN

Mark heard a car and hurried to the living room window to look out into the frosty dusk. Rafe's. He drove up faster than usual, hit brakes and light switch, and skidded to a stop. The door popped open, Rafe jumped out, it slammed, and he started for the house at a trot.

"Is it Rafe, Mark?" Tris called from the kitchen.

Shit man! Mark felt a thrill run through him. *Rafe's contact must have the stuff!*

Rafe took the porch steps at a bound and burst in, grinning hugely. "He's got it!" he shouted. "He called me and he's got it! The suitcase from Allah! We can pick it up tomorrow, or tonight if we want!"

He closed the door behind him then. Phil and Tris came in from the kitchen, Mary a step behind, all talking excitedly. "The suitcase from Allah!" said Tris, and turned to her husband. "See! I said it was an Arab."

"That's a figure of speech," Mark said. "I'll bet it's not an Arab. The Arabs like revenge too much not to carry it out themselves. It's probably KGB."

Raphael Dietrich laughed. "I'll never tell." He sobered then, just a little. "We've go to decide some things now. You want to eat first or what?"

"Talk, Rafe," Mary said. "I'm too excited to eat."

"Yeah!" Phil and Tris said the word together.

An unexpected chill ran through Mark: this was it. Tomorrow—the day after at the latest—they'd be dropping the world's third atom bomb. "I'll go with that," he said. "Talk first, eat later."

They took seats, Tris and Phil leaning forward on the old sofa, Mary and Mark in overstuffeds, Rafe sitting backward on a wooden chair. "Okay," Rafe said. "It's a long drive. If you want to drop it tomorrow, we need to go get it tonight. I know where the place is, so Mark and I can go together in the pickup and trade driving. The two of us will load the thing. If we leave right after supper, we can be back by one or two in the morning.

"Or we can drive there tomorrow; whichever you want. You're the ones been so anxious."

He looked at Mark. Mark felt like he had to take a crap. "Let's do it tonight," Mark said. *And get it over with*. They turned to Phil and Tris. Phil's face was suddenly very sober; Tris was looking at him questioningly.

"Shit!" Phil said. "Tonight, I guess. I tell you what; just now I got the wim-wams."

Rafe laughed again. "You and me both, Phil baby, you and me both. They'll go away though when we see that nice mushroom cloud, and know that the boom is the death knell of nuclear power in the United States. If not the whole world."

"Yeah!" Phil said. The word carried no enthusiasm.

"So we'll bring the stuff here. Then Mark and me can get a few hours sleep before we take you guys and go load it in the plane. We ought to load it about the time it's first getting light out. There probably won't be anyone around the field that time of day to wonder what we're loading."

No one said anything for a moment. "Is that it then?" Mary asked, looking around. "Let's go eat before the food gets cold."

At Belgrade, the president's small travel staff remained at the American embassy, as usual, while the president, with the ambassador, carried out their official functions. And as usual, several messages arrived for the president. Zale looked them over. One, from Milstead, described briefly the initial congressional and press reaction to his technical breakthrough statement in the Warsaw speech.

Zale didn't give it to him. There was little the president could do about it from there, and it could be a distraction. He'd give it to him when they left Ankara, ready to start home.

The modified old four-place Cessna was flying at 3,000 feet above the west shore of Chesapeake Bay, heading south at 110 mph. The back door was gone. Freezing air snarled through the empty doorway—their bomb bay—but the numbness Tris felt had nothing to do with cold. It had everything to do with the object on the rack beside her.

She'd been visualizing a suitcase bomb, and they'd received it in something much like a metal suitcase. But inside had been a 203mm nuclear artillery shell, rigged with a cargo chute. And an artillery shell looked so overtly, blatantly deadly! In this instance it was twenty kilotons worth of deadly.

She'd almost died after Rafe and Mark had gotten it on the plane. Rafe had taken a short-handled sledge hammer from the pickup and slammed the base of the shell with it as hard as he could!

He'd grinned when she'd screamed. "I was just activating the rear fuse," he'd said over the engine noise, then leaned over Phil's shoulder. "That made the computer inside think it's been fired out of a cannon. The front fuse will activate automatically in twenty minutes. It can't go off till then. Drop it from 3,000 feet, like we talked about. It'll take an impact to explode it, but it can't go off before twenty minutes. It'll take you about fifteen minutes to arrive over target. Then Tris pushes the dump lever and out it goes. Right? You'll have five minutes then to get the hell out. Five minutes is about nine, ten miles, plenty far enough that the shock wave won't wreck you."

Then he and Mark had gotten out, and stood watching as the plane took off.

Phil's voice took her attention off the deadly cylinder beside her. "We're coming up on it," he said. She could see the Calvert Cliffs nuclear plant about two miles ahead, sitting in a break in the cliffs. "Be ready. When I raise my right hand, you grab the dump handle. When I chop it downward, dump her."

She said nothing, only nodded. The gesture was lost on

him; his eyes were on the plant, as hers were. In a few minutes, five or six, the plant would be ruined—in her imagination a seared and glassy circle.

It was an endless ninety seconds. Phil's right hand lifted, and she clutched the dump lever with hands water-weak. His head was almost pressed against the side window as they drew over the plant, but she didn't notice; her gaze was fixed on his hand. Chop!

Tris pushed the lever, harder than necessary, and the heavy shell, with its cargo-chute pack, slid down the now-tilted rack and out into the icy propellor blast. As she pulled in the static line, she heard the engine roar increase, felt the speed surge. Her guts, which had been tense before, had knotted when she'd released the bomb.

Moving forward, she took the seat beside Phil, pulling off her mittens, unzipping her mountain parka at the throat, and belting herself in. The plant was directly behind, and she couldn't watch the parachute.

Another minute passed, and another; it should be hitting the ground about now, she thought, but nothing had happened. She wondered how much time they had left on their twenty minutes, whether anyone had seen it come down, and if they had, what they were doing.

Phil had been losing altitude, as planned, to gain additional speed and hopefully get below radar pickup height. They were only a hundred feet or so above the bay, with the brow of cliffs cutting off sight of the plant, when the bomb went off. Phil had deliberately avoided watching, but had just glanced out the window at the rear-view mirror when it happened. The flash seemed to sear his eyeballs, even just seen in reflection, through glass, and for a long moment he saw nothing but after-image while he flew on reflexes.

All Tris saw was Phil's face. Her own tightened, and she clung to her seat with both hands. The shock wave, when it caught them, wasn't as bad as she'd feared, and by that time Phil could see again, fuzzily. In a vague, disassociated way, he wondered if his eyes were permanently damaged.

He looked in the mirror again, and blurred though his vision was, he could see the cloud of dust rising on its stem, bigger and more impressive than he'd expected

from something no larger than the artillery shell. It rose
and rose.

They continued flying south, without exultation, almost
without speaking. Phil visualized Air Force pilots sprinting
to fighter planes at Langley Field, and Andrews, and
probably Dover. When they reached the broad mouth of
the Potomac estuary, he climbed to 500 feet.

The pasture they were looking for on the other side was
surrounded by woods, but Phil had no trouble finding it.
The landing was rough but not dangerously so. By that
time his vision was nearly normal. He taxied the elderly
Cessna to the edge of the trees; then they climbed out
and, still not talking, hurried to a sagging shed nearby, at
the end of a wooded lane. They'd padlocked their old Ford
Tempo in it more than two weeks earlier.

The shed was cold, smelled dusty, and Phil felt appre-
hension as he slid behind the steering wheel. He put the
key into the ignition, made sure the transmission was in
park, pumped the gas his standard six times for cold
morning starts, and looked back through the open door,
where Tris stood waiting. Somehow she seemed to think
she needed to close it after them, as if they were back
home in Ohio and this was their garage.

He turned the key then. Nothing. The starter didn't
even grunt, didn't even click! He switched it off again,
then back on. Nothing.

He didn't try a third time. Didn't even try to get out of
the car. Didn't even swear! The battery's dead, he told
himself, the battery's dead. After a minute, Tris came in
and looked through the window at him.

"What's the matter? Won't it start?"

And he'd be blind tomorrow; he was sure of it. It would
happen in his sleep.

"Phil? Phil, for chrissake! Answer me!"

"It won't start," he said, and somehow got out of the
car. "The battery's dead."

They left the car. They left the plane. By now, Phil
knew, fighters would be in the air. The Cessna had been
picked up and tracked by the radar ring encircling the
capital; they knew right where it had landed. Police cars
were on the road, headed this way.

Tris led him back into the woods, where they'd have cover. They'd walk parallel to the road, she told herself. Walk till they were well away from here, then hitchhike.

She wished they hadn't been too excited to eat breakfast, or that they'd thought to bring a lunch.

The lane met a blacktop road, and she wasn't sure which way to turn. She should have brought the map from the car, she told herself, and turned to Phil. "Which way do we go?"

Phil didn't answer.

"Phil? Phil! Say something!"

"Either way," he said. "Either way."

She turned right and they hiked on through the woods, keeping the road in sight to her left. It was the first time since she'd known Phil that she'd walked faster than he did. Or that he'd walked slower than she.

TWENTY-EIGHT

In Belgrade the president spoke with Yugoslavian Prime Minister Planinc and his Ministers of Industries and Planning. The next day, in Ankara, he spoke with Turkish Prime Minister Ozal and his Ministers of Development and Defense. He made no further public addresses. It was right after his Ankara meeting that he learned of the Calvert Cliffs disaster, less than an hour after it happened. There too, John Zale gave him Milstead's messages on the flap in Congress over his Warsaw speech.

From Ankara he flew to Frankfurt, where he transferred to Air Force One and took off for the States.

He'd thought about spending a day or two at Camp David, resting; he and Lois had never been to Camp David. But this was definitely not the time. He did pause long enough at the Air Force base in Frankfurt for a shower, and a rubdown by a military masseur.

He slept all the way from Frankfurt to Andrews Field, outside D.C. By the time he got back to the White House, it was little more than an hour short of breakfast. He dropped in at the White House kitchen and arranged for his breakfast to be delivered to his desk, then took another shower. After that he walked to the Oval Office and found waiting for him a brief preliminary report on the probable environmental impacts of the Calvert Cliffs bombing. He read it quickly, then began drafting a short speech on the disaster.

At eight o'clock Milstead came in, and the president agreed to meet with Brosnan, Kreiner, Bushnell, and Bender. They were the senior members from each party and each house on the Select Committee on the Emergency. The president also asked that Speaker of the House Lynch, and Senate president pro tem Grosberg be included. If the repeal bill couldn't be stalled in committee, perhaps Lynch and Grosberg would agree to stall it on the floor until he was ready to release his "breakthrough."

Milstead commented that the nuking of the Calvert Cliffs plant had drawn media attention almost entirely off the Warsaw speech.

At 0825, Milstead returned to tell him that the people from Congress would be over at ten o'clock if that met with the president's approval. It did. Haugen told Milstead to sit in on the briefing with them; that he needed to know too.

The president finished the last intelligence summary and looked at the clock. He'd been itching to talk to Dirksma. His secretary had said the director would be in about nine, and would call. It was 0854; that left six minutes or so. Haugen reached for the next report: the weekly summary of the Public Works Administration. It had lots of tables, but the summary table was the only one he gave more than a glance to. Then he scanned the summary list of narrative points: principal complaints, principal accomplishments, major difficulties . . . It was going better than he'd expected. Quite a lot of people were actually trying to make it work, to get something done, use it for more than a paycheck. Not everyone by any means, but a lot of them. Maybe he was seeing a resurgence of responsibility.

The security phone buzzed; he keyed it on and Dirksma's face appeared on the screen. The time readout at the bottom said 0859:37.

"Good morning, Mr. President. Are you interested in a report on the Blackburn investigation now?"

"Why not?"

"I thought perhaps your time was tied up with yesterday's nuclear bombing."

"Nope. There's nothing I can do about that except make appropriate noises. What have you learned?"

"There's quite a bit of it. I've had a full written report prepared—tabbed, indexed, and summarized. It'll be on its way to you in a few minutes, by courier."

Courier. Why not by modem? the president wondered.

"In brief though," Dirksma was saying, "we have depositions by three people at the CIA stating that when he took over as director, Dr. Blackburn assigned three men, men who'd written critical reports on him, to work with the guerrillas in Malaysia. That's considered the most dangerous project they have. One refused and resigned; no one seems to know where he is now. After being flown out of Manila, neither of the other two ever reported back, which, considering their experience and other qualifications, is surprising. We suspect they were actually killed enroute.

"Next, we've interviewed several people who've given us verbal data on several offenses Blackburn allegedly committed as an agent. There's no reason to think we couldn't establish some of these as fact, if we wanted to seat a grand jury. But a lot of sensitive information would be involved—a lot of contacts would be put at risk if anything was leaked—and you know the grand jury record on confidentiality."

Dirksma paused as if contemplating grand jury leaks.

"Later, as a field project supervisor, Blackburn also worked on a research project to develop a reliable means for erasing memories and data regarding especially sensitive matters, in covert operations personnel who were going to leave the agency. We've got several notebooks of material on this; it was in a personal code, but we had no trouble breaking it. We've verified some of the contents, and there's more than enough incriminating evidence there to jail him, if he hadn't suicided. He brought foreign employees in to experiment on, and a couple of them died. We have no evidence that the procedures were ever used by the agency though, not even while Blackburn was director. Their legality is extremely dubious, even if they worked properly, and for erasing memories, they simply were not accurate. They could leave you with a vegetable or an amnesiac or an unpredictable psychotic, any of which could have brought about an investigation."

The president stared grimly into the CRT; Dirksma went on with his report.

"But maybe the most interesting thing was that he set up a private office, and presumably a private practice, in Waterbury, Connecticut. He only flew up there occasionally, and whatever he did there, he apparently kept no records and operated on a cash-only basis. We may have a lead though; we're pulling the string on that. The lab there contains the same kinds of equipment as his lab at Langley—the same stock of hypnotics, an electroshock table, and a wheeled control unit that's a lot more technical looking than usual for electroconvulsive therapy. All very expensive. We're looking into the possibility that he set it up with equipment obtained with government purchase contracts.

"And that's the bare bones of it, Mr. President. Blackburn's death still hasn't been made public, and he has no close family except a sister whom he apparently didn't get along with. Unless you prefer otherwise, we'll leave it that way, on the legal basis of national security.

"Meanwhile we'll keep digging. This could lead to some very important information."

After they ended their conversation, the president buzzed Martinelli. "Jeanne," he said, "get me General Cromwell, please."

While he was waiting, he picked up the next report, and read the cover. *A Summary of Public and Other Surveys on Justice and the Law*, by Allenby, Mildred S., University of Iowa School of Law. Haugen's eyes lit up; he'd been looking forward to this one. It should help him pitch his legal reform package when it was ready.

The people from Congress weren't overjoyed with the

promise of silence the president exacted before briefing them. But they were impressed with the briefing, and assured him they could hold off on a repeal bill vote for at least a week. The bombing, they said, would help on that; it certainly established a continuation of dangerous disorder.

A week, Haugen thought to himself, would be more than long enough.

Cromwell arrived with Gupta after lunch. Haugen rolled his chair to the file cabinet beside his desk, talking as he sorted through the hanging files.

"I certainly stirred up a hornets' nest," he said. "I got caught in my inexperience. For some reason it never occurred to me that people here wouldn't accept my remarks without evidence."

Somehow, Jumper Cromwell found the admission reassuring. Not because it showed Haugen as willing to admit error, but because it showed him able to commit error.

The president pulled out two copies of a bound report and turned back to his guests. "I'm going to tell the two of you something that, for security reasons, I didn't tell the people from Congress." Grinning, he handed the report to the general and the physicist. "Here. Give a look. It's a draft of the presentation we planned—that Duluth Technology put together—for release to the press. It's been waiting till the first installations are in operation."

Frowning, lips pursed, Cromwell opened the report and began to read the frontal summary. His brows unknitted, rose. "Jesus Christ, Mr. President! This is bigger than transistors!" He stared. "And you're going to give this to the Soviets? The Chinese?"

"The Chinese. The Soviets already have it. That's the part I wasn't ready to talk about to the congressmen."

Cromwell's mouth opened.

"And let me correct something," Haugen said. "I don't have complete proof that the Soviets have it, but the evidence is compelling."

"But—if they have this, why don't we see evidence of it?"

"The evidence is there. It's just that no one's paid attention. To the Soviets it's an ultra secret part of a weapon system. They haven't used it beyond that because they don't want us to know there is such a thing."

Cromwell looked warily at the president. "What weapon system? And why don't they know we've got it ready to release? Christ, they knew about the Manhattan Project in World War Two before President Truman did! Let's face it: They've got the best military intelligence system in the world, bar none."

"To answer your first question, the weapon system is their scalar resonance network." He looked at Gupta. "You told me the transmitters required huge amounts of electric power. And that the Soviet transmitters were more powerful than ours were until super conductors came along." He turned to Cromwell. "So why was that? And remember I asked Jim to check and see if there are nuclear reactors at those locations? He found out there aren't. There isn't even evidence of high capacity transmission lines.

"They're generating their power on-site, without nuclear reactors; without any visible power generating system at all."

He looked intensely at Cromwell. "And if you know enough to build and use scalar resonance to manipulate weather and induce earthquakes, then you have the basic concepts that allow you to develop the geogravitic power converter. All it takes from that point is some tangential investigation and enough luck and persistence. Or maybe Tesla's notes."

Cromwell stared. "Shee-it!"

"I got into it with sort of a Sherlock Holmes approach," the president went on. "Six years ago, reading on Tesla, I ran across a quote from a 1931 *Time Magazine*; I can damn near recite it verbatim. Tesla said he was working on a new *source* of power that, as he put it, would clear up a lot of puzzling phenomena in the universe. That's what he said: the universe. Then he went on that this was a source no previous scientist had turned to, so far as he knew. And that when the concept first hit him, it was a tremendous shock.

"Of course, Tesla was never a man to understate things, but I always read him with an open mind, considering the things he actually pulled off.

"Unfortunately he could also be coy. It's a valuable ancillary skill for an inventor.

"Anyway, he said it was an entirely new and unsuspected power source that would be constant day and night and at all times of the year. The apparatus for converting it into electricity would be simple, with both electrical and mechanical features, and it had nothing to do with the power of the atom."

Haugen chuckled. "Tesla didn't think atomic energy would ever be practical. He missed on that one.

"Anyway, I looked at what he'd said from every angle I could think of, and drew nothing but blanks. I tried doodling on paper, idly, waiting for something to appear out of the doodles; that's worked for me a time or three. Nothing. Then, one morning in the shower, this idea hit me: gravity! And I got goose flesh like hell wouldn't have.

"I never questioned whether I was right or not, just went on the operating assumption that gravity was it. So how had Tesla expected to convert gravity into electricity?" Haugen spread his hands. "Something simple, he'd said. Simple but apparently not easy. If it was easy, he'd have designed and built it, and died rich instead of poor.

"But I knew he'd been interested in scalar waves and resonance, including resonances transmitted through the Earth."

He chuckled. "Unlike a lot of people, I don't strain when I'm working on something. If the ideas aren't flowing, I work on something else. But I keep putting my attention back on the problem area, on the target so to speak, especially when I'm ready for bed at night. And every now and then, pop! I'll get an idea on it, most often in the morning, in the shower or on the ceramic throne, or maybe shaving.

"And that's the way it worked. After a few months I had enough of the concept to start actual research and development."

Cromwell looked at Haugen in awe. "And this thing really works? Christ on a crutch! It'll change the world!" His eyes went thoughtful. "OPEC isn't going to like it worth a damn, and neither is Standard Oil. Consolidated Edison is going to hate it!"

"Yeah. But the environmentalists will love it, and so will

everyone who pays an electric bill. And world oil reserves will last a helluva lot longer; their main use will be as raw material in synthetics manufacture. That and aircraft fuel for a while. I've even designed and patented a prototype car that'll run on it, with as much power as you'd want."

He grinned at the general. "Tractors, ships . . . And cheap, Jumper, cheap! When Tesla's AC transformer made electricity practical, it remade technology within a few decades, with relatively cheap, clean, safe, transmittable energy. This will make at least as big a difference, and a lot more quickly because of the technical base we've got now. And because this is cheaper, a lot cleaner, and you don't need to transmit it if you don't want to; you can even ride around on the generator.

"And all that without considering what it's going to do to physical theory."

Cromwell wasn't ready yet to ask what it would do to physical theory. Gupta didn't ask either; he looked as if he was already working on it mentally. "And it's ready to release?" Cromwell said. It was part question, part statement.

"Jumper, we'll have one powering an entire municipal electric system within a few days. And others are being installed, plus we've got a couple of warehouses full, ready to ship."

Cromwell sat still, awed. "Gravity! When do we get antigravity?"

Haugen laughed. "Hard to tell. Me, I'm just a jackleg engineer. Wait till the theoretical physicists start playing with this; antigravity might not take all that long."

Some jackleg engineer, Cromwell thought. Then a question occurred to him. "How come . . ." he said slowly, "How come this hasn't leaked?" And with the question, he felt a twinge of doubt. If this was real, then without the constraints of a government security apparatus, surely it would have leaked. Maybe Haugen was nuts, had dreamed all this.

"If the government had developed it," Haugen replied, "or some big university, it *would* have leaked. Almost surely. The GRU monitors them constantly; you don't need me to tell you about that. Companies like mine though, not connected with the arms industry, they apparently don't pay much attention to. And I've been calling it a geopetroleum sounder; no big deal. Told my people, those who didn't need to know the truth, that we were making them for the Arabs."

He chuckled. "As for the Patent Office—I patented it as part of something else that's not very interesting: as the power component of a track layer for heavy transport on swamplands."

Cromwell nodded. "Another thing's come up," he said. "There's a fuss over at Foggy Bottom."

"Right. The congressmen asked about that too. It seems to have started with my firing Ambassador Tyler. The man was an utter fuckup; ignorant, insolent and arrogant. An example of someone who can parrot back course material on an exam without having any idea of what it means or how to use it.

"And Coulter sponsored him. Good old Coulter, who also sponsored Blackburn. I'm offloading him, Jumper. I don't trust his competence and I don't trust his purposes. Grosberg and Kreiner are helping Milstead sort out three or four candidates for the job. Then Charles will get dossiers prepared on them."

Cromwell nodded. The president's comments had reminded him that Trenary had been sponsored for Air Force Chief of Staff by Campbell, and Campbell was Coulter's buddy. And now Trenary seemed to be.

"Sounds good to me," he said, then told the president about Trenary's upset, and the Trenary-Campbell-Coulter connection. Haugen looked interested but didn't comment.

As Jumper Cromwell came out of the president's office, his bodyguards fell in beside him. "Guys," Cromwell said, "you people better take damn good care of that guy in there. We sure as hell can't afford to lose him."

The general had hardly closed the Oval Office door behind him when the president's phone buzzed. He answered it.

"Mr. President, Director Dirksma is on line one."

"Thanks, Jeanne, I'll take it."

Dirksma's face popped onto the screen. "Mr. President, a man and woman have been arrested in Virginia. The man claimed they were the ones who dropped the A-bomb in Delaware. Of course, several others have confessed to the same thing; you expect that sort of thing after a spectacular crime. But the woman agreed with him, and they knew right where the plane was parked. They're the McCoy.

"The woman named three other people who were involved as accessories, and where they could be found; we've got two of them now, a husband and wife, and they've confessed too. The third one, a man, had blown."

The president eyed Dirksma thoughtfully. "So far, so good. You people do excellent work.

"Now I've got another job for you. It's not a criminal investigation; a lot of it can probably be done without anyone having to leave the Justice Building." He gazed levelly at the FBI director. "I want you to put together the background of Secretary Coulter."

"The Secretary of State?"

"Right. I want his full professional history, people and organizations he's been associated with, that sort of thing. Especially any history he has with Blackburn and Defense Secretary Campbell. And Air Force General Ewell Trenary. And I want to be informed as you go; don't wait till you've got the whole thing put together before you call me. Any questions?"

"No questions, sir. If any occur to me, I'll call, but that seems to be pretty straightforward."

"Good. I'll let you go now; I know you're busy."

The president disconnected, got up and started for the coffee machine; then changed his mind; he'd been pouring too much gunk in his stomach. Instead he walked to the pool-gymnasium area. He'd been exercising again, spasmodically, but not enough and not often enough. It was time to correct that; he'd promised Lois he'd take better care of himself.

TWENTY-NINE

On his second morning back, the president got a full report on the nuking. The bomb had landed in a plant parking lot; there were living witnesses to that. It had looked like an artillery shell. A guy in the lot had thrown it in the back of a pickup truck and sped away with it, horn blaring, as if realizing what it was. It had blown almost a mile away, and damage to the nuclear generating plant was not massive. There were no radiation leaks from the plant; the radioactivity released was entirely from the bomb.

A northwest breeze had carried the radioactive cloud across Chesapeake Bay and the southern Delmar Peninsula. Panic had been widespread there, where many people thought Washington had been nuked and nuclear war begun.

After the briefing, the president boarded an army helicopter and overflew the site, an action of no obvious functional but considerable political value. Afterward he met the press at the army's nuclear cleanup camp near Prince Frederick, where he delivered a two-minute address and dealt with a few questions. Then, with the first lady, he visited the refugee center near Washington, and the injured at Walter Reed Medical Center.

They were back at the White House for supper. And while he'd gotten no "work" done that day, it occurred to Arne Haugen that what he had done was as important in the functioning of a president as anything else would have been.

After supper he worked on his "new technology" speech.

THIRTY

Barron Tallmon reached for his buzzing intercom and touched the pulsing button. "This is Barron," he said. The screen remained blank. By contrast, the television in the corner of his darkened living-dining room was alive with motion and color, though he'd keyed down the sound to take the call.

"Barron, this is Massey. I'm in my office, about to watch the speech. Come down here. I may have thoughts for you to take notes on."

"Yes Mr. Massey." As he said it, Tallmon glanced at the digital clock built into the face of his set, and touched the countdown key on his remote; one minute and fifty-three seconds before nine.

"I'll be there momentarily."

"Do so."

Tallmon took the barely-touched TV dinner into his kitchenette and put it on the drainboard. *I shouldn't have waited so long to eat,* he told himself. From a stand by his apartment door, he grabbed an ever-ready clipboard, pen attached, then hurried out. A minute later he knocked at the door of Massey's sitting room/office.

"Come."

He entered. The room was lit only by the television and a small glow panel turned low beside a window. Massey spoke without taking his eyes from the screen. "There is scotch and seltzer on the sideboard if you'd care for some."

Massey had repeated the invitation innumerable times over eighteen years; the answer had always been the same.

"No thank you, sir." It occurred to Tallmon to wonder what Massey's reaction would have been if he'd said "yes sir." There would be no reaction, he decided as he took a chair a half dozen feet to Massey's left. Then, clipboard on his knee, he turned his own attention to the set.

". . . and perhaps some comment on the reported coup attempt in the Far East Command of the Soviet army." The familiar, resonant voice of CBS's Weldon Germaine paused, and dropped to an undertone. "The president has just come into the room."

The picture switched to Arne Haugen as he walked across the room and sat down at a desk. His gaze went to the camera facing him and seemed to look out at Tallmon.

"Good evening, ladies and gentlemen, fellow Americans. I have several important things to talk to you about this evening. My press secretary, Mr. Okada, tells me it's preferable to talk about only one subject in a talk like this, and I can see the logic in that. But at the rate things have been happening, tonight I need to talk about more than one."

He chuckled then, seemingly not aware of it, as he looked down at the ruled yellow sheets on the desk. Then he looked back up at the camera, his gaze and attention focusing.

"I'm going to talk to you briefly about foreign trade and a foreign affairs action I'm taking. And after that I'm going to tell you about the new technology I mentioned in my Warsaw speech; I understand there's been a lot of curiosity about that.

"But before I talk about any of those things, I need to talk to you briefly about the goal I have as your president. It's a goal I take so much for granted that I had to be away from America before it occurred to me that I needed to tell you about it."

He seemed to gaze out at Tallmon for a pair of seconds before continuing, seemed to catch and hold his eyes, and for a moment it took the man by surprise. "I have a vision of America," the president said. "Nothing magical, nothing utopian, it doesn't have heavenly choirs. But I want to tell you about it, tell you what it seems to me that America might become. If you agree with me on it; if you decide to make it that way or let others make it that way."

The president paused. Tallmon glanced surreptitiously at Massey. Massey's expression was detached interest—no stranger to his pale, aristocratic face.

"I visualize an America," Haugen was saying, "where the law defends the rights of its people, and at the same time enables them to grow and evolve individually and as a nation. Where education—" He paused for emphasis. "Where *effective* education functions freely and creatively to *help* them grow and evolve as a continuingly unique and special part of the community of Planet Earth." Another pause. "An America where the individual has more freedom than ever to shape his or her life according to his or her own developing purposes. And . . ." He slowed, enunciating the words one after the other. "Where that individual growth and development is not threatened by arbitrary bureaucratic regulations, but is constrained only to the degree necessary to protect the reasonable rights of others."

Again the president paused, eyes intent on the camera, as if looking through it at his audience. Intent but not intense, calm instead of zealous.

"An America active, rich in ideas, where new things are tried, and new ways of doing things, with no more than essential regulation. Where personal and group experimentation is respected or at least tolerated. Where the future takes form by persons and groups choosing from many alternatives or creating new ones. Where government planning agencies have no power to dictate the future. Where government's role is to ensure freedom and reasonable opportunity to grow. Where the board rooms of giant corporations cannot play big games with the economy and dictate people's choices to suit corporate ambitions." He paused again for emphasis. "Where arrogant elites do not undertake to program the nation, and through it the world, into a machine which they intend to drive."

Once more Tallmon slid a rightward glance from the corner of his eye and saw no response. Or had the expression hardened a little?

"All of these," Haugen was saying, "government agencies, corporations, self-appointed elites—all of these should be free to propose, experiment and expound, but not to coerce and dictate to the people.

"And I see the key to this future as reduced restrictions, greater individual responsibility before the law, and greater tolerance of differences, even greater respect for differences. Which is to say, the conditions which the founders of this nation intended and which a self-interested establishment has degraded.

"In about a month I will announce reforms of our legal system to move us in that direction.

"That's enough about that for now though. Let's look at foreign trade next: I've had a lot of urging to put tighter restrictions on foreign imports and even to cut off most of them entirely; cut off almost all but the importation of oil and strategic minerals.

"Decades of movement in the direction of totally free world trade have helped put us where we are. The free-trade theory is still attractive; it *seems* as if it should work. And it might have, if everyone had worked at it. Some nations tried; America tried. But too many others, for very real political and economic reasons, restricted imports while taking full advantage of freedoms to export. Many competed in world markets while paying their workers far lower wages than others did, which enabled those countries to sell at cutthroat prices. But which on the other hand enabled them to develop their primitive economies into more or less modern economies—to join us in the late twentieth century. And a few countries deliberately dumped commodities on world markets at a loss, to destroy competition.

"Let me give you just a few examples from the many I could have chosen. West Germany put restrictions on foreign poultry and dairy products that effectively held out American poultry and cheeses. Taiwan, Hong Kong, Indonesia, and more recently India exported very large volumes of clothing to us, made by workers whose pay for a day was less than American workers made in an hour. The result was that American employment in the manufacture of fabrics and clothing was cut to a small fraction of what it had been. And as some of you are aware, the economies of Finland, Sweden, and Canada crashed after the Soviet Union, selling at a loss, dumped huge quantities of coniferous timber on the world market to ruin their competitors.

"Of course, as world recession slipped toward world depression, the support for free trade fell off. Most countries acted to protect their producers at home by increasing restrictions and raising tariffs on imports of anything they produced themselves. Some reacted more extremely than others. The United States, under President Donnelly, reacted less extremely than perhaps any other country.

"I have been urged to increase both tariffs and restrictions, and I have also been urged not to. I won't go into the arguments here, except to say that recently our wage levels have dropped to the point that the prices of imported goods no longer seriously undercut the prices of goods made in America. Meanwhile the popular movement to 'buy American,' urged by President Donnelly, has helped noticeably. So the advantages of increased restrictions are not as great as some people would like to believe.

"In my second week in office, I asked the Congress for its best recommendations, and the House and Senate jointly set up a select committee to winnow through the pros and cons and hammer out a program. They've done that. And it's a convincing program but not a dramatic one. It recommends only a few moderate adjustments to the formula President Donnelly established under the authority granted him by Congress last year. The overall effects should be about the best we can get, under the circumstances. I'm instructing the Secretaries of State, Commerce, and Agriculture to carry out the Congressional recommendations.

"As for foreign policy actions, I have only one to announce. I am closing all Soviet consulates in America and discontinuing their trade missions; this evening they were given six days to leave the country."

The president paused to let it sink in.

"This is not intended as a hostile act. I am definitely not contemplating breaking off diplomatic relations with the Soviet Union or any other country. It is simply a recognition of certain realities.

"A country has consulates and trade missions in foreign nations for two purposes: One is to serve its trade interests. And the second—the second is to gather intelligence by monitoring publications and broadcasts, by recruiting spies, and by providing contacts for spies. Because we now have very little trade with the Soviet Union, their consulates and trade missions here serve little purpose except to gather intelligence, both legally and by spying. By shutting them down, I am disrupting their spy network and closing several of their monitoring centers, and we can expect them to take half a year or more to regain something approaching their present intelligence effectiveness.

"Hopefully, by then we'll be ready to trade with them on a significant level again, and to reopen their consulates here."

The president paused, then spoke more slowly, more emphatically. "Let me repeat, this action is not an act of hostility, although we can expect the Soviet government to claim that it is. That is part of their standard political response to foreign actions they don't like."

He stopped, glanced down at the papers on his desk, then back up at the cameras. "And now for something more positive, probably the most important announcement I will ever make. It deals with a major step toward renewed prosperity."

Unawarely, Tallmon leaned slightly forward at this.

"But you'll have to be patient with me," the president said, "because I'm going to set the stage with some background for it.

"The greatest boost to recovery from economic depression is new or improved technology of a kind that means more goods and services available and more jobs. What you do is *out-create* the depression. If we can produce more goods more cheaply without reducing incomes, we've beaten the depression. Some people might say this is impossible. It's not, as you'll see.

"For years we've had a worsening problem of environmental pollution. To keep pollution from getting worse, controls have been imposed. And directly or indirectly, the cost of those controls has to be paid for by the products, which has made those products somewhat more expensive. That was one cause of inflation.

"Another major cause was our dependence on petroleum for fuel, for energy. Oil prices more than tripled a year ago, making electricity, heating, and transportation much more expensive."

The president paused to sip lemon and water, then looked at the cameras again. "How would you like electricity so cheap that most homes will be heated with it? How would you like to have transportation costs drop below anything you've seen for decades? Without smog from power plants or automobile motors? Without nuclear wastes? How would you like to see these things happening in a large way within a year? That's what our new technology will give us. And the world's limited oil supplies will be left for other uses.

"The new development I've been referring to is called the geogravitic power converter; the GPC for short. You can think of the GPC as converting gravity into electricity without in any way reducing gravity. And it provides that electricity far more cheaply than any other system. The generators are cheap enough that every town and village can have one. In every nation, under congress or king, parliament or dictator, free enterprise system or marxist dictatorship.

"My technical staff and I, at Duluth Industries, completed its development less than a year ago.

"And now we get into the reasons for secrecy. At that time we recognized serious problems in getting it released for use on Planet Earth. There are financial interests who would see in it the loss of much of their influence and some of their wealth. There is also an intricate complex of laws and regulations that could be manipulated to serve as barriers, and a disinformation system that could be used to discredit it. And finally, the government could have slapped it with a *Top Secret* classification that would effectively and finally have buried it."

Tallmon dared another glance; Massey's face was rigid now. Oil formed the most important single element of his wealth.

"To get around these barriers," Haugen was saying, "we used creative imagination of a different sort." He grinned broadly. "At that time, of course, I hadn't even imagined being president, so I had to be sneaky. I came up with a two-part plan. I would secretly make a number of converters and present some of them quietly and secretly to several communities and businesses on terms they couldn't refuse. In the United States and also in foreign countries. And then, to make sure, I would franchise it to various other nations, to make them there. That would almost ensure that we could make and sell it in America.

"Today the town of Bear Forks, Minnesota, has a GPC in place on its municipally-owned power distribution system. In fact, it went on line at 7 P.M. this evening, Central Time, providing all the electricity for the town, its huge taconite refinery, and the rural area immediately around it.

"And the generator was hauled there on a bobtailed ton-and-a-half truck.

"Converters have already been shipped, air freight, to the six countries I visited recently, with technicians to help install them. Within the United States, dozens more are ready to ship to areas now being served by nuclear generators. I expect all nuclear power plants in the country to be closed down as obsolete within months.

"This is vastly more effective than demonstrations and picketing. And infinitely less destructive than the nuclear bombing carried out by psychotics in Maryland the other day.

"And the GPC is only the beginning, because it is based on discoveries new to basic physics. Scientific and technical descriptions will be in the mail tomorrow to colleges and universities, to private and governmental research facilities, all over the world."

The president paused, sipped lemon and water again, looked thoughtfully over his half glasses, and went on. "There is another side to this, of course. Bear Forks will no longer buy power from the coal-burning plant belonging to North Shore Edison. Which presents that company with a problem that will get worse as the towns of Duluth, Two Harbors, and all the rest get GPCs.

"And now you can see one reason that the financial establishment resists revolutionary new developments, unless it can see a way of controlling them and getting richer from them. And why I made it available all over the world so they couldn't suppress it."

Excitement had sneaked up on Tallmon as he listened. It was an unfamiliar feeling, yet he was too absorbed to notice.

"So what will this mean to the people who work for North Shore Edison?" Haugen asked. "It will mean a whole new set of industries and new jobs. Small villages can afford a GPC. Numerous businesses, and they don't have to be big, will be building the GPC before long. Which means jobs and payrolls. Smaller models have been built and tested and can be cheaply manufactured, that will be affordable for use on farms and ranches and ships.

For example, a small GPC will soon cost less than a new tractor, and provide more power.

"Furthermore, the high-performance, smog-free, relatively cheap electric car and tractor is now possible. A prototype has been tested and works beautifully. Any automaker can build it, and releases giving details are now being provided to the news media. Our cost analysis indicates that a family-size car can be sold at prices in the neighborhood of $4,000, in terms of last year's dollars.

"And we've only begun to explore the new physical principle that this grew out of. Research facilities of all kinds will soon be turning physics inside out, and within a very few years, new industries should be springing up all over."

The president sat silent for a moment then, as if to let what he'd said sink in.

"Of course, this won't mean the end of problems. I doubt that people will ever run out of problems. But it means the end of some serious old problems, and more important, it marks the beginning of a new advance in human achievement.

"To further help that advance, I'm setting up the Office of Scientific and Technical Innovations. Its purpose is to *test*—not simply read and pass upon, but test—proposals for new scientific and technological directions and developments. Its director will be Dr. Eddie Wing, a science consultant, and Eddie will be looking for new approaches and ideas, especially the kinds that open whole new areas, like the transistor, the microchip, the geogravitic power converter.

"Eddie's staff will receive bonuses for valid innovations found and supported. Nothing will be rejected out of hand on the basis that it's too far out, too unorthodox. Validity will be decided by tests—does it work or doesn't it?—and not by compatibility with current scientific orthodoxy. So any proposal you submit had better include practical tests that can be run on the principles involved.

"And for staff, we are not necessarily looking for authorities in the various scientific and technological fields. But competence, open minds, and active imaginations are a necessity."

The president steepled his thick fingers and seemed to

contemplate them for a moment before looking again at the camera.

"You might ask *why* such an office," he went on. "Why shouldn't people with innovative ideas take them to some corporation? They can, of course. But in too many corporations, the truly innovative is not welcome and may not even be recognized. Had I not been able to manufacture the GPC myself, but taken it instead to some major corporation, it would quite possibly have been buried as something that might hurt other areas of corporate investment. Or corporate interests might have handled it to maximize profit and corporate power, rather than human benefit.

"Mainly what we're trying to avoid here is valuable new ideas getting buried in corporate limbo. To get them developed and financed, or contracted out for manufacturing with requirements that will see them available for wide and beneficial use at honest prices.

"And that's all I have to say this time. In the future I'll be talking to organizations like the American Bar Association and the American Medical Association, but when I talk to them, I'll be talking to you at the same time.

"Thank you for listening."

The president got up then and walked off camera, and the picture cut to a New York studio where Weldon Germaine and Connie Cartwright sat waiting to comment on the speech. Massey touched a key and the picture flicked off; for a long half minute the two men sat in the semidark. Tallmon was looking openly at Massey now, waiting. The face he watched was set in granite, veneered with gray wax.

"That man is incredibly dangerous." Massey said it without looking at his lieutenant. "I want him dead. See to it. Make sure. Let as many contracts on him as it takes."

He didn't move to get up though, and Tallmon, sensing that his master wasn't done, kept his seat, waiting for the rest of it.

"Meanwhile, see that the media increase their attacks. I cannot have this nonsense taking root among the masses."

THIRTY-ONE

The president was swimming slow-paced powerful laps in the White House pool, the breast stroke in one direction and a side-wheeling backstroke in the other. He'd been swimming daily for several days, and his endurance was improving, though less than he'd expected. *Getting old*, he thought. Swimming parallel to him along the opposite side was Stephen Flynn. Their laps were out of phase— Flynn was swimming on his side, and the president did a modified racing turn at each end. The sound of their strokes and exhalations were loud in the enclosed space.

Lester Okada had entered the natatorium, and stood watching for two or three minutes without making himself known. The room was warm and steamy, and Okada felt a fine dew of sweat form on his face. Then the president stopped at the deep end, breathing heavily, and after a moment hoisted himself onto the pool deck. It was then he became aware of Okada.

"Good morning, Les. Something?"

Okada grimaced slightly. "There's always something, Mister President. I need to ask you some questions before I talk to the ladies and gentlemen of the Fourth Estate this morning."

"Go ahead."

"Mister President, I know these people pretty well; I know how they think. After all, I was one of them a few years ago. Some of them are going to take the position that your talking about the geogravitic power converter, in your last speech, amounted to using your position to promote your commercial products."

The president's brows formed a gnarled ridge above his

eyes, then gradually relaxed. "If anyone asks that question, tell 'em it's too stupid to dignify with an answer."

Okada waited a moment before responding. "Do you really want me to tell them that?"

The president grinned. "Sure. Tell them you asked me, and that's what I told you. And if they seem unhappy with that, ask 'em: Does that bother you? And if one of them says yes, tell him he needs to develop a thicker skin. Tell them they insult politicians and other public figures often enough, and that what *I* said was at least the truth. Okay?"

Okada looked at the president. "I'm not sure if you're kidding me or not, sir."

Haugen's eyebrows arched this time; then he laughed. "No, I really mean it. You can reword it if you'd like, to suit your style, but that's the message. That's probably what I'd tell them if they asked me."

He got up from the edge of the pool deck, and at the other end, Father Flynn got up too. "Anything else, Les?" Haugen asked.

"Yes sir. Last night you didn't address the rumors about the OSS. The rumors that you've got everything over there in a turmoil, and that the FBI is running a purge there."

"Okay. Don't answer any generalities unless there's an advantage in it. If someone says something about 'everything in a turmoil over there,' ask them what they mean by 'everything in a turmoil.' " The president made quotation marks in the air with his fingers. "And then don't answer any more questions till one of them's answered yours. When they have, then pin them down on the next generality, like what they mean by a purge. Or however they put it. Tell them the FBI has been investigating one person there, ex-Director Blackburn."

"Suppose they ask about Blackburn, sir?"

The president stood thoughtfully for a moment. "If they ask the question, tell them the truth. This is one we don't want to be cagey about. Just don't let them walk on you. Don't answer bullshit questions; pin them down to real-world questions and answer those.

"And don't let them play prosecuting attorney with you. Take a lesson from Wheeler. When that arrogant asshole Samuelson got too offensive, he had him removed and never let him back in. And 200 million people applauded."

The president paused. "And speaking of the real world, better check with Dirksma at the FBI first, and make sure it's still just Blackburn he's investigating in the OSS; he hasn't updated me the last couple of days. But I think he's finished asking questions across the river anyway."

Okada nodded, not entirely happy. "Another thing, sir. Is there anything further I should know about the State Department? I expect I'll get more questions about it, too."

"Tell them you've said all you have to say about that. That Mr. Tyler and I had serious disagreements on his performance in Poland, that our discussion became heated, and that he said he could no longer function as ambassador there. That I then relieved him from duty and he has since resigned from the State Department. That's what you told them yesterday, right?"

"In substance, yes sir."

"Good." He looked the press secretary over. "You're doing a good job, Les, and I appreciate your staying on here. If they surprise you with something, trust your judgment, whether it agrees with mine or not. Chances are you'll say the right thing. And I'm seldom hard on honest mistakes."

Then the president and Flynn went to the dressing room.

"Mr. Okada's afraid of you, Arne," said the Jesuit.

"You're right, he is, a little," Haugen answered. "But mainly he's afraid of the White House press corps. What scares him about me is that I ask him to be tough with them. He's a good, decent man, Steve, and he's capable. He's even shown he can be hardnosed in a pinch. But he has this consideration that he has to be nice to people." The president pulled off his trunks, wrung them out, and hung them on a peg. "And it's preferable to be nice to people," he went on. "It really is. But it's trouble when you feel as if you *have* to be."

"What are they going to say when you announce that you're firing Secretary Coulter? After saying the trouble was with Ambassador Tyler."

The two men walked into the well-lit, white-tiled shower room.

"Tyler and Coulter are two separate troubles. And I can't tell the press I'm firing Coulter until I tell Coulter. That would be a helluva thing to do."

Haugen turned the water on and gave his attention to adjusting the temperature, then ah-ahed with pleasure as the coarse hard spray beat on his back. "I should have another report on Coulter from Dirksma today," he added. "Then I'll know what I can say about my reasons. And I can contact my selection to replace him. Rudolfo Valenzuela."

"I don't know him."

"He's the Dean of International Studies at Miami of Florida. Milstead put together an interesting dossier on him."

"At Miami. Is he Cuban?"

"His parents were; they left during the Battista regime and settled in Puerto Rico. He started out as a poor black kid quarrying marble with his dad. Heavy damn labor." Through the spray, Haugen grinned at Flynn. "Reminds me of me; maybe that's one reason I like him so well. Then he joined the army—101st Airborne; served in Viet Nam. Decorated, made first sergeant, then went to school on the GI Bill, like a lot of guys." The president turned off the water, and stepping out of the shower room, took a towel from a stack of them. "He was Deputy Secretary for African Affairs under Wheeler, and served as Wheeler's envoy to Cuba after Castro died. He's the one who worked out the agreement that Wheeler closed with Colonel Lopez."

Valenzuela sounded to Flynn like a good choice—experienced and effective. And being black *and* Hispanic, he'd have certain advantages at home from the political point of view. It occurred to Flynn then to wonder why Coulter had been appointed secretary—what his qualifications had been. He asked the president.

"You'd have to ask Donnelly. When Wheeler died, Alford stayed on at State until the end of Donnelly's partial term; then resigned. He had health problems. Then Donnelly appointed Coulter. Coulter'd been a professor of political science at the University of Colorado, and I suppose they'd gotten to know one another back there when Donnelly was in state politics."

Haugen hung his towel on a peg. Someone unseen would come within minutes and the wet towels would disappear, to show up anonymously later on, among others, laundered soft and white and neatly folded. He put on his shorts, then took his shirt from a hanger and thrust thick hairy arms into the sleeves.

"It's not the greatest time to change secretaries over at State," he added. "But it's better than keeping someone who's got strange fish of his own to fry." He pulled his slacks on and buckled his belt. "And I'm perfectly willing to have malfeasance charges filed against him, if Dirksma comes up with proof of anything."

Scowling, Paul Willard Randolph Massey tossed aside the editorial section of the *New York Times*; it landed on top of three others. Reading it, one might almost think the *Times* approved of Haugen, praising as it did with faint and equivocal damns. And two of the other papers had been no better.

He looked at the clock: 2:41. In nineteen minutes, Keller and Johnson were due to arrive for their meeting.

He got up from his chair and began to pace. Normally Massey was a mild and patient man, but Haugen's speech had stirred some deep and restless poison in him. Pausing, he stared unseeing through the wall-size window toward the Statue of Liberty and wondered what Barron had done toward getting more satisfactory performance from the press.

He was becoming frustrated with Tallmon again. And he couldn't threaten him with "Merriman" because Merriman seemed to have disappeared. Nor had he taken time yet to find anyone else with Merriman's expertise. He wasn't sure there was anyone else.

It was the kind of thing that, ordinarily, Tallmon would take care of for him.

Massey felt suddenly tired. Things were becoming difficult, and he no longer had the force he'd had ten, twenty years ago. Perhaps he should pass more of the responsibility to Keller and Johnson. He gathered himself then, and inwardly shook off the thought. Not now; not yet. This was just a mood; he'd feel better tomorrow at home.

Barron Tallmon had not been about to send the thick, 9 X 12-inch envelope with the mailman, nor even mail it at the village post office in East Roughton. Not addressed as it was. Instead he weighed and stamped it and took it all the way to Waterbury, dropping it in a curbside box outside the main post office. Before he pulled back into traffic, he glanced at his dashboard clock: 2:41. He wondered what Massey was doing at 2:41.

Not that it made any difference to him, Tallmon told himself. Massey had no teeth; he used other people's teeth. And outside of politics and finance, Massey didn't know the ropes, didn't have the contacts to hire the teeth himself. He, Tallmon, was the one Massey depended on to arrange the occasional assassination.

Except, of course, for Merriman. Merriman with his dangerous people. Massey knew Merriman. But Merriman had dropped out of contact. Maybe he was in a cell somewhere, or maybe dead. Considering the kinds of things Merriman did to people, neither one would be surprising.

THIRTY-TWO

Besides the de facto members, the National Security Council meeting was attended by specialists from the Department of State and the CIA. Coulter wasn't there; Haugen had fired him two days earlier, along with Campbell at Defense. Actually, he'd requested and accepted their resignations. Haugen had appointed Assistant Secretary Harold Katsaros as acting secretary of state, bypassing Coulter's deputy. An assistant secretary recommended by Cromwell was acting secretary of defense.

And Stephen Flynn was there, sitting out of the way, observing.

Also there, as a consultant, was Rudolfo Valenzuela. He hadn't agreed yet to take over at State, but he hadn't said no either. Apparently he wanted to test the water; at least he'd agreed to sit in today. The principal subject of the day's meeting made it an ideal time to have him there, for he was exceptionally knowledgeable about both South Africa and Cuba, and could even be called a personal friend of Colonel Juan Augustin Lopez, Cuba's president.

The basic briefing on the first topic had been little more than an oral summary of the written report. Strong military forces of the *Republiek van Suid-Afrika*—the RSA— had rolled into Namibia. Namibia was ruled by the Marxist-oriented native SWAPO, and increasingly, SWAPO had been supporting sabotage and guerrilla activities in the RSA.

To the north of Namibia, in Angola, the Cubans had approximately 20,000 mercenaries, hired from the Cuban government by the Angolan government. This was the largest Cuban armed force outside Cuba since Lopez had evicted Moscow's advisors, reopened diplomatic relations with the United States, and signed a trade agreement.

And while the Cuban government was no longer influenced by the Kremlin, it still supported indigenous revolutions. Lopez was quite prepared to send his Angolan force south into Namibia to help SWAPO against the Afrikaners.

"Suppose they do?" asked the president. "What then?"

"It'll make a battlefield out of Namibia," said the State Department specialist. "There are a lot of Namibians who aren't political. They'll be caught in the middle. And the Cubans will take a drubbing, which Lopez won't like. He'll be looking to us to intervene."

"Is that right, Jumper? The South Africans would drub the Cubans?"

The general nodded. "Absolutely. First of all, the Cubans there are short on armor and air support since they crowded the Soviets and East Germans out. Most of the armor and planes had been Soviet, and the Sovs took almost all of it home with them. And the Afrikaners are not only well equipped for war there; they've been ranked fifth in the world in the quality of their army, between France and the United States. Although I could make a good case for ranking us ahead of them."

"Huh! Where does Cuba rank?"

"Eighteenth. Which is damn good for a third world country. To give you an idea, the Soviets are rated thirteenth. But eighteenth is quite a way below fifth. And in Angola, as I said, the Cubans are short on armor and air support."

"Then why would Lopez send his people south? I presume his contract with the Angolans only holds good for Angola."

"It's partly a matter of face: The Cubans have a Latin style of honor. And while they've pulled out of Moscow's Comintern, their government is still basically Communist; just independent-minded Communist."

Valenzuela spoke then. He was a fairly big man with a deep resonant voice, powerfully built but a bit overweight. His hands were even larger than Haugen's and just as beefy. "I'd be surprised," he said, "if Colonel Lopez wouldn't like a way out. Which might be something we can provide him with to our advantage."

"Tell us about that," said the president.

"Namibia used to be a German colony, until 1915 I believe it was. There's still a sizeable German population on the coast there. More important, after World War Two, West Germany traced down all they could find of the old native colonial army veterans and paid each of them a healthy bonus. In native terms, that was true wealth, and it made a strong impression on the Namibians. I was impressed at how highly they regarded the West Germans."

"What are you suggesting, Dr. Valenzuela?"

Valenzuela turned to Katsaros and grinned. "What do you think we could get out of the Germans, Hal?"

"I think," said Katsaros thoughtfully, "that we might talk the Germans into providing a squadron of A-111G ground-support fighters and possibly one of F-16 interceptors. To operate out of the airfield at Walvis Bay; the South African army will probably control Lüderitz before we could get the Germans there. And assuming we succeed, well, the Afrikaners have a lot of respect for the West Germans. I'd be very surprised if they'd risk fighting them." He turned to the president and smiled. "Ask General Cromwell how the West Germans rank in the quality of their armed forces, Mr. President."

One of Haugen's eyebrows raised. "How about you telling me?"

"They rank first, sir. Just ahead of Great Britain and Israel."

"Huh! West Germany and Great Britain first and second! Interesting. Supposing the Germans agree. Then what? I don't suppose they'd want to stay there indefinitely. How would we follow up on that?"

"Then we get President Lopez, or his foreign minister, to lean on SWAPO to stop agitating, while we lean on the RSA to move out of Namibia."

"And you think Lopez would be willing to do that? And SWAPO?"

"I wouldn't guarantee it," said Katsaros. "But I think there's a very good chance. Lopez must know the difficulties his troops would face there. And I'm sure SWAPO does too. Most of Namibia is desert grassland and open scrub—poor country for fighting a tough, mechanized army like the RSA's. Especially one with air support."

The president frowned thoughtfully. "It looks to me as if the best we could hope for was a return to the old status quo then, and I don't see how that could last long. My impression is that the Afrikaners get more intransigent year by year; that they don't even pretend anymore. And the blacks get less willing to accept the way things are."

No one said anything. Haugen turned to a CIA specialist. "Werner, your brief didn't say anything about the RSA having nuclear weapons, so I suppose they don't. Right?"

"That's right, Mr. President. We can feel pretty sure they don't, regardless of rumors to the contrary. First, they don't need nuclear weapons, and they've made a point of saying they don't want them. Frankly, they're afraid the rest of the world would gang up on them if they did. But the key reason for our assumption is that their information security isn't good. There are too many white South Africans who, more or less secretly, are anti-government. And not just whites of British or Australian or other non-Afrikaner backgrounds; they include more than a few Afrikaners too. So if they ever get nuclear weapons, I'd be damned surprised if someone didn't leak it to us, or to the British, in very short order."

Haugen nodded and looked at Katsaros. "If they're going

to have a war down there within a few years anyway, mightn't it be better if they did it now and got it over with? In a few years the RSA might have those nuclear weapons."

"Mr. President," said Katsaros, "I'd prefer to prevent any war if we can, or any war I can envision off-hand. On the admittedly optimistic principle that if we delay hostilities, something may occur to cancel a war there indefinitely. The circumstances tending to bring about a war may change. We didn't invade Cuba, and after thirty-odd years, Cuba disconnected from the Kremlin. We didn't invade Nicaragua, and the Sandinistas, under Cuban pressure, also disconnected from Moscow. Then centrist Sandinistas took control, and suddenly that problem was gone."

Haugen didn't respond at once. After a few seconds he looked at Valenzuela. "How does that sound to you, Doctor?"

"Every case has to be considered on its own set of particulars. But certainly in this case I agree with Secretary Katsaros."

"All right," said the president, turning back to Katsaros. "Then if we go that route—if we ask Lopez to intervene with SWAPO—who in Namibia do we ask to allow the Germans to come in? Assuming the Germans are willing. How do you propose to actually do this?"

"First," Katsaros answered, "we ask the Germans if they're willing. They're the bigger question. Then, if the Germans are willing, we talk to President Lopez, because we need his agreement. His people would be the ones to talk to SWAPO. Then, if Lopez is willing, we lay it on the line to the RSA."

The president frowned and looked at Valenzuela. "Dr. Valenzuela, what is the state of mind in the Republic of South Africa just now? Among the whites?"

Valenzuela didn't hesitate. "Among the majority of the white population, the state of mind is ruthless determination not to yield an inch on apartheid. And during elections, they've removed from government anyone with any visible tendency to compromise. The liberals have been gone from government for decades, the moderates for years. So among those who govern, the state of mind is three parts ruthless determination and one part desperation. Desperation because in government they have a better view of the situation, and they're the ones who have to make things work, or try to.

"There is also a minority of whites with moderate inclinations, who don't say much except to each other. These are people who don't see their way free to leave, at least not yet. South Africa is their homeland. They have property, position, family ties, generations of family history there. And a high standard of living. What they don't have is influence or hope. I have little idea of how many they are, but they are there. I've talked to a few of them, and to some who've left. We cannot expect anything from them, however."

The president nodded. "Ruthlessness and desperation, you said. So what can we expect to accomplish by talking to the South African government? Except to buy time?" He didn't wait for an answer; the question was rhetorical. Instead he asked, "What is the state of mind of the black Africans there?"

"That's harder to say," Valenzuela answered. "Our communication is with the educated few. A Bishop Desmond Tutu, a Wilfred Mpumelele. But the really important blacks there are the illiterate tens of millions who have no one we can read as a barometer. So we judge as best we can from riots and demonstrations, and those are abnormal situations, not representative. Then there are tribal differences. And the men who clean streets no doubt feel differently about things than the farm hands, who look at things more or less differently than the mine laborers. While what we might call the reservation blacks will have their own attitudes.

"But I believe we can assume that there is increasing unity, a generally lower flash point, and a greater potential for widespread violence, really terrible violence, than there was a few years ago."

The president nodded and turned again to Katsaros. "And you still believe we should try to cool this situation, and hope something happens to prevent a future war there?"

Katsaros nodded without hesitation. "Yes sir, I do. And we should try to make things happen to prevent that possible future war."

Haugen nodded. "All right then, go for it," he said.

"You have my approval and support. But off the record, I'm not optimistic. Not very hopeful and definitely not optimistic."

He fixed Katsaros with his eyes. "I'll want to see some sort of follow-up plan aimed at preventing a holocaust later. And if we're going to have a plan, we need some sort of long-range goal to start with. Work on it.

"Now. Are we done with this topic?" His gaze swept the table. "Apparently we are. Our next topic is the Soviet situation in Iraq-Iran." He turned his attention to the CIA specialist on that subject. "Mr. Batzer, how reliable is that estimate of Soviet casualties? Twenty-three thousand looks like a lot, considering their weapons superiority."

"It is a lot, Mr. President, but actually it's conservative. It's really 23,000 killed, missing, and *disabled*. It doesn't include wounded treated in the field or at field hospitals and returned to duty; just those evacuated from the war zone."

"Where did you get the data?"

"Mostly from our wide-gullet broadcast recorders. We get all kinds of radio traffic on them, even the breakdown reports from trucks on the road. With regard to casualties, we have order-of-magnitude checks based on an abundance of SR-71 and satellite photography."

"And what's the basis for the prediction that the Soviets won't be in Baghdad for at least a week?"

"That's a judgment call based on a complex of factors: Soviet logistics problems, like heavy early snows in the Zagros, and continued interruption of roads by raids and bridge destruction. And the number of Iraqi units—quite a few of them, actually—that have joined with Iranian units to fight the Soviets. Sort of a 'let's get together and bust the Russian infidels' attitude. The return of the refugee Iraqi fighter squadrons from Saudi Arabia, where they'd fled earlier when the Iranians broke through. And thirty or thirty-five thousand Kurdish irregulars, a lot of them down out of Turkey, taking advantage of an opportunity to fight Russians.

"When it comes to technology, organization, and discipline, the Soviets have every advantage, and they'll win just about every face-off. But the Iranians and their allies have the edge when it comes to morale, or maybe fervor's the word. . . ."

By 1040 hours they'd completed the agenda. The president looked the group over. "Before we break up," he said, "let me state that I have a lot of respect for the people sitting here now. Dr. Valenzuela, I hope you decide to accept my offer of the secretariat. I'm sure that Mr. Katsaros would prove a very competent and ethical Secretary of State, but it seems to me that you are the man for the hour. And if you decline to serve as secretary, I hope you'll agree to be my special envoy to El Presidente Lopez on this South African matter."

After the NSC meeting, Flynn and the president swam slow laps for twenty minutes, showered, and had lunch in the Oval Office to the twelve o'clock news. The pundits of television were being critical today, not in any big resounding way but about some of the inevitable flubs and fumbles in the public works program.

The current biggie had the president shaking his head in awe: For some unstated and impenetrable reason, some nitwit district supervisor in the PWA had had a bridge built that went over nothing. The video camera showed it, a modest three-lane structure of steel and concrete that would have been about right for a fifty-foot-wide river. But there was no river. Not even a creek. Not even a dry wash. Just Texas panhandle ranchland confidently waiting for spring.

"The human mind," the president said in mock awe, "is a wondrous and mysterious thing." He made a mental note to have someone's ass run up the flagpole for that, unless they had a compelling explanation.

When they'd finished eating, Flynn looked at the president.

"Arne," he said, "I've got a question about this morning."

The president switched off the set. "Okay. Let's hear it."

"You approved the proposal to get the South Africans out of Namibia and postpone a nasty war there. But you seemed to think that postponement wouldn't have any lasting effect. And that the war, when it did come, might be worse for the postponement. What decided you to approve?"

"Politics, Steve. International image. Aided and abetted

by the slight hope that postponement might turn into cancellation, but that wasn't the decisive factor. The bigger factors were, one, that getting the Afrikaners out of Namibia will make us look good. And two, it could inspire a little more hope for future peace. Also it's a precedent for squelching a military takeover of a neighbor; we're short on precedents like that these last few decades.

"And it'll make the Cubans feel important, which they are, and put them in a peace-keeping role."

The president looked for another factor but didn't find one. "That's about it."

Father Flynn nodded, then sipped his coffee thoughtfully.

"What're you thinking?" asked Haugen.

"When I asked the question, I really hadn't looked past the matter of a South African war; I was looking at it in isolation. But you're right."

He paused then. "And one other thing."

Haugen's brows raised.

"Just postponement is worthwhile, all by itself. I'm sure that God judges it so."

Haugen nodded.

Flynn wondered what the nod meant—whether the president agreed, or was acting agreeable, or simply acknowledging the statement. But he didn't ask. There were times when it was best to let things be.

Fairly often, Lois Haugen prepared supper herself, in the little kitchen Jacqueline Kennedy had had built off the family dining room. Often it was a very simple meal; this time it was a mixture of American and Scandinavian elements—Swedish sausages, plump and savory, buttered corn bread, and green salad, with the inevitable coffee, decaffeinated. When the sausages were gone—there'd been only two each—and they were sipping coffee, she asked about his day.

"Not bad," he said, "not bad at all. We think we may be able to avert a nasty war in Namibia, and Valenzuela agreed to take over as Secretary of State. I'll be surprised if he doesn't do a damn fine job, and it'll be good PR, too. The media will stop yapping about my firing Coulter and talk about Valenzuela, whom they're almost sure to approve of.

"And Milstead tells me the number of threats on my life has about doubled lately, so I must be doing something right." As he mentioned the threats, he watched his wife's eyes.

She never flinched; in fact, she smiled. "You must indeed," she said. Then: "I'm glad you're swimming instead of jogging these days."

He nodded. He'd thought about dropping exercise; physically he didn't have the recuperative power he'd had even a few months ago. "And one other thing," he said. "Jumper Cromwell got something very interesting in the mail yesterday, and gave it to me after the NSC meeting." He got to his feet. "I brought a photocopy for you to look at."

It was on the dining room mantel, above the flickering fireplace fire. Getting it, he gave it to Lois, who opened it—a sheaf of xeroxed sheets bound in a ring binder by Cromwell's Pentagon secretary. The title page read: *Redeclaration of Purpose, the Archons, 1928*, by John Simmons Massey. She looked questioningly up at her husband.

"It explains itself," he told her, and smiled slightly. "When you've read it, Jumper's report on the Holist Council will take on a whole new dimension."

She set it aside. "Dessert first, if you're willing to help me eat it. I broke down and asked Mr. Birmingham to send up a quart of French vanilla; it's in the bottom of the refrigerator, softening. We can't overeat *too* badly with just a quart."

He grinned at her. "Ice cream, the principal vice of senior citizens. Sounds good." He gestured as she moved to get up. "I'll fetch it. I'm a president, not a king."

In three minutes he was back with two soup bowls of ice cream and a squeeze bottle of fudge topping. "If we're going to load up on calories," he said, "we might as well do it right."

It didn't take them long to finish it, and when it was gone, he left for his office. Lois took the tray back into the kitchen. Then, with the ring binder, she went into the sitting room and began to read.

THIRTY-THREE

The President's January 12 address on legal reform, before the American Bar Association special conference.

Thank you, ladies and gentlemen, members of the bar, for having me here. I appreciate the opportunity to talk to you. I want to point out though that what I say here is said not only to you but to the rest of the nation. Many other Americans will be as interested as you are, because my subject is legal reform, and it affects them as much as it does you, if less directly. Others won't be much interested in what I say, but almost all of them will be very interested in the results.

I'm going to open with a story; I believe that's how guest speakers usually start. I have a friend, an attorney, who used to belong to the same wrestling club as I did, when we were still willing to subject our bodies to that kind of stress. One day while we were warming up, someone said to him, "Jack, does it bother you to hear what some people say about the legal profession?"

And Jack said, "Like what?"

"Well, like what a bunch of crooks lawyers are supposed to be."

"No," said Jack, "it doesn't bother me that they say things like that. What bothers me is, there's so much truth in it."

Incidentally, I called Jack Mestrovic and got his approval to tell you that story.

Now, I didn't come here to insult lawyers. I opened with that story simply to illustrate a common view: that the profession of law, including the judiciary, is riddled with dishonest—sometimes criminally dishonest—people. And that there is some substance to that public attitude.

An attitude which is only a part of the widespread public distrust of our justice system.

So tonight I'm going to talk about legal reform, a new package of law which will go into effect very soon.

Before I talk about this legal reform package, I'll describe very briefly how it was developed. As you know, I'm an engineer, not a lawyer. But with my customary immodesty, I approached legal reform by roughing out a program myself, based on how things looked to me. I did this my very first two weeks in office, because without reform of the legal system, I could see little hope for the future of democracy in this country.

From my opening anecdote, one might get the notion that I ascribe the problems of the legal system to dishonest lawyers. Dishonest lawyers *are* an element in the situation, and so are the opportunities to exercise greed within that system. But the major faults lie in basic assumptions and procedures so taken for granted that many Americans assume they are unchangeable, perhaps chiseled into stone on Mt. Sinai, or programmed into the universe, or at least written into our Constitution.

Which of course they are not.

Perhaps the most basic of these working assumptions seems to have grown out of royal word-splitting. The king, let's say, wanted to get rid of Someone. Legally. So he said the law really meant such-and-such, and that Mister Someone was in violation of that law. Off with his head! So it seemed very desirable, in the interests of justice, to be extremely explicit in legal language. To leave a minimum of opportunity for interpretation. And what interpretation was necessary would be done by someone who was not the king and who was not controlled by the king. Or the president, if that's what you have as head of government.

It would be done by independent judges. Which *seems* to make sense.

Most of this is not written into the Constitution, however, let alone having been given by God to Moses. The Constitution stays pretty much out of the subject, except to assure certain rights, such as jury trials, and to establish the Supreme Court. It leaves judges free of presidential control.

How well has this worked, here in these United States? The answer is the state of justice and the state of the public defense in this country: It's kind of worked, but it labors harder and harder, costs more and more, and runs slower and slower. And all too often it doesn't get where it's supposed to go. If a truck ran like that, we'd overhaul it or trade it in.

And frankly, ladies and gentlemen, in today's crowded technological world, if we can't get the legal system to work better than it has been, then everything else we might do toward restoring the social, political, and economic health of our country will be wasted. The land of the free and the home of the brave will continue to become, more and more, the land of the frustrated and the home of the rebellious.

Did you get that? You need to. We all need to.

You might ask what made me think I was qualified to draft a program of legal reform. First of all, I'm an engineer, a designer of systems, and a solver of problems. And like most citizens in this country, I have opinions on law. A citizen doesn't need to be a lawyer to look around and see how well or how poorly our legal system is working.

What is our legal system supposed to do? Make us a buck? Give us a game? Basically the legal system— the laws themselves, the enforcement agencies, and the system of courts and judges—has the purposes of defense and justice. Of defending the individual and society from harmful acts, and providing justice to individuals and groups.

Obviously our system could have been far worse.

It's been good enough that people have been willing to ride with it. But more and more it's been struggling. Good people within the legal system keep bailing, but it keeps settling in the water despite their earnest efforts. My job is to keep it from foundering, and democracy with it. And that's what I've undertaken to do.

So I looked at what seemed to be right and wrong with it, and what common sense suggested could be done about it, and then I wrote it up. Next I worked it over a couple of times and then showed it separately to three attorneys. After swearing each of them to secrecy. Each of them is prominent and experienced, and none of them knew I'd shown it to the other two. I pointed out to each of them that what I'd given him was a trial draft, a playing with ideas. And that what I wanted particularly was their opinion on whether it could be made constitutional. And workable. And what parts served justice and what parts didn't. I asked him to read it while I sat there with him—or her in one case. To read the whole thing before commenting.

So they read it while I waited. Then they commented and I taped what they said.

I should also mention that all three of those attorneys were people whom I knew to be more or less critical of the legal establishment. Their positions and experience, on the other hand, were considerably different one from the other. And I'd heard that one of them was a frequent reader of science fiction, so I hoped that she, at least, could take a rather free-wheeling viewpoint.

I suppose this is a good time to tell you who those three attorneys are. You all know their names: Judge Curtis Liederman, Professor Ellen MacLieth, and Senator Bob Lawes.

After we'd discussed the rough draft, I worked it over again a couple of times, making substantial changes, and called all three of them in for a joint conference. After we'd read it over together, I told them I wanted each of them to draft his own version of it—to give me a workable system that included what I considered basic principles. And to do that without consulting one another.

Their results were very similar. Then we all got together and spent a day talking them over, after which the three of them drafted a final form which we edited together.

So that's how the package came to be. The next question is, what's in it? What does it say?

I'll get to that. But first I need to talk about the problems, starting with laws and the police. What kind of system is it that requires an officer to enforce laws that shouldn't be? Laws that don't make sense, or are harmful? Or unenforceable? We require too much of a police officer when we ask him to use double-think—when we ask him or her to justify, to himself or herself, police actions that are not justifiable. Or when we throw his or her careful work into the trash through some judicial stupidity.

I've heard it said that the only thing wrong with law enforcement is that it's in the hands of humans. Actually it was Arnold Mansford who said that, to several million of us on television a year or so ago. Arnold, what would you suggest? Robots? If robots were available that were sophisticated enough, advanced enough, and we turned to them for our police services, it would be—a disaster. No one should be enforcing the law who can't exercise subjective human judgement. As someone involved in research and development on robots, I assure you that humans are infinitely preferable to robots and computers for dealing justly with anything as complex, variable, and subtle as human behavior and human society. For dealing with anything so unamenable to accurate mathematical expression.

Yet in training police officers, and in managing police forces, too often the model striven for seems to be the robot. As if the ideal policeman should operate as an organic robot. This, along with unreasonable demands, and the inequity, unenforceability, and arbitrary stupidity of so many laws, especially as they stand interpreted, tends to warp too many officers toward emotional dullness—toward the non-human, insensitive condition of the robot or computer.

What is needed in law enforcement is intelligent, fair-minded officers well informed in the principles of justice and well trained in the functions of police. Men and women trained and permitted to be tolerant but tough, *understanding but responsible*. And the system of laws should be one they can feel honorable, if not always comfortable, about enforcing.

As for the courts, all too often they have frustrated the citizen looking for justice, or looking for guidance in behaving reasonably and within the law. Too often the courts have frustrated intelligent efforts to improve conditions, and all too often they have also frustrated the police. Despite the efforts of many good men and women in the legal profession, American courts are too often a failure and sometimes a disgrace.

Incidentally, I am not saying that the police should have the right to do whatever they wish. The purpose of law is not the convenience of law officers, and necessary restrictions will remain. Actually, most of the laws constraining police behavior will remain, but some laws will change, and the courts will change.

We cannot reasonably expect the legal system to be perfect, but it must be adequate. And as it stands, it falls too far short of providing reasonable defense and justice. In the guise of justice, the system has sometimes led to injustice, very often delayed justice, and all too often no justice. Ask many of the people who've been there. Too often it has undermined both order on the one hand and reasonable liberty on the other.

How did this happen? It was a matter of cooperation between legislators and citizens who either were shortsighted or had some degree or other of tunnel vision. And by activists and special interest groups. Some operated with avarice, some with the best of intentions, and all too many with intolerance. Too often the battlecry has been "Pass a Law!" Or more exactly, "Pass *My* Law!—the law that will give me an advantage. Or the one that fits my prejudice." And lawmakers passed these laws by the uncounted thousands.

Many of those laws, considered singly, seem like good ideas. But taken en masse, they grew to be a legal disaster that too often has strangled rights and perverted or denied responsibility.

And the legal profession, acting within the justice system, and in legislatures and the Congress, has failed to keep things from getting worse. The popularity of "Dirty Harry," and of vengeance movies, tells us something about the public attitude toward our legal system.

So I'm making some changes before it's too late. Before the people, in final disgust, turn to real-life Dirty Harrys and to gun law.

The Constitution doesn't allow the federal government a whole lot of authority over state courts. Although it gives us more than some might think, and we're taking advantage of every bit of it. So the reforms I'll talk about deal mainly with federal courts and laws and to some extent with those of the individual states. And I invite the American people to demand that their legislatures pass similar legal reforms.

Some attorneys will applaud these reforms, and some will howl. I invite the American people to consider the howling as a reflection of pain in attorneys' bank accounts. Also, keep in mind that many legislators are lawyers, and that some of them will give all sorts of reasons not to reform state law. Don't let them get away with it.

The adversary system has made of our courts a sort of intellectual football field, with the prosecution and the defense declaring war on one another in order to win, and to hell with justice. So we have changed the ground rules to get away from this. These changes will also reduce the seeming endlessness of some trials, as well as outrageous court costs and legal fees.

Also, while a judge may, as before, find a public person guilty of contempt of court, a citizen or a higher court now may charge a judge with contempt of public.

In the new system, the term "guilt" is not used. The jury will find the accused either *at fault* or not at fault, based on whether they judge that the person committed the illegal act or didn't commit it. Good intentions, ignorance, insanity, have nothing to do with fault.

However, they may modify *culpability*. In deciding culpability, the main considerations are fault, how reasonably avoidable the act was, what the person's alternatives were, and what his intentions seem to have been.

And the penalty depends on culpability and on what harm, if any, was done to someone.

The new system also considers that individual freedoms are too precious to be sliced and hacked at by people and groups who feel that people must be protected from themselves. Let me restate that. The legal system is no longer the tool of people who feel compelled to control others—people with a compulsion to protect you from yourself whether you like it or not. The Constitution does not authorize the federal government, *or the state governments*, to impose that kind of control on citizens.

In this regard, I invite you to consider the ninth amendment to the Constitution, which states: "The enumeration in the Constitution, of certain rights, shall not be construed to deny or disparage others retained by the people."

Three examples should be enough to let you see what I mean by keeping the law out of areas of *self*-harm. If you are eighteen years old or older and want to ride your motorcycle without a helmet, you have the right to. Or if you are less than eighteen and your parents are willing, you have that right. But as a motorcycle operator, you can require your riders to wear one.

And if you want to drive without fastening your seatbelt, that's your right too. Of course, your insurance company may pay less, by a reasonable amount, if you're hurt or killed when not strapped in, but you have the right to ride that way, with this exception. A driver can insist that his or her riders buckle down.

Also, taking harmful drugs is no longer a crime, but laws controlling the *dispensing* of harmful substances remain in force. And you will soon see new and forceful government action against the importation of illicit drugs. The Coast Guard is the only branch of government authorized by international law to stop, search, and seize vessels at sea for smuggling. A warrant is not, and has never been, required for this, and reasonable force can be used.

However, the Coast Guard has had far too few ships and planes for the job, so I have temporarily transferred the necessary ships, planes, and personnel from the Navy to the Coast Guard.

Almost no states have laws against suicide or attempted suicide, and such laws are voided by this reform. But there is an *indirect* prohibition against suicide that applies almost everywhere in America: Suicide is severely punished by insurance companies, which generally refuse to pay "death benefits" in cases of suicide.

If someone wishes to end his or her own life, that is their prerogative. To live or not to live, within the individual's ability to do so, is his or her most basic right. And it is a right that supercedes the desire of anyone else—*anyone* else—that the person remain alive. Even that of a spouse or parent or dependent, and certainly an insurance company.

Yet an insurance company also has the right to protect its shareholders and policy holders from someone who, let us say, might pay $100 for a $100,000 life insurance policy and then kill himself, enriching his beneficiaries. To legalize that would be like granting a license to steal.

So beginning this February first, insurance companies may not refuse payment of indemnities for suicides. *But they may reduce payments*, based on reasonable actuarial formulas, and considering the premiums paid and the coverage. The intention of this is not to punish suicide, but simply to protect the insurance company and its policy holders and share holders from financial damage.

None of this applies to church prohibitions against

suicide. A church may withhold its sacraments from a suicide if it wishes—that's a matter of religious freedom.

Incidentally, if any of you are considering killing yourself, keep in mind that suicide is not reversible. You can't change your mind the next day. And the condition you sought to avoid by suicide may not have seemed nearly so terrible the next day. Or it may be remedied next week! It might be better to get counseling from a pastor or a therapist than to take cyanide. But it's your life.

Unfortunately this speech may inspire a brief flurry of suicides. But more than a few of them would be covert suicides anyway, masquerading as accidental deaths. Others would become tomorrow's drug overdose statistics. Or murders.

Now let's consider the interpretation of law.

A legal precedent is the way some judge in the past interpreted how the law applied to some specific case. In the courtroom, judges and attorneys use legal precedent to guide their arguments and decisions. And while legal precedents are sometimes the product of high wisdom and often of common sense, they may also prove to be foolish, certainly in some of their applications.

And laws, as interpreted with the help of legal precedent, were supposed to be followed exactly. "To the letter." So what happened? People, generally lawyers or with the collusion of lawyers, found ways to sneak around the intent of the law by finding chinks and crannies in the language of the law. They found ways of interpreting the law to circumvent the intention of the law.

Sometimes, when a law or its interpretations were destructive, finding a loophole was the only way an intelligent action could be carried out. But all too often it amounted to cheating, to getting an advantage over others, and the broader welfare be damned. And the person or group who could afford a coven of clever lawyers could operate more freely, even much more freely, than others could. Thus wealth gave one an advantage in legal matters.

There are multimillionaire lawyers around who built their fortunes on this kind of thing. Mostly it wasn't illegal, although sometimes it may have been. You can look at it as gaming, but from a justice point of view it's destructive. And the legal profession didn't treat it as an ethics issue; that would have hurt too many of their bank accounts. So even if you've been an honest, ethical lawyer, you still share responsibility for the tar of public disgust, because you did not take effective action to reform your profession and the legal system.

I really regret saying that, because I've become aware of how hard some of you have worked to reform it.

So now we are requiring all courts, not just federal courts, to apply laws *as the laws were intended*. Where the original intent is not clear from the language of the law, intent will be decided according to the conditions and situations that the law was written to deal with. The intent of the law will always outweigh precedent to the contrary.

Cracks and *unintended* loopholes will be disregarded. Also, I'm asking the Congress and other legislating bodies to make a clear statement of their intentions in passing any new law, stating those intentions first in terms of broad principles and then of immediate specifics.

The most basic and most important changes in the system will be in the courts. These apply mainly to federal courts, until the people and their legislatures install them in state law. The package you'll be given after this talk describes in what ways this reform affects courts other than federal courts. Now, with that in mind, here are the new ground rules:

The role of the judge is changed considerably. Although the judge has not usually "judged," he or she has weighed too heavily in the courtroom. As a generality, the judge has had more authority than has proved wise for one person to have in court. The judge, like anyone else, has prejudices and blind spots, and today perhaps a snootful of cocaine. In your own studies, you have indicated that cocaine use among judges and attorneys has become a serious problem in justice proceedings.

The judge has been the court executive who guided the proceedings and assessed what the penalty would be. Usually it has been the jury that has judged guilt or innocence, but its decision has had to be *within the limits of what the judge says the law really means and how it applies*. And at times, judges have rejected a jury's decision of guilt or innocence.

Our changes will help the jury judge the case with greater justice and speed. The jury now will also decide the penalty, within certain guidelines, *and penalties will commonly include restitution and amends*. And the jury will have the authority to *decide the law*—to decide for itself how the law applies, within broad legal guidelines, considering the stated or apparent intent of the people who made the law.

The judge is required to explain and to advise the jury on the law. He may point out precedent. But the jury may ignore his advice and reject precedent. The judge has no authority to order them, nor tell them what they should do, nor try to coerce them, in matters of the law. The jury is free to interpret the law according to the jury's own view of its intent and its application to the case, subject as always to appeal.

And very important, the jury will have the right to insist that the court ask certain questions of the accused; and of the principals in a civil suit; and of witnesses. The procedures for doing this are described in the reform package. The jury can even require that the attorneys and the judge answer the jury's questions, where the jury feels it necessary to clarify what the truth is and what justice requires.

Because we are looking for a maximum of justice. We are no longer treating a courtroom as a gaming place for lawyers.

And we are looking toward justice as justice is viewed by the citizens. On the whole, courts dominated by judges have not done an adequate job, and I believe that citizen jurors will do better.

Incidentally, the jury will have another right. If a jury agrees that a law, or part of a law, is ridiculous, or poorly written, or for any reason is a poor law, they can recommend that it be reviewed for possible cancellation, alteration, or replacement. They must judge the case at hand according to the law as it is, but they can recommend that the law be reviewed, saying why. There will be review panels for that purpose.

The most severe penalty will be imprisonment without liberation until judged by a board of citizens as safe for society. And the safety standards will be more stringent than often has been the case. Let me repeat, that is the most severe penalty.

Earlier I mentioned restitution and amends. There you have one of the principles this new system stresses: personal responsibility. I want to emphasize that. Whether convicted of a misdemeanor or a felony, the person convicted is likely to be assessed restitution, to be paid to the individuals or institutions they have harmed. And they can be required to make appropriate amends to society. If nothing else, their amends will include court costs.

This is not a matter of additional punishment. It is a matter of being responsible for the damage one has done, as judged by a jury of citizens.

Which brings up a related matter. If a crime so attracts publishers or film makers that they want to buy the book rights or film rights from the criminal, the proceeds that normally would go to the criminal as author or coauthor or story source will go first toward restitution to the injured, and if any is left, it will be paid to the court as an amends to society. The agent who handles it can of course receive a reasonable commission, and any writer who assists with the manuscript or script can receive a reasonable fee. But kickbacks will be treated as felonies.

And now about civil law.

This nation has a history of lawsuits and even criminal charges being filed which proved to be clearly unfounded. Sometimes suits have been filed to harass or defame someone. Sometimes they have been

made simply for publicity. And frequently they have
been filed in hopes of getting an out-of-court settle-
ment from someone who wants to avoid the time,
expense, and publicity of a court case. From now on,
filing a clearly unfounded case will be a good way for
a lawyer to get himself tried on felony charges, fined,
disbarred, and possibly imprisoned.

Which brings us to what may be the most disgraceful area in the American legal system: liability
claims. Some decades ago, I recall a case where
three teenage boys saw a tractor in a farm field in
Kansas. The farmer had driven home in his pickup
truck to eat lunch. The boys went out into the field,
trespassing, started the tractor and drove off with it.
One fell off and was run over, suffering severe injuries.

So— His parents sued the farmer!

And the court did what? Did they charge the boys
with trespassing? No. With illegally driving the tractor? No. With reckless driving? No. They awarded
the injured boy's family half a million dollars. In
1960, that was equivalent to about two million of last
year's dollars.

Say that their lawyer got thirty percent. That happens in liability claims. So let's say that after taxes
the family itself ended up with what amounted to
one million of last year's dollars. Invested through a
reputable brokerage firm, that could easily provide
an income of $80,000 a year. So here was a kid who
broke the law, and as a result his family had an
income far far greater than the average family's.

Here was a teenage boy who not only was not held
responsible for his own actions, his own foolishness
and heedlessness, his own lawbreaking, but who was
rewarded for it!

I won't tell you what I think, and what most
Americans think, of the lawyer. Or the judge. Or the
court. Can the legal profession possibly interpret
this as justice? One can hardly avoid wondering if
the judge received a kickback from the lawyer, who
morally smells like a profiteering criminal.

Perhaps more remarkable was the case of the man
who swallowed, or half swallowed—an office staple

puller! It's not easy to half-swallow a staple puller.
It's not easy to imagine a grown man putting one in
his mouth! He very nearly choked to death, and
surgery was necessary to remove it. Then, with the
help of a lawyer who deserved to be put in jail,
he— *Sued the manufacturer because the staple puller
did not have the warning: harmful if swallowed!* And
more incredible yet, he was awarded $400,000 dam-
ages! I don't know what the lawyer's cut was of that
award. Twenty percent? Thirty?

A large majority of Americans consider such legal
actions outrageous and shameful. Your own public
surveys have established that unequivocally. Yet apparently the American Bar Association considers such
actions ethical. Right? Because through its membership, it has had the necessary power to end them,
and hasn't done it. However you might rationalize
this, it seems clear that the fat bank account has
outweighed ethical considerations in your organization.

And whose money is given away in these outrageous grants? The insurance company's money? In a
way, yes. But really, it was everyone's money who
bought insurance, which is most families, because
their premiums had to be made high enough to pay
for the judicial stupidity, the judicial irresponsibility, the you-help-me-get-mine-and-I'll-help-you-get-
yours greed that resulted in such awards. The many
many such cases cost everyone who bought insurance a great deal of money. Everyone except the
gougers.

And worst of all, it degraded public confidence
and helped make the law and the courts contempt-
ible in the eyes of many Americans.

Of course, many liability suits are proper and just.
People do injure others, intentionally or through
ignorance or carelessness. In such cases the person
being sued should be held accountable for their actions, and damages assessed which are just and reasonable. But it is not acceptable that people be
rewarded for their own carelessness, their own stupidity, sometimes their own avarice, even their own
trespassing, at the expense of the rest of us.

So we are finally starting to get rid of these expensive comedy shows. Damage awards will depend on *actual* damage, *actual* liability, and reasonable legal fees. And if cases are brought which are as flagrantly predatory as the examples I mentioned, the case will not only be thrown out; the lawyer will be disbarred and the plaintiffs quite possibly fined.

Only *actual* damages will be rewarded, not punitive damages. I'll repeat that. Only actual damages will be rewarded, not punitive damages. If punishment is appropriate, then instead of punishing with punitive damages, criminal charges will be filed and punishment carried out that way.

The majority of liability cases fall under state instead of federal law. But this legal reform package has considerably extended what cases can be tried in federal courts. And it makes certain new requirements of state and local courts. As a matter of fact, we have gone to the very limits of constitutionality on this. But the federal government has just so much authority and no more. So if you, both lawyers and citizens, like what I've said here today, then use all the pressure necessary to get similar reforms written into state law. If your local legislator gives you alibis instead of action, then find someone who will give you action and elect him to the legislature.

And I hope you'll write your senators and representatives to Congress, letting them know how you feel about this. I'm sure they'll want to know. Perhaps your newspaper will list their addresses, and those of your state legislators.

Now one last thing. Although a decent system of defense in law, a decent system of justice, is much more important than the self-interest of any establishment, it is conceivable that a few people in the legal profession may try to sabotage this legal reform and make it fail. I would advise against that. The government will cheerfully file criminal charges in such instances. A judge guilty of malfeasance may find himself on a prison farm, experiencing the joys of field labor of the sort he may himself have meted out to other criminals.

And that's all I have to say on this reform. To you members of the bar, I'm sorry if, at times, I've seemed to lump honest attorneys with the dishonest. I've worked closely now with three of you who are deeply interested in correcting these things. And they have referred me to studies made by others of you who have worked long and hard at trying to correct these problems. It's too bad that so many others of you blocked their efforts or at least did not pitch in and help them push.

To the many non-attorneys listening to me on television and radio, to a considerable degree I am putting the federal justice system in your hands, as jurors. I invite you to write and tell me what you think of these changes.

Thank you all for listening to me.

THIRTY-FOUR

They unloaded from the smooth quiet of Air Force One at Houston: the president, four cabinet secretaries, Senate president pro tem Louie Grosberg, House speaker Ken Lynch, and six Secret Service men. They were met by Brigadier General Harvest Ballister and his aide, and transferred to an army helicopter, a Sikorsky S-70 outfitted for VIP shuttle duty. For this mission it would be known as Army One.

The people from Washington had been briefed before they'd left the capital. They had the general picture, of which a key part was Ballister. Large, black, young for a general, he was in charge of the internment camps that held people arrested under martial law for rioting and associated violence. Or those still being held. The biggest single element were blacks, though there were plenty of "anglos" and Hispanics.

The chopper lifted and swung away northward, crossing the city's eastern suburbs, then flew out over a pattern of forest, housing developments, and farmland where morning sunlight glinted on occasional ponds. On their line of flight, scattered housing developments continued for miles from the city, the traffic from them funneling conveniently down country roads to the divided concrete strips of US 59 and thence to Houston.

After about fifty miles—twenty minutes—the last developments had been left behind. Ahead stretched national forest, broken here and there by logged-off patches and by their destination, the square, fenced enclosure of an internment center. The initial tent camp had been replaced by a war-time style military hutment built partly by its inmates, its shacks more suitable for winter than the tents would have been.

Except for three uniformed greeters, no one seemed to be there as the S-70 settled to the helipad. The sound of rotors and engines stilled, and the passengers got out, squinting in the sun, zipping jackets against a thin chill breeze.

"This, gentlemen," Ballister said, "is the San Jacinto Internment Center, one of sixteen still occupied. Except for the "D" camp in Nevada, this one's the farthest west; they're scattered from here to South Carolina."

He turned to the reception party. "This is Captain Roberg, the camp commander, and this is his project officer, Mr. Castro." After Roberg had introduced his master sergeant, Ballister continued. "Captain, the president and these other gentlemen have seen a brief written summary of the internment camp system. Why don't you show us around and give us the specifics of your particular operation?"

Roberg did. First they looked into one of the huts, covered with green asphalt siding. Inside at each end was a small, wood-burning, sheet-metal stove and a dozen single-deck bunks, everything orderly, everything clean. The messhall was of similar construction, but much larger. The latrine-laundry-shower house was scrubbed and odor-free, the big, stainless steel washers and dryers wiped clean, the porcelain washbowls and commodes shiny white.

Outside again, Roberg pointed. "And that," he said, "is the classroom building. Unless you insist, I won't take you inside now; it would disturb the classes. What I'd prefer to do next is show you some of the project work the men have done."

They got back on the S-70, and guided by the brawny-looking Castro, a Forest Service superintendent on loan, viewed several hundred acres of new loblolly pine plantations planted by the internees. Then they flew over hundreds of acres more of older plantations from which the competing scrub had recently been chopped, the stubs painted blue with biocide to discourage regrowth. Roberg had the helicopter land at one where crews were currently working.

Castro gave them a quick rundown on the projects while curious internees cast glances toward them. "The Sam Houston National Forest," he said, "had about three year's worth of projects backlogged, because of federal budget problems. This internment operation's gotten us caught up on a lot of it. We'd have done the work by machine, if we'd had the money, but the internees have been using handtools, which has the advantage of being more exact, and easier on the ground, than using heavy equipment.

"There are still 187 men here, alternating ten-hour work days with six-hour school days. We work half of them one day and the other half the next, and they've been doing better work than we'd ever imagined they would. The first week we had a lot of trouble with them, but that grew out of the hard cases—the Type D troublemakers. Then those got segregated out and shipped to Nevada, and the rest of these guys settled down pretty quickly."

Category D, the president thought. Category D was out west now, in desert mountains, working and living under heavy guard, doing things like improving primitive access roads with hand drills, sledge hammers, picks and shovels—the techniques and tools of seventy and eighty years earlier.

Castro was still talking about his San Jacinto crews. "They're pretty good-natured, as good as you'd expect any crews to be. They get paid by crew production points, with individual bonuses, and both crews and individuals get deductions for poor work. They really put out. The crews make a contest out of it, and the crew members lean

on anyone who goofs off or does sloppy work. But that
hasn't happened much since the first couple weeks."

Flying back to camp, the president's thoughts went back
to the Type Ds. Each one was a person. And presumably,
somewhere beneath the hatreds, fears, violences—the general insanity and ignorance—somewhere beneath all that,
presumably there was some decent nucleus, something
that could be clean and creative.

Or were some people born evil? Irreversibly and in-
nately hateful and destructive? He acknowledged to himself that it might be, but the concept didn't seem necessary
to explain the phenomena, not considering what some
people went through, some children.

*But we don't know how to clean the shit off to let that
nucleus show. Not with anything like reliability, we don't.*
It seemed to him that if someone could do that, could
come up with a practical, efficient system to salvage Type
Ds, it would be as important in the long run as the GPC,
transistors, and the budding field of gene splicing. Because as they were, Type Ds produced nothing but trouble, destruction, whether they operated in the streets,
with physical violence, or slyly, in board rooms or government, using lies and collusion. They were the instigators,
if not the leaders, of trouble, the generators of scorn for
whatever was good, whatever was being done to better
things. And they were probably a major source of other
people's mental problems.

What had Godfrey called Blackburn? A mind-fucker.
That was one kind. Blackburn had been a Type D with a
tie, gray flannel slacks, and blue blazer.

Haugen sheered away from the subject then. It seemed
to him a morass which, in an absence of data, he was not
prepared to deal with. He wondered if anyone was re-
searching the subject, making any progress. He'd talk to
Wing about that.

The presidential party arrived at the messhall after the
internees had begun eating, and following Haugen's lead,
the visiting party stood in line to get their food. Then they
sat on benches at an oil-cloth covered plank table, to eat
from sectioned trays that had probably been waiting in
some army warehouse since at least the Viet Nam War.
The food was plain but nourishing, the cooking decent,

and there were seconds—not bad for these times, the president thought.

After an initial half-minute or so of gawking, most of the internees gave their full attention to eating again.

The Secret Service men were edgy and watchful as they ate, concerned with possible danger to the president. These internees were clean and quiet just now, but a few months earlier they'd been torching buildings, cars and buses, stoning firemen, some of them shooting at police and troops. Special agent in charge Rogers had intended to post his men near the door, to watch the room for any possible threat, but the president had told them to eat with the rest of the government party. They'd done as he'd ordered, most of them resentfully, although they hid it. They had a duty, the responsibility of protecting the president, and didn't appreciate having obstacles put in their way.

After the meal, the internees on their study day had till two o'clock to loaf and nap. The teaching supervisor, Warrant Officer Willard Light, took the presidential party through the classroom building, a building considerably longer than the messhall but with the same asphalt siding. There was a large room for assemblies and for showing films, plus a library-reading room and several smaller rooms. There was a large globe in every room; ancient army typewriters from god knew where, perhaps thirty in all; books and chalkboards; abacuses to learn the principles behind arithmetic; modeling clay; stacks of cheap paper; several ancient personal computers. . . .

General Ballister had just previously been in charge of army technical training. And more relevant, before that he'd been in charge of remedial education in the army, a post he'd held with exceptional success. He'd overhauled the system, innovating freely and brilliantly; it was that which had gotten him the command of internment centers. The teaching supervisors were products of his training system, as were the teachers themselves.

Mister Light stated that the average reading skill of his students had already increased by two grade levels, that mathematical skills had increased even more, and that average IQ had risen a dozen points, which said something about IQ tests and human potentials. And most important, the attitude toward classroom learning had improved radically.

The president wondered what the results would have been if the Type Ds had still been there; poor, he suspected.

After touring the classroom building, the presidential party had gotten back aboard the S-70 and taken off for Houston. Then, in the air on Air Force One, they'd had a meeting and made their decisions. In part they'd already been more or less determined: The Type Ds would be formally charged with the appropriate felonies and tried, and their status changed from internee to convict or free person. Martial law would then be cancelled. The remaining internees could be returned home, or they could stay where they were, as Conservation Corps employees instead of internees. The fences and watchtowers would come down.

Grosberg and Lynch were more than a little pleased. The Congress had wanted to cancel martial law, but most had felt constrained to retain it as the basis for keeping the internees interned. And this seemed a major symbolic step toward normal government.

THIRTY-FIVE

"Thanks, Jeanne, I'll take it." The phone had interrupted the president in the midst of his morning routine; he touched the flashing key. "What can I do for you this morning, Steve?"

"May I speak with you for a few minutes, Arne? Personally? It's something that's been weighing on my mind since your speech the night before last."

"Sure. Come on down."

"Thank you. I'll be there in two minutes."

The screen went dark. From the third floor to the Oval Office in the Executive Wing, two minutes would be good time even for Flynn's long legs, Arne Haugen told himself. He got up to check the hot water supply in the coffee station, then made himself a cup of coffee. He'd just sat down again when Flynn arrived.

"Have a chair," Haugen said. "Tell me what's on your mind."

Flynn sat. "It's what you said about suicide."

"Oh?"

"This argument may not mean much to someone who's not a committed Christian, but I know you're a man who respects others, respects their beliefs. And I need to tell you mine about this—mine and just about every other devout Catholic.

"You see— There's a law above the law of man; Natural Law, the Law of God. Life is something given to us by God to care for, to live and to cherish. And suicide is murder, Arne, self-murder, a mortal sin. It's not that God or the Church would prolong suffering, but life is sacred, and shouldn't be deliberately destroyed. Even by one's self."

The priest looked painfully earnest. "Suicide is *not* a private act, you see, even when done in private. It's a form of violence against family, neighbor, and society."

Arne Haugen ignored the brief impulse to mention the crusades and inquisitions. Those had been long ago, in more barbaric times, and no doubt the Church had long regretted the bloodshed and anguish it had caused. Instead he nodded. "But Steve, I didn't recommend suicide," he pointed out reasonably. "I tried to discourage it. My purpose was and is to reestablish principles of personal liberty and responsibility."

"I know. And I appreciate that. But . . . law has an influence on morals. And so do the words of someone as widely respected and admired as yourself. So people are likely to commit self-murder who otherwise would not have. You see."

The priest stopped, but the president kept quiet, sensing more to come.

"But what concerns me most deeply," Flynn went on,

"is that self-murder is not only a mortal sin, one that damns the suicide's soul. Self-murder also ends the murderer's life, *so that he or she cannot confess the sin and ask for absolution!*"

Jesus, Haugen thought, *believing that, no wonder he looks so troubled.* "I see your point," he said, "and I make you a promise. I'm supposed to talk to the press briefly at noon, and I'll tell 'em what you've told me. As the Catholic point of view. As something they should know about. It'll be on the Networks.

"How's that?"

For a few seconds the Jesuit mistrusted his voice. Then he said, "Mr. President, as Professor Rabinowich would have said, you are a mensch."

Haugen grinned. "A mensch? I hope that's good."

Flynn smiled back. "It is, Arne, it is."

Arne and Lois Haugen were enjoying a nightcap when the first automatic rifle fire erupted, three separate bursts, near enough to hear clearly inside the thick-walled White House with its tempered-glass windows and heavy drapes closed against winter. *From Lafayette Park again,* the president told himself.

Things were quiet then, and he didn't take the trouble to call the marine command room on the top floor. If there was anything he needed to know, they'd call him.

The next shooting was nearer, seemingly on the north lawn not far outside their window, and he heard glass breaking. The firing repeated in fast, vicious bursts as he waved Lois to the Center Hall, then crouching, moved quickly to his bedside table, took his .357 magnum from its drawer, and followed her out, both wearing light robes. Two Secret Service men were there, pistols in their hands, one listening on a hand radio. There was more gunfire, then quiet. The four of them stood in the hall, three with guns in hand. After a minute, the agent with the radio looked at the president.

"Some armed men got inside the grounds somehow, sir. The marines don't know if they . . ."

He was interrupted by more gunfire, overlapping bursts, muffled in the interior hall. The four of them looked at each other in the following silence.

"They didn't know if they'd gotten . . ."

This time the gunburst that cut him off sounded closer, perhaps on the south lawn. Haugen grinned.

"They didn't know if they'd gotten them all," he said, finishing for the agent. "Maybe they have now."

He'd barely gotten it out when the alarm began—not the great blaring nuclear attack alarm, but a constant high-pitched howl. The president scowling, the first couple went quickly to the emergency elevator, and with the bodyguards rode it down to the deep, heavily-reinforced shelter, where Flynn soon appeared, along with the staff members on duty at that hour. The president was glowering now—a rare occurrence. He had the distinct notion that the danger had been over before the alarm went off.

He and Lois sat up for a few minutes, then went to bed in their shelter quarters. Not long after they got to sleep, the all clear sounded. They could have stayed where they were, but the president got up so Lois did too, and they went back to their apartment. The ice had mostly melted in their drinks there. They finished them dilute, then went to bed.

His eyes were closed when he heard a distant explosion. *To hell with it,* he thought, and a minute or two later was asleep.

In the morning, as soon as he'd wakened, he called the marine command post. "They were ninjas, sir," the captain told him. "Apparently eight of them, wearing black. Japanese; real ninjas." He sounded impressed. "They seem to have jumped from a plane at high elevation and body planed in before pulling their chutes. We found their equipment. Some of them landed outside the fence, but three came down inside."

The captain still sounded wound up, Haugen thought.

"The first one we saw," the marine went on, "was in Lafayette Park. He carried ten kilos of air-miscible high explosive in a flat backpack. When we discovered that, that's when the alarm was sounded. We didn't know if there were any other human bombs or not. If one of them somehow got inside the White House, or even to the north portico . . .

"One of them came down way over near the Lincoln

Memorial, and he carried HE too. Apparently he was
disoriented and didn't know where he was; anyway he
blew himself up by the reflecting pool.

"It was so dark last night, we'd have had a hard time
finding them if it hadn't been for our night visors. They
were using the trees for cover, sneaking along—eight of
them, including the one that blew himself up."

The president wasn't sure how long the captain would
have talked if he hadn't interrupted. "You people handled
things very professionally, captain," he said. "I'm very
proud of you all. Tell your men for me at muster."

Then he hung up, chuckling. It had been a long time
since he'd been as excited as the captain seemed to have
been. And excited was a great condition, when you handled it well.

Unless he had an NSC meeting in the morning, Jumper
Cromwell usually read the news as soon as he'd finished
the daily intelligence and situation summaries. The Joint
Staff had people who looked through some twenty newspapers
each night and morning, clipping news articles, editorials,
and columns, pasting them on large sheets and photocopy-
ing them for senior officers.

Today the news ran heavily to the night's attack on the
White House. There were pictures of the dead assassins,
masked in black, and a couple with masks removed. Cromwell grunted. The frigging newspapers seemed thrilled to
be writing about actual ninjas. The marines who'd shot
their asses off got almost no space, at least in the clipping
sheets.

The editorial pages still were fixated on the president
though, and on his speech of two nights before. As Cromwell read, his usually mild temper heated. When he finished, he reached for his phone, drew back, then with a
move of abrupt decision dialed the White House. It wasn't
a confidential matter, so he went through the White House
exchange, the operator there putting him through immediately to the president's secretary.

"Just a moment please, general," Martinelli said. He
waited. Seconds later, the president's face popped onto his
phone screen.

"Good morning, Jumper. What can I do for you today?"

"Have you seen the papers this morning, sir?"

"The usual: read a summary that included some Xeroxed excerpts. Two of 'em: yesterday's and today's."

The usual. It seemed to Cromwell that the president would have read more than that, with so much attention being given to his speech.

As if he'd heard the general's unspoken thought, or read his expression, the president went on, "I'm not as interested in what the editorial writers think as I am in the reaction over on Capitol Hill. Most of Congress is lawyers, you know. What in particular bothered you in the papers this morning?"

The general suddenly realized that Haugen was grinning! It occurred to him that perhaps the people who put the summaries together might be shielding the president from the worst shots.

"How does this sound?" Cromwell said, and began to read. " 'It is abundantly clear that the president has no intention of returning the government to normal constitutional processes. President Donnelly, apparently under extreme pressure from the Pentagon, turned the government over to a man he'd never heard of—General Cromwell's president who, under the ill-advised Emergency Powers Act, has made himself the dictator of America. This would have been bad enough if he'd been content to preside over the normal, proper organs of government.

" 'But Dictator Haugen is trying to redesign government according to his own strange notions, and has overturned some of the most basic precepts of American democracy.

" 'No reasonable person can claim that the emergency still exists. The only significant violence today grows out of public outrage at his presidency. It is time for Congress to impeach, to throw out, this amateur president with his perverted and un-American ideas, before he does more damage.' "

Cromwell shifted his gaze to Arne Haugen's image on the screen. Haugen was looking calmly back at him. "Mr. President," said Cromwell, "I'd say it's time to exercise the sedition act."

"Against Mr. Sanders?" Haugen asked.

It was Sanders' column, though Cromwell hadn't said so. "You'd already read it then," he said.

"Yep. They included it in full, in the summary. Said it was pretty representative of what they called "the more irate" segment. But it's not actually seditious; he doesn't advocate revolt or disorder.

"I thought Eichmeier's syndicated column was a lower blow than that. According to him, I'm practically guilty of manslaughter because Chief Justice Fechner had his stroke listening to my speech. You knew he died yesterday, I suppose." The president paused. "At least I'll have a chance to appoint his replacement, someone who doesn't seem hostile to me."

Cromwell nodded. "Did you see the *American Daily Flag*?" he asked.

"Just the last paragraph or so of an editorial. It ended something like, 'The American People could be forgiven, or even congratulated, if they rose up and threw this tyrant out.' That does come fairly close to sedition, I'll have to admit."

"Are you going to do anything about it?"

"Nope. The media reaction overall was really pretty mild; some of it was actually friendly. And as far as the *Flag*'s concerned, ninety-five percent of the people who read it were already saying that, or worse, or at least thinking it." He paused.

"And consider just how far I went in that speech, Jumper. Now *that* was extreme!"

Cromwell didn't speak at once, but it was clear from his expression that he was forming a response. Haugen waited.

"Mr. President, you have the basis for a counterattack that has nothing to do with the sedition act or prosecutions of any kind. You have my report on the long-term activities of the Holist Council executive board. And now you have their bible—the Archon book; that damns them with their own words. Why don't you just read parts of those in a fireside address?"

"I probably will, when the time comes. But not now. For one thing, it would be a red herring. Almost none of the editorial writers or columnists or TV news analysts have ever heard of the Archons. Probably none of them have. I'm sure that most of them don't know much about the Holist Council either, and very few of them are connected with it. They're expressing their own views, whether we like them or not.

"I talked to Okada last evening after I got back from Texas, and again this morning. We discussed a statement he'll be giving the media today. In front of the TV cameras. He'll be saying the right things back at them. Like, it would be interesting to know who was willing to spend the kind of money it took to hire, equip, and fly in the ninjas. And to import a nuclear bomb. Okada'll probably sound harder than usual; he was really pissed by Sanders and Eichmeier, too.

"Meanwhile, tomorrow Morrisey and Spencer will start another survey, this one on public response to my legal reform. I'm looking forward to that. It'll be a lot more useful to me than TV or the papers. Or even than the letter tally we'll be getting over the next few days."

Cromwell felt a little better. The president was a remarkably deliberate man, and so far his judgments had been damned good.

The president changed abruptly to a different subject. "D'you know one of the troubles with this job, Jumper?" he asked.

The shift took Cromwell by surprise. "No. What?"

"There's so little direct action. A president hardly has any hands-on involvement; I work through proxies almost entirely. I have to; it's the only practical way. But sometimes I feel like I'm half spectator and half manipulator." He laughed. "And half worrier; it's a job and a half. I'm never out where it's happening; no time for it."

His voice changed, became brisk. "I need to hang up, Jumper. I've got another call flashing."

Haugen disconnected, and touched a key on his security phone. Dirksma's face appeared on the screen. "What have you got, Peter?" the president asked.

"Mister President, we've found a connection between Blackburn in his secret, private practitioner personna, and a financially prominent person. Very prominent. Under the name 'Dr. William Merriman,' Blackburn had done occasional work for Paul W. Massey. We don't have details yet, just the connection. We got onto it from a bug that General Cromwell got installed, illegally I suspect, in Massey's residence. Except for a couple of underworld names that were mentioned, no one here paid much attention to it—not until we learned Blackburn's alias.

"Of course, we couldn't use any evidence acquired this way in a court action, but it's certainly giving us some leads to follow."

"I know about the bug," the president answered. "I approved it under a provision in the Emergency Powers Act. But I agree that we shouldn't use it in court, if it comes to that."

He paused to jot on a note pad. "I'll send you photocopies of a couple of things today: a report Jumper had prepared, and a copy of something sent by the person who installed the bug for Jumper. Neither is clear evidence of criminal activity, but they give perspective to a lot of things. Including the connections you just mentioned."

Haugen stopped. A chainsaw had started just outside. "Peter, I need to see about something. Are we done?"

"I believe so, sir."

"I'll hang up then. Thanks for the information."

The president disconnected and strode out of his office and into the yard, followed by two concerned-looking Secret Service men. Nearby, a man with a hardhat was about to make a notching cut in one of the trees on the White House grounds.

"Hey!" shouted the president, "what're you doing there?"

The man turned, saw who was coming, and cut the ignition on his saw. He wore coveralls with a Parks shoulder patch. Awkward, not sure what to do, he saluted. The president saluted casually back.

"What're you doing?" the president repeated, this time with no trace of indignation.

"Mr. President sir, we're supposed to cut all the trees around here."

"How come?"

Another man was hurrying over from a panel truck nearby. "Can I help you, Mr. President?" he asked. He was a tall, powerful man, sure of himself.

"Yes. This gentleman tells me you're planning to cut the trees here. Who told you to do that?"

"Sir, Mr. Cambert, my supervisor. He said the Secret Service ordered it."

"The Secret Service!?" The president's voice had raised half an octave.

"Yes sir. They're afraid somebody might use those trees for sneaking up to shoot you. That's what Mr. Cambert said."

The president assumed a serious expression. "I see. Well, I certainly appreciate their concern, but I don't want these trees cut down." He gestured. "You see those marines? They take good care of me. Were you in the service?"

"Yes sir. Airborne sir, like you. Twenty years ago."

Haugen looked at the sawyer. "How about you?"

The man straightened. "I got out of the navy last year, Mr. President. I was on the missile cruiser *Ticonderoga*."

Two other men with saws were standing by the truck, waiting to see what would happen.

"Well, you can imagine then," Haugen said, "that those young marines are pretty darned competent. And we know what they did to the ninjas last night. So what I want you to do is go back and tell Mr. Cambert the trees will have to stay; that the president said so. Tell him I'll take care of it with the Secret Service so there's no squawk."

"Yes sir, Mr. President. I'll tell him that. And the boys and me are glad we don't have to cut 'em. We were just saying what a shame it would be."

The president surprised the two by shaking hands with them. Then he watched for a minute as the crew loaded gear into the truck, before grinning at an embarrassed Agent Trabert. "Glad you guys are so interested in my health," he said, and started back for the executive wing.

It was felt in Anchorage as a distinct jar at 0632:21 hours, Alaska Time, followed exactly twenty seconds later by another equally strong. At about that time, those who were looking and had a good view westward saw the explosion, a ruddy flash in the wintry predawn somewhere near the horizon, fading to a faint reddish glow that quickly died. Fourteen minutes later the sound of it reached the city, a boom that woke the sleeping.

Mount Spurr had exploded, blowing more than half a cubic mile of rock to powder and sending it miles into the sky. It also converted some 300 million cubic yards of glacier into vapor and water—roughly 100 million tons of water which, mixed with dirt, roared down mountain slopes and ravines, carrying with it thousands of blasted trees. Seconds after the explosion, Chakachamna Lake, large by most standards and thickly iced over, was hit by an avalanche of incandescent gas and dust, moving at several miles per minute, that instantly burned the deep snow away, opening the ice with an immense snarl of steam, and torched the shock-flattened trees that it touched. Minutes later the water arrived, debouching onto and into the lake, preceded by the booming of great boulders swept by it down the ravines.

Dawnlight came soon after, then daylight. Shortly before 11 A.M., Alaska Time, the leading fringe of the ash cloud arrived at Anchorage on a fair west wind. Ash and a midday twilight began to settle on the city. By twenty past eleven the street lights were on. At noon the prohibition against nonemergency traffic went into effect, and snowplows moved out, their lights flashing blue in the gloom, to begin the job of plowing ash from the streets. By 2:40 in the afternoon, snow began to fall, muddy snow. Ordinarily it wouldn't have been quite sundown yet, at sixty-one degrees north latitude on January 14. On this day, however, it had been dark for nearly three hours.

There had been no warning. The mountain's innards had grumbled recently, but not alarmingly. Seismographs had noted nothing threatening until seconds before the first shock. The few humans in the mountain's vicinity had had no warning at all.

Sixty miles south, Mount Redoubt erupted too, but not explosively. A fissure or fissures opened in one flank. Glacier burst from steam pressure, lava flowed stinking forth, snow melted, and water and boulders scoured its ravines. The event was trivial, compared to the explosion farther north.

When the report reached the White House, President Haugen had just begun swimming laps with the first lady and Father Flynn. Milstead hadn't interrupted him for these presumed acts of God. The chief got little enough relaxation; after lunch would do. Thus the president and Flynn learned of the eruptions while eating to the twelve o'clock news.

Acts of God—eruptions, great hurricanes, tidal waves—can be more engrossing than acts of man, and Haugen and Flynn watched intently. By that time it was daylight in Anchorage, and planes had already overflown the devastation, taking such pictures around Mount Spurr as the light there allowed. The more impressive footage was of the Redoubt Volcano. The dust cloud from Mount Spurr was drifting east, not south toward Redoubt, thus a rising sun lit the scene redly through sooty fumes and steam. Lava still ponderously flowed, the snow retreating ahead of it, and debris-filled mud lay in great fans of ruin at the foot of the ravines.

It was midafternoon in D.C. when James Gupta at the NSA called the president. The seismograms associated with the eruptions, he said, were peculiar in several respects, and taken together left no doubt in his mind that this quake and eruption were triggered by scalar resonance.

"What's the certainty level?" Haugen asked.

"The probability is well above the ninety-nine percent level—better than 0.999."

"Hm-m." The president frowned. "Why Mount Spurr?"

"I have no substantial idea, sir."

"How about an insubstantial idea?"

"It could have been a demonstration—the Soviets reminding us of what they can do. In a location that did no severe damage to populations or property."

"To what purpose?"

"It could be to worry us, in advance of some Soviet move in Europe or Asia. To make us hesitant, more reluctant to mount a countermove."

The president's look was thoughtful, perhaps tinged with skepticism. "If you say the quake and eruption were created by scalar resonance, I'll accept that. But we already knew what they have the power to do, and they know what we can do if we choose to."

"True."

Briefly Haugen said nothing. "Well, I won't wrack my brain over it. At least not until we have more data." He paused. "And just to be sure, check on our own resonance transmitters; I need to be damn certain we didn't do it. Check that right away and get back to me on it."

Gupta's answer was delayed slightly. Obviously the order bothered him. "Yes sir," he said.

"How long will it take you? I presume you know exactly who you need to check with at each location."

"Yes sir, I do. I should have the information to you within the hour."

"Good. They'll probably think you're crazy for asking. Tell them the president wants to be absolutely sure before he takes certain steps."

Gupta nodded very soberly, wondering what those "certain steps" might be. When they'd disconnected, the president buzzed Cromwell, just down the hall.

"Jumper," Haugen said, "I need to talk with Colonel Schubert again. Tomorrow morning. Any problem with that?"

"I'll have to check, but I doubt it very much."

"Fine. Let me know."

It was hard for Arne Haugen to put his attention back on the proposed tax reform package the Joint Committee on Taxation had sent him. But he persisted until it had his complete attention. It was detailed and well written, with glossary and appendix. The discussion seemed very thorough and the proposal very rational. *Why,* he asked himself, *didn't earlier committees come up with one like this?* The reason, when he thought about it, seemed obvious: The difficulty of getting it through a Congress beset by a hundred special interest groups, or a thousand, almost all of them persuasive and some of them convincing, arguing or wheedling for modifications and compromises. And all wielding influence in the form of political support, and frequently potential campaign contributions.

His phone buzzed again. "What is it, Jeanne?"

"Your daughter's on line one, sir."

The president felt a pang of guilt as his finger moved to the flashing key; he hadn't called Liisa since—since the Christmas that hardly was. Her face appeared on the screen, a face more resembling his own than Lois's—good but not pretty.

"Hi, sweetheart. How's it going in far away Grand Forks?"

"It's cold here, daddy. Six below at noon."

"How's Ed doing? And the kids?"

"Ed's fine. He's still acting department chairman; Professor Becker's not recovering as quickly as expected. I just wanted to let you know that Joyce is expecting. I'm going to be a grandmother."

She didn't sound very enthusiastic. "Huh! That's interesting. Any more talk about a wedding?"

"Nothing definite. Well, in a way. They've definitely decided to, but they haven't set a date. Not even a month." She paused. "Joey only makes a dollar an hour. He does pick and shovel work for the P.W.A."

"What does Ed think of all this?"

"About Joyce's pregnancy? He doesn't know yet. Joyce just found out for sure this morning, though she's suspected for the last couple of days. Joey's supposed to have been taking that new oral male contraceptive that the FDA approved last year. Either it didn't work, or Joey forgot."

Probably the latter, Haugen thought. Ed considered Joey Lund a world class bumbler. Likeable but a klutz. The president grinned at his daughter, strangely lightened by her report, as if it somehow lent perspective to things. "Life gets complicated around here, too, honey. Have you told your mother yet?"

His security phone began to buzz, and a code number had formed on its screen.

"No. I thought I'd call her next," Liisa said.

"Good idea. Liisa, the National Security Agency is trying to get me on my security phone. I need to hang up. Thanks for the news, and for thinking of me."

"You're welcome, daddy. 'Bye."

"Goodbye, honey."

He disconnected and reached for the security phone. *Life does get complicated all right*, he mused.

THIRTY-SIX

The word from Gupta had been unequivocal and negative: The American scalar resonance transmitters had not triggered the Mount Spurr eruption. They'd stood unused for weeks; for years except for bimonthly equipment tests.

Then the president had the Washington-Moscow Direct Communications Link—the "Hot Line" office—arrange a conference between himself and Premier Pavlenko, via the video "red phones" that Wheeler and Gorbachev had had installed.

The first thing next morning, Haugen and his guests rode the emergency elevator down to the bomb shelter beneath the White House. There, in a rather small but comfortable room, he took a seat beside a State Department interpreter. Out of sight of the video pickup sat General Cromwell, Secretary of State Valenzuela, and Gupta of NSA. And an unintroduced Colonel, Schubert/Bulavin, who'd come in with Cromwell. The president nodded at a major watching from the control room through a small glass window. The major nodded back, and no doubt signaled a sergeant.

For a moment, the telephone screen paled diffusely, then a picture flashed into being. The face of Marshal Premier Oleg Stepanovich Pavlenko looked out at the president.

It was 1600 hours in Moscow, with its year-round daylight saving time, and 0800 in Washington.

"Good afternoon, Marshal Premier Pavlenko," Haugen said in Russian.

"Good morning, Mr. President."

Pavlenko appeared to be a man about sixty years old,

mostly bald, thin-lipped, wearing thick, wire-rimmed glasses.

"What is it you wished to talk about?" he asked.

Haugen's interpreter, wearing headphones, translated into English scarcely a thought behind the Premier. The sound volume in Russian was subdued, too quiet to follow, to avoid confusion in listening to the English translation. Haugen didn't feel confident enough of his Russian fluency to try carrying on a sensitive exchange in the language—an exchange that could conceivably become technical. He, Valenzuela, and Schubert/Bulavin would listen to the original Russian afterward, on tape.

The president answered now in English. "We have had a great volcanic eruption in our state of Alaska."

The face that looked out at him wore no identifiable expression; it was simply cold. The eyes were colder.

"I have heard."

"My specialists have assured me that it was not an unassisted act of nature. They tell me it was triggered by a very large and explosive release of energy via scalar resonance."

"Why are you telling this to me?"

"We here in America did not trigger it. And there are only two nations with the ability to. Therefore it follows that someone in the Soviet Union is responsible. I am calling to ask why it was done. Assuming that my information and my assumptions are correct."

The thin lips smiled slightly, but the eyes did not change. "Mr. President. We have contingency plans of every sort here. Including plans for delivering attacks of various sorts and intensities on many countries. If I were to carry out such an attack, I would not choose a location where the damage would be so meaningless."

"Then the Soviet Union is not responsible for the eruption yesterday?"

"No." The slight, cold-eyed smile returned, perhaps a trifle wider this time. "You have my word on it."

"Thank you, Marshal Premier Pavlenko," the president replied, in Russian again. He deliberately kept expression from both his face and his voice. "You can imagine how reassured I am. Perhaps we shall talk again sometime under more relaxed circumstances."

The image in front of him snapped off, and the president signaled the major that he was done. Then he looked at the men sitting away from the pickup.

"Did you learn anything?" asked Cromwell.

"Not much. Let's listen to the recording." He touched the playback key on the console, and after a brief delay, Pavlenko's Russian came from the set. When it was over, the president sat back. "How I read it is that Pavlenko is quite happy for us to believe he's responsible. He'd like us to worry about possible future attacks on locations where an earthquake or eruption would be a lot more serious.

"I presume he has it in mind to do more than he has. He could have scalar warfare in mind, but it's probably something else, because of the risk that scalar war would go nuclear. Or he may be testing us, feeling his way a step at a time." Haugen looked around. "Do any of you have any comments?"

No one spoke; heads shook.

"All right. Then we might as well leave."

They did. Most left the White House entirely, but Schubert/Bulavin went to the Oval Office with the president. When the president had poured coffee, they sat down.

He gazed at the ex-Soviet spy, ex-Soviet major general, ex-Soviet deputy ambassador. "What kind of reputation did Pavlenko have in the Soviet army when you were there?" he asked. "As a person."

"He was considered a dangerous person to work under. Fanatical, totally patriotic, and liable to punish severely for a first error. Particularly if it could be interpreted as an expression of moral corruption." Bulavin paused. "Moral corruption isn't really a good translation. He had a reputation for cruelty and for abusing women. Let's say he was harsh toward official corruption—corruption political and financial."

"I got an impression of him, on the phone," Haugen said. "One of the reasons I like video phones so well; they make it easier to evaluate the person you're talking to. There's a concept I ran into once, in reading, that might apply here: *reasoning psychotic.*"

Bulavin's eyebrows lifted.

"Reasoning psychotics apply more or less rational intelligence to carry out insane purposes," the president continued. "If they're single-minded enough, they can be very effective; effectively destructive, ordinarily. Could that describe Pavlenko?"

The Russian answered thoughtfully. "Perhaps. I've never known Pavlenko myself. I've seen him, but never talked to him."

The president nodded. "Do you have any idea what his motives might be in setting off a volcanic eruption in Alaska?"

"None whatever. I must tell you, I had no idea at all that such a thing was possible, until last night, when Vice President Cromwell briefed me in preparation for this morning. In Russia I'd heard rumors of a great secret weapon, with installations in the arctic and near Riga, and in Kazakhstan. But in the GRU, it is easy to be cynical. And if it was true, then it was the kind of thing you're wise not to speculate about."

"Have you known General Gurenko?"

"Gurenko?" Bulavin sounded surprised. "Yes. Rather well, although our contacts were professional, never personal. He was in charge of the San Francisco residency when I was a young operational officer there. A very fair officer, but of course very ruthless. As I was. As the GRU goes, he was a good officer to work under."

"What's his attitude toward Americans?"

Bulavin reflected for a moment. "It was not something we discussed. But he wasn't a xenophobe like Pavlenko and so many others. He'd lived abroad too much for that, particularly in the States."

Haugen nodded. "I've been assuming you're with the Defense Intelligence Agency now; that or Army Intelligence. Is that right?"

Bulavin smiled a one-sided smile. "While General Cromwell was the CJCS, I was his intelligence aide. Since then I've had an 'open assignment' on the Joint Staff. Before he was chairman, I was briefly with the Defense Intelligence Agency, but there were two problems with that. One was the need to keep my true identity confidential; only three people there were allowed to know it. And more difficult, more basic, there was the understandable problem that

the seniors there—the people who knew who I was—
didn't fully trust me. So they made limited use of my
particular qualifications.

"Any intelligence organization is very sensitive to the
danger of double agents, and most intelligence officers,
here as well as in the Soviet Union, are very afraid of
making errors. Too much is at stake."

"Why does Jumper trust you?"

"I'm a man with an exceptional memory. Not an eidetic
memory, but exceptional. So when I defected, I was able
to provide an extreme amount of detailed and valuable
information on the Soviet military and government. I've
been called the most valuable defector ever. And so far as
I know, in no case has any of my information proved
false."

Again the one-sided smile. "Beyond that, it seems to me
that the general is a man who tends to trust his intuitions."

That fits, Haugen said to himself. That sure as hell fits.

"Are you up to date on Gurenko?" Haugen asked. "Is he
still commanding officer of the GRU?"

"He was as recently as January fourth. If there'd been
any change, I would probably have heard."

Haugen studied the Russian thoughtfully; Bulavin sat
quite relaxed through it, studying him in return. Then the
president made a decision.

"Colonel Schubert, what's your given name these days?
Not Nikita I suppose."

The Russian laughed silently. "Kurt. Even on the Joint
Staff, I pass as German-American. In this identity, my
family is Baltische Deutsch, from Narva. That explains my
occasionally odd English and non-standard German."

The president was surprised to see a twinkle in Bulavin's
eyes. "Did I say something that amused you?" Haugen
asked.

The Russian shook his head. "No. It was the discussion
of my new identity. Working for General Cromwell was a
marvelous hiding place for me. In the Soviet Union, no
one would imagine a defector being made an aide to the
chief of the general staff."

Haugen nodded. "I suppose not. Not many Americans
would imagine that, either. I'll tell you what: I'm going to
call Jumper and have him arrange to borrow you. For me,

although we won't tell the Joint Staff that. Then I'm going to get him over here today, along with LaMotte and Barry for their data and contacts. You and LaMotte will find or create a secret communication line to Gurenko, if at all possible, and see if you can interest him in carrying out a coup in the Kremlin."

His eyes found Bulavin's and held them. "Does that sound at all possible?"

Bulavin sat quietly for a long several seconds. "Mr. President, a year ago I'd have said no. Not remotely possible. Either making contact with him or getting his interest. And assuming that by some miracle we did both of those, I could not even have conceived of his actually carrying out a successful coup. Not even as chief of the GRU. I'd have said that the chance was absolutely zero, and I'd have been right.

"But now, with things as they are there, I can conceive of it." Bulavin grinned. "Just barely, I can conceive of it. And to try— That would be the challenge of a lifetime!"

"Good." The president reached for his phone. "Then we might as well get started."

THIRTY-SEVEN

The president burst out of bed to the high-pitched sound of an alarm—not the building alarm—that continued for several long seconds, punctuated midway by a bang a little distance off. Lois was sitting up, staring at her husband crouched in the darkness.

"What is it?"

He straightened. "I'm not sure. Did you hear the explosion? The instruments on the roof may have picked up something, maybe a rocket, and used the ECMs to blow it up." He took his bathrobe from a chair beside his bed.

"I'm going to go find out. Do you think you can get back to sleep?"

She got up. "I think I'll read till you come back. Then you can tell me about it."

He left thinking what a cool head she had, and took the stairs to the third floor command room. The first lieutenant in charge of the watch was startled to see the bathrobed president come in.

"What happened?" Haugen asked.

"Sir, a rocket was fired at the White House. We shot it down. We also got a read on the origin, and sent a gunship; I haven't heard them shooting though. The enemy may try again later; do you want to evacuate?"

"No. How loud does your alarm need to be?"

"It's more than loud enough now, Mr. President."

"Right. How loud does it *need* to be? I presume the watch on duty is always awake."

"Yessir! Always!"

"Then what's the function of the alarm?"

"Well, sir, it lets us all know and—it galvanizes us."

"Umh. I see. How loud does it need to be to do that? You galvanized me, too, and when you're going to bed in the morning, I'll be going to work."

"I see your point, Mr. President. I'll set the volume down to—how would a third be? If there's time to evacuate, we'll hit the building alarm anyway."

"Okay, try it at a third. And thank you, lieutenant, for your good shooting. I'm glad you and your men are here."

He strolled out on the third-floor promenade then. The night was still and overcast, the temperature up around forty. Some civilian staff were out too, gathered in a loose group, gazing across the city. He joined them.

"A little excitement, eh?" he said.

"Yes sir," one of them answered.

"I told them to cut back the volume on their alarm. No need to shock everyone in the building unless we need to head for the shelter."

"Yes sir." The man turned to look northward again. "It would have been interesting to see the shooting. They must have blown up whatever it was; I heard an explosion."

"They did. And a marine gunship went after whoever

fired it. I'm going back to bed now; the excitement seems to be over. Have a good night."

As he headed back to his apartment, he wondered what form the next attack would take.

Seven hours later the president was briefed by Secretary Valenzuela. The Republic of South Africa had stopped their advance in Namibia when the West German squadrons had arrived. But they refused to withdraw unless the United States, Britain, and West Germany recognized their right to pursue raiders north across the borders into the black nations they raided from. And also their right to hit raider staging areas in the black nations. Otherwise the Afrikaner army would stay in southern Namibia.

It was an impasse, and Haugen had no solution to suggest. Unless someone came up with something, the Germans and Cubans both would be unhappy. He half wished now that he'd refused to intervene. But only half wished. It was unlike him to half-do anything; it seemed part of a vaguely depressed feeling that had settled over him at times lately.

He told himself, after Valenzuela left, that he needed to get himself together again. He should feel pretty good about things. The economic recovery was progressing steadily if slowly, unemployment was dropping, public morale was better than anyone had expected, and the repeal bill had failed by a goodly margin in both houses of Congress.

And the new Morrisey and Spencer public opinion survey had come out even more favorable than the one before, though the difference wasn't very big.

He knew one thing that was bothering him; Pavlenko and the eruptions. Suppose the Soviets released a few megatons of energy in the Yellowstone hotspot! That could make Mount Spurr or Mount St. Helens look like cherry bombs.

They probably wouldn't hit Yellowstone though. It had the potential to produce a year without a summer, worse than the legendary year of eighteen hundred and froze to death, after Tamboro Volcano blew in 1815. Something like that would hurt the Soviets worse than it would America, though the ashfall would cause enormous damage in Montana and Wyoming.

And there was always the San Andreas Fault. No one planning a scalar resonance attack would overlook that as a possibility. Or the Juan de Fuca subduction zone off the coast of Washington; if that one had the potential energy many geophysicists thought, a quake there would hit eight-plus, maybe nine, on the Richter scale and wreck Seattle, Vancouver, Victoria . . . that whole section of coast. There'd be not only the quake, but the tsunami, and the harbor waves trapped in Puget Sound and the Straits of Juan de Fuca and Georgia. And if Mount Rainier let go as a side result . . .

He tried to shake off the thoughts, but they snapped back at once. No one knew for sure whether the Juan de Fuca had built a lot of stress or not: The subduction might be relatively smooth. But even a quake of 6 would be bad news.

He wondered how Bulavin and LaMotte were doing on getting a line in to Gurenko. Or how Gurenko would respond if they succeeded.

He sat back in his chair. *I'm getting nothing done this morning—nothing except wallowing.* Occasionally back home, when necessary to get rid of a fixation, he'd drive out of town and walk in the woods, seeing how many different things he could spot. Bobcat dung, fungal conks on trees, a porcupine half hidden in the foliage of a white pine, fly amanitas sprouting from the forest floor, the chiseled out nest of a pileated woodpecker in a big old balm of gilead . . . But here if he tried to walk in the park, the Secret Service would go crazy.

So he got up and walked around his office instead, spotting things in the pattern of his carpet, an assymetrical leaf on one of the plants, the details of the carving on the mantle of his fireplace. He reached out and raised the presidential flag standing next to the Stars and Stripes in his window embayment. He'd never paid attention to its pattern before; now he examined it thoroughly.

After four or five minutes of this, he sat down again to his speech on business and the IRS. Pavlenko and scalar resonance transmitters were still in the back of his mind, but for now they were out of sight.

That night there was a 60mm mortar attack on the

White House. The first shell missed, landing on Lafayette Square. The second wrecked the East Wing theater; the third hit the North Portico and converted their bedroom windows into granules; the fourth hit a third floor storage room.

By that time two gunships, their crews on ready and on board, their engines warmed up and waiting, had lifted. Flares were fired. But the mortar crew got away. Apparently they'd fired from a roof somewhere, then went inside out of sight. Maybe they'd heard the choppers coming.

At 0917 hours the next morning, the FBI, backed by a platoon of paratroops, arrested three men who shared a small apartment. The mortar tube, base, legs, and sight were found in a closet, along with two cloverleafs, one empty and one with two remaining mortar bombs. Television newscasters interviewed the angry neighbors who'd turned them in. By midafternoon, an ugly crowd had gathered outside the D.C. jail, demanding to be given what they termed "the bombers." The news shots showed ropes and baseball bats, and no doubt more than a few had knives and razors. Nothing happened though; they seemed to be making a statement and blowing off steam.

The pictures shown of damage to the White House were sobering, the commentary somber and condemnatory, contrasting this action with the progress of national recovery. Domestic staff interviewed were angry, not fearful.

Perhaps, Haugen thought, a corner was being turned. Anger wasn't the highest of emotions, but it was better than fear or despondency.

That night an elderly F5-B jet fighter, which had not replied to repeated radio challenges, was shot down over Virginia, approaching Washington from the south. It had worn the American Air Force emblem, but the identification number didn't pass a computer check, and no F5-Bs were stationed in the eastern United States. Its single 500-pound bomb had not yet been armed and did not explode on impact. Examination of the wreckage the next day identified it as a plane reported stolen, perhaps "bought," from the Columbian Air Force by drug lords.

The CIA had reported that something like this was

being talked about as a response to the recent destruction and capture of boats and planes carrying drugs to the United States. And to the new policy of searching seamen leaving ships, and of certain cargoes on the docks; and of other actions being taken to reduce the inflow of drugs.

The media treated these things soberly too, and gave time to Coast Guard footage of boats and planes being challenged and searched. And a few firefights. For now, at least, the Emergency Powers Act was not the focus of attention.

The next morning the media had something new to occupy them. The South African government admitted that thirty-seven-year-old Wilfred Mpumelele had died in prison "of undetermined causes." By nightfall, riots unprecedented in South Africa were spreading like fire on oil.

THIRTY-EIGHT

Excerpts from the president's January 20 fireside talk on the economy and taxes.

. . . .A very important part of our economic problems has grown out of government spending. Where does government money go? For decades a very large segment has gone annually to defense. That's unavoidable in these times, if we want to remain a free nation. A larger segment has gone to do things for people which it's been considered must be done, and considered also that they can't do for themselves as individuals.

A third segment of government spending might be termed the slopover of money appropriated for the first two: that slopover which we call government waste. Citizens and the media look around and see— Government waste.

Waste is an inevitable part of government activities, just as waste is part of the activities of businesses and of almost every family above the lowest poverty level. The trick is to keep the amount of waste relatively low. In government, this has been attempted by trying to monitor purchases and payments, keeping track of almost everything.

But to do that, to monitor government expenditures in detail, costs a lot of money. And on top of that, the red tape and paperwork that the monitors demand of every government operation, in order to monitor them, makes it more difficult and expensive to get productive work done.

This is rather like the red tape and paperwork that the IRS requires of businesses in order to monitor their income and expenditures. Which makes it more difficult and expensive for a business to get out its products. But I'll get to that later in this talk.

This effort to control government waste adds greatly to the operating costs of everything from highway construction to the Veterans Administration, from aid to dependent children to NASA and the military. This effort can, and I suspect often does, cost more than it saves, and sometimes screws things up royally in the process.

So we're going to reduce and simplify monitoring. The monitoring agencies and offices are going to spot-check government operations, especially where there are good opportunities for substantial waste or dishonesty. And they will follow up on any substantial waste or dishonesty that they uncover.

Where unreasonable waste is found, three possible whys will be looked for. First, an operating system can be intrinsically inefficient. That is, the way it's set up, you can't run it without a lot of waste. Second, there can be careless waste, the kind that results from not giving a damn. Actually that's a form of dishonesty. And third, there is dishonesty

for gain—for the gain of the government employee
or a contractor or whatever.

In the case of an inefficient operating system, we'll
correct the system—perhaps reorganize it—and may
ask for bids from private contractors who think they
can do it more economically. Where we switch to a
private contractor, normally we'll require that the
contractor staff-up his new operation from among the
federal employees whose old jobs are being discontinued. In the case of carelessness, training and disciplinary action will be used. Where there has been
dishonesty for gain, criminal charges will be filed
and people will be arrested. . . .

. . . .The "Wall Street" scene was pretty complicated. I've had four experts brief me on it, one at a
time. One was a prestigious professor and two were
prominent brokers. The other was a merger specialist. I taped the briefings, and after each of them, I
sat down with two of the government's in-house
specialists. We'd listen to the tapes of the last briefing and I'd ask questions. Then I was ready for the
next expert. I wasn't totally ignorant to start with,
but I learned quite a bit.

What I'll talk about here are just a few of the
points, to give you a sense of it. I'm doing this
because many of you know very little about what
Wall Street does. Then I'll tell you what we're doing
to reform its operations.

First, the stock markets. They serve very important functions. Stocks are pieces of ownership, shares,
in a corporation. The stock markets provide a system
for financing business expansions. They help stock-
brokers find buyers for shares or bonds that the
owners want to sell. And they provide a service for
people who want to invest, usually to invest as a
source of retirement security.

Tens of millions of you lost your investments in
the crash; lost the security those investments were
intended to offer. But over many decades, many
millions of people retired very comfortably on just
such investments: sometimes investments they ar-

ranged themselves, but more often the investments that their pension funds consisted of.

The stock markets generally do not help new businesses get started. New businesses, if they are not sole ownerships or partnerships, are usually privately-held corporations whose stock cannot be sold in the stock markets. . . . Their startup money is commonly venture capital, and such investments are often quite risky. The venture capitalist often takes big risks with his money in hopes of big profit. It is often the venture capitalist who finances the new ideas of business pioneers. Later, when an established small company wants to expand, it may apply for the right to offer stock for open sale on a stock market. . . .

Now on Wall Street there were brokers called "futures traders," who dealt with fairly unpredictable commodities. Let's consider a corporation whose business includes buying and selling corn. For example it buys corn from farmers' cooperatives. No one can predict a year ahead of time whether next year's corn crop will be excellent, good, or not so good. Or whether, in more normal times, there'll be a profitable export demand for corn.

Futures traders buy corn that hasn't been harvested yet, or even grown yet, perhaps not even planted yet. They buy these "corn futures" assuming that there'll be such and such demand for corn, and such and such supply. Then they own lots of corn that they can sell when it eventually is harvested.

Though commonly they'll sell before that; they'll sell what they bought, which is not corn but "corn futures."

Futures are bought with borrowed money that the traders never see or touch. The transactions are simply paper transactions, or actually, over the last couple of decades, computer transactions. They buy when they judge that prices are going to rise, and they sell when they feel that prices are topping out, or as soon as they start to fall, to make maximum profit.

Their very legitimate function is to provide money, in the form of credit, to farmers, banks, grain elevators—whoever or whatever might already own an ungrown or unharvested corn crop and needs money for some purpose such as expansion or machinery. And that is a useful service. On the other hand they manipulate the market without ever raising a crop, without ever delivering a shipload or carload of corn. . . .

Futures trading is not a reprehensible activity. I've used it here as an example of the sort of things that go on, in the money game. Smart, perceptive people spot a need and use ingenuity to fill it. A useful financial service is provided, sometimes with harmful side effects.

And sometimes use is made of it which is at least dishonest and may be criminal. Because there is the possibility of getting BIG money easily and quickly with a strategic bit of dishonesty.

Futures traders are brokers of a special sort. Brokers more generally buy and sell securities such as stocks and bonds, and serve as valuable pipelines for investors. . . .

Let's say Mr. Jones worked for a beer distributor. Mr. Jones owned his own truck and delivered beer to stores and taverns in his city, while Mrs. Jones worked as a secretary for the distributor. They worked hard and made pretty good money, they weren't extravagant, and they wanted to put some of their money where it would provide a good retirement income. Stocks and bonds.

And having neither the time nor the inclination to become educated in investment, they hired an investment firm, a brokerage firm, to invest their money for them. The brokerage firm had a team of trained, salaried brokers who performed this useful service for thousands of people like the Joneses. And they performed this service skillfully and ethically, so that over the years, Mr. and Mrs. Jones developed a nice investment portfolio, and at age sixty retired to Sun City to live happily ever after.

Except that "happily ever after" didn't work out that way, because the stock market crashed and there weren't any more checks coming in.

So the whole area of what is loosely termed "Wall Street" has been under review by a joint committee of Congress. And also, separately, by a small select group outside of government. These committees aren't thinking about replacing the system. Basically the system works, it exists ready made, and it's starting to function again, although relatively slowly and cautiously these days. What the committees are working on is modifying the system to decrease the risks, and preliminary drafts of their reforms are being critiqued now.

There is another element of the stock markets that we are doing something about already. That is the criminality in the system, and I'm going to tell you about that now. Some of this criminality is subtle and hard to detect. You might see evidence that something criminal was happening, but not just what or by whom. Over the years, changes were made in brokerage and other business procedures and in monitoring techniques, to make financial crimes harder to commit, and financial criminals easier to catch. But the payoff possibilities were BIG. And while most brokers were ethical, the temptations were too strong for brokers with flabby ethics or a snootful of cocaine.

So I'm adding to their risk in a different way. The white-collar criminal who breaks federal law, be he stockbroker, banker, government official, corporation executive—what have you—will be imprisoned on a special basis.

In the past his imprisonment was almost always on a special basis too, if he went to prison at all. The white-collar criminal was rarely a violent or vicious man; he tended to be mannerly and quiet. And he often had influential friends. So he was given privileges and decent quarters in prison. His work duties were clean and easy. He typed and filed in an air conditioned office and generally worked less hard than secretaries do on the outside. Less hard than he had as a broker or corporation executive or lawyer or judge.

Alas for him, the new special basis is different than the old. Under new law he will enjoy the hospitality of a prison camp for white-collar criminals in the Gila River Valley of Arizona. There the crooked broker will work long hours chopping weeds in the cotton fields. Side by side with crooked lawyers and crooked judges and crooked corporate executives.

Now this is not "cruel and unusual punishment" in the language of the Constitution. Prisoners, though rarely white-collar prisoners, have done the field labor on prison farms in this country from the beginning. In fact, the white-collar prisoner will be doing the kind of labor that cotton farmers long took for granted before mechanization and chemical herbicides.

He will also enjoy the comfort of an old army squad tent, shared with others, and sleep on a folding cot. Just as so many soldiers and marines have done in war-time. He will live and work under hardnosed but not brutal supervisors, and eat plain but healthy food. Very plain. I'm told that brown rice and beans, along with some fruit and green vegetables, powdered milk and coarse bread, make up a balanced diet. Not bad in times like these. And counseling will be available to him, if he wants it— counseling psychological or religious.

Barbed wire fences will be his walls, watchtowers his monuments. Dustdevils and desert crags will be his scenery. He will learn all about sweat and dirt. And in case he develops a sense of physical daring, there is a mine field outside the fence. We're done with building enormously expensive federal prisons except for prisoners who require stone walls.

And if his wealthy friends hire a rescue mission, they will find the guards equipped with anti-tank rockets and Stinger anti-aircraft missiles.

As a matter of fact, we have white-collar criminals in federal prisons right now who, on Thursday, will be on a plane to Gila Bend to learn all about mucking out irrigation ditches and chopping weeds with a hoe and picking cotton by hand. And you may be pleased to know that, over the past week, we've rounded up a lot of white-collar criminals who've been free on suspended sentences because the jails were considered too crowded. Actually there were a lot more of them free than in jail. They'll be among those flying to Gila Bend.

And when they're released, they'll have a new perspective on the basis of wealth, which is honest production. For let it be understood that production of goods and services is the only basis there is of wealth. That's what wealth is: goods and services. Money is simply pieces of paper used to represent goods and services. The goods may be cotton, for example; the service may be the honest brokerage of cotton futures or the transporting of cotton. Whatever.

Production of the various goods and services *is* the basis of wealth.

Up till now, much of the wealth stolen by the Wall Street criminal has remained his—converted into stock, real estate, and so forth. That too has now changed. In future cases, his personal wealth will be confiscated and put into a superfund to help make restitution for what we might call the "people damages" of white-collar crime—the damage to people.

This seizure of property will be only what is necessary to cover what a jury decides is proper restitution and amends, plus court costs. And of course, seizure will not be resorted to if the criminal himself arranges restitution, which he will be allowed to do.

Admittedly, in some cases this conversion of his estate will be hard on his family, who've been used to the affluent life, but they will be eligible for help from the superfund on the same basis as any of his other victims.

And let me add that none of this is done in a spirit of revenge. Although I'll admit to feeling a certain vengeful satisfaction from these laws. No, the biggest single reason is to emphasize and instill, within the society of big money, the concepts of *responsibility* and *accountability* for one's actions. And the concepts of restitution and amends. It is also—and this is a key part of it—it is also to *discourage* white-collar crime, not only on Wall Street but on Main Street. Not only in brokerage houses but in banks and government offices.

And beyond that, this is to demonstrate to you,

the people of this country, that there is no longer a special moneyed class to whom the laws and penalties do not apply the way they do to the rest of you. The theft by a white-collar criminal is often of very large sums—occasionally even huge sums. His penalties will no longer be paltry. . . .

One other thing I want to touch on tonight is federal taxes and the IRS. Congress, presidents, and the innumerable lobbies have had much more to do with the federal tax mess than the IRS has. The IRS has simply had the unenviable job of trying to collect.

Unfortunately, in trying to cope with the mess, the IRS has too often been guilty of decisions having less to do with justice than with making their difficult job easier.

Some officials in the IRS have been arbitrary and high-handed, making decisions far outside the intent of Congress. We fired a number of them last fall, and we've jailed others whose actions were criminal. President Wheeler, you may recall, charged several such officials with malfeasance and abuse of office, charges very hard to make stick at that time. For one thing, judges tended to be afraid of the IRS. So in most cases the charges were dropped when the officials agreed to resign.

Well, those charges have recently been reviewed, and where appropriate they have been revived. There have been several arrests. And when the courts have heard the cases, I'm sure the cotton fields along the Gila River will have some additional workers. And if you listen closely, you may hear President Wheeler laughing and clapping clear up in heaven.

But the real problem has been the tax laws, not the IRS.

I admit that I wince whenever I use or hear the term "tax reform." Such atrocities have been committed under that name! But I've read the prefinal drafts of the new tax reform law, and it *really is reform*. The new law will have nothing in it of tax "penalties" for being in certain businesses, and tax "breaks" and "incentives" for being in certain others.

Incentives and breaks are actually government subsidies. In the future, business subsidies and penalties, if any, will be entirely separate from federal taxes. They will not be allowed to complicate and generally muck up our federal tax system. The new tax system is intended solely to provide money to operate the federal government with. Any additives would be abominations.

And in the future, I hope the voters will be smart enough to throw out of office anyone who tries to complicate the system again, for whatever purpose.

The Congressional Committee expects to have the final draft done on this reform bill within a few days. I'll then decree it into law with no delay, and we'll draw up and issue a whole new set of operating guidelines for the Internal Revenue Service, ready for next year.

This will make life a lot simpler and easier, and more pleasant, not only for the taxpayer but for the IRS! Of course, paying taxes is never a joy, but why make it worse than it needs to be.

So I believe you're going to like this new federal tax law. Look it over. Perhaps you'll be letting your state governments hear about reforming state taxes along the same lines.

And that's all I have to talk about tonight. I opened this speech by saying it was time to fill you in on what Haugen's been doing with his time recently, here in Washington. Now you know. Thank you for listening to me, and good night.

THIRTY-NINE

Paul Massey sat grimly watching the six o'clock network news on WTFD-TV. The trial of the three mortarmen who'd shelled the White House got the biggest play; it was visual and exciting. But the president's speech, and responses to it, got a lot of attention too.

Massey had spoken little since watching the speech the night before. Rumors had been rampant on Wall Street for days of a major investigation by the Securities and Exchange Commission, but he'd felt no concern. There'd been big SEC investigations before, and none had touched Massey. He'd been too well buffered.

But Haugen's speech had frightened him, he who couldn't remember feeling frightened since early childhood.

When the weather forecast began, he clicked the set off and keyed Tallmon's apartment on his intercom. A few seconds later, Tallmon's face appeared on the comm screen.

"Yes Mr. Massey?"

"I want to see you at once. In my office."

"Yes sir. At once sir."

Massey sat and waited, even his face immobile. When Tallmon came in, there was no offer of scotch and seltzer, just the order "sit," and a gesture at a chair facing Massey's. Just "sit"; Tallmon knew then that this would be a very unpleasant meeting. But he'd changed since he'd begun his covert revolt; he could confront Massey's displeasure now, however expressed. He sat.

"Haugen is still alive. The attempts on him were clumsy."

Tallmon didn't tell him that, of the publicized attempts, only the ninja attack and the rocket attacks had been by his contractors. The others—the mortar attempt and the

308

fighter plane attempt—had been independent efforts. He also didn't tell him that only two other contracts were pending.

"Yes sir."

"Explain."

"The explanation seems to be that the White House is exceedingly well protected, sir, particularly electronically. There have been attempts on his life that were cut off before they got far enough to make the papers, and he scarcely leaves the White House."

"I do not employ you to explain failures." The phrasing was acid but the delivery monotone.

"Of course not, sir." Tallmon didn't trouble to remind Massey that an explanation of failures was exactly what he'd demanded.

The eyes that probed Tallmon's bland exterior were no longer rational.

"And the media; you were to direct a media war on the man. Yet the worst that I see in the papers is carping and innuendo, and the television criticism is mostly even weaker. There has been no concerted attack, while the clumsy assassination attempts have actually inspired a degree of sympathy and indignation.

"How do you explain *this*? Certainly not protection."

"May I speak frankly, sir?"

Massey's response was a long look and a short reply: "Do so."

"You have considerable influence, sir, but only limited power. There is a difference. In a sense, you are like the Pope: Important people listen to you, but they may or may not do what you want. You have no army to coerce them with, and in times like these, they are much less likely to comply."

Massey said nothing, just looked. Tallmon continued. "You inherited machinery of a sort for brokering power, but it wasn't designed for times like these. That was probably your great grandfather's biggest oversight.

"I was able to contract with people whose service is assassination; they are in the business. But the newspapers, the networks. . . You might influence their boards of directors, their chairmen, to a degree, but they are more interested in selling papers than they are in advancing your grandfather's philosophy and plans—a philosophy and plans they do not even know. And their editors are another step away from you; they don't know you at all. They know only their publishers, and often do not heed them. While their writers do not know the publishers; they know only their editors.

"Even those that you own, like the Bassett Chain, and the Foremost News Network before it lost its license, operate independently to some degree. There are none who undertake to follow your orders as slavishly as I. They have their own points of view, and their own interests to advance."

He shrugged. "When Haugen has made what they considered serious mistakes, they have jumped on him, perhaps more heavily because of your influence. But so far his mistakes have not been serious enough to result in serious difficulty for him."

Tallmon's voice had been quiet from the beginning, and patient. Now it became faintly sympathetic as well. "In a way, sir," he went on, "your true power is like a glacier; your great grandfather designed it that way. He and his associates set certain things in motion, to move ponderously in a certain approximate direction. Piece by piece they undertook to program the entire American nation to move in that direction, and things *have* moved in that direction. A considerable distance. They planted an orchard of institutions and nurtured their beginning, then allowed them to grow and bear fruit in their own time. They never intended to fight a war for power; cultural evolution was their mode, with themselves as the cultural engineers, so to speak.

"They never devised an effective steering mechanism for their glacier, nor designed any weapons other than financial—no instruments of quick and decisive, far-reaching command. They let it move inexorably on its own, confident that they or their lineage would be in a position to seize the crown when the time came."

Tallmon thought of adding that to seize a crown required a man of action, but he didn't.

"And the people you've engineered into positions of power," he added, "even Coulter, are not your puppets, but only people you influenced, who might be expected to act in appropriate ways."

As he spoke, Tallmon's eyes never left Massey's wooden mask. Surprisingly, Barron Tallmon felt a stirring of something like love, as if for a harsh father come upon hard times in his declining years. "Your great grandfather," he continued, "was a genius, a man of vision and resource. You inherited his wealth and his organization, but you did not inherit . . ."

Massey interrupted. "How do you know so much about my great grandfather?" The eyes burned cold and bitter.

"I read some things in your personal safe." Tallmon gestured at the concealing picture on the wall. "The book on the Archons, and other things."

"Then you spied on me." Massey's voice was still quiet, still expressionless.

"Yes sir. I used a tiny surveillance device to obtain the combination."

Quietly, Massey's hand had drawn out a desk drawer. Now it brought forth a pistol, with a silencer that made it seem larger than it was. Tallmon watched the muzzle move to point at him. And wasn't afraid. *This is what we've been working toward all these years*, he thought. He would have to hurry to tell him his act of ultimate treason.

"And I photocopied them," Tallmon added. "And sent the photocopies to General Cromwell. So far, he hasn't even seen fit to do any . . ."

The crooked finger tightened, firing the pistol, the .32 caliber slug striking Tallmon in the center of the chest. His mouth fell open, not from surprise, for he wasn't surprised, but in death. The bullet had pierced his breastbone and heart, and then the chairback. After a suspended second, what had been Barron Tallmon folded forward and toppled off the chair.

Massey sat expressionless for perhaps half a minute, looking coldly at the body. Then he put the muzzle in his mouth and pulled the trigger again.

FORTY

The air was thick with large wet snowflakes, and Jumper Cromwell had ridden to the White House in a chauffeured staff car. Even with slippery streets, a car seemed better than a helicopter in the heavy snowstorm. He got out in front of the South Portico, where a snowman greeted him with widespread arms—brooms—and a jaunty grin dug into the snow face as if with two fingers. It wore a scarf whitened with new flakes, and a snow-covered basket resembling a coolie hat that shielded the bottle-cap eyes.

The new roof on the East Wing Theater had been completed over the weekend, Cromwell noticed. The mortar attack had done the first hostile damage to the White House since the British had burned it in 1814, and surely the most aggravating. The trial was already over, and the three men sent to Alcatraz Penitentiary, renovated during the Wheeler Administration.

Cromwell had deliberately arrived nearly a quarter hour before the NSC meeting was scheduled to begin. He walked briskly to the Executive Wing through eight inches of white, stomping the snow off his feet in the small portico there. Then he went in, returning the salutes of the marines at the door, and entered Martinelli's office.

"Good morning, Jeanne," he said. In these days almost everyone addressed her as the president did.

"It is if you like snow," she answered cheerfully. "Shall I let President Haugen know you're here?"

"Yes, if you please."

She did, then looked up again at the general. "You can go in now, sir."

The president had rolled his chair back from the desk

312

and watched Cromwell enter. "What do you think of the weather?" he asked with a grin.

"It looks like your marines like it. They built a snowman in your south yard."

"Huh! That wasn't the marines; that was Lois and me. We got up early to play in the snow. The snow in Duluth is usually too dry to make snowmen; we figured we'd better take advantage of the opportunity." He grinned. "We don't expect to be here another winter. Not past New Years."

Cromwell's eyebrows raised. "In that case, sir, you've got less than a year to find a new vice president and break him in.

"Meanwhile I've got an interesting piece of agreeable news for you."

"I'm always open to good news. What is it?"

"Trenary. We were talking yesterday, and he told me he'd been wrong about you. He liked your speech the other night, I guess. About Wall Street and the IRS. What he actually said was, 'That old sonofabitch is sharp and tough, and he's good for the country.'"

"Well I'll be damned! I kept thinking I needed to replace him, and never got around to it."

He chuckled. "When I find myself putting something off, something I'm not afraid of, I usually leave well enough alone. I tell myself I've probably got a good reason for putting it off, that I just haven't spotted yet."

He gestured at the coffee station. "Cuppa?"

Cromwell glanced at the clock and shook his head. "I don't suppose you saw the papers this morning?"

"Just the usual summary." Haugen grinned again. "We seem to be getting better press lately. Maybe getting shot at helps."

He got up. "We might as well go. And thanks, Jumper, for telling me about Trenary. Maybe some other people are changing their minds about me. Favorably."

They strolled through the west wing, past the old press area, then took the elevator to the "second floor." In a sense it was more of a third floor—ground, first, second— and Haugen used the Cabinet Room there for NSC meetings. A number of staff aides had been ordered to attend, and no one was late despite the weather. At 0930 sharp, the president opened the session.

"All right," he said, "I guess we're all here. The meeting will come to order." He looked at the new CIA director. "Barry, update us on the South African situation."

Roy Barry stood up. "Yes sir. It's been a bloody week there. The RSA government slapped on a complete press censorship of course, and their usual ban on cameras around civil disorders was applied over the entire country. They also slapped on travel restrictions: stopped all air traffic in and out. Crews of foreign ships weren't even allowed on the dock except to handle hawsers."

He smiled. "But we have some cameras a little out of their reach, not only in overflights but from embassy and consulate roofs. And of course, eyewitness descriptions from informants, via embassy and consulate communication centers, not to mention radio monitoring. There were extensive fires in and around Johannesburg and Bloemfontein, and they were pretty bad in Durban, though not so bad in Pretoria and Cape Town. A number of small towns were largely or entirely burned out."

He paused. "It was incomparably worse than the troubles we had here. And there were pitched battles in the black townships, with a lot of shooting. The blacks had succeeded in caching considerable guns and ammunition, including anti-tank rockets which somehow we hadn't gotten an inkling of.

"There've been pitched battles in the townships before of course, but nothing at all like these. And equally relevant, this time the blacks made some obviously planned and fairly disciplined armed raids into white districts. The fires there weren't just a matter of blacks with work permits running amok. Outsiders came in shooting, some in cars and trucks.

"The blacks got more than they dished out, of course; they were outgunned, untrained, and their organization is still rudimentary. But they dished out a *lot* more than they ever had before. They made considerable use of gasoline bombs, and mostly they didn't pause to watch or loot. It was hit and go on to the next block. Apparently white deaths ran well into the thousands; white police and military casualties alone clearly ran into the hundreds. Black deaths ran into the tens of thousands. And property damage . . ." He shrugged. "It has to have been well into the billions.

"The RSA called all their troops home from Namibia, partly because of stepped-up raids out of Mozambique. And even Zimbabwe, which has been pretty cautious about harboring guerrillas. But the raids weren't as heavy as we'd thought they might be; apparently the blowup caught them unprepared to take full advantage of it."

He stopped and looked around the large table. "That's it in a nutshell," he said, and sat down.

"How is the white population taking all this?" Haugen asked him.

"The word is that the number of people trying to get air reservations or ship passage out of the country is way up. Apparently a lot of the moderates have decided it's time to leave. Of course, there's always the problem of selling their property, but a lot of them undoubtedly got burned out anyway. And property isn't going to be as big a holding factor as it's been in the past; I think we'll see a considerable white exodus over the next month or two.

"But the ordinary Afrikaner is probably more grimly determined to hold out now than he ever was."

"Val," the president said, turning to the Secretary of State, "what have you got to add to that?"

"Not much, Mr. President. A number of countries have registered official condemnation of what they've generally termed 'the genocidal response' to 'the black demonstrations.' That includes all the eastern bloc and African countries of course, and a lot of others."

"Umm. Anyone else have anything on this?"

No one did. The president meant meaningful contributions, and they knew it.

"All right. Val, is there anything you need from this conference now? Anything we need to talk about here?"

"No sir. I've sent the statement you approved. I believe that's as far as we should go for now."

"Fine. Barry, what's new on the Soviets that we should know?"

The CIA director stood back up. "Nothing everyone here hasn't seen in the intelligence summaries. There've been scattered mini-mutinies in the Soviet invasion army.

Nothing overt: the 'sit down and pretend the equipment doesn't work' kind. At least sometimes with a little strategic sabotage to make the breakdowns convincing. It would be worse if the army hadn't been careful to transfer all Soviet Moslem troops out of the invasion units.

"And there was a major mutiny, an officers' mutiny, in their East Asian military district at Khabarovsk. We don't have any information on what inspired that, but it ended in a pretty respectable fight."

Haugen said nothing, but he was feeling a little more hope for his Gurenko plan.

"Meanwhile," Barry was saying, "the Kremlin continues to shift their mobile ICBM launchers around, and they've sent up eleven anti-satellite and anti-missile satellites in the past week, in contravention of the Wheeler-Gorbachev agreements." He shrugged. "It could be posturing, or they could be planning a nuclear strike, but even if they are posturing, it could turn into something real."

He sat down again. "Thank you, Barry," the president said, and turned to Cromwell. "General, anything to report on the strategic alert?"

Cromwell shook his head. "No sir. Even a yellow alert is something of a strain on personnel at first, but they get used to it. And after a while they get less alert."

"Anything more we ought to be doing?"

Only Valenzuela spoke. "I'd recommend you talk to Pavlenko."

"I'll get with you later on that." He turned to Paul Van Breda, his new defense secretary. "You too, Dutch."

It occurred to Haugen that Van Breda hadn't yet been told about the scalar resonance weapons. He should be. But not in front of all these people.

They went from the subject of the Soviets to the same old Malaysian troubles, and then to the renewed Moro uprising in the Philippines. The Malaysian situation was three-cornered, involving the Moslem government, a fundamentalist Moslem insurrection, and a Buddhist separatist movement. The Wheeler government's policy had been to help keep the government in power and get it to conciliate the Buddhists. Under Donnelly, Covert Operations had been phased out, and Haugen was disinclined to get them reinvolved.

The Moro uprising was simpler: The Moslem provinces in the southern Philippines wanted independence, though apparently they'd settle for autonomy within the Philippine republic. After brief NSC discussion, the president decided to confer on the subject, via telephone, with Ireneo Malaluan, the islands' reform president. Haugen had at least some common ground with Malaluan; he'd participated in the liberation of his home province, Batangas, half a century earlier, and had a speaking knowledge of Tagalog, gained partly there and partly from a Filipina housekeeper he and Lois had employed for several years.

After that, the conference reviewed ongoing projects and adjourned by 1120.

It seemed to Haugen that they were living a dual existence. In some respects, foreign as well as domestic, things seemed to be going better and better. They were going to hell in South Africa of course, but people had been expecting that, and it didn't seem to threaten the United States. On the other hand, the Soviet threat seemed more dangerous, if harder to evaluate, than during the Khrushchev-Kennedy confrontation in 1962.

After the meeting, the president and Secretary Valenzuela gave the new defense secretary a minibriefing on the UFOs and scalar resonance. Van Breda left looking even more sober than before.

At lunch, Father Flynn asked permission to teach a night school class in written English for some members of the domestic staff whose literacy was poor.

"Getting a little boring around here, is it?" Haugen asked.

"Not boring so much as—unproductive for me."

"Sure, go ahead. Sounds like a good thing to do. And I appreciate your company; I'm glad you didn't ask to leave."

Flynn nodded.

"President," Haugen mused. "*Emergency* president. Lots of death threats and assassination attempts, no speaking trips—I've never been so house-bound in my life! Tell you what, Steve: I'm still having fun, but I'll be more than happy to leave."

Yet even as he said it, and true as it was, it seemed to

Arne Haugen that he'd never again have the freedom of movement he'd had before.

It was just a little after lunch when the president got a call from the CIA. The Kremlin had announced that, since the "Iranian genocides" had been driven from Iraq, Soviet troops were no longer needed there. The Soviet army was beginning an evacuation that would probably take it back across the central Zagros to the Iranian cities of Qom and Hamadan, and perhaps farther.

And the next morning, both his intelligence summary and his news summary informed him that a Syrian army coup had overthrown the pro-Soviet government.

Judas Priest! he thought. *Things are happening fast!*

A pang of anxiety struck him. He had such hopes for what he was doing! The nation *was* climbing out of the economic hole it had dug for itself. It *was* showing new morale. Manufacture of GPCs had begun, or soon would, by licensees in Greensboro, Detroit, Seattle, and three foreign countries. A number of corporations, including Ford, GM, Chrysler, and International Harvester were falling all over themselves to complete production designs for geo-powered cars, tractors, and trucks. Eddie Wing's summary reports told of intense excitement developing around the new research in what they were already calling Tesla matrices, and what it implied in fields as diverse as cosmology, "space" travel, and apparently, human consciousness.

The whole darn human species was promising to leap to a new and higher level!

And suddenly it seemed to him beyond bearing if nuclear apocalypse, or any apocalypse, should trash it all.

FORTY-ONE

The president's office phone buzzed. He reached, touching the flashing key. "What is it, Jeanne?"

"Mr. Guild is on line one, sir."

His legislative affairs assistant; he'd replaced Blake. "Thanks." He tapped line one. "What have you got for me, Manny?"

"Mr. President, I just got back from the Hill; I was talking with Speaker Lynch. He expects a new bill to be submitted today to repeal the Emergency Powers Act, but he doesn't expect it to get out of committee.

"He also commented that the repeal lobby is losing a lot of steam. The recovery is going so well, a lot of its business supporters have apparently decided to quit rocking the boat. He wanted you to know that."

"Thanks, Manny. Is that it?"

"Yes sir."

"Fine. Thanks for letting me know."

"You're welcome, sir."

Haugen tapped the key again, disconnecting. It still surprised him that Congress, as a whole, was agreeable to a president having so much authority. Of course, they were the ones who'd originated the Emergency Powers Act, and the vote for approval had been lopsided in both houses. And they had the power to repeal it. But still . . . He wasn't sure how he'd feel in their shoes.

He returned his attention to the intelligence summary. More than 60,000 white South Africans who'd applied for exit visas had been interned and their property confiscated. Presumably the Pienaar government considered it a matter of social discipline, but if you leave people no avenue of escape, you inspire mutiny, and if mutiny isn't feasible, then sabotage.

And 60,000 of them! A great time to be in the barbed wire business there, if you had a strong enough stomach.

He read on: Raiding out of the north had increased, mainly from Mozambique, and the raiders were routinely pursued across the border by South African defense forces without restriction. The South African air force had bombed and strafed raider staging areas in Mozambique. Several of their aircraft had been shot down by surface-to-air missiles.

It was easy to see why so many moderates wanted to get out. Things were sliding toward the day of final reckoning there.

He turned a page. Food riots in the USSR, even in Russia. And more sabotage. If it was true that the Kulish government had invaded Iran partly to stoke up Russian patriotism, what might the more militaristic Pavlenko government do? He wondered briefly what things might have been like if Gorbachev had lived. Gorbachev's reforms had gone even further than Khruschev's, and he'd been less reckless and more sagacious in foreign affairs. But Gorbachev hadn't lived.

He wondered where Kulish was now. Presumably still loose. If the Pavlenko government ever got hold of him, they were bound to make a big show out of it. It would be a distraction from the troubles there.

He read further. The Soviets were still shifting their mobile missile launchers around. They hadn't orbited any more missile- and satellite-killer satellites for more than a week, but that could mean they didn't have more to send up just now.

Haugen became aware of physical discomfort: a weak watery feeling in his hands, and a knotted stomach. *Anxiety,* he told himself. He reached for his security phone and keyed Cromwell's Pentagon number. No answer. On the system line, Cromwell's secretary answered; the general, she said, was away from his desk. Could he call the president back?"

"Right," said Haugen. "On the security phone."

All he wanted to ask was if Cromwell had heard from Schubert/Bulavin. He could check with the OSS of course, but he didn't want them to know that the president was anxious. It'd be bad for his image.

* * *

Hammaker called him before Cromwell did. South African fighter planes had just bombed and strafed the government district in Maputo, Mozambique's capital. Haugen wasn't surprised; it was the sort of thing to expect. *So why,* he asked himself, *does it make me feel so ill at ease? And what the hell is going on with me anyway?* It seemed to him he'd never felt so negative before in his life.

Then Cromwell phoned him back. Schubert was still out of the country, and he hadn't heard from him.

The best thing for anxiety, Haugen told himself, short of resolving the problem, was work. Quickly, without further cerebration but simply recording mentally, he read through the rest of the intelligence summary. Then he began to outline his scheduled speech to the American Medical Association.

That evening, Gupta called the president. Immediately afterward, the president called an NSC meeting for 0800 the next morning. Pavlenko seemed determined to push him to the wall.

FORTY-TWO

The NSC meeting was as small as any had been during Haugen's presidency. Besides the actual council members, only three persons attended: Milstead, Gupta, and Father Flynn. There were no aides; the president had things to say that were best said to a minimum of ears.

The attendees came in looking more serious than usual, as if the president's mood of yesterday had infected them over the phone. Actually he felt better today. A shaft of

winter sunlight reflected off Gupta's mahogany bald spot—
like a sign from God, Haugen told himself. Too bad Flynn
couldn't see it from where he sat.

When they were all seated, Haugen opened the session.

"Dr. Gupta," he said, "tell these other people what you
told me."

Gupta got up. "That much and more, sir. Gentlemen,
starting the night before last, there's been a marked shift
in the jet stream. Certain characteristics strongly suggested that the shift was artificially induced; so I had
instrumented aircraft sent to investigate. Our uncertainty
level went to zero: The Soviet government has used scalar
resonance transmitters to shunt the jet stream into a particular course, and it's likely to hold that course as long as
they maintain their artificially induced high and low pressure cells.

"This has started an arctic air mass moving south through
western and central Canada. Most of the plains, midwest,
and east will be severely affected, all the way to the Gulf.

"From the Great Lakes southward, particularly southward, we can expect heavy precipitation along the front.
From about the Ohio River south, snowfall accumulations
will be very heavy . . ."

The president interrupted. "From the Ohio River *south*?"

"That's right, Mr. President. Farther north there'll be
less moisture available, so less snow. South of Tennessee
or northern Alabama, a lot of it will fall as rain, turning to
snow later, and along the Gulf Coast the rains will be
torrential. And then, when the front passes through, it's
going to get cold. Damn cold!

"We're looking for at least fifteen inches of snow in
Tennessee and maybe as much as twenty-five or more.
And there'll be freezing temperatures all the way south
through Florida. For as long as the pattern remains."

And the country was already suffering from lack of fuel
oil. The president shook his head.

"In other words," he said, "we're looking at the beginning of a weatherwar. Is that it?"

"Yes sir. You could call it that."

"What would happen if we used our own transmitters to
disrupt the pattern? Can we do that?"

"We could. Last night I ran a number of alternative

scenarios with our computer models, assuming a variety of Soviet responses. And while our prediction models aren't designed for a sequence of manipulations and counter-manipulations, some of the results seem to be worse than doing nothing. So frankly sir, I'm a little afraid of what might happen if we tried to break it up. If the Soviets would simply let us break the pattern, I'd have no qualms. But I can't see any reason why they would."

"And there's no natural explanation at all for this jet stream shift? Could the Mount Spurr ash drift have anything to do with it?"

"No sir. And actually, two jet streams are involved. A northern and a southern. We're sure that location of the northern one is the result of Soviet manipulation: The pressure cells could hardly have formed naturally where and when they did in the pressure milieu immediately preceding them, and our on-site instrument check detected low-grade heat extractions to maintain them in place."

"All right. Can you people produce comparably severe weather for Russia?"

"I've run some models on that too, sir. We can give Russia her worst snowstorm in maybe fifty years, and follow it with a helluva coldwave."

"What will this do to the weather in central and western Europe?"

"Italy, the Balkans, Turkey—they'll all get fairly prolonged heavy precipitation—rain near the coast, and snow inland and at high elevations where they normally get snow. A maybe once-a-decade size storm there. It'll pretty much miss West Germany, but it'll be heavy in Poland and Czechoslovakia. And Finland. It'll be very heavy in Rumania and worse to the north and east, then slacking off past the Urals.

"I'm talking about something like thirty inches or more in the region from maybe Odessa to Minsk, Volgograd to Gorkiy, slacking off past the Urals. And with winds and drifting. It'll be a calamity.

"That'll be followed by a cold wave of the sort they get maybe once in ten to twenty years."

The president looked the council over. "Comments?"

"What will the Soviets do," asked Valenzuela, "when we've done that?"

"Good question." Haugen turned to Gupta. "I don't suppose you have an answer for it?"

Gupta shook his head. "It's impossible to say how the Soviets will react."

"Any other comments? Jumper, what's on your mind?"

"They've got more transmitters than we have; twelve to three. What will that mean if we make a contest out of this?"

"The twelve to three difference in transmitters won't mean much for the United States and Canada," Gupta answered. "Not if the Soviets stick to weatherwar. They can create and maintain bad weather over a lot more of the world than we can, but I don't see that as an advantage to them.

"Of course, they might decide to create some earthquakes and eruptions, and our highly susceptible west coast areas have a lot of people in them, while the most susceptible Soviet area, the Kamchatka Peninsula, has very few. The Caucasus would be our best retaliation site. But seismic warfare is likely to escalate into explosive energy releases anyway, and then go nuclear, and I can't visualize the Kremlin taking that risk."

Haugen could visualize it. He pursed his wide mouth, then exhaled gustily. "Now I think we know why they triggered the Mount Spurr eruption; Pavlenko assumed we'd be afraid to retaliate against this." He scanned the serious faces around the table. "Okay, I'm going to make a tentative battle plan. Jim, I want you to monitor the pressure cells they've created; see if they're maintaining them in place. If they're still in place twenty-four hours from now, give the Kremlin a blizzard to remember.

"Any disagreement?" He looked around, his eyes pausing for just a second on the silent Jesuit, but it was Valenzuela who responded.

"What would you think of communicating with Pavlenko first?"

"Not much, Val. I'm convinced the man is psychotic. Any sign of sweet reason, he'd read as weakness, and escalate, try to drive us to our knees. On the other hand, if we confront him, he may back down." *Or will he? If he's psychotic?*

An emergency phone rang beside the president. He

picked up the privacy receiver. "This is the president. What is it?"

The others watched the president as he listened. His face paled. After about a minute he said "thank you," hung up, and looked around. "Gentlemen," he said, "what appears to have been a neutron cluster warhead was exploded over Pretoria, South Africa, a few minutes ago. Considering the weapon, and the population of the district, the dead should number something like half a million. And Pretoria being the administrative capital of the RSA, we can also assume their government's been wiped out.

"Satellite data shows it was fired from coastal forest in southern Mozambique. We can assume the Mozambique government got the missile and the launcher, and certainly the warhead, from the Soviets. It looks like Soviet intimidation—something to scare the world. The American and European publics especially. And most particularly me.

"Any possibilities I've overlooked on this?"

Valenzuela shook his head slowly. "It's inconceivable that the British would have provided it, or the French. Or the Israelis. The evidence is that no one else can make that kind of warhead."

The president nodded. "All right, let's adjourn this meeting. Val, you need to draft a statement for the press concerning the Pretoria tragedy. Not pointing a finger at anyone; we'll let others do that. And let me see it before you release it."

He turned to Gupta. "Jim, don't wait twenty-four hours. Crank up your blizzard today."

Arne Haugen and Stephen Joseph Flynn watched the noon news together. The fatality estimate was 540,000, white and black. The camera footage was gruesome. It was summer in South Africa, and daylight saving time; the warhead had exploded during evening rush hour, and it had not yet been dark when the television helicopters had overflown Pretoria. The streets were full of wrecked and stalled cars, the downtown sidewalks littered with dead. Small bodies lay strewn about a playground.

There was little visible damage to structures, and radioactivity was minor, but the death toll was staggeringly complete. There was no visible trace of movement; apparently it was too late in the day for vultures to be abroad, and smaller birds had not yet infiltrated from outside the death area. Tomorrow would be uglier, Haugen told himself, and the next day worse.

"What is there to say?" asked the president.

Father Flynn shook his head. He couldn't think of anything.

FORTY-THREE

Sergeant Kurt Marais stood at the .50 calibre pintle gun, knees slightly bent, braced against the movement of the solitary armored personnel carrier as it rolled down the graveled South African road. The summer rains had been sparse, and six large tires and the air stream raised a long, conspicuous train of dust.

Except for themselves, the road seemed abandoned. Apparently every white in the region who hadn't been called up in the mobilization, or killed, had headed south.

The APC was traveling at 20 mph, fast enough considering they weren't going anywhere in particular, and the low speed conserved fuel. The day before, they'd found the Hoopstad base abandoned and its diesel fuel gone. The company had pooled the fuel it had with it then, abandoning six of its sixteen vehicles, carrying the extra men mostly on top, and headed south for Bultfontein. A bunch of bloody kaffirs with rockets and automatic weapons had ambushed them from a hillside, and been routed of course, but not before the company had lost two vehicles and twenty-eight men.

They'd found Bultfontein abandoned too, with no more

fuel than there'd been at Hoopstad. So again they'd pooled what they had left, filling the tanks of three and partly filling another. Then Captain Temborg had asked for volunteers to go on foot, to go shooting kaffirs until they were dead themselves or out of ammunition. Every man had shouted or growled his readiness—they were all from Pretoria, and most had had family there. Temborg had chosen the youngest.

They'd spent the night at Bultfontein. There'd been kaffirs about, their calls eerie in the darkness. But there hadn't been enough of them to feel like attacking the APCs. At dawn the men on foot had moved out. Most of the rest had headed south for Bloemfontein—it was anyone's guess what they'd find there—but Marais' machine, the one with less than half a tank of fuel, would never make it. So with Temborg's blessing, Marais had driven off with his squad, on their own, to kill kaffirs.

Only once had they seen any near enough to go after. The ground there hadn't been difficult—a field of fresh-cut sorghum stubble—and the APC had given chase. He'd ripped eighteen with the pintle gun, its huge slugs killing almost every man they'd hit. Or as good as killed them. But mostly the kaffirs seemed to be keeping away from vehicle roads, staying to rougher country. So Marais had shot cattle, any he'd seen within range; they were all kaffir now anyway. And soon he'd be out of fuel. Then they'd have to abandon vehicle and pintle gun, so there was no reason to spare its ammunition.

Most farms they'd passed had been burned out, and a couple of times they'd seen recognizably human bones scattered about, picked clean by the vultures or jackals. Only the scraps of clothing suggested whether they'd been black or white. Marais had seen several burned out cars and trucks, too, and an abandoned tank—an ancient Comet holed and scorched. What it had been doing where it was, was anyone's guess. Its fuel tank was empty, of course.

The Willemsdaal couldn't be far ahead, Marais thought, though how near he wasn't sure; the kaffirs had pulled down and burned the road signs and mileage signs. His fuel wouldn't last long, and there should be a live stream in the Willemsdaal, where they could camp, and plan what to do next.

Marais watched carefully as they approached a set of fire-gutted farm buildings with trees in the yard, about a hundred meters from the road. Even at that distance, the whitewashed walls were soot-grayed. He caught a glimpse of movement there, but before the sound of gunfire could arrive, before he could swing his machine gun toward it, a bullet slammed him. His knees gave way and he slid down inside the APC, shocked semi-conscious for a moment, then felt the vehicle speed up as two of the men untangled his limbs and pulled off his shirt. A moment later the vehicle turned toward the buildings, lurching across the dry and shallow ditch. Old Brant had clambered up to man the pintle gun, and Marais heard its deep staccato slamming, drowning out the lighter sound of kaffir automatic rifles.

Then the APC braked, stopped, Brant continuing to fire the .50 calibre as the others went out the troop door, their own automatic rifles in hand. All but a cursing Celliers, who'd slapped a pad of surgical sponge on the hole in Marais' upper chest and was wrapping him round with bandage. The firing intensified; a grenade roared, and another. Then it quieted. There were a few single shots.

Marais felt no great pain, but it was getting harder to breathe, and he was weak and dizzy. Something fell on him, something wet. He was on his back, and focused his gaze on the gun hatch. Brant too had been shot, had fallen partly over the coaming, and blood had run down his body, his leg. Now it was starting to trickle off his boot.

The squad was returning, men climbing back into the vehicle, swearing excitedly or mechanically. Marais was going to ask if there were any more casualties, but it was too much work to speak, almost too hard now to keep his eyes open. It occurred to him that he was dying.

The president's January 26 address on health, before the executive council of the American Medical Association.

Thank you, gentlemen, for allowing me to talk to you. I should point out that what I say here is being said not only to you but to the rest of the nation, although the subject will be more immediate to you than to most people. The topics I'll talk about specifically are malpractice suits, the cost of health care, the assurance of medical competency, and the right to die.

Regarding malpractice suits: I presume that most of you know about the changes in our legal system. Malpractice suits will no longer be a rich field for harvesting by unethical attorneys. A physician can no longer be successfully sued when he is without fault, and attorneys now have a strong incentive to avoid clearly groundless suits. Punitive damages will no longer fatten an attorney's bank account.

The insurance industry has been informed of what the government expects from them in the way of rate reforms over the full spectrum of liability insurance, including medical malpractice insurance. Exactly what the new rates will be, we should know very soon. They will be a lot lower.

Physicians will continue to be held responsible and accountable for their competence and ethics, of course. Legal reform does not change that. The main effects of legal reform on the area of malpractice will be to avoid wrongful lawsuits and help relieve the profession and the general public of unconscionable costs.

Modern medical costs remain intolerably high. This is not a serious problem for the wealthy, of course, but the great majority of Americans are not wealthy. Medical costs for middle-income Americans can be a crushing, impoverishing blow, or in some cases a constant impoverishing drain. The poor may find free treatment available to them, but involving such difficulties of transportation, for example, and occasionally such resentment on arrival, as to discourage seeking and receiving it.

At the same time, competent physicians deserve a high level of reward. The cost and demands of their education, and of equipping a medical practice, have to be recovered. Their work is often very demanding and their hours can be long.

Also the development of a new medicine can cost a pharmaceutical company many million dollars, which they have to earn back. Hopefully those companies will be more willing to work on development when they don't have greedy litigation lawyers hanging like hyenas around their perimeter, hoping to get rich off some rare, unpredictable, and unavoidable side effect.

And incidentally, I've had letters from a lot of lawyers who are as glad to see liability law reforms as the rest of us are.

But despite the coming reduction in liability insurance costs, and the marked reduction which that will allow in medical and hospital fees, those fees will still be too high for many families. For one thing, there is the cost of modern high-tech medical equipment.

So there appears to be no prospect that overall medical and hospital costs can be reduced to a level we'd like, without serious reduction in the quality of care. The best we can do seems to be to spread the costs differently, so that no one need go without necessary care or be impoverished by it.

And personally I prefer to avoid a government-operated system of social medicine if possible.

So I am asking this council to assemble a committee of physicians, management specialists, and lawyers to draw up a blueprint for a system of health care that will spread the cost in a blanket national insurance system. In occasional consultation with the Department of Health and Human Services. And if your committee doesn't come up with a complete and satisfactory system by the first of April, I'm going to decree a government-run program of socialized medicine, for which a blueprint is already available.

Because the field of human health is not the sole concern of any one group or profession. We are looking at the matter of life versus avoidable, unwanted death; of human suffering and human dignity. Areas I know most of you feel strongly about, and most of the rest of us too. Areas where inequities can sour a society, make it bitter with a sense of injustice, and weaken its fabric.

Now, regarding competence, the medical profession reputedly has been guilty, sometimes flagrantly guilty, of covering for certain members who are incompetent. Your profession performs a broad spectrum of activities. Some areas often demand very discriminating diagnoses, other areas less. Some require very high surgical skills, some require exceptional recall or high endurance, etc. This is generally recognized. Physicians and surgeons must be restricted to activities at which they are actually competent.

Except of course in unusual emergency situations where no good alternative seems reasonably available. As an extreme example, a veterinarian may never have seen a human appendix, but does have considerable surgical skill and a great deal of knowledge about mammalian bodies. And in an emergency where no physician is available, a veterinarian would be justified in performing an appendectomy to save a human life.

Next I want you to look at something that is only indirectly connected to medical costs and competency. Some of you, let's face it, are not entirely rational on the subject of human life. Frankly, human bodies do wear out. And human beings sometimes wish to be allowed to die. It is neither sane nor ethical to insist on keeping a human consciousness trapped in a painful, nonfunctional, *burdensome* body, when that consciousness, that human beingness, prefers to die. Almost every state has recognized that now, and has enacted law requiring health professionals to honor a patient's preference for death, under certain circumstances and at the patient's specific request. But too many of these laws are inadequate in their protection of the right to die. Therefore the Secretary of Health and Human Services will appoint a committee to draw up guidelines for a national law protecting that right.

The committee will include geriatricians and other physicians, psychologists, nursing home operators, and lawyers, and it will hear representatives from the elderly and the general public. But it will not include or hear representatives of insurance companies. Insurance companies have legitimate and important problems and considerations, and these must be dealt with fairly, but they cannot be allowed to deny the right to die. Their problems must be solved without interfering with that right. We will not allow people to be held in needless, unwanted suffering, against the threat of insurance cancellation, so an insurance company can get a few more premiums before having to pay a death benefit.

Already this is not the problem it once was. We're going to handle it the rest of the way.

I'm sure all of these matters will be worked out in a manner acceptable to the medical profession and the American people. I'll leave you now with Dr. Guzman, our new Secretary of Health and Human Services. She'll talk specifics with you.

And I thank you for your attention.

The president switched off the 11 P.M. news from Duluth's KDAL-TV and picked up his cup of the hot buttered rum Lois had made for them. The weather was getting a lot of attention lately, he thought drily. It hadn't been warmer than −12° F for four days in Duluth, hadn't gone as high as zero even in Chicago, and the high and low at International Falls for the day had been −29 and −51. Siberian, he told himself, or damned near. He'd authorized diversions of military fuel oil reserves for domestic distribution—weatherwar was war too, of a kind—but they wouldn't last long. He'd also ordered increased pumping in domestic oil fields.

The latest emergency powers repeal bill had been killed in committee, just as Lynch had anticipated.

He wondered how much fuel oil had been saved by the installation of GPCs in power systems. Not a lot yet; nothing compared to what it would be next year at this time. If there was a next year.

The Soviets had a certain advantage in a war like this one: so many households there heated and cooked with wood. Of course, a lot of wood-burning stoves had been sold in America during the past year, but probably not more than ten percent of American homes could heat with wood or coal. He'd seen TV features on families that had moved into the garage these last few days, had cut or broken a smoke-hole below the roof peak or in the roof itself, and kept a fire going on the concrete floor. Camera operators had gotten tired of showing people carrying or wheeling home bundles of firewood or bags of coal from distribution yards. The neighbor who owned a wheelbarrow, one commentator had observed, was more valued then the neighbor with a Cadillac.

It was going to be a bastard of a winter if the Soviets didn't back down, but he would not escalate this covert war.

When you find yourself running low on options, Haugen told himself, *you look to your long shots.* And Bulavin had gotten back that evening; Cromwell and LaMotte would be debriefing him now. Maybe there'd be good news in the morning.

FORTY-FOUR

The poshed, command model Kamov Ka-25 helicopter hurried along about one hundred and fifty meters above the undulating steppe toward Voronezh. It might almost as well have been at 3,000 meters, because General Serafim Petrovich Gurenko wasn't giving the snowbound landscape much attention now. In two days of hopping from base to base, he'd already seen and heard all he needed to. This morning it was time to return to Moscow.

That the roads were plugged with snow was bad enough. But in the Soviet Union, the railroads were far more important than highways, and on them too, almost nothing moved. Trains were nearly buried by drifts, visible mainly where the winds had scoured the snow away. Snowplows chuffed and pushed so slowly that their sooty coal smoke formed no plume, but simply rose up, then spread, to settle on and around them. Most were not rotary plows, but pushed and punched their way behind tall, V-shaped blades. When they came to a grade cut, they hunkered, virtually stalled, for the cuts were drifted full, the depth of the snow equalling the depth of the cut, be it three meters or six.

Military traffic was utterly stopped—supplies, troop trains, all of it. And there was little sense of urgency. Urgency comes with purpose, desire, and there was little of that beyond the purpose and desire to survive. In the cities they might riot, but the time-honored peasant rule was tighten your belt, wait, persist. And on the collective or in the city, those whose purpose reached beyond simple survival were mostly ignored, unless they had authority, and even authority was heeded mainly until it was out of sight.

Gurenko's eyes paused on a village, one of many on the steppe. It was the coal smoke that had caught his attention, pooled over the low buildings by the frigid inversion layer. Snow had blown across the open plain until it met some obstruction or depression; there it had been dumped by the wind eddies. Thus, beneath its smoke, a village appeared as little more than a complex pattern of drifts and scour holes, with walls and roofs showing mainly on the windward sides.

By now the peasants would have dug, tunneled where necessary, to the shed to feed and milk their family cow. But the collective's livestock would still be waiting, hungry and freezing, in their lean-to shelters.

Gurenko had not visited the rangelands of Kazakhstan; that had been out of his way. But the conditions there would be worse. The death toll of cattle and sheep could only be guessed until spring uncovered them, but it would be bad. How bad depended on how many had found their way to shelter, or been driven there when the storm warnings were broadcast. No doubt many herdsmen had died too, caught by blinding blizzard, unable to find their way to safety.

Ahead low hills appeared now, and patches of scrubby woods. Voronezh would soon be in sight. There he would transfer to something faster than this machine, fly to Moscow, and do what had to be done. Or try to. For the storm, and this bitter cold that Pavlenko had brought upon them, had forced him to look, and to see more surely, how deeply his country had foundered these last few years. Till now, he'd equivocated, rationalized. Now it was time to place his life on the line.

Marshall Premier First Secretary of the Communist Party of the Soviet Union Oleg Stepanovich Pavlenko walked down the wide and polished corridor noticing neither its grandeur nor its beauty. He was not much given to aesthetics. Nor did he notice the ever-present guards standing stiffly at intervals along the polished hardwood wall panels, their AKM rifles at present arms.

He had seen the reports, from every republic, every oblast. No one was doing anything! No one but the army! They were all waiting for someone to do it for them; their God maybe! Waiting for spring to come! By God, they should be out there with their shovels, with tea spoons if that was all they had, clearing the railroads! He knew these damned people; they wanted him to do it for them!

Well, he *had* done it for them. He did not remember the names of the exact places, but his technologists knew. Nor had he asked the concurrence of the others; now he would simply tell them. He was tired of that puking Predtechensky, who wished always to argue; and Makarov, who always nodded but who, behind his back, whispered and plotted; and Goncharov, who seemed to be turning against him lately. . . .

Today he had taken the irreversible step. Today they would either overthrow him or they would get on their bellies. And tomorrow he would begin making a nation of those treacherous and willful minorities, and of the disobedient, bull-headed Russian people who could so easily say *yes*, then turn around and do the opposite.

He was the only one who had any sense of history, of destiny. The first since Comrade Stalin. The rest of them, one after the other, had been nothing but apparatchiks.

His aide opened the door for him, held it, and Pavlenko stepped through into the council room. The others were there ahead of him. A haze of cigarette smoke was already forming. He nodded curtly and took his place at the head of the burnished Circassian walnut table.

His hawk eyes swept the congregated Politburo. Three were there besides the members: Bogoslovsky from the Transport Ministry, a whiner; Morozov of the Armed Forces Inspectorate, who'd grown surly of late; and Feldstein of the newly reconstituted OGPU. Being a Jew by birth, Feldstein was vulnerable to certain prejudices, thus his loyalty was more reliable.

They sat there with each his own trivial business to

press. In a minute he would tell them what he had ordered, and they would forget all about what they'd wanted to say. His eyes moved to the clock on the wall opposite him: 0906 hours. It would be happening just about now! Leering, he rapped his gavel on its ceramic plate and called the meeting to order.

When the president went to bed, he'd plunged deeply into sleep. It was less than an hour and a half later, at 0116 hours, that the phone drew him unwillingly awake. He fumbled the receiver from the cradle.

"This is the president."

"Mr. President, this is Jumper. A heavy quake has hit the San Andreas Fault, actually two of them almost simultaneously, at 7.7 and 7.3 on the Richter Scale. The first reports are that San Bernardino's in bad shape, and San Francisco's taken a lot of damage. L.A.'s taken some too."

Jesus Christ! Haugen found himself thinking, *let it be natural.* But it couldn't be, not two at once.

"A lighter one hit Seattle at almost the same time," Jumper continued. "It was still fairly strong—it read 5.3. The epicenter was where the Juan de Fuca plate rides beneath the North American. All three were artificially triggered."

"Right. Jumper, is Bulavin with you?"

"He's in the debrief room; we were almost finished when I got the call."

"Call Gupta right away and get him on a security conference call with you and me and Bulavin. I'm going down to my office right now."

He disconnected and got off his bed. Lois was staring at him from her own. "Pavlenko's given us an earthquake, Babe," he said. "Three of them in fact. Be glad the White House isn't in San Bernardino."

Frank and Will were the Secret Service men on duty in the Stair Hall. They followed the bathrobed, slippered president down the stairs. "Big quake in California," he told them. The rest of the way he was silently blessing the nation's luck: Seattle's and Tacoma's especially. The geologists had worried for years that enormous stress had built up along the Juan de Fuca subduction zone—it was either that or subduction had been unusually smooth. The fear had been that when it let go, the quake might be close to the theoretical maximum of nine-plus on the Richter Scale! With an actual reading of 5.3, apparently it had been smooth.

There was an exasperating but actually short wait to get Gupta tied in on the call. The NSA office at the Nevada Test Center had phoned him as soon as they'd read the quakes, and he'd already been on his way to his office at Fort Meade when Cromwell had phoned. When the general called the White House again, the president could see Bulavin sitting beside him.

"Colonel Schubert," Haugen said, "it's 0938 hours in Moscow now, right?"

"Yes, Mr. President."

"Then the Politburo's likely to be in meeting now?"

"Yes sir. Almost certainly, and for at least half an hour to come."

"Jim," the president said, "do you have a detailed diagram of the Kremlin?"

Gupta's eyebrows raised. "I'm sure we do, sir; in the computer."

"It's there," said Cromwell.

"How detailed is it? Would it show the building where the Politburo meets?"

"It shows every building there," Cromwell answered, "with floor plans."

"How accurate is it? And how fine is the coordinate system?"

"Sir, it's part of our computer-generated planetary coordinate system, so it's as fine as you want it to be. As for accuracy, it's probably within inches; a couple of feet at most."

"Jim, how accurately can you place a Tesla energy release? Or let's make that an energy *extraction*, to minimize damage."

Gupta's mouth formed an *oh*—he realized what the president had in mind. "Either one can be centered within a ten meter radius anywhere on Earth," he replied. "Without ranging."

"And what's the smallest radius of effect you can give me?"

"It depends on the effect you want. The temperature within the heat extraction sphere will be virtually at absolute zero at the moment of extraction—say minus 458° Fahrenheit. So there's going to be a damned sharp temperature gradient around it that will suck heat out of the surroundings. But if the extraction sphere is entirely enclosed within a certain room or rooms, it won't have a lot of effect outside those walls.

"The sphere needs to be large enough to account for the error of location and to include the entire room, or almost the entire room. So the sphere is sure to intrude into other spaces—a hall probably, and one or more adjacent rooms. Within the sphere, it'll be as if the walls aren't there, as far as the temperature effect is concerned. But a twenty-meter extraction sphere won't have much effect outside of four or five rooms, assuming they're large."

The president's intent eyes moved to Schubert/Bulavin, sitting beside the general. "Colonel Schubert," he said, "can you locate, on the general's diagram, the actual conference room where the Politburo meets?"

Bulavin's eyes seemed to gleam at him through the CRT. "Definitely, Mr. President."

"How long, Dr. Gupta, does it take your people to set coordinates on a scalar resonance transmitter and do a heat extraction?"

"The people are on alert there now. They can do the job within five minutes of a call."

The President of the United States stared silently at nothing for maybe three or four suspended seconds. "All right," he said. "I want you three to get your information together and instant-freeze the Politburo. You need to work fast, while they're still in conference. I'll notify Nevada and authorize it. Is there anything else I need to do on this?"

Gupta shook his head. "No sir. I'll order a target zone of twenty-five meters, to make sure we cover any possible error."

"Let me know when it's done," Haugen said. "I'll be here in my office."

"Yes sir."

Haugen cut the connection, then his fingers called the Nevada NSA code to the screen and he rapped it on his keyboard. The man at the other end looked sober as hell. The authorization procedure took less then thirty seconds, and when it was done, the president slumped back in his chair to wait for Gupta's call. It didn't occur to him to make himself coffee.

Hopefully the order he'd just given had nipped World War Three in the bud. But if the Politburo had already adjourned, he may have ensured it instead.

FORTY-FIVE

The president had gotten back to bed at about 0230, after calling Milstead to arrange a flight for him to the west coast. After the earthquakes, he needed to be seen in San Bernardino and San Francisco, and Seattle. He'd asked Lois to come with him, but she'd been tired lately, and when the phone had wakened her, she'd been sweating, and had pain in her stomach. She'd go to the White House clinic instead, and have Colonel Singleton check her over.

Haugen wasn't feeling so energetic either. After finally getting back to bed, he hadn't gotten to sleep again until nearly 0330, then had gotten up two hours later, taken a very brief cold shower, and been shuttled by chopper to Andrews Air Force Base. He'd shaved on the plane after takeoff, then eaten breakfast and followed it with two cups of strong coffee.

He wondered if Milstead had gone back to bed at all, and if he'd make an opportunity for a nap that day. Knowing Milstead, he'd probably work on through. He'd turned out to be an excellent chief of staff, and his temporary continuance had become, by mutual and unspoken agreement, an arrangement for Haugen's full tenure in the White House.

Sunrise caught up with Air Force One over Cincinnati. The president took a brief break from the economic update he'd started to read, and removing his reading glasses, looked south out the window beside him. The Ohio River had frozen over after the snow storm, its bare ice looking black from the air. No doubt it was spotted with ice-fishing shelters not visible from 20 thousand feet. To the south, beyond Covington, the farmlands of northern Kentucky stretched white under more than twenty inches of snow.

Apparently it was a lot worse in Russia. Here the high-ways had been cleared within two days, most lesser roads within four.

It was midafternoon in Russia. At noon Moscow time, no news had come out of the Kremlin, but apparently his hit on the Politburo had worked. His daily intelligence summary had been delivered to Air Force One before he had, and it had commented that for some reason, the normal daily releases from the Soviet Central Committee weren't appearing. Even from the ministries, the normal flow of bureaucratic communications was down to a trickle. Clearly something very major had happened, but just what, the CIA had not yet learned.

This time, Haugen thought, he knew what the CIA did not. For the first time it occurred to him that this might influence Gurenko's decision.

Bulavin had been in Berlin, working with one of LaMotte's people there. They'd actually gotten a message to Gurenko eight days earlier, at a terrible risk to some-one, some unknown Russian hero or heroes. What Gurenko's reaction had been, they'd had no clue. Bulavin had waited for some possible response, but there'd been none, and he'd come home. Probably the only reply they could expect would be action or inaction.

After the strike at the Politburo, the president had ordered the Tesla transmitters shut down. The high pressure cells they'd created should decay rather quickly, Gupta had told him, but when an actual thaw would come to Russia and the Ukraine was another matter.

Again the president picked up the report and began to read. He'd read it and two others when someone knocked at his compartment door, and he swiveled his chair to face it. "Come in," he called. It opened and John Zale looked in.

"Sir," Zale said, "we just got a message from Washington. Moscow's announced that the Politburo has appointed a General Gurenko as premier and Party chairman. Secretary Valenzuela would like to talk to you about it."

The Politburo! For a moment, the president had felt a pang of anxiety. But of course, Gurenko would have appointed a new Politburo, to legalize his position. He must have made plans and preparations enough that with Pavlenko and the old Politburo snuffed out, he'd been in a position to move quickly. While everyone else in the Kremlin was still in shock and confusion.

He might even think that the old Politburo had been snuffed out to enable him to take over!

And Valenzuela hadn't been told about the hit. But even on security equipment, now was not the time to enlighten him. Haugen nodded to Zale. "Thanks," he said, picked up the privacy receiver, and touched the flashing key. "Good morning, Val," he said. "John told me Gurenko has taken over."

"That's right, Mr. President. It is uncanny how quickly he moved. I'd have expected a month or more of machinations. In fact, I didn't expect him to try at all. We need to make some kind of public statement, as well as a formal one to the Soviet ambassador."

"Right. You prepare them, and let me see them before they're released."

A thought struck the president then, and his stomach tightened. Was it possible that Gurenko didn't know about scalar resonance, or didn't know that his own government had struck first with it? For a moment he felt an urge to have the pilot return to Washington.

Instead he said, "And Val, call the Soviet ambassador right away. Tell him I'm on the West Coast, visiting the earthquake areas. That we know Pavlenko caused the quakes, and that with Gurenko in charge, we do not intend to retaliate further. That there is no need for war. He probably won't know what you're talking about, but tell him that anyway."

Valenzuela wouldn't know either, the president realized. "I want you to record this," he added. "Can you?"

Valenzuela's face was exceedingly sober as he nodded and reached. "Recording now, Mr. President."

"Good." The president repeated his message. "That part about not intending to retaliate further is extremely important. Some things happened last night around one-thirty, on fifteen minutes notice, that you haven't heard about. I'll brief you when I get back. Or you can talk with Cromwell; he was part of it.

"But call the ambassador first, right away, *muy pronto*,

and let me know as soon as you've finished. Is there anything you need to ask before you do that?"

"No sir."

"Good. I'll be waiting for your call."

Haugen disconnected. What *did* Gurenko know and not know? Surely he knew that the previous ruling body had been quick frozen. Instant frozen; the heat had been removed instantaneously from not only their environment, but everything in it including their bodies. There'd been no gradient heat loss, no shivering, no moments of shocked realization, just . . . instant death.

Gurenko was bound to be concerned that his new government might be hostage to the same kind of attack.

Haugen became aware that his body was tense—shivering with tension. He took deep breaths, focused on relaxing, and felt the tension drain away. He'd visit the disaster areas today, fly back to the White House this evening, sleeping on the way, and call Gurenko as soon as he got there.

He buzzed the orderly the Air Force had provided; he'd have the man make up his bed. Then, after Valenzuela called back, he'd take a long nap. Just now sleep seemed the most profitable way to spend a few hours.

FORTY-SIX

It was after one o'clock the next morning that the president got back to the White House. During the day, he'd made repeated use of the communications equipment on Air Force One, and Valenzuela and Milstead were waiting for him at the White House helipad with Valenzuela's top interpreter. And with Grosberg and Lynch; it was time for the leaders of Congress to know what was going on.

At the president's radioed instructions, Milstead had alerted the Hot Line office, which had alerted its Moscow counterpart. Haugen excused the interpreter, then gave the other four a fifteen-minute mini-briefing on scalar resonance, the weatherwar, the source of the earthquakes, and what had happened in the Kremlin. They were four very sober men when he'd finished.

"So you fought a war and assassinated an entire cabinet without recourse to Congress," Lynch said.

Grosberg glanced sharply at the Speaker of the House, but there'd been no antagonism, nothing accusatory, in Lynch's words. They'd been thoughtful; even awed.

"Right," replied Haugen. "And it's something the American people need to be informed about. I started work on a press release flying back to D.C., but it may be a couple of days before I'm satisfied with it. Meanwhile Congress needs to know, or that part of Congress you decide on. I'll send over the complete text of the press release shortly before I give it to the media. You'll have time to comment before it's released."

Together then they went down to the bomb shelter, to the Washington-Moscow Direct Communications Link. The President of the United States took a chair in front of the video pickup, then signalled the duty officer. An image flashed into being.

The man who looked out at him reminded the president of Bulavin, and seemed little if any older than the defector. The face was broader, but like Bulavin's, lined and hard-looking, tempered in the harsh and relentless school of Soviet military intelligence.

"Good morning, Premier Gurenko," Haugen said in Russian. His tone was carefully serious and not quite impersonal. "My congratulations on your success."

Gurenko nodded curt acknowledgement. "And my congratulations on yours." His American English was almost unaccented. "I have taken a few minutes this morning to watch television coverage of the earthquake areas in your west coast states. And of your visit there. It is regrettable, but perhaps inevitable, that things had to go so far."

And that, thought Haugen, was quite a statement for a Soviet premier.

"It is indeed." The president was still speaking Russian;

now he paused. "Here I am speaking your language while you speak mine. I'm quite willing to continue like this, but you're more accomplished in English than I am in Russian. It might be best if we both continued in English. With your agreement, of course."

Gurenko nodded. "Your Russian pronunciations are quite good. But you are an engineer; your Russian vocabulary may not extend to matters of government."

So they both spoke English, their courtesy constant but matter-of-fact. They conferred for more than an hour, and before they had finished, they'd agreed to meet in Zurich in ten days. Ten days would give Gurenko time to establish fuller control of his nation, and it would give the Swiss government, and the Russian and American embassies in Switzerland, time to set up the demanding machinery, including security, that a summit meeting required.

In a reversal of the usual procedure, there would be no preliminary conference of diplomats to set things up. In Zurich, they themselves would work out a broad agreement, and a general agenda for subsequent conferences at the foreign ministry level, which would work out the details.

They did not talk about relaxing their military stance. After what each government had done to the other in the last twenty-four hours, it wasn't surprising. But there'd been no sense at all of truculence or suspicion.

Valenzuela would have preferred a longer lead time than ten days. There were various other governments to consider, and he'd have liked to confer with them in advance about their various interests. But he sat quietly. Now was the time to move, he knew, while things were fluid. And Arne Haugen had displayed genius at making things go right.

When it was over with, Haugen, Valenzuela, Grosberg, and Lynch, along with Milstead, went to the Oval Office and relaxed with their choice of bourbon, Scotch, or something hot, discussing briefly what had to be done soonest. In the morning, Grosberg and Lynch would inform their minority party counterparts, and the chairmen of their respective foreign affairs committees, of the forthcoming summit meeting. Okada would release a brief announcement of the upcoming summit to the press at noon.

Also tomorrow morning, Valenzuela would talk to the ambassadors of China and Iran, who were bound to feel twitchy about any possible meeting of minds between Washington and Moscow. He'd assure the Chinese that there was no possibility of agreements infringing on their interests, and the Iranians that they would be conferred with on anything that came up about Iranian interests. If anything did.

He was to stress that the President of the United States wanted the maximum of possible worldwide satisfaction with whatever results the conference might produce, and that the ultimate goals were peace and national self-determination.

The British ambassador would also be contacted; the United Kingdom had been America's firmest foreign policy supporter for a dozen years, in times as embarrassing as Iran-gate and as tense as the showdown between Wheeler and Gorbachev. If the prime minister wanted a quick informal meeting, in say Ottawa or Vancouver, that could be arranged, although privately the president couldn't visualize what they might talk about before the Zurich meeting. Afterward there'd be plenty to talk about.

The five of them dispersed then, and Haugen walked slowly up the stairs, his bodyguards following. Their day had been as long as his.

"When are they going to relieve you guys?" he asked.

"There's a new shift waiting upstairs," Wayne said. "They'll take over when we get there."

There was, and his traveling bags stood beside the door, deposited there by John Zale when they'd gotten back. The president shook hands with Wayne and Gil, then tossed a salute to their replacements before he went into the second floor Center Hall, into the family area, leaving them behind. He felt now as if the air had gone out of him, the starch. He was tired but also relaxed and enormously gratified with the day. It occurred to him that he wasn't fully feeling yet the impact of all that had happened; that later, perhaps in a week or month, this day would loom bigger than any other in his life. *Maybe*, he thought as he opened his bedroom door, *I'll even get to read about it in a history book before I die—see what posterity will make of it.*

Lois was not in bed. She'd fallen asleep in her favorite wingbacked chair. Gazing at her, she was as lovely to his fond eyes as on the day they'd married. Her skin was no longer smooth and snug, but there was a softness to it. And paler, he thought, than he'd ever seen it; she'd been an outdoors person all her life, till they'd come to the White House. It occurred to him that the restrictions on life here, in this difficult time, had been harder on her than on him.

He'd intended not to waken her if he could help it. But she'd be stiff in the morning if she spent the whole night in the chair. He touched her shoulder, spoke quietly to her, and as she stirred, he bent and kissed her cheek. Her eyes opened.

"You're home," she said, and smiling, straightened, then got up and kissed him, a kiss that was tender but also sensual. For a moment it seemed to the president that she might be making a pass at him, but if she was, she sensed how drained he was, and let the moment go by.

"Would you like some tawny port?" she asked. "I'd have made hot buttered rum if I'd known when you'd get home."

"Port would be fine," he said. "I'll be getting into my sleeping shorts."

They shared a drink while he summarized for her his talk with Gurenko. He'd already told her, very briefly the night before, about the hit on the Politburo, wondering at the time how Father Flynn would take it when he told him.

Lois in turn described the TV coverage of the earthquakes and his visit to the disaster areas.

She didn't mention her visit to the White House physician, and her husband didn't think to ask. He was starting to nod off before he'd finished his drink.

FORTY-SEVEN

Arne Haugen slept till 1040 hours, wakening at the insistence of his urethral sphincter. He noticed, when he got out of bed, that Lois's was empty. The door was open into the private north hall, her way of telling him that she'd gone herself to prepare their breakfast. He relieved himself, showered and shaved, then dressed. Walking into the Center Hall, the smell of bacon frying led him into their private dining room. Lois was in the adjacent Kennedy Kitchen, and he looked in on her.

"Hi, Babe. How did you know I was up?"

"I went in to wake you and heard the shower." Grinning, she pointed at a dishtowel humped over something on the counter. "I baked bread last evening. Your favorite—anadama. It's been awhile."

He went to her and kissed her.

"Kissing the cook is always a good idea," she told him, shrugging loose, "but there is good timing and bad timing. Right now I have to check the bacon." She took the frying pan from the hot burner, and after a moment raised the lid. "Done," she said, then peered under another.

"As boss of the kitchen," she added, "I hereby direct you to pour the juice and get something agreeable on television."

Something was bothering her; a slight acidity underlay her bantering this morning, something he seldom felt. He thought he knew why. When they'd first moved into the White House, he'd told her they'd be out by Labor Day—possibly by the Fourth of July if things went well enough or badly enough. And domestically they were going well enough, but he was talking in terms of "the end of the year."

Last October, of course, he hadn't known about weather-war and seismic war. And he had a better idea now of what might actually be accomplished, and what it would take. And who could he trust to follow through on the programs he envisioned? The education reform he'd soon be springing on them?

After he got back from Zurich, he'd take a few days off and they'd vacation in the mountains at Camp David. Spend weekends there as often as possible. She'd feel better about things then.

So, obediently, he went pitcher in hand into the small dining room, where as always, places had been set by one of the domestic staff the evening before. He poured cider, returned the pitcher to the refrigerator, then checked the television computer for eleven o'clock programs, settling for the Boston Symphony on Public TV.

While he was adjusting the volume, Lois came from the kitchen with a plate of bacon and a platter of fried eggs. Firm-yolked, he was sure, though sunnyside up. By the time he'd poured coffee, she was back again with sweet anadama toast, covered to stay warm.

He held her chair for her while she sat down.

"My! What a gracious gentleman," she teased. "If only my husband could see you; maybe he'd learn a thing or two."

He nodded. "That's what all my girlfriends tell me. At the table or in the boudoir. Ah well, when a girl marries a cedar savage . . ."

He sat down and stared at the platters. "Do we have breakfast guests I haven't heard about? That's enough to feed a logging crew!"

She shook her head, still smiling, but softly now. "I decided to overlook the calories—that both of us would really splurge on our favorite breakfast."

By the time she'd said it all, her voice had begun to falter, and Arne Haugen had gone watchfully sober, not asking, letting her tell him in her own time.

"*Fan ta'n!*" she burst out. "*Haugen, ja' har rili gått och gjört dä nu.*" ("Damn it, Haugen, I've really gone and done it now!") Tears had begun to flow, and he stared, waiting for what would follow.

She dropped the Minnesota *bondspråk*. "Arne," she said, "I have cancer. Of the lymph system. And it's not operable. Colonel Singleton did a scan yesterday, and it's metastasized; it's spread to a lot of different places. He called a specialist over from GWU, and I'm to go there today for extensive examinations. So they'll know what they can do about it.

"They said my symptoms hadn't been typical for my age; that they should have shown up sooner." She tried to laugh then. "You've told me how young I've stayed. Now look!"

The president stared at her, his vision blurring till he could no longer see the tears flowing down her cheeks. She went on.

"And honey . . . I don't want to go away from you!"

She broke down then, crying quietly but hard, her body shaking with it, while he sat miserably, unable to think or even wipe his face. After half a minute he heard her giggle, then hiccup. His hand found his napkin and he mopped at his eyes. She was grinning shakily at him.

"I didn't plan to tell you till we'd finished eating. Now go ahead and enjoy your breakfast!"

She broke down again, and getting up, her husband walked around the table and knelt beside her, circling her with an arm, holding her against him. Saying nothing till her weeping had eased again. "You and I have never had a genuine crisis in the family before," he said quietly. "We'll just have to get used to it. We'll handle it all right, you and I."

She nodded, then kissed him, their wet cheeks touching. "Well," she said, "I'd better go wash my face. Maybe I'll feel better then."

After a few minutes they actually ate a bit. She was to see Colonel Singleton after lunch, and they'd ride the half-dozen blocks to the university hospital in Singleton's personal car, to avoid notice if possible.

"And sweetheart," she said, "you've got a lot of things to take care of downstairs. For a lot of people. We'll let the doctors take care of me."

After a little bit he did go downstairs. The Secret Service men could tell something was wrong. So could

Martinelli, and so could Milstead when he came in. But once the president got underway, he worked as well, and as rapidly as usual, although his family crisis was never far from his consciousness.

At mid-afternoon he stopped at Singleton's office and left a message for the doctor to call when he got back. Half an hour later Singleton called, and Haugen had him come to the Oval Office. Treatment would be immunotherapy, the colonel said. She'd be in the hospital for at least a week; perhaps as long as two.

Only time would tell what the treatment would accomplish, but the first lady was in most respects an unusually healthy woman. Certainly her case was far from hopeless. Dr. Hummerick, at GWU, was one of the best in the evaluation and treatment of lymphomas, and he estimated that the odds were perhaps thirty percent for a complete remission. The least they could hope for was a considerable palliation, and perhaps years of not uncomfortable life continuance.

Well, the president told himself when the doctor had left, *thirty percent's not bad. We'll see how it goes.*

Meanwhile though, death seemed more serious to him now than it ever had before.

That evening, as he and Lois often had, he invited Father Flynn to supper. And told him. Flynn hadn't heard yet; remarkably the situation hadn't leaked, not even her hospitalization! Partly, the president told himself, because the White House Press Corps was no longer located inside the White House; that and the loyalty of the staff.

When he and Flynn had finished dessert, Haugen excused himself to call Liisa. "Hi, honeybunch," he said. "How're you guys doing?"

"Just fine. It went up nearly to zero in Grand Forks today! Up to minus three degrees!"

Haugen laughed. "Don't feel too bad," he said. "Think of it as minus twenty Celsius."

She made a rude noise at him.

"How's Ed?" he asked. "Can he pick up the other phone?"

"Just a minute, daddy." He heard her call out, away

from the voice pickup. "Ed, the President of the United States wants to talk to us both."

Her husband picked up the phone in his office, an old-fashioned instrument without visio, and Haugen told them about Lois. "If it's practical," he said, "I'd like to fly the two of you to Washington tomorrow for a few days. Lois would really appreciate it; she was feeling pretty down today."

It was Ed Ruud who replied. "Geez, Arne, it would be awfully darned awkward for me to go tomorrow. But I could batch while Liisa goes, and fly there myself on Friday night for the weekend."

"Sounds good. And I was hoping Liisa could be here while I'm in Zurich," Haugen added, "meeting with Premier Gurenko."

"Sure, daddy. I want to be there."

"Absolutely, Arne. Jesus Christ! We both want to do all we can to help."

"Thanks, both of you. I'll wire you the money tonight. It'll help your mom, and take a lot of pressure off me."

When he'd disconnected, he phoned a money-order, enough to more than cover their costs, then settled down to talk with Flynn again.

"Lois would like to see you too," Haugen said, then grinned. "But it's best not to arrive in clerical garb. We wouldn't want her to think you were there to administer the last rites."

Flynn winced at the attempted humor. "Of course." *And I'll pray for her,* he told himself. *She'd appreciate it, even if she didn't expect it to do any good.*

Neither man said anything for a while. Then Flynn broke the silence. "There's been a lot of suffering this winter," he said. "South Africa and Iran torn by war, the rest of the world by depression, hunger, fuel shortage. And now we've had weatherwar." He shook his head. "It amazes me when I read the public opinion surveys; I wonder if morale here is really that good, and if people really are that optimistic."

"I haven't read one since the weatherwar started," Haugen replied. "Morale may not be so good right now." He paused for a moment, then looked at the priest with surprising intensity. "But it'll bounce back. And d'you know why?"

Flynn shook his head.

"Because they feel, most of them, as if the country has direction now, that it has goals, that it's going somewhere they want to go. Even if they don't know just where that is, any more than I do. And they feel as if they're part of the movement. When you feel like that, hardships are likely to temper you, strengthen you instead of breaking you. Especially hardships you share with the rest of the country.

"That's why people put up with me, though probably not many have sorted it out for themselves. Our goals pretty much coincide. And that's why Congress hasn't shut me down yet, and why the media haven't really tried to scuttle me. I really honest-to-god believe I've been the man for the time."

Again neither man spoke for a bit. *He's right*, Flynn said to himself. *And that's been the key to what he's accomplished. He's a product of this nation, and through him it . . .*

The president interrupted the priest's thoughts. "Stephen," he said, "I have something to confess to you. I don't feel as if it's a sin, but I murdered some people the night before last. Or maybe *murdered* isn't the right word, but I ordered some people killed: a room full. At least a dozen, and almost certainly more."

The statement startled Flynn, but he said nothing, merely nodded attentively. Then the president told him what had caused the west coast earthquakes—no surprise to Flynn, really—and what had happened to Pavlenko and his Politburo.

"It wasn't revenge," he went on. "I can tell you that with total certainty. It was a kind of war. I felt justified in cutting off the man who'd decided to escalate and attack with earthquakes, and might decide to escalate again. In a way what I did was *de-escalation*, but it was also a coldblooded ambush of a kind. No pun intended."

The president paused, examining. "The only one I really wanted to get was Pavlenko. The others just happened to be in the room with him, at the hour when I knew where he was—where he could be hit. But it was probably a good thing I got them all. It set it up for Gurenko."

"And it's possible to do that kind of thing now?" Flynn said. "Reach across the world and snuff lives out like that?"

"I'm afraid so. In this case though, it may have saved a lot of other lives."

"It's not this case that dismays me," the Jesuit said. "It's the instrument that dismays me."

"Me too," the president answered. "But there it is. I believe it was fore-destined, the day that man became man. It was inevitable that we'd learn to do this—do all these things.

"And it seems to me that humankind needs the same sort of mental breakthrough—or spiritual breakthrough if you'd rather call it that—that we've made in physics and engineering. A breakthrough comparable to nuclear fusion, scalar resonance, the GPC, the superconductor."

It struck Haugen then that that's what the Christian churches claimed had happened two thousand years earlier: the great spiritual breakthrough. But it hadn't worked, or hadn't seemed to. "Ultimately," he continued, "good government, decent government, can't solve our dilemma. At best it provides an environment in which it can be solved. And really, when I look at it, that's mostly what I've tried to do as president—provide the environment.

"And preaching can't solve it. Humankind's been preached at for longer I'm sure than any church that's still around."

The Jesuit nodded, and caught himself at it. There was *cynicism* again, the cynicism that sneaked too often into his heart, his mind, about the efficacy of the Church and the salvation of man. Yet there was also the *Revelation to John,* that troublesome book. Unless God changed his mind, someday the world would be destroyed. And all men would *not* be saved. *We must strive to save them all,* he thought, *but we must accept our failures as well as our successes.*

The president wasn't done yet: After a moment's thoughtful silence he went on. "Eddie Wing's received three different research proposals," he said, "on what the Soviets call psychoenergetics; pretty much what the science fiction writers call psi. And remotely, I might even see a tie-in with the underlying field the GPC actually draws on.

"And there's hardly a snowball's chance in hell that any of them would be approved by any 'proper' university or 'well-administered' foundation, where the powers-that-be are too afraid of their reputations to fly anything like that." He paused thoughtfully. "Or maybe there is a chance, barely, with all the wild activity in physics lately. But I'm not betting on it. I've told Eddie to go ahead on all three.

"I'll be keeping close track of what they find, and I want you to. Look at it for tie-ins with religion, any religion; you're schooled in that."

The priest nodded. "Of course, Arne. I'll be glad to." *For God works in strange ways*, he added silently, *through strange and often secular instruments*. The Jesuit felt a chill flow over him, perhaps on omen of sorts. *And this is a good man*, he told himself. *Perhaps through him I have an opportunity here to do something very large in the service of God*.

They talked of other things then: the economy's steady upward creep, the problems and successes of the new legal system, Haugen's ideas on education and what his task force was doing with them, and what might be accomplished in Zurich. And after a bit they said good night, the priest going to his room.

The president headed for a few more hours at his desk. There was so much to accomplish, sometimes it was hard to stop working and go to bed. *Maybe I should get more sleep*, he thought. *My energy level isn't what it ought to be*.

FORTY-EIGHT

The Swiss were practiced, skilled, and diplomatic at coordinating foreign security contingents with their own police. Thus Zurich was as safe for Gurenko and Haugen as could reasonably be managed. From the airport, Zurich was a short drive south along the river Glatt, and small groups of military police were stationed along the way. The highway and city street on which the foreign entourages would travel had been briefly cordoned off, well before dawn, and the route carefully checked for mines and other devices. Reopened for morning traffic, it was kept under constant surveillance. Other vehicular traffic would be excluded during the passage of the official convoys, and as soon as the armored limousines had passed, the road would be opened for normal traffic again.

Both Soviet and American parties arrived at the airport in midmorning, when traffic was well past its peak. Then, under the watchful eyes of Swiss marksmen, some of them on roofs, they were driven, with police escorts, to the Züricher Hilton, where the conference would be held.

Days earlier, after their staffs had presented them with what they considered the needs and problems involved in such a meeting, Gurenko and Haugen had talked twice more on the hot line, establishing ground rules. And when they arrived in Zurich, it was with modest staffs of subject-matter specialists—smaller than their advisors had urged.

They met in person for the first time at 1100 on the day they arrived. Gurenko began by speaking Russian, and Haugen English. But then, on a whim, Haugen switched to Russian, and as if by agreement, Gurenko to English. In confused embarrassment, the Russian interpreter suddenly

357

realized he was translating Haugen's Russian into English for Gurenko.

From that point, the interpretors did little except, mainly in Haugen's case, clarify terms. (Haugen had been practicing his Russian. On his daily visits to the hospital, he and Lois had spoken little else, and he'd had a State Department Soviet specialist come over for a half-hour each day to discuss technical matters with him in Russian.)

Gurenko and Haugen even took lunch together, separate from their advisors, talking mostly about things outside the conference agenda. Supper involved the two heads of government and their staffs, and at Haugen's and Gurenko's insistence, everyone was required to talk. As the vodka, Scotch, and bourbon flowed, some talked a little loudly.

There was a Mrs. Gurenko, Xenia Federovna, and she'd come to Zurich with her husband. Based on an inspiration someone had voiced at the first supper, on the third day she flew to Washington to meet with Lois Haugen at the hospital, and stayed for two days.

So far as any of them knew, there'd never been a summit conference even remotely like it before. The American and European media covered it like a festival, with unprecedented access to the principals and their consultants. Not at the meetings themselves, of course, but outside the meetings. And the Soviet media were allowed a degree of reportorial freedom that at first they hardly knew what to do with. But they got the feel of it quickly enough.

After six days it was over. To world television viewers, its ending left a vacuum almost like the closing of the Olympic games. The event was over; all that was left were the results, the agreements.

The Soviet Union had been in the poorer bargaining position, partly because the industrial-transportational machinery was scarcely operating, partly because parts of the empire were not safely under control, and partly because the Russian people themselves, the backbone of the empire, were in a sort of passive noncooperation that could turn violent, given the problem of food shortages. And there was a real prospect that troops would refuse to fire on civilians if massive rioting developed in Russia itself. If that happened—chaos.

So while there might be grumbling in the Soviet military council that Gurenko had been soft, had given up too much, presumably there'd be nothing more than grumbling. The generals could see that the nation's resources had to be focused on the internal situation.

In America, the far right would call Haugen a communist sympathizer because he hadn't insisted on the impossible dismemberment of the Soviet Union and the Soviet military, while the left-wing was already complaining that Haugen had thrown away most of the gains of the past sixty years. But neither wing had wide support.

The existence of the scalar resonance transmitters was made public in a joint statement, saying nothing of their recent use and only generalities about their physics. (Colonel Paul Fairbairn's previously ignored book, *Tesla's Unknown Legacy*, became an instant best seller. Based only on speculative analysis, it had the principles remarkably correct, though of course it lacked the technical details.) Each great power would retain two scalar resonance transmitters, to be staffed by joint crews. They'd be used to ameliorate or divert seriously damaging weather, such as severe droughts or major hurricanes. Requests would be channeled through the World Meterological Organization, an affiliate of the United Nations.

All Soviet military forces would be removed from East Germany, Poland, Czechoslovakia and Hungary. All American military forces would be removed from the continent. This agreement was contingent on Britain and Canada also removing their remaining forces, but there was no doubt at all that they would.

The question of Soviet forces in Iran was only touched on. The United States took no position on it other than to commend the stated Soviet intention of withdrawing entirely north of the pre-invasion border as promptly as conditions permitted, and surely by mid-April.

The Soviet Union felt serious concern over the possibility of political and military unification of the two Germanies, in the train of the Soviet military pullout. Russia, after all, would lose much of its leverage on the buffering Warsaw Pact nations. The United States therefore agreed to cosponsor a conference of the Warsaw Pact and NATO nations, to ensure the development of no new military threat—the two Germanies were not specifically named—in central Europe.

A plebiscite, supervised by Australia, India, and Egypt, would be held in the Afghan SSR, as "a state whose incorporation within the Soviet Union had been a coercive act by the disgraced, imperialist Kulish government." The Afghans would be given a choice of remaining in the Soviet Union, or independence under temporary UN assistance, with all Soviet forces withdrawn. This, more than anything else, impressed the world of Gurenko's good intentions.

It was much the most daring and dangerous agreement Gurenko made—it could inspire demands for independence in SSRs that were integral, instead of peripheral, to the empire. But insurrection was flaring in the Afghan countryside and towns alike, and problems with military morale and discipline had convinced Gurenko that the risk was necessary.

The United States and the Soviet Union would hold an NCB (nuclear-chemical-biological) disarmament conference, to be seated no later than April 1. Other nations could be jointly invited to participate. First-order objectives and ground rules for the convention were agreed upon; the objectives included on-site inspection procedures, and both Haugen and his conference staff felt that real progress might be made this time.

Several other subject areas were discussed; it was agreed to put them on hold for the time being. Gurenko insisted privately that the commitments he'd already made had put him at a significant degree of risk with the Soviet army.

Privately, "off the record," Gurenko told Haugen of two internal reforms he intended. That summer there would be a new Soviet constitution, and he would announce a new level of Soviet statehood—"*Associated* Socialist Republic." In these, the Communist parties would be independent of the Communist Party of the Soviet Union, with separate and largely independent bureaucracies and their own domestic policies. The native language could be used as the language of government, with Russian as a secondary official language to be taught to children in the schools. The three Baltic states—Lithuania, Latvia, and Estonia— would be granted this status first, both as showcases and to debug the system; other Soviet Republics could earn the status by accomplishments in production and education.

Haugen was hopeful but not awfully optimistic that this would work, though he concealed his doubts from Gurenko. He'd read voraciously and omnivorously most of his life, sometimes two books an evening. History and nations had been favorite subjects of his, and he had a huge volume of information available to his remarkable recall. He knew that at the end of the Second World War, the Stalin government had hauled to Siberian labor camps approximately 1.5 million of the five million Balts and Estonians who'd survived the war—thirty percent. These had been replaced with Russian colonists. Government was put almost totally in the hands of Russians, who'd favored the Russian colonists over the native people in every way.

That had been a half century earlier. The iron Russian grip was said to have lightened in recent decades, and since the Russian conquest, two new generations had been born to both the native people and the Russians who'd been forced on them. And there must have been intermarriages. But ethnic hatreds often die slowly, and it seemed likely to Haugen that, given the opportunity, many Balts and Estonians might in their turn discriminate against the Russians among them and against the Russian language.

He hoped they wouldn't. If they did, the Russian fist might clench on them again.

And of course, the new and independent Communist parties might change so much so fast, they'd spook the Russians.

Time would tell.

At least the cold war seemed definitely over for the time being, Russian imperialism had cooled, and the new ruler was neither paranoid nor xenophobic. And as important as any other trait, Gurenko, more than any of his predecessors, was more a rationalist than an ideolog.

So Arne Eino Haugen felt pleased with the world and himself when he got an Air Force One and took off for home.

FORTY-NINE

The president knew a couple of things as soon as Martinelli told him who was on the line. One: Something was bothering Cromwell, who, since becoming vice president, had seldom phoned him from outside. And two: whatever he was calling about probably wasn't officially urgent, because he'd called through the White House switchboard instead of directly by security phone.

The general, he decided, was calling to make a point, and he was prepared for Cromwell's response to his usual "what can I do for you, Jumper?"

"Mr. President, I'd like to make a suggestion."

"All right."

"I've been keeping a close eye on Valenzuela ever since you appointed him secretary. He'd make a hell of a good vice president."

Haugen laughed. "I think so too. You still want to weasel out, do you?"

The answer came a little stiffly. "No sir. I want to see more suitable presidential material as vice president."

"Jumper . . ." The president paused. "Excuse my honest-to-god lousy choice of words. I know you're not trying to weasel, and I know how you feel about being next in line. I've been watching Val with that in mind. From the start. I'll take it up with him when we get together this afternoon. He's coming over here to watch Weisner's talk to the UN with me.

"But if I died this minute, you could appoint a vice president and resign tomorrow. You know that."

Cromwell shook his head. "It would look to the people as if there was something wrong with the job. As if it was too much for anyone but you."

362

The president nodded. "I see your point. I'll tell you though, Jumper, if someone shot me today, you'd make a helluva good president. Better than most have, I guarantee it.

"Meanwhile I can't give the job to just anyone, and I don't know how Val will feel about it. I wouldn't be surprised if he told me he's never even imagined the possibility. But if he's willing, I'll let you know. Then you can send me your resignation, to be effective on the date of his approval as vice president. Okay?"

There was a perceptible lag before Cromwell replied. "Yes sir; thank you sir. I'll look forward to hearing."

The president knew what caused the lag, too. "I know I could approve Valenzuela myself," he added, "and I would in an emergency. But I'm not going over Congress's head when it's not necessary."

"Of course, sir. I agree entirely."

You do indeed, the president thought. *And there we have the difference between the mind and the emotions.* "Anything else, Jumper?"

"That was it, sir. Thank you."

They disconnected. Arne Haugen looked at the clock on his desk: In an hour and a half or so, they'd be bringing Lois home from the hospital, with a live-in nurse for a while. Gate security was to notify him when the limo arrived.

He picked up the intelligence summary he'd been reading when Cromwell had phoned. There was a lot to do, as always. He'd finish this, handle his IN basket, touch up his educational reform speech for Friday, go to his twelve o'clock press conference across the street, then come back and listen to Weisner's speech on television.

Marianne Weisner, the chief United States envoy to the United Nations, sat in the General Assembly, waiting to be recognized by the chair.

The resolution before the assembly had been authored by the representatives of the United Kingdom. The Security Council could have taken action on its own, but it had decided to wait for a request by the General Assembly, to allow the African nations in particular to address the matter.

The African nations hadn't been as hostile as widely

expected. *And some of the hostility expressed was more form than substance,* she told herself. North of the Kuvuma, the resolution even had some support, expressed confidentially.

The secretary general called on her, and she stepped to the rostrum, switching on the microphone in front of her there.

"Almost everything there is to say on the subject has been said," she began, "so I will simply résumé, stressing some considerations I regard as central to our decision.

"The white South African has been forced back into a small portion of the large territory he so recently held. But he defends that small portion with great tenacity. To drive him into the ocean would be terribly costly in human lives, both black and white.

"Of course he can be beaten now, and killed. Much of his motorized equipment is already stalled, out of fuel, and we can be sure his ammunition supply is not endless."

She looked them over, the assembled faces, the mixture of national costumes among western business suits. They were different in inner ways, too, but all in all they were far more alike than they were different, brought to a considerable common ground by education. And so she knew them rather well.

"Really," she went on, "what we are looking at is a choice, a choice between vengeance and justice. Civilized people recognize the difference between the two, and in this assembly we are civilized people. So where does justice lie?

"Since the evacuation of those who wished to flee, almost all the remaining whites in South Africa are Afrikaners. South Africa is the homeland of the Afrikaner, as it is of the black people there. The Afrikaner was born there, as were his parents, and their parents, and theirs, in most cases for more than three hundred years, a dozen or more generations. He has no other home."

Her glance, which could be fierce when it suited her need, swept the assemblage mildly.

"His crimes against his fellow humans are not the issue. We know what they have been, and we have seen them bring ruin upon him. What we are considering is not what the Afrikaner has done, but what are our future actions will be. Not the momentary satisfactions of revenge, but the long-term benefits of justice.

"While genocide is a term often misused to stir emotions, genocide also happens in reality. And those who, in their understandable bitterness, would wipe out the Afrikaner, lineage and language, push him back against the sea and kill him, driving any survivors into scattered exile—those people are advocating genocide.

"That genocide has occurred many times throughout history does not make it right. And I believe we have outgrown such barbarous behavior.

"And consider the alternative, the resolution before us. Granting the Afrikaner the territory between the Great Kei River on the east and the Sunday and Zeekoe Rivers on the west, from the Ocean northward to the Orange, would allow him a territory of 32 thousand square miles, scarcely seven percent of what he once called his. It is sufficient to support his numbers, probably not much more than two million now, for he uses land skillfully and has a good command of technology. And the world, and his neighbors, will never let him dominate and enslave or abuse black people again."

She paused to look around once more, her glance stopping here and there on African representatives, most of whom she knew, most of whom knew her.

"I hope," she said, "that all of us here will vote for the resolution presented by the United Kingdom, as a unanimous statement of principle and justice, and as a step toward a better future for all of us on this planet."

On his television screen, the president watched her sit down to courteous and general applause. Ambassador Weisner was a handsome woman of forty-eight, with a master's degree in biochemistry, a doctorate in law, and remarkable energy. Haugen, not having paid much attention to the UN, had paid little attention to her until Coulter had complained to him about "that Weisner woman" who "sometimes seems to think she represents Israel instead of the United States."

The president had already decided Coulter would have to go, but he'd looked into her performance anyway. And been impressed. Coulter's complaints had no substance.

They'd grown out of the same strange mental program that controlled most of what he'd done.

Now he turned the sound down and looked at Valenzuela. "What do you think of her?" he asked.

"She is both wise and skilled. It was entirely her speech, you know; I merely read it and concurred. She picked a theme, civilized behavior, and left out things that might have offended the black South African, like the Afrikaner as a source of jobs and technology. She scarcely mentioned him as a fighter, cornered and dangerous."

He shook his head. "There's no doubt at all that the General Assembly will give the necessary two-thirds majority, and the Security Council is prepared to act regardless. Now if young van Louw can hold his position against the die-hards . . . But I'm certain he will. Their families are with them there, and it will even allow them their blessed apartheid within their own small land. Though life without a subject race to exploit may require considerable adjustment.

"But still the Afrikaner probably will prosper."

The president nodded. "It'll be the white South African who lives on a reservation, not the black, but in this case the land will be truly his. And you're right; he has the technology, the skills, the discipline; I expect he will prosper. Maybe after a bit he'll even be a good neighbor. Or am I being sentimental?"

Absently he sipped tepid coffee. "What would you think of the lady as vice president?"

"Marianne? What that really means is, what kind of president would she be, if it came to that." He looked at the question, then at Haugen. "I believe she would be quite effective. I take it General Cromwell still wants out and you're considering her."

"No, I'm considering someone else. But the someone else might want to consider her." He put down his cup. "I'm not going to stay on past this year. I'm not indispensable, and I'd like to take Lois out of here."

His eyes captured Valenzuela's, and at that moment, Valenzuela knew what was coming.

"How'd you like to be vice president, Val? For a little while. And after that, president. The Jones Act made Puerto Ricans eligible way back in 1917; Cavanaugh as-

sures me there's no question about your constitutional
eligibility.

"It's a kind of spooky feeling, I know, to become president this way. Or it was for me. But why did it feel that
way? Because culturally, something feels missing: I didn't
run for office! Any office! I didn't go through the standard
procedure. Background? Hell, Hoover was an engineer,
Grant and Eisenhower career military men . . . Reagan
was an actor and Wheeler an ex-professional football player,
for chrissake! You have as good a background, your credentials are as good, as almost any president this side of
George Washington."

The president grinned at his dark secretary then. "Or
maybe you're rarin' to have a go at it. Maybe I'm wasting
my sales pitch. Whatever. I've watched you enough to feel
sure you can handle the job, handle it well, and I'm sure
that Congress will approve you."

"Hmh!" Valenzuela smiled slightly. "You'd be a hard act
to follow, Mr. President. But yes, I would accept the vice
presidency. There may be times I'll regret saying it, but
I'm willing." He laughed then. "You realize of course that
you're talking about a black Hispanic Catholic president
and a female Jewish vice president."

"Why not?" Haugen laughed too. "What the hell, we're
up to it now. It's not that much wilder than a president
who didn't speak English till after he started school."

"You know," he added grinning, "Abe Lincoln would be
proud of us."

He reached for the phone. "I told Jumper I'd let him
know what you said. He's probably got his resignation
typed up and ready. Then I'll call Milstead and he'll get
your nomination drafted. We'll get this underway right
now."

At Lois's suggestion, Arne had invited Flynn to supper.
Flynn had spent time with her every day in the hospital.
She'd gotten him to talk about his life: his childhood, so
different from Arne's, his growing interest in becoming a
priest, a teaching priest . . . even two of the spiritual
crises in his life. She thought of him now as a close
personal friend.

She wasn't able to eat much yet—soup prepared in the

White House kitchen under the direction of her nurse, a gentle salad, custard. Therapy had been hard on her body's systems, though much harder on the lymphomas that threatened them with extinction. But for the men in her life she'd ordered stroganoff sent up from the kitchen, "in honor of our newfound affinity with things Russian," she told them.

It felt so good to be out of the hospital, done at least for a time with the therapy. And the White House staff were always good to her; there was real affection here. Now, she thought, it would be pleasant to go for a drive along Lake Superior, in passing to look out through cliffy, fir and birch-framed vistas across steel-blue water . . . But this winter even Gitchee Gumee's storm-tossed winter seas would be bound, restrained, roofed over now with ice, and the roadside picnic tables buried under snow.

She remembered north shore drives in winter. Except in the very hardest of them, Superior's broad expanse stayed open year round, even when harbors and bays were covered by thirty inches of ice. If you drove very far along the north shore, you usually could see open water, blue in the sun or gray beneath cloud, with a shelf of ice a mile or two wide along the shore.

And at some place or places where the road passed near the bouldery beach, she and Arne would stop, get out. The shelf ice provided much easier travel than the rugged, stream-cut land and the often brushy forest, where the snow lay deep and soft. With its snow firm and wind-packed, the ice was a travelway, tracked by moose and deer and wolves, and at last by their own skis and ski poles.

It seemed to Lois Haugen that they would never do that again, but there was no sense of loss in the thought. They'd lived and nurtured a good and rare life together, she and Arne, one that neither of them had imagined before they met, or even when they married.

Things had their time and place. How had the song gone? It seemed to her it had been rooted in the Bible. "There's a time for all things—a time for life, a time for death, a time for love, a time for hate." Something like that. She wasn't sure which time this was, for life or for death.

She couldn't visualize a time for hate. Children used the word as synonymous to "don't like," but the word was not the thing. She could remember anger briefly flaring, and transient resentments, largely during childhood and youth. But hate she knew only as a spectator, mostly by reading about it, and wondered if that was unusual or common. Perhaps hatred was more common in books than in the lives she'd seen being lived around her.

Arne's laughter drew her attention outward, as animatedly he told a story from his youth to Stephen. "And old Inge laughed and said, 'Yesus Christ! Dey vere stinging me so terrible bad, you know, dat ay yumped over two fences and a hayrake.' "

Flynn laughed too, and Lois, who knew the story, joined them.

"Sometimes I miss those days," Arne said. "And those characters. And when we leave here, sometimes I'll miss this too." He turned to Lois, smiling. "We'll be out of here before Christmas, Babe, I promise you. And I'll shoot for Thanksgiving." His smile widened. "See! I'm moving the date back this way now. We'll spend next winter in Hawaii if you'd like, the way we used to say we would some day."

FIFTY

The presidential convoy was forced to slow as it approached the Washington Hilton. On Seventeenth Street, demonstrators, their signs bobbing up and down or waving, flowed across in front of the Metropolitan Police cars. There was not a large number of the demonstrators— probably no more than two hundred. Nor did they seem hostile as a group, though no doubt a few individuals were, for among the signs they carried were a couple that said BETRAYED! But mostly they bore messages like UKRAINAN FREEDOM! and DO NOT FORGET LITH-UANIA!, and even REPARATIONS FOR IRAN!

Inside the armored limousine, the president nudged Lester Okada with an elbow. "Les," he said, "tape what I tell you."

Okada's hand emerged with a pocket recorder.

"If it comes up with the press, make a point to them that these people, these demonstrators, have my sympathy. Most of them fled a hated police state, or their parents did, some just a jump ahead of the secret police, and they've wanted to see their homelands free ever since. Their anxieties are understandable. But the United States doesn't rule the world; it doesn't have unlimited powers. And I don't command the Soviet Union. Even Gurenko doesn't have unrestricted command there; he's limited by what the Russian people and the Soviet army are willing to go along with."

The demonstrators had been kept well away from where the president would get out, but a small crowd of orderly bystanders had been allowed closer, standing behind a rope barricade and a cordon of Metropolitan Police. Closer still were media people—photographers and television crews, the so-called "body watch," there mainly to get pictures if someone attacked the president. Outwardly impassive, Secret Service men stood facing the onlookers. The limousine pulled up within ten feet of the canopied entrance, and Wayne and Gil got out to stand by the open, bulletproof, limousine door, shielding the president as he emerged and walked into the building.

Once inside, the two bodyguards breathed just a little easier. Now they could see anyone in a position to harm the president. The corridor had been cleared, except for the other Secret Service men posted there, but in a minute the president would be in the convention hall, where seventeen hundred people would be sitting. A morning like this aged a Secret Service man five years.

The President's February 13 address on education reform, before a special meeting of the American Association of School Administrators.

Thank you, ladies and gentlemen, for the opportunity of speaking to you. Because this is a speech on education reform, it makes sense to give it in front of a gathering of school administrators. But most Americans are interested in better education, and perhaps a hundred million of them are listening at their television sets and radios.

Since I addressed the American Bar Association, groups have probably gotten nervous about having me speak at their meetings. But I'm really not an ogre; I'm not out to get anyone. I'm simply going to discuss what we'll be doing together to improve the literacy and abilities of the United States and its citizens.

So here I am, and I thank you for meeting with me.

Most of us, as children and youth, had teachers we remember fondly, who stimulated our interest in this or that subject or in learning in general. Teachers from whom we learned a lot or who helped us learn a lot. We also remember teachers whose ineptitude or hostility made us dislike or disdain them more or less heartily, who wasted our time and theirs. Teachers from whom we developed at least a temporary distaste for the subject they taught, and in too many cases a dislike for school. Some of them, in their incompetence, ridiculed and degraded pupils.

Mostly though, there were teachers we liked well enough, and from whom we learned quite a bit.

Some of that latter class of teachers might have been a lot more effective if they'd had a better environment to teach in. Or if their students had been better prepared in the lower grades. Or if they'd been free of arbitrary administrative idiocies of the kind that all too many teachers can tell about at length.

Of course, often those administrative idiocies grew out of unfortunate laws and court rulings, and problems with strange parents and ineffective teachers. All too often, school administrators have found themselves in a Catch-22 situation.

And of course, there are problems with children.

In any school system that undertakes to teach any and all children, there are certain children who simply don't seem able to learn very much. Putting it plainly, for whatever reasons, some of them seem to be stupid. Others have attention spans near zero. Others, from families that may be poor or may be affluent, are so discouraged by what they see around them and do not understand, that they consider education a waste of time.

While all too many hate school. Hating school is undoubtedly a major cause of juvenile delinquency and adolescent drug use.

There was a time when children who didn't learn were failed repeatedly, until at age fourteen or so they were allowed to leave school. And did leave, perhaps with the fifth grade uncompleted. In more recent decades, children like those have been passed forward indiscriminately, often to graduate from high school illiterate or semiliterate, actually unable to do third grade work. Their activity in school was not learning. At best it was suffering in silence, and all too often it was interfering with teachers and other students.

How brutally boring it would be to spend five or six hours a day in classrooms, understanding little and learning less!

Another gross failure of our educational system is the semi-education of those many many young people who obviously can learn, and do learn, but who finish school with serious gaps in their education. Who are, for example, nonfunctional mathematically, can't divide or multiply or tell you what a fraction signifies; *or never learn to learn effectively;* or are ignorant of history or government or science, or the basics of how societies and economies function. And commonly don't realize they are ignorant! Or think it doesn't matter. *This is truly disgraceful—the central and perhaps most critical disgrace of our education system, and a danger to our future.*

We've been more or less aware of this in America for decades, yet nothing effective has been done about it. Our teachers colleges have turned out far too many teachers who cannot, or at least do not, teach effectively. And if the institutions that teach the teachers don't know how to teach—well, there you have one reason we're in trouble. Of course they impart some useful teaching knowledge and techniques—any interested parent or grandparent is aware of this—but the teachers colleges have utterly failed to solve the problems, and have contributed to some of them.

I strongly suspect that many teachers would have been at least as good if they'd never attended classes in education, if they'd simply been trained in the subject matter they teach and allowed to use their own intelligence and judgment in their own way. And I further suspect that some would have been better teachers without courses in education.

Our school districts have hired many incompetent teachers, perhaps for lack of enough good candidates, and inflicted them on our children and teenagers. And some of these incompetents prove very hard to get rid of, once they've gotten tenure.

Well, that's enough review of the situation. A couple of months ago I rough-drafted a critique of American education, with some notes on what I thought might be done. Then I called in three prominent educators who've been publicly and responsibly critical of the system, and asked them to critique my write-up. . . .

. . . I'm going to present you with the main points [of this reform]. When I'm done, a detailed package will be handed out. It's being mailed today to school districts, legislatures, and colleges nationwide.

Some of you may be wondering what the legal basis is for federal law on education. After all, the Constitution, by default, leaves public education, if any, to the states. But the Constitution also guarantees various rights to individuals, and the courts have long since determined that education is necessary to provide some of these in today's world. Also, almost all school districts and states in America receive federal aid to education in one form and another. Beginning next year, to receive federal aid of any kind to education, states will have to abide by these reforms.

So here is a summary of them.

From this date there is only conditional tenure for public school teachers. The condition is competence, based on the progress of their pupils. Teachers will not be allowed to teach a subject that they don't teach effectively.

Likewise, administrative employees of a school district have only conditional tenure. They have to be competent too. I'm sure that all of you are aware by now of the changes in the federal civil service law requiring competency. Perhaps you live in a state that has followed the federal lead in this.

So how will we get competent teachers?

Degree programs at teachers colleges, and teacher certification will be subject to national standards. Our examiners will be testing the subject matter competency of graduates. And we will publicize the overall statistics of each teachers college. Can the would-be math teacher do and explain math? Can the would-be English teacher parse a sentence?

The stress will be on the ability to produce pupils who know and can use the subject matter of their grade level. So teaching candidates must be thoroughly trained in the subjects they're going to teach. There will be very strict limits on what courses in education and in the psychology of education can be required, either openly or covertly—because curricula heavy on these courses do not produce a high percentage of effective teachers.

Without the ballast of required courses in education, the required curriculum for a school teacher should take a full-time student no more than three years.

In lieu of most required courses in education, and regardless of any elective courses in education they may have taken, all new candidates for a teaching certificate—not a diploma but a certificate authorizing them to teach—must serve a year as a full-time, minimally paid *teaching intern*, working with several teachers in two or more schools for experience. When the internship has been completed, the candidate will be advanced to *associate teacher*. Interns and associates will meet in seminars with invited master teachers, to discuss the techniques and problems of teaching. This system should be a major improvement over required courses in education and educational psychology.

And this brings us to a very important point: Beginning with the next academic year, teaching candidates must score well on tests of their subject matter competency. Those who pass will be certified as intern-eligible. *There will be no college requirements whatever for acceptance as an intern.* If an applicant who has never been to college passes the tests, that applicant must be entered on the roster of intern-eligibles, and ranked according to score.

In other words, and this is important, a teachers college, or a university school of education, will no longer be a place where you go to get a degree, *but a place where you go to develop competence as a teacher.* You may get a degree, as a sort of trophy, *and feel justly proud of it,* but it will carry no weight on the job market. An employer cannot even ask if you have one, or record it if you tell him.

Now where does quality control enter into all this?

"Quality control? Who ever heard of quality control in education?" Exactly. Now you have. Cosmetics manufacturers are required to have strict quality control to avoid injuring people's skin. Surely education should have quality control, to prevent injuring or short-changing our society, our young people, and our future as a nation.

Therefore, every child will be examined at the end of every semester to find out how well he or she has mastered the material and skills taught that semester. The child who doesn't do well enough will have to restudy the material in either the next semester or in summer session, until he or she has mastered it.

And teachers, and schools, and school districts, will be rated according to the performance of their pupils. If a teacher or school or district has been shortchanging pupils, they can be required to upgrade their competency in the areas of weakness.

Now, none of what I have said so far has dealt

directly with the problem of children who do not learn in school, or who do not learn much. Some of this problem grows out of poor situations at home. And an important factor has been a seriously flawed education system.

Another important part of it has been a society, and many families, that don't respect and encourage learning.

So far, school psychologists and school counselors have not proven effective in handling learning problems. I'm sure that many counselors and psychologists can point to successes in upgrading student performance. But the sheer volume of student problems in our schools, and the sources of many of those problems, are far beyond what we can expect school counselors to handle, even assuming they have the tools.

On an optimistic note, it seems to me that as a people, we have changed, these last months, that we are getting our priorities turned around.

Now, back to the pupils who fail a semester exam. Let me repeat: They will restudy *the subject they did not understand* until they've mastered it. They will *not* have to redo the entire grade. To redo the entire grade wastes time and humiliates the pupil. They shouldn't even have to restudy the parts of the subject they already know. The pupil will be allowed to move up in the subjects he or she passes.

Pupils who are a continuing behavior problem will not be allowed to degrade the classroom for other pupils. The school will be required—*not allowed but required*—to remove troublemakers from the general classroom. Just what will be done with them then will depend on the problem and the causes. We don't want to simply abandon them, and some good and experienced people are working on developing a practical pupil-salvage system. But meanwhile, as an unsatisfactory coping action, incorrigible pupils can be assigned to disciplinary groups where the principal subject drilled will be self-control.

Finally there is a very basic change that will be tested in fifty schools beginning with the next school year. We expect it to help a great deal in starting kindergartners and first graders on the right foot.

I refer to spelling reform—the use of spellings which approximate the way the words are pronounced. The present irrational system of spelling American words is a major barrier to children's learning to read and their ability to study.

Let me give you some family and personal background on this. My parents each learned to read before they came to America—my father in Norway, my mother in Finland. They learned at home. It wasn't difficult; in Norwegian to a large extent and in Finnish especially, the words are spelled the way they're pronounced, which makes reading much easier to learn.

Thus my mother had read much of the New Testament in Finnish, aloud to her parents, before she began school at age six. You can imagine what this did for her vocabulary.

My own experience was similar. Before I started school, I'd learned to read both Norwegian and Finnish. When I started in our little one-room school, I learned to read English very quickly *because I had a working sense of how reading was done*. And unlike some children who started school already knowing how to read Norwegian or Swedish or Finnish, I was not indignant at the English spellings. I thought they were hilarious—dumb but hilarious.

They no longer amuse me.

By the end of the first grade, I was well into the Fourth Reader, and later I, and others, were allowed to learn as rapidly as we wanted. For that, thanks are due to the willingness of two very able teachers: Miss Shogren and later Miss Knaizel, who were not constrained by idiotic rulings from a district office denying us the right to forge ahead. When some of us, in grades three or four or five, had finished the eighth grade reading and history and geography books, these beautiful young ladies loaned us their personal books, and borrowed by mail for us, wholesale, from the county and state libraries.

That is called helping pupils learn. Shameful to

say, in many schools it's not allowed now; not standard, you know.

But spelling reform! Some of you may be thinking, *Good grief! If this spreads, I'll have to learn to read all over again!* Or, *My children won't be able to read any of the books we have.*

No, that's not the way it works. If you already read fairly well, you could pick up a book with the new spellings right now and start reading it. In a few minutes you'd be reading it easily. And if you're an English-speaking adult with a severe reading problem, you'd probably be able to read a book in the new system with a half-hour's coaching.

The letters themselves are those you're already used to. The main difference is that words will be spelled very much the way you hear them. And once grooved into reading, your children will easily pick up reading other books.

Incidentally, we're going to have some adult-level books published in the new system so that people can see what it's like. They should be out in time for Christmas.

How did we come up with this new system?

English and American spelling reforms have been talked about for centuries. They've been resisted in the past by publishers and educators who were unwilling to adjust, while hair-splitters have feuded over what kind of alphabet to use.

We've been practical and kept it simple. Three specialists in language have worked together to compile a new spelling book, starting with a vocabulary for first readers. They used only the twenty-six familiar letters of the English alphabet, with marks over two of the letters in order to fit the alphabet to American vowel sounds. And they've kept the spellings as simple as possible—much simpler than the system we're used to.

One of these three persons is from Chicago by way of Logan, Utah; one is a Yankee from Keene, New Hampshire; and the third is a lifelong resident of South Carolina. They represent the three principal varieties of spoken American: middle American, yankee, and southern. Mostly, they've agreed on the spelling for each word. Where they didn't agree, they've followed middle American pronunciations because that's what most Americans speak.

These are practical people who recognize that no system will be perfect—*that what we are after is simply something that will make it much much easier for American children to learn to read!* We've had too much of this idiocy of making learning far more difficult than necessary for our six-year-olds. A difficulty that often seriously hampers their education from then on, and plagues many of them through the rest of their lives!

A lot of our other troubles and frustrations in education will be greatly reduced, over the years, by this simple spelling reform.

If your school is interested in getting into the program and hasn't been included in the selection of fifty, get in touch with your school district. We'll try to include it.

And basically, ladies and gentlemen, school administrators, that's the picture on education reform. I consider it as vital as legal reform to the future of a democratic America. The material that will be handed out to you contains the details. Personnel from the Department of Education will meet with you tomorrow to answer questions. You'll have read the material by then.

Now— What I have to say next is directed mainly at the millions of Americans watching on television or listening on the radio. One of the most urgent things we have to do in this country is provide an education system that our children will enjoy, not dislike—a system that will interest them and actually educate them. We need to educate our children decently so they can function in the twenty-first century, so this country can compete with nations like Japan and Germany, where education has been truly respected. And so they can make tomorrow's world better than today's.

Most teachers and most school administrators will take hold and make this new system work. Many of them became education professionals because they feel strongly about education.

Inevitably though, some will drag their feet, and a few will try to sabotage the new system by screwing things up and bad-mouthing it. Eventually they'll be culled out for poor job performance. But meanwhile it's a new system, and at first there'll also be some honest misunderstandings and difficulties in operating it. There'll be some honest confusion, and at times it may be hard to tell the saboteurs from people who just haven't gotten used to operating in a new way, or have just gotten their toes stepped on and are blowing off honest steam.

So don't be surprised at some stumbling around at first, or at some noise and complaints. This new system will work quite decently if enough of you—teachers, administrators, parents, pupils—just drive on through the initial confusion. Things will settle out soon enough.

And that's all I have to say for now. Thank you all for listening to me. I wish you well.

The applause fell far short of thunderous. Quite a lot of it was mechanical; quite a lot was more than that. Scattered through it were singlets and small pockets of enthusiastic clapping and even a few cheers, but these did not spread.

The president was willing to settle for that. He left the podium and went out through a door at the rear of the room. Secret Service people closed in behind him, two others preceding. Lester Okada had been waiting, listening out of the way beside the door, while in the corridor with more agents, an army physician stood; there was always a doctor with the president while away from the White House. Then, surrounded by Secret Service men, the president, Okada, and the doctor were escorted down the hall to a small room. There they would wait briefly until departure security was fully in place—the entrance area cleared, the armored limo and other vehicles situated and ready, and route security notified that the president was on his way.

There were assorted hot rolls and coffee in the room,

with butter, honey, jam, sugar, and cream. Okada and the president had black coffee and ignored the rest; the Secret Service people were too intent to take any of it.

"You sounded very convincing, Mr. President," Okada said.

Haugen sipped coffee, then looked up, his expression uncharacteristically dour. "I hope so. I probably made as many enemies today as I did with legal reform. But it'll be worth it in the long run."

Okada didn't try to make more conversation. After a couple of minutes, the SAIC, the special agent in charge, looked into the room. "Everything's ready, Mr. President. We should leave now."

Unsmiling, Haugen nodded and stood, and they left the room, walking briskly down the hall to the VIP exit. The limo's open door was perhaps eight feet from the end of the entry canopy. The usual crowd was waiting behind ropes about eighty feet away, some of them calling or cheering when they caught sight of the president. Television and press cameras were aimed from media groups about twenty feet away on either side.

From one of the camera groups, someone shouted to the president in Finnish, poorly pronounced but recognizable—"Hyvää päivää, Herra Presidenti!"—and for a moment Haugen, surprised, stopped to wave.

That's when the shooting started, and the president went down under Secret Service bodies. There were screams, shouts, oaths. After no more than three or four seconds, he felt people get off him, felt hands half lift, half drag him into the limo. The door slammed, the heavy vehicle surged forward, sirens began to ululate.

Gil saw a large smear of blood on the president's left cheek and temple, but no apparent wound. "Pete," he snapped to the driver, "the George Washington Medical Center, fast." That was standard when there'd been shooting, with or without evidence of injury: Head for the nearest major hospital, just in case. The driver, also Secret Service, radioed rapid orders, first to the escort vehicles, then to the hospital.

Gil's face was tight, grim. While throwing the president to the pavement, he'd glimpsed the physician's face bursting crimson; it could be his blood on the president's cheek. "Are you all right, Mr. President?" he asked.

"Damned if I know." The voice was weak, the words blurry. "No. I'm not. I'm hit. Left arm . . ." His voice cleared then, though it was still weak. "Jesus Christ! Something's wrong with me!"

Something was! The president's breathing, the agent realized, was shallow and weak, and the smell reminded him of gutting a deer. *It's more than the fucking arm!* Gil told himself. *Jesus Christ, don't let him die on me.* He clamped his teeth. *Why in hell did the doctor have to get it?*

There was a medkit in the limousine. Gil opened it, removed heavy shears designed for the purpose, and began rapidly to cut free the president's jacket and shirt, enough that the medics could easily strip the garments away. Blood was soaking the left sleeve now, and as Gil exposed the hairy torso, he found more than just the sleeve bloody. The hole in the chest moved and bubbled with every breath.

The president looked at him, and for a moment the vagueness cleared somewhat from his eyes. "Gil," he said. "And you. Listen up." He gestured weakly with his head at a second agent sitting gun in hand on the other end of the seat, watching intently out the window for possible further attack.

"Larry!" Gil snapped, "listen up!" Then: "We're listening, Mr. President."

Haugen gathered himself, then enunciated slowly, clearly. "I appoint Valenzuela vice president. Got that? Valenzuela vice president. Otherwise Cromwell would never forgive me. Tell Milstead."

An awful chill flowed over Gil Rogers. "Yes, Mr. President. You appoint Valenzuela vice president. I'll tell Mr. Milstead."

The president let his eyes close.

The hospital was scarcely more than a mile from the Hilton; in under three minutes from the shooting, they were at an emergency bay, where a gurney waited. Gil stayed with the president, gun in hand now, all the way to surgery.

Then, hard grim eyes paying no attention to the other agents there, he squatted outside the door until someone brought a folding chair. He'd been assigned to protect the president that day, and the president had been shot.

FIFTY-ONE

Corridor traffic was sparse but purposeful. Within minutes, several doctors entered or left the president's operating suite, under the hard, evaluative eyes of agents. Occasional other hospital personnel passed by on unrelated business. Another agent arrived, relieving Gil Rogers, who left to be debriefed. Overall, the mood in the corridor was one of tense waiting.

The hospital lobby was briefly overrun by media people, until hospital management had the Metropolitan Police clear them out. Then thirty were allowed to return inside. About half an hour after the president had been wheeled in, Lois Haugen arrived, pale and thin, with Cromwell beside her. The eyes of the cameras followed them compulsively toward an elevator, and one team—cameraman and interviewer—moved to intercept. One of the Secret Service men stepped between and snatched the microphone.

"I ought to shove this up your ass," he said. Bitterly. And audibly. There was a patter of applause from people waiting in the lobby. The newsman, flushing, retreated, and the agent tossed the microphone after him.

Cromwell recognized the agent; he'd seen him on shift at the White House. Frank something. *He'll probably get a reprimand from uplines for that*, Cromwell thought as they got on the elevator. *I'll write him a commendation. If I have to be president or acting president, I might as well get some satisfaction out of it*. When they got out on the president's floor, he drew one of the other agents aside and learned Frank's last name, Shapiro. "Shapiro's a good man," Cromwell said. "Tell him not to worry about what happened in the lobby."

They were led then to a small sitting area near the operating room. To wait.

Stephen Flynn had hesitated to go to the hospital. Even in lay garb he might be recognized. He'd almost surely be recognized if he was with the first lady's party, and he could imagine what the media might make of that. "Priest with stricken president." But he wanted to be on hand, in case there was anything he could do. If Arne *was* dying . . .

So he called the hospital, that they'd be expecting him, then went by cab. Wearing his "camouflage"—a business suit. It was a bright still day with the temperature surely more than fifty degrees: God's earnest money on the coming of spring. Truly, Gurenko had turned off the winter machine. Flynn wouldn't have been surprised to see a robin on the hospital grounds.

None of the news people so much as gave him a glance. He showed his driver's license at the reception desk, where they checked by phone with the presidential party, then sent him up with an orderly to guide him. On the president's floor, an agent checked him out at the elevator, then using a little belt radio, called the agents in the waiting area. One of them came to get him, one who knew him; they were taking nothing for granted.

Lois met him with a smile. "They just told us," she said; "his condition's been upgraded to serious. He's going to be all right." She paused. Her eyes had welled, but her voice never quavered. "I thought he would. Because I'm going to be, and I don't believe God intends us to be separated—not for long anyway."

The debrief of the three Secret Service men who'd brought the president to the hospital, uncovered the fact that Haugen had appointed Valenzuela vice president. Milstead was notified at once, and Milstead called Valenzuela, who then became acting president and was sworn in. Cromwell learned of it when he returned to the White

House, and was surprised, almost dismayed, to feel a pang of disappointment before the wave of relief.

Radio, television, newspapers, all covered the situation closely and soberly. The president had been shot twice. One bullet had struck his raised left arm, fracturing the humerus but not touching the brachial artery, and one had struck his chest, penetrating an intercostal space; punctured the pleura and the left lung; broke a rib in back; then broke and holed the scapula, emerging much flattened. The most serious danger had been death from profound shock.

Two other people had been shot: Major James Jackson, Army Medical Corps, and a Secret Service man, Agent Wayne Trabert. Neither wound was critical, but Major Jackson's face would require reconstructive surgery; the bullet had had a hollow point.

There had been just one assailant. He'd carried press credentials and a Walther PPK 7.65 mm pistol whose seven-round clip he'd emptied in less than two seconds. A television camera woman had struck his arm upward in mid-burst, otherwise more people would have been hit. She'd also sunk her teeth into his jaw and hung on. Then a Secret Service man had slammed into them, bearing them to the pavement, where he covered the assailant with his body while others closed around them to keep people from killing the gunman.

The assailant's name was Crainey Branard. He was a TV newsman from Tulsa, Oklahoma, and a convert of the Stalwart in God Church of the Apocalypse. President Haugen, he said, was endangering the day of judgment, and the millenium during which Christ, after wars and terrible plagues, earthquakes, and meteor falls, was to rule on Earth for a thousand years.

The founder and head of the Church, Reverend Delbert Coombs, would appear on television that night to lead his five million followers in mass prayer for the president's recovery. To the network news team that interviewed him in his Cincinnati office, the reverend stated his belief that President Haugen would be one of those saved by the Lamb of God on Judgment Day. When asked what he thought the Lamb would do about the gunman, he said simply that he hoped people would pray for Branard too.

Branard, though he may have been insane, had done a very respectable job of planning and execution, even to having bought a Finnish pronouncing phrasebook and a Finnish-English pocket dictionary, and practicing a greeting to stop the president for a moment between hotel and limousine.

By midafternoon, the president, awake but sedated, was allowed a short visit by his wife. Afterward, when she left the hospital with General Cromwell, the television cameras showed her serene and confident, despite her unaccustomed thinness.

FIFTY-TWO

Over the next two days, the sedated president drifted in and out of consciousness. But even when conscious, he was mostly only vaguely aware of the comings and goings of hospital personnel, the ever-present nurse, and the Secret Service man who sat by the window, jacket open, shoulder-holster bared. Haugen knew that Lois had been there off and on, and Liisa unless he'd dreamed it.

On the third day, sedation was reduced, and he was considerably more alert. Lois visited him briefly, and somewhat later, Liisa. Her mother, Liisa told him, was visiting other patients.

"You've got mail, daddy," she said, and showed him an envelope. "It's from 'Stenhus, Littlefork Minnesota, 56653.'"

It had already been opened by his letter office staff, which handled the thousands of items received for him daily. This one they'd recognized as one he should see. Removing the clip they'd closed it with, Liisa drew out a much folded sheet of ruled tablet paper. "Can you hold it?" she asked.

"You'll have to read it," he said. "I don't know where my glasses are."

She held it up and began.

Dear Haugen,

Well, you done it that time, forgot to duck. Like in that fight you had with Martin Kjemprud and he broke your nose. I thought you were going to kill him that time. It is the only time I ever seen you get really mad. There is some people around here that are worried you are going to die. They don't remember you as good as I do. I told them sure he's going to die. Someday. But he is too goddamn tough and mean to give that Brainerd sonofabitch the satisfaction of killing him.

They said the country can't get along without you. I told them if it can't get along without Haugen, then to hell with it. What the hell more does he owe it any way.

Up at the falls they are making those little size generators you invented, like the size for places like here at Littlefork. So we got one here. The electricity is just the same as it always was (ha ha) but the bills aren't so big anymore. A lot of people had quit getting electricity but now they got it back again. I heard they even got one ordered down at Effie. I don't know what the hell they are going to pay for it with in Effie. When they get one at Craig, I guess they will be every where then.

This is just about the coldest winter any one ever seen around here. Up on Kabetogama (spelling?) the ice is way to thick for a 5-foot augur, they got to break out about another 8 or 10 inches out of the bottom with a spud and you better have a long spud. People are ice fishing anyhow, because times are still hard but they are better than they were. It is only about 4 foot thick on the river because the current keeps wearing it away you know.

The snow ain't very deep though, not much above

my knees. About up to the ass on a squatty little guy like you. It come early. Then it got to cold to snow.

People around here been doing better than in the cities I guess. They been outlawing deer and moose to eat when they got gas to get out of town, and I ain't heard about nobody getting arrested for it either. I think the cold going to kill off a lot of the deer any way before spring. Charley Stuvland said they ate a wolf at his place to see what it taste like and it was tough and dry.

That is all I got to write about. You get healed up fast and come up here, but not before spring. It's going to be the middle of May before the ice is off the lakes if then. Then we'll see how good the muskies come through the winter.

> Your old friend
> Vern

"That's a pretty nice letter, daddy," Liisa said. Somehow it had touched her deeply; she wasn't sure why.

Arne Haugen chuckled faintly. "Yes, it is."

"I'd better go now, though. The nurse told me not to stay more than a few minutes. You need lots of rest. I'll be back later."

When she'd gone, the president closed his eyes. But he didn't go to sleep immediately. He was thinking about something Stenhus had written: Some people said the country couldn't get along without him. And Vern said if it couldn't, then to hell with it.

Vern was right, but he couldn't know how good it had been—how much he'd enjoyed it. He'd never really looked at that himself till now.

Lois Haugen looked into the small room on the maternity hall. The girl inside was black, round-faced, and perhaps, Lois thought, fifteen years old. She stepped in.

"Hello," Lois said. "You don't seem to have any visitors; is it all right for me to come in?"

The girl didn't respond for a long moment, her eyes suspicious of this stranger; finally she nodded. Lois went to a chair by the bed and sat down. From there she could see plastic tubes coming from beneath the sheet.

"Did you have a baby?" she asked.

Again the delayed nod, curt this time.

Somehow Lois didn't ask about the child. Instead she said, "How do you feel now?"

The gaze remained suspicious, the lips silent.

"Maybe you'd rather be alone. Shall I go?"

"You can stay." After a moment the girl put a hand lightly on her abdomen. "I had a caesarean."

"Ah. I had one of mine that way."

"Mine died."

This time it was Lois who lagged. "I'm sorry," she answered simply.

"It's probably better this way." The girl shifted beneath the sheets. "My father lost his job last summer, and all he's got now is the PWA. He was really mad when I got pregnant, but we're Catholic, so . . ."

She sized her visitor up, the years, the ring finger, the expensive business suit that fitted too loosely, as if she'd lost weight. But the woman carried no religious tracts and didn't seem critical, and the girl had tired of morning television; she went on. "The baby started comin' last evening, all of a sudden, and the paramedics brought me here. The nurse says I nearly died."

Again she looked Lois Haugen over. "What are you in the hospital about?"

"My husband's here. But he's sleeping just now, so I thought I'd walk around and see who might want someone to talk to."

"What's he in here for?"

"A man shot him. Twice."

The interest strengthened, the eyes sharp now. After a moment the girl spoke again. "You're the president's wife, aren't you? Mrs. Haugen."

"Why yes, I am."

The girl's sudden laugh was cut short by pain. After it had passed, she said, "My brother Trevor's not goin' to believe this! He got in a fight last week—sort of a fight—with my boy friend about President Haugen. Trevor was in one those internment camps, after the street fighting, and after that he worked in a CC camp, down in Alabama. He said your husband kept the country from burnin' up and everybody starving. Then Caddy said the president's

just another Whitey, and with times so hard, the country
might as well burn up. So Trevor hit him." The girl
grinned at the memory. "Knocked Caddy flat on his ass.
Caddy didn't say anything, just got up and walked out.
He's scared of Trevor."

She pointed at the television that looked down on her
from high on the wall. "I watched the news this mornin'.
It showed Vice President Valenzuela. Do you know him?"

"Oh yes. We had supper together last night."

"Why did President Haugen make a black man vice
president?"

"Mr. Valenzuela has a lot of wisdom, and knows a lot
about government. And the world. And Arne—my husband—
says he's a highly ethical man. He'll be the next president."

Again the eyes studied the first lady. "Trevor said President Haugen was born and grew up in a log cabin. Was
someone lyin' to him?"

"It was made of logs all right; I've been there. But I'm
not sure whether you could call it a cabin. It had four
small rooms, a kitchen, and an attic. The children slept in
the attic. They heated the house with a stove made from
a steel barrel, and they burned wood in it. The toilet was
outside, behind the house, and they pumped water from
an outdoor well. When he was little, they still hauled their
water from the river with a horse."

The young eyes were shrewd, and curiosity had grown
to interest. "How did he get rich then?"

"Well— He's a very intelligent man to start with, and
after he got out of the army, he went to college. And—he's
got the gift of being able to invent new things that people
want."

"What did he invent?"

"The most important thing is a new kind of generator to
make electricity. In the towns that have them, electricity
is cheaper than it used to be. And he . . ."

A nurse came in while Lois was talking, closing the door
behind her. "Excuse me, Mrs. Haugen," she said. "Feleen,
I have to get you ready for the doctor to examine. He
wants to see if you're ready to move to a ward, where
there are other young women."

Lois Haugen got up. "I'll go now, Feleen," she said.
"Thank you for talking with me."

"That's all right." The girl grinned. "People aren't goin' to believe me when I tell them the president's wife came in to see me."

Then the nurse pulled down the sheet, and Lois left.

The employment figures had been climbing, but things were still awfully hard for millions of families. Yet it seemed from the surveys that morale was good, and that Arne had been important to that, even crucial. Now this young girl, with the story about her brother, had made it real to her.

If Arne wants to stay on in the White House, she told herself, *I won't say a peep against it.*

As a White House resident, Father Stephen Joseph Flynn was entitled to eat there, and mostly he took his meals with the domestic staff, who also ate there. But today he felt like eating alone, so a cook made him a roast beef sandwich and Father Flynn took it to his room. There he poured hot water from his electric pot onto a tea bag, turned on his small TV, and settled down to watch the twelve o'clock news.

He ate slowly, absently, while watching. The American Federation of Teachers had officially expressed its expected mixed reaction to the Haugen Education Reform Act. They were unhappy about the limited tenure provision, their spokeswoman said, but pleased at provisions that would remove chronic trouble-makers from classrooms, and with decreased administrative dictation to teachers.

The Reverend Ferris Bradwick of the Christian Reform Convention was generally pleased, but disappointed that it had not provided tax deductions for tuitions paid to church-operated schools, or addressed the issue of legalizing prayer in the public schools.

A class-action suit had been filed for a woman in Providence, Rhode Island, to strike down what her lawyer termed "the unconstitutional provision for segregation of students who exercised their freedom of speech in the classroom; and their forceable inclusion in "penal classes." He'd requested an injunction to stop it until the courts had an opportunity to strike down the law.

Attorney General Cavanaugh said the provision referred to called for the removal of disruptive students from regular classrooms, and authorized their assignment to corrective groups if they continued to be disruptive. He doubted that an injunction could be obtained, and if one was, he anticipated that it would be struck down by a higher court.

The anchorwoman then pointed out that, with the present makeup of the Supreme Court, it seemed doubtful indeed that the suit would succeed, or that any such injunction would be allowed to stand. She also commented that, as a mother of two junior high school students, she was pleased with the law.

The priest finished his roast beef sandwich and his tea, washed his plate and cup and put them away, then got ready to go to the hospital. He decided to walk this time. It was less than a mile, the weather was nice, and the exercise would be good for him. He hadn't used the pool lately—didn't feel quite right about using it in the president's absence.

Flynn didn't suppose Arne was watching newscasts yet. Perhaps he'd give him a rundown, if it seemed he might like one. After all, most of the news was good.

FIFTY-THREE

Arne Haugen recovered faster than expected. In a week he walked around in his room, with the doctor's permission and an orderly's support. Two evenings later he walked, unsupported, with Lois to the TV lounge at the end of the hall, to watch Dustin Hoffman as Oberst Markus Dietermann, in *The Sweet Breeze of Spring*.

Lois was with him a lot. The hospital had given her a room there, and they talked a good deal. Stephen Flynn had made it three-cornered a few times.

Two days later, Acting President Rudolfo Valenzuela came to see the president, at the president's request.

They borrowed an empty room, one that could hardly have been bugged—there'd been no chance to. Two Secret Service men requisitioned a pair of upholstered chairs for them from the staff lounge, and hustled them down the hall, arriving just ahead of the president and his stand-in.

"So you like the job," said Haugen when the bodyguards had left the room.

Valenzuela's chuckle was a resonant bass rumble. "Under the circumstances I do. I can imagine it becoming quite different when things are more strongly political again. But that could be very enjoyable too, very stimulating."

The president nodded, then seemed to change direction. "I wonder if anyone ever saw a winter as wild as this one before," he said thoughtfully. "A fall and winter. Politically, economically, meteorologically . . . seismologically. There's hardly anything in America that hasn't been turned on its ear."

For several minutes, Arne Haugen kept the conversation casual, and Valenzuela wondered why. Maybe he was letting his subconscious prepare. The president had wanted him here today, this afternoon, had wanted a secure room to talk in, but what he was talking about could have been said in front of anyone. Whatever the point was, and Valenzuela suspected what it might be, the president was in no hurry to get to it.

After a few minutes, Haugen changed directions again. "How do you like living in the White House?" he asked.

"Quite well. Although we don't feel we're really living there. We're *camping*, in the Lincoln Suite. It's a bit like living in a museum; it took a day or two before we felt comfortable about sitting on the furniture." Valenzuela grinned. "Milstead suggested either the Queen's or the Lincoln Suite. Manuella was attracted by the Queen's"—again the chuckle—"but I, for some reason, preferred the Lincoln."

"How have you gotten along with Grosberg and Kreiner, and Lynch and Powell? Or haven't you had much to do with them yet?"

"They briefed me on current Congressional affairs, early

on. I hadn't realized how legislatively active they are on the hill these days. Your legislative bombshells have gotten all the attention. Since then I've met with them twice, briefly, and so far we've gotten along very well."

"What's the latest from Zurich?" Haugen asked.

"Progress is reasonable. Encouraging. We've had no real barriers thrown in front of us. Hal Katsaros is in charge; he's acting secretary again."

The president nodded. "And the new court system; how's it going?"

"The bugs and snarls are less now. Mr. Cavanaugh assures me there are no problems which actually threaten the judicial processes. In fact, he said it's probably running as smoothly now as a year ago, and with better results.

"I've also talked with Chief Justice Liederman, and it is his opinion that it will engender similar reforms in almost all the individual states within the next two years. You are probably aware that last Friday, North Carolina became the seventh to do so, and very similar reforms are already pending in eleven more, including two of the three largest, California and Texas."

Haugen nodded. Minnesota, long a stronghold of populist philosophy, had been the second state to pass one.

Valenzuela's expression became quizzical now, and he changed the subject. "General Cromwell has shown me his report on the Holist Council, and the very interesting booklet written by the senior Massey. Along with the tie-ins that Director Dirksma found between Massey junior and Coulter and Blackburn/Merriman and others. Including the Calvert Cliffs bombers. He told me he is still waiting for you to make these public, and he's wondering why you haven't."

The president gazed mildly at Valenzuela. "If you were me, what reasons might you have, if any, for sitting on it?"

"Hm-m. Just now, none of it seems terribly relevant . . . It would be—a public distraction, I suppose. Despite the Archons having had a very large impact not only on this country but on the world and on human life in general. Basically they're out of it now. Massey is dead. And Keller and Harburt and Johnson, for their years of insider trading violations, have been removed from Wall Street to the Arizona cotton fields.

"All that's left are their after-effects."

Haugen nodded. "That's the way I look at it. And you made the right distinction—they *seem* irrelevant. Actually they're relevant enough, but their relevancy isn't immediate." The president shifted in his chair, as if restless. "And I do intend to make them public. I've even chosen the time and place—unless someone releases them ahead of me."

He stopped then and looked Valenzuela over. "You've been sitting there waiting patiently for what I asked you here about. So. Are you ready to be president for real now? With the title as well as the duties?"

Valenzuela grinned at the president. "I am."

Haugen grinned back. "Good." He leaned forward, a bit carefully, and extended his good hand. They shook on it. "I'll have Okada call a press conference for me next Monday. That'll give you and Milstead seven days to get ready; and me seven days to get stronger. It would have the wrong effect to resign as an invalid; I'll do it on my feet, from the Oval Office."

He paused. "You've known this was coming. If not now, then almost certainly sometime this year. D'you have a vice president in mind?"

"Marianne," Valenzuela said. "She has an instinct for discerning the correct action in a situation. And politically, the combination of her and myself would truly mark this as a new era." He paused, eyeing Haugen. "A new era that you have taken us into. You and the circumstances, of course."

"And Jumper," the president added. "Jumper was the key. You know when he sprung this on me on a stormy night last October, it startled hell out of me; I was totally unprepared. So I put him off till morning; wouldn't answer yes or no. But after he left the hotel and I went to bed, I lay there feeling all sorts of stuff going on subliminally, and I knew then I was going to do it. And I wasn't scared; I was excited. Then I went to sleep and dreamed furiously all night long. Getting ready.

"It seemed to me that I was the right man, or a right man, for the time and place. And I figured that if Jumper was willing to ride with his knowingness, and choose me on short acquaintance when there were all those hungry politicians available, experienced in government, lots of them bright and skilled . . . He had to have a hell of a lot of self-confidence and balls." The president smiled and shook his head. "There's more to Jumper than people notice. That's why I kept him as vice president so long when he didn't want the job. Until I found someone else I liked for it as well."

"You might want to tell him that," said Valenzuela.

"It'd be better if you told him. He never believed me. And he'd know I'd told other people what I thought of him; that I hadn't just been stringing him along." Haugen shook his head. "I don't know why he was so afraid of becoming president. It occurred to me once that his name might have something to do with it—Cromwell. But he's named after Thomas, not Oliver."

The president's voice had become tired; now he shifted in his chair again. "I guess we've said what we need to here." Gingerly he got up, leaning forward to get his weight as much as possible over his knees, then pressed down with his right hand on the arm of the chair and stood.

"The country may not know it," he added, "but it's time to graduate from having the general's president in charge."

Actually, he could probably function for a year or more, he told himself. But his condition would be conspicuous before then. He'd been noticing it for a couple of months, himself, and had ascribed it to the job.

Then, on Friday, he'd had that physical exam that Singleton had urged. He needed to tell Lois about it. Today would be good. But it was no time to tell the nation.

FIFTY-FOUR

Resigning wasn't just a matter of writing a statement, signing some forms, and saying "I quit" before cameras in the Oval Office, but Haugen didn't make a production of it, either. He simply told the nation that "the old man" had been waiting to "sleep late, lie in the sun, and fish a lot." And since the recovery had really picked up steam, and people were making things go right, and he had a vice president who could not only do the job—Cromwell could have too—but who was happy to do it, it was time for him to leave.

It didn't involve a turnover of government, with extensive briefing of the new president. Valenzuela had been part of the government, and had been acting as president for more than two weeks. And like Haugen, he inherited a functioning, in-place executive office staff that was dedicated and efficient. Only John Zale and Stephen Flynn left when Arne Haugen did, and neither had been part of the regular executive staff.

It was a breezy morning in mid-March when Arne and Lois Haugen, private citizens, disembarked from the shuttle copter at Andrews Air Force Base and walked thirty yards to the Rockwell T-39. Arne suspected it was the same executive jet that had brought him to the capital less than six months before. That had been at night in a rain storm; now white clouds sailed briskly across day-blue sky, the air seeming to chill whenever one of them cut off the sun.

The government was flying the Haugens home to Duluth, with the six Secret Service agents assigned to them. (Stephen Flynn had left for Albany the day before to visit his parents.) The Haugens departure had not been announced, and the press was not there. They'd said their goodbyes to the White House domestic staff, and to Milstead, and to Martinelli who, wet-eyed, had hugged her ex-boss—gently, for he still wore a cast and had pins in his left shoulder blade.

President Valenzuela could not see them off. He'd left the evening before on Air Force One, to meet in Vancouver with Prime Ministers Byrnes and Beliveau of Great Britain and Canada. Vice President Marianne Weisner and Jumper Cromwell were the Haugens' farewell committee.

The Air Force personnel were courteous and respectful, as always, and when the Haugens had boarded, Arne shook hands with all of them. Then, after the preflight routine was completed, the small jet took off. The city passed beneath, both Arne and Lois watching as it gave way to a patchwork of developments, woods and fields. Shortly the landscape became dominated by long low mountain ridges extending southwest to northeast, covered mostly with winter-bare forest. Somewhere down in that general region, Arne knew, was Camp David; he and Lois never had gotten there.

He looked across at her. She seemed pensive too; obviously they had adjustments to make. He decided to start his as of right then, with a reading binge, and from his travel bag took a paperback novel: *Once More Into the Wishing Well*. The cover showed a banded, jovian planet, and a ship that had just launched a spherical probe. Undoubtedly manned. Liisa had brought the book with her when she'd arrived to help her mother organize their move.

Anderson. How long has the old master been writing? Forty-five years at a guess, Haugen told himself as he settled back to read. *After all those years, all those books, his muse is still healthy, still keeps up its varied flow.*

His last thought before immersing his attention in the novel was to wonder if he had a muse? He'd soon find out. Or perhaps the term didn't apply to reciting memoirs onto tape.

Muse or whatever, he wouldn't ask any long-term production of it.

FIFTY-FIVE

They stayed in Duluth only a week, then spent a couple of days in Grand Forks with Liisa and Ed, and two more in Canoga Park, California where their son had a computerized film animation lab. From there they flew to Maui, where a friend had made available his vacation place near the beach.

They were on Maui for ten weeks, with a break of several days in Honolulu where Lois had further immunotherapy. The treatments had not cured her cancer, but simply reduced it; the retreatment was to keep it controlled. She declined more heroic treatment.

Arne's problem was amyotrophic lateral sclerosis. The symptoms were more definite now; his fine movements were a little slower and less precise. It would be downhill from here on.

Even so, he exercised, walked, swam, and stretched, but somewhat more moderately than before his presidency. His recuperative powers were noticeably less. And he read some of the mail sent to him, including an occasional letter from friends in government—Valenzuela, Grosberg, Liederman, Cromwell, Dirksma.

His principal activity, and Lois's, was preparing his memoirs. Including the history of the scalar resonance transmitters—their early Soviet development, the evidence for ET visits, the history of Soviet-USA technical exchanges, weatherwar, seismic attack, and the strike against Pavlenko.

He'd already sold limited North American rights to Random House, Commonwealth rights (excepting Canadian) to Ploughshare Books, and all other international publication rights to Iwaki House in Japan. While he could hardly imagine that the Valenzuela government would slap an injunction on the book under the Official Secrets Act—for one thing, the media had already speculated convincingly that there'd been a weatherwar and a seismic war—he had a history of making sure of things. And it was time that the public got the information, now, in the warm sunlight of an expanding economy and national confidence.

The two of them worked on it four or five hours a day, outdoors in the ocean breeze, beneath a sunscreen. Arne taped; Lois sat at one computer and typed; he rewrote on the screen of another. Once a week a private courier flew to each publisher, carrying what they'd finished. It went fairly rapidly and without real effort. Every second week, disks and hard copy came back, edited and with questions, and twice his editor flew to Maui from the wilds of Manhattan.

Then, in mid-June, they flew first to Honolulu, then to Los Angeles and D.C. The two houses of Congress were seating a joint constitution committee to develop constitutional amendments for consideration by Congress and ratification by the state legislatures. The results could range from a rewrite—a new constitution—to no change at all.

And the leadership had invited Arne Haugen to make the keynote address.

The ex-president looked a little leaner and a little older than they remembered him, but walking to the lectern, he seemed as vigorous as before, and tanned from his weeks in Hawaii.

When he reached the lectern, he looked the audience over—the members of the Senate and House, the president, the Supreme Court, the cabinet, and as always, the media and selected guests. It occurred to him that if someone blew the place up now, or laid in a quick-freeze, Jumper Cromwell might end up head of government in spite of himself. But no; his eyes didn't find Marianne here. Perhaps that was a deliberate safeguard.

He turned and nodded to Ken Lynch, who'd introduced him. "Thank you, Mr. Speaker," he said, then faced his audience again. "I want to express my appreciation to the Congress for inviting me, because I do have things to say. And to the people of America, who's guts and resilience and adaptability have brought us so far in our national recovery that now the nation can really attend to its future.

"I'd like to stand up here and give you a short, warm, possibly sentimental address, or maybe a pep talk. But instead I'm going to say what needs to be said, because I don't intend to speak to the nation again.

"We're sometimes advised to live in the present. It's the only place we truly can live, because only in the present can we act. We are always in the present; it's a moving point that travels with us through time, and its track is the past.

"We create our future by what we do in the present. It can be a future of slavery and poverty, of poison and degradation, or one with a high degree of justice and freedom, opportunity and satisfaction. And it will depend to a considerable degree on the wisdom exercised in this year in this building, by the members of this congress and its constitution committee."

He paused to scan the chamber, his eyes stopping on Tim Brosnan, who would chair the committee. "History can be an important source of that wisdom. Recent work in the new universal field theory suggests that when we have learned to separate our intuitions from our prejudices, our inspirations from our aberrations, then our intuitions will be more reliable than data. And my own intuition is that this is correct. But that's still theoretical physics, it's not yet technology, and at least for now, government must pay attention to what the past has to teach us.

"Too often, human beings have learned the wrong lessons from the past. Repeatedly, history has been used as inspiration for hatred and vengeance. And you will find people who would have you poison this Constitution with the bitterness of yesterday. It would be unfortunate if something like that happened, but I'm confident it won't. There is too much wisdom in Congress for that.

"Somewhat more than two hundred years ago, a gathering similar to this one was seated in Philadelphia to do the same sort of thing this Congress will do—it decided on the ground rules for the United States of America. And they wrote a constitution that, with the Bill of Rights, allowed as much personal freedom as they thought was compatible with the overall welfare. A constitution that was basic enough, wise enough, with enough understanding of human nature, that given an occasional amendment, it functioned well for more than a century, and more or less adequately till quite recently."

Haugen paused to sip lemon water before going on.

"Some of you have read a 'Modern Constitution for the United States of America,' a document developed by the Holist Councils Panel for Constitution Reform. That proposed constitution is based on principles drastically different from those in the constitution we're familiar with. Basically, the Holist constitution assumes that the American people are too ignorant, unruly, and foolish to be allowed the ultimate power. Or any real power. It assumes that all decisions, including who holds office, must be in the hands of an assumed elite.

"But the people do have that power, regardless. If somehow the Holist constitution, or anything like it, was proclaimed for this nation, after the troubles we've recently experienced and the renewed hopes we've more recently tasted, there would be riots to make those of last fall seem like Sunday School picnics, and I doubt that the military would prevail against them even if it tried. Which I doubt. And the elitists would be lucky to get out of the country alive.

"That would be quite in keeping with the view expressed by the founding fathers of this nation. Writing their views for their editing and signatures in the Declaration of Independence, Thomas Jefferson declared that when a government clearly intended to reduce a people under despotism—" he paused, looked around, then suddenly beat the air with a thick finger in rhythm with his swelling words—"then 'it is their right, it is their duty, to throw off such Government.' "

Again he paused, looking about, almost fierce, almost glaring, then relaxed and spoke more softly.

"I mention that only to make the point that the power resides in the people regardless of any constitution, and things will go much better if we keep that always in mind, operating on that principle. I feel utterly confident that this Congress will not consider such a constitution. I know this Congress well enough to have no fear of that.

"But I *am* concerned about the lobbies, the special

interests, that will clamor in the corridors and wheedle and coax. That is and should and must be their right. But they are experts, usually highly paid experts, at influencing and confusing. And they are here for only one purpose: To gain advantages for their employers, their special interests, and most often those advantages will reduce liberty, add heads to the bureaucracy and complexity to government.

"So I beseech this Congress and their committee: Do not let those lobbyists dilute the liberties, the responsibilities, and the powers of the American people. Listen to them with a skeptical ear and a hard heart. Hear their points, which may be good, *promise nothing*, then turn your backs on them and walk away. After making sure your wallet is still in your pocket."

He stopped talking for a long moment then, to scan again the assembled congressmen, his eyes stopping here and there. "I see three members of the Holist Council's Panel for Constitutional Reform seated among your members: I even noticed the name of one of them on your joint constitution committee: Senator Morville.

"They have every right to be here. But I do want to point out a few facts to them, and to any who find that Holist constitution attractive. First, we have climbed out of depression partly by backing away from elitism and providing new power and responsibility to the people as individuals.

"There are some who say that we reversed our decline by calling in a dictator, and there is some truth in that. But it succeeded only because, in this case, IN THIS CASE, that dictator started at once to return responsibility and power to the people.

"Actually they'd never lost it. The people always had the power in America; they just hadn't been exercising it. Too many had been brainwashed into thinking it belonged to someone else. But when things got bad enough, they started exercising it again. They started in the streets. And if the army and the marines had begun to agree with them, and refused to fire on them, we might have plunged into a mob-ocracy, which could have turned into a brutish feudalism.

"So Americans, if you want to keep this land a land of

justice and opportunity and freedom, see that your constitution provides workable democratic ground rules. Follow
the lead of the Constitution we've had all along, and this
time take responsibility for what happens afterward without waiting for things to go to hell."

He stood quiet for several seconds; the chamber was
utterly still.

"Because the biggest trouble with the one we have is
that we allowed it to be corrupted, partly by 'gimme-
ism,' which I've talked about before, partly by a legal
system that put too much power in the hands of a legally
knowledgeable elite, and partly by"—

Once more he paused. "I hate to say it, but partly by
conspiracy. Last winter we uncovered a long-standing,
deliberate conspiracy that we kept quiet about until the
investigation could be completed."

Haugen stopped there and looked his audience over
carefully. "Conspiracy. A loaded word. Let's unload it
before I give the particulars. Usually conspiracy implies
illegal acts, criminal acts. But drawing up the Declaration
of Independence was a criminal act within the British
Empire, and Paul Revere was a conspirator when he rode
to warn the minutemen. So there are conspiracies we've
admired.

"The conspiracy I refer to here, however, the conspiracy that helped corrupt our democracy, was *not* illegal.
The men who conspired acted within their rights, though
against ours. They called themselves the *Archons*. The
term Archons was originally applied to the ruling aristo-
crats in Athens before the Athenian democracy. Later, in
the early Christian church, the term 'archons' was applied
to a theoretical kind of spiritual beings who were higher
than the angels.

"So we see how our American archons viewed themselves.
Originally there were six of them, and their names were
from the who's who in American finance in the late eighteen hundreds. Their heirs were with us till this year. I'd
like to read to you what they were up to, in the words of
their founder, the man they acknowledged as their leader."

Haugen held up a looseleaf folder. "The original to this
photocopy has been sent to the National Museum," he
said, then opening it, began to read aloud. "The title page

reads, 'Opening Address to the 1928 Meeting of the Archon Fellowship,' and it is signed 'John Simmons Massey.' " Haugen turned a page. "Copies will be available; I'll give you some excerpts. These are Massey's own words. They start out:

> The recent book *Holism and Evolution*, by General Jan Christian Smuts of the South African Union, has given us perspective and a comprehensive framework for a refinement and reaffirmation of our initial Statement of Principles as written and agreed upon in 1880.

Haugen looked up. "Eighteen eighty. We're not dealing with something new here." He looked down at the booklet again. "Massey goes on to say:

> Given that the Peoples of the World are, for better or for worse, its mutually dependent Co-Inhabitants; and that the average Citizen of whatever Nation is neither rational nor gifted with suitable Intelligence or Foresight; and that there are those of us who *are* so gifted, as witness our general Competencies and Successes and the breadth and boldness of our Reach, as reflected in our accrual of Wealth, Power and Honours; it therefore behooves us to assume the Helm and steer the Species of Man toward a new and higher Condition and Polity and then to rule it. It is our Destiny and the Destiny of our Species that we do this. And it is Time.

Again Haugen looked up. "It is desirable and usual that men of competence, able men, dominate government. The more competent, the better. The question is, how much power should they have? And subject to what popular control? I'll look at that with you shortly, but just now I want to get back to the words of John Simmons Massey."

He picked up the binder again.

> Since we agreed upon that wording, 48 years ago in April of 1880, many things have changed, includ-

ing in large part our membership, but the truth of those words is more evident than ever.

And during the nearly five decades since that concordat was signed, we have made much progress. Indeed we have created, or seen to the creation of, a broadly functioning foundation for the attainment of our goal. Furthermore, within a decade we can expect to see very major progress following the unprecedented economic depression that will soon strike this nation.

It has been a matter of establishing, or of directly or indirectly gaining control of, appropriate institutions; of selecting, encouraging, and supporting the right people; and of course of indoctrinating with our principles more and more people who are or will be executives, professionals, or otherwise influential and powerful people.

And as far as possible getting others to do our work for us. Of letting those people, those offices, those institutions, forward our programs on their own.

And most particularly, appointing the right people to key chairmanships in prestigious universities. For it is from those universities that our most influential leaders will come. And not only do those chairmen influence bright young minds from their lecterns. They hold the keys to appointments! And advancement! And curricula! And to who sits on what committees!

To be sure, this manner of operation has meant that our control has been extremely loose, and efficiency undeniably low. But close control has not been available to us. And efficiency has been low only in a narrow sense, for our progress has been steady, while our investments of time and money have not been extreme, and have often been profitable even in the short run.

Our victories have not been cheered, of course, or even noticed, but it is necessary that we be surreptitious. We cannot afford that our goals be known.

And in time—in good time—we will take our rightful seats as government, perhaps not in our present lifetime, surely not in mine, but in a later one unquestionably. Meanwhile, for years yet to come, those whose actions we depend on must operate on their own determination, with their own energy and whatever wisdom they have, stumbling and sometimes turning aside, with mostly loose and often indirect guidance from ourselves.

Haugen stopped to sip water, then looked up. "I'm going to skip ahead now. Massey went on to say:

I mentioned General Smuts, whom I had the pleasure of meeting during his recent tenure as Prime Minister. Like some others, Smuts, with his doctrine of Holism, advanced our work without even knowing of it. For those of you not familiar with it, it takes the position that the universe itself is a vast developing organism moving step by step through a sequence of increasing integration.

Unfortunately Herr Smuts did not discuss the human fraction of that organism beyond the individual human being. But the kernel is there in his work. We may regard the entire human species as a sort of poorly developed, scarcely integrated organism with individual human beings as its cells. The roles of tissues then are filled by the trades and professions. And the destiny of man is to be an advanced organism, finely coordinated, ruled by a "brain" in the form of rational and absolute government.

Ex-president Arne Haugen looked up from the binder. "So there you have it—the philosophy of the Archons as expressed by their founder, John Simmons Massey. And it is also the philosophy behind the Holist Council. Because the Archon Fellowship is, or until recently was, the ruling body, the executive board, of the Holist Council. Now let me read to you what Massey had to say about the operating principles of the Archons:

It is obvious that when government is ours, we will need to be heavy-handed at times, particularly in the early years. But a man coerced, threatened, forced to do the right thing beneath the whip or at gunpoint, will seldom perform as well as the willing worker doing his duties because he believes in them.

On the other hand, a man who does his duties neither believing nor disbelieving, but simply because they are his duties, is even more to be desired. Because he does not question or decide, but simply obeys. So we must continue to entice, to nudge, to tempt the professions of psychology and psychiatry and pharmacology, and indeed science as a whole, to develop the roots of knowledge which can produce that kind of unquestioning human cell.

Not that we want such citizens yet, of course. We do not want an obedient public until *we* are the government. But it is appropriate to develop and test the theories and techniques. . . . '"

Haugen stopped reading, stood unmoving for a moment, then closed the notebook and looked up. "Those are the words of John Simmons Massey, then the world's richest and most influential man, spoken and written down on Anhinga Island, Georgia, April 19, 1928. He died three years later, to be succeeded by his grandson Charles and later by his great-grandson, the late Paul Willard Randolph Massey.

"As for the actions of the Archons—before the turn of the century, that small group of extremely rich men began to establish chairs of philosophy and medicine, of pharmacology and psychology, of journalism and economics and law, in a number of our universities. And of course, their financial power allowed the Archons to dictate who should hold those chairs—who the chairmen should be that developed and controlled curricula, appointed professors, granted awards, influenced who got advanced degrees and honors, and so forth.

"And they filled many of those positions with men of good will and good intelligence, but who held certain viewpoints and could be influenced. They depended heavily on people of good will, people well known for their good will, though they preferred men of ill will in certain positions of power.

"In time they would expand by forming what came to be called the Holist Council, made up of scores of able and often prominent men. And very few of those men knew there was such a thing as the Archon Fellowship, or what kind of overall program their projects were the pieces of.

"And out of all this grew important aspects of our society, our government, our law."

Haugen leaned his forearms on the lectern, looking not at all like an Old Testament prophet; looking instead, just now, both intimate and mild. "I'll admit this has sounded more like a prosecutor's oration than a keynote address, but let me take it a little further and tell you what the Archons have been up to recently.

"Up till now I've stressed those Archon activities that were legal. But not all of them were. Not many months ago we had a psychotic, Dr. Carlton Blackburn, as head of the CIA. Having worked his way there through Covert Operations. Investigation found him guilty of a gruesome pattern of sadism and murders, and he suicided rather than face trial. Under the pseudonym Dr. William Merriman, Blackburn had secretly set up a private weekend psychiatric practice in Connecticut, where he did pain-drug-hypnosis conditioning for the victims of his private clients. He was also the brain behind several murders disguised as natural deaths. Notably for the late Paul Willard Massey, who until last winter was the head of the Archons and the chairman of the Holist Council. Massey, as you recall from the news coverage, committed suicide last January after murdering his long-time executive secretary for Holist affairs.

"Four others of the Archons were arrested for insider trading and other financial crimes. One suicided before he could be tried. Three are in prison. Two have talked freely to the FBI, filling holes in our evidence.

"And now we come to terrorist violence. The kingpin in the terrorist group that nuked the Calvert Cliffs power plant was arrested by the FBI last January and told us who he got the bomb from. We kept this confidential, to give the FBI an opportunity to follow the track of the bomb, which in fact was a 203 mm artillery shell stolen from a French army ordnance bunker. The shell was then put on the market, and the successful bid was from—" He looked around. "Paul Willard Massey's executive secretary through a short series of vias that were not hard to verify, once we'd questioned Massey's confederates.

"Well. Enough of that. You now have some insights into the people and the intentions behind the Holist constitution.

"I want to point out to you that there will always be people with what we may call the Archon attitude; persons who consider it only proper to enslave their fellow man. And—*people have a right to think like that*. And they have a right to meet, and to plan, and to carry out the kind of *legal* acts that the Archons carried out! If they don't have those rights, then liberty is dead in America.

"Most of what they did was to nurture and spread and channel traits and weaknesses already present and operating in human beings. Including greed and arrogance and fear and irresponsibility. But also their opposites—decency, the desire to help, willingness to do things for others. They made use of all of these, bad and good, bending them to their purposes. And we cannot legislate against having a philosophical and political program that operates within reasonable laws; not and retain any meaningful human liberties. We cannot outlaw people like the Archons, we can only beware of them.

"The Archons, in failing, have reminded and warned us of what we can expect and what we need to watch for. And the best protection against people like them is a strong public respect for freedom, opportunity, and justice, and a rejection of 'gimme,' and 'it's all your fault,' or 'it's all their fault.' You and I are as responsible for what happened as they were.

"In this universe, freedom cannot be separated from responsibility. To try to have it otherwise is ultimately to fail. And that includes not only freedom without responsibility. It also includes demanding responsibility without granting the freedom to carry it out.

"I hope very much that the joint constitution committee, and the congressional deliberations that will follow it, will keep that in mind.

"Because the people, to carry out *their* responsibilities, must have the freedom to carry them out. Thus I urge that this committee and this Congress will establish a clause or constitutional amendment providing for national referenda in which the citizens of these United States can express their will directly into law.

"I hope this committee and this Congress will reject elitism, even benevolent elitism, and see to it that opportunity and accountability are assured to all the people.

"Incidentally, the basic definition of *elite* is 'those who are the most skilled. The best.' Elite is a great thing to be. The baseball elite plays in the All Star game; the elite of that elite will be voted into the Hall of Fame.

"*Elitists*, on the other hand, are those who believe in *elitism*. And elitism is *rule or domination by an elite group, or a* supposedly *elite group, or the belief that such a group has the right to rule*. And elitism is a dangerous road for at least two reasons: Elitists, even if they are truly elite, overrate themselves. They consider their own opinions to be correct and that others should abide by them. There will then become standard ways to think and act, and the nation will stultify, decay, and come apart.

"The key to a successful future for mankind, I'm convinced, is a pluralistic society, a nation that allows as many ways of doing things as feasible, within the limits necessary to keep people from trampling each other's rights. A multiform society that is tolerant of differences, protective of differences, that even encourages differences. And a creative society, one that encourages new developments, in science, in art, in technology. A society that encourages man to explore outward into the galaxy, and inward into whatever we might find there.

"As your president, I tried to start things in that direction. But now it is up to you the Congress and you the People to either carry it through or reject it."

Arne Haugen paused and looked thoughtfully into the cameras in front of him. "And that, my fellow human beings, my fellow Americans, is all I have to say today, except to wish you all well. And to make it clear now, in case it hasn't been apparent, that it was an incredible adventure to serve as your president. I loved it; I ate it up; and I wish for each of you something that will mean as much to you as being your president meant to me."

Afterward there was a reception, and to the anxiety of their Secret Service detail, the ex-president and first lady mingled with the crowd for nearly an hour before leaving.

Again the executive jet flew them, and their body guards,

to Duluth. It was home, and summer had come there. They would rest a few days, two or three, because their health was slipping, then polish up the Haugen presidential memoirs—it was not a large book—and turn them back to the editors.

Arne had already assigned authority to his attorney and to Ed Ruud to handle any problems in publication if he wasn't able to himself.

FIFTY-SIX

It was 0950 on a sunny, late September morning. At the sound of the door chimes, agent Frank Shapiro put down his magazine and stood up, not to answer, but be ready. A minute later, John Zale came into the room from an inner hall, carrying a package. "The galley proofs for the chief's book," he said, holding it up. "The courier's here to get them."

Shapiro nodded, but he stayed on his feet, going to a window from which he could see the courier's parked car. The Haugens had been staying pretty much secluded. When they'd first arrived back in Duluth, the ex-president had granted an interview to a local TV station, and another to the newspaper, but since then, nothing.

Shapiro had been aware that something was wrong with Haugen's health, but he hadn't known what until he'd overheard Haugen's daughter talking with *her* daughter. Lou Gehrig's disease. He'd looked it up then. Arne was going to get weaker and weaker, bit by bit losing control of his body, dying slowly. Shapiro wasn't looking forward to the next couple of years, especially the last one.

Although Arne still looked pretty good. He'd shrunk a bit, as if he'd been cutting down on the calories, but he no longer swam, or worked out at all as far as Shapiro knew. And he'd lost his old vigor, and that hard, strong look the White House detail had commented on to each other when he'd first come to Washington.

It was Lois who'd lost ground conspicuously. The world knew of her cancer now, had known since they'd gone to Maui. She'd been in the hospital again, two weeks earlier, for another brief round of therapy. Just before that, she'd sent off her own manuscript—the story of the White House domestic staffs, she'd told him, dating back to Jefferson.

Frank wasn't looking forward to watching her weaken and die, either. Lois and Arne were as well-liked by the agents as any first family had been—better than most.

He saw the courier go down the short sidewalk, get into the car, and drive down the horseshoe drive to the road. In his mind's eye, Shapiro tried to visualize the yard deep in snow, the temperature far below zero; he was from Sarasota, Florida.

"You'll like winter here," Zale had told him. "Once we've had a pair of touring skis on you, you won't want to leave."

Arne said it was winter here by Thanksgiving, and Thanksgiving was only two months away. It had already been freezing at night.

One evening the week previous, the agents on duty had donned sweaters and jackets and gone out on the front lawn with the Haugens, to sit quietly on lawn chairs and watch the aurora borealis, their non-alcoholic drinks almost forgotten in their hands. It was an evening Shapiro would remember the rest of his life; it had left a sense of closeness with the Haugens that he never expected to feel again with someone he was assigned to protect.

A door knob moved behind him, and Shapiro turned. Arne and Lois came into the room. "Frank," Arne said, "we need to talk to you and Gil. Is he in the front hall?"

Gil was in charge of the Haugen detail. Frank spoke into the small radio he carried clipped to his belt, and a minute later, Gil came into the room.

"Why don't we all sit down," Arne said.

They did, the agents somehow ill at ease.

The ex-president smiled at them. "Guys," he said, "Lois

and I have talked it over, and we want you to go back to Washington. We like every one of you, but it's time for us to be on our own. Anything you want to say about that?"

"Yes sir," Gil answered matter-of-factly. "Crainey Branard isn't the only nut in the world who might decide you ought to be killed. That's why we're here. And—" He paused, then went on. "You're more vulnerable now; you don't get around physically the way you did a year ago."

Arne nodded. "All too true. Lois and I have considered both those facts, but we've decided to take our chances."

"There's another thing," Gil said.

"Yes?"

"We're not authorized to leave you. If you ordered us off the premises, we'd leave, but we'd still try to keep the place covered from the street or wherever."

"We understand that too; we assumed that's the way it was. So what I'd like you to do is phone Secret Service headquarters in Washington. Get me connected with whoever I need to talk to to get protection discontinued."

Gil thinned his lips. "Before I do that, Mr. Haugen, is there something we can do about whatever's bothering you? About having us here? Maybe we can talk it out."

Arne Haugen grinned. "Gil, Frank, you're friends of the family. And more considerate than some friends might be. But—" He shook his head. "We've made up our minds. We'd like to be alone, unwatched. We'd like to be able to go somewhere, if we want, without you fellows following."

Gil nodded unhappily. "Okay, sir. I'll place the call for you." He went to the phone on a nearby table and, Arne Haugen standing by, dialed a sequence of digits. On this particular line, it connected him with the Protective Division of the Secret Service.

"Mr. Kossuth, please," he said. "This is Agent Rogers in Duluth, Minnesota." The screen went blank. After a moment, a man's face flicked onto it. "Mr. Kossuth, this is SAIC Rogers, with the Haugen detail in Duluth. Mr. Haugen would like to talk to you."

Arne repeated his wish to Kossuth, who at first assumed, as Gil had, that there'd been some friction or annoyance. When Haugen had made clear that this wasn't the case, Kossuth transferred his call to the director. Again, patiently, the ex-president repeated his request, answering essentially the same questions. The director too was less than happy, but the ex-president was within his rights. It was agreed that the detail would be discontinued at noon, central daylight time.

When the conversation was over, Haugen called the other agents at their local residences, and Gil and Frank phoned their wives. The Haugen cook, forewarned and assisted by the Haugens, prepared a lunch worthy of one of the better restaurants—a mini-smörgåsbord. Then, along with the Haugens and Zales, the agents and their wives enjoyed a farewell meal.

While they were eating, Valenzuela phoned. The Secret Service had called, telling him of the Haugens' request, and Arne explained to him too. "Arne," Val said, "you are a national resource." But he didn't press.

That afternoon, when the agents had left, Arne Haugen dictated letters of commendation for each of them, and Zale ran them off on Haugen's elegant bond stationery. Afterward, Lois typed two letters to Arne's dictation—instructions to his lawyer with a copy for Ed, and a short one to Jumper Cromwell. Arne's typing was clumsy these days; his coordination was slipping more than his strength. And these were letters that were not for Zale to know about. When they came out of the printer and Arne had added his now-crabbed signature, she addressed and stamped the envelopes and sealed the letters in them, and Arne put them out for the mailman to pick up when he came by the next noon. He specifically told the housekeeper not to mail them on her way home. He didn't want them delivered prematurely.

Lois also typed a long letter from both of them to each of their children.

That evening the couple went off by themselves for a late supper in the Skyview Restaurant atop the four-year-old Saint Croix Hotel, overlooking Lake Superior. The restaurant's walls and roof were seamless molded Duluth Thermoglass, a Haugen product. They'd reserved one of the small, semi-detached rooms. Again the aurora was superb, from the recent solar flare activity. When they'd finished their meal, he turned the light off and they sat quietly watching, hands clasped loosely atop the table.

*   *   *

The next morning they drove up the north shore. The sky was clear, the view softened by autumn haze. The breeze was offshore, and only modest waves broke upon the beach. Here and there, gulls wheeled, mewling.

They stopped at a highway restaurant just outside Silver Bay, for midmorning coffee, and took a table facing out a window, that they might not be spotted for who they were. The waitress recognized them, but Arne pressed ten dollars in her hand and said they wanted privacy. She nodded. He suspected that silence would not be easy for her.

As they waited, they looked down the hill at the big taconite refinery, with a huge ore ship at the dock. Shipments had increased to near full capacity, he'd read, and people thought of the depression as over. Unemployment was at eight percent "and falling," much of it in tourism; people hadn't gotten back into vacationing much yet.

Some locals were drinking coffee and eating pie, talking and laughing. Pulpwood contracts were being let in the jackpine and aspen up north of Isabella, and logging had started on a big sale of fir and spruce on the Tofte District. Arne enjoyed listening to them. They weren't too unlike the men he'd known as a youth, although had he spoken Scandinavian to them, or Finnish, probably none would have understood a word of it.

When the Haugens walked to the cash register, one of the men glanced at them and his eyebrows raised, but he said nothing just then. A lanky blond man, aproned, came out of the kitchen to take their money, and he obviously recognized them too. Outside, holding Lois's car door open for her, Arne was aware of faces at the windows, staring out, and he grinned without looking up at them.

North of Silver Bay, the highway took them higher, winding along the contour of steep and sometimes cliffy slopes well above the shore, and across occasional small gorges whose streams cascaded and foamed and plunged their way down from the plateau to join their clear waters with the icy lake. Farther north, the highway came down close to shore level again, sometimes within sight of the water, at others bordered by forest on both sides.

Before long they saw a large rustic wooden sign ahead, the letters routed into it announcing "Bjerke's Resort."

Arne turned off there, the driveway taking them through birch and balsam and spruce. The lodge was built of lathe-turned pine poles, neatly fitted at the corners. A smallish stream, quiet here so near its mouth, flowed past to join the nearby lake. A row of cabins faced the stream, a dozen yards back from its edge. Rowboats were tied along the bank.

Arne parked and they entered the lodge, where a tall, rawboned man with iron-gray hair and a large mustache watched them in from behind the counter.

"Hallå Haugen!" he said. *"Er dette faktiskt din kone?"* ["Is this one really your wife?"]

"Ja visst!" ["Yeah, sure."]

The man grinned. ["That's what you said about the other ones."]

["No, this one is really her. We're on our honeymoon."]

Bjerke looked at Lois. "Well," he said, "good luck with him. He ain't so bad when you get to know him." He took a key from the array on the wall. "You folks got cabin number two. Why don't you let me take your bags for you? While you go in and order dinner."

"No," said Arne, "I'll take them." He grinned. "I'm not that old yet."

The two small suitcases Arne took to the cabin were even lighter than they appeared. He put them on the luggage stands without opening them, and after a bath-room break, they went back to the lodge for dinner, a term applied here to the midday meal. One of the Bjerke granddaughters waited on them, young, blond, and pretty, pink-cheeked through her tan. When the food arrived, he and Lois ate slowly, saying little, but often their hands touched.

When they'd finished, they went back to the cabin. Lois lay down to rest, while Arne went out and looked over the boat that went with the cabin rental. It was graceful, clinkerbuilt, with tholepins for two rowers.

The cabin had a tiny shed built on. Haugen unlocked the door and checked the gas in the outboard motor there. It was full, they always were, and so was the can. Sig Bjerke didn't overlook things like that.

As Arne closed the shed door, his mind went to Stephen Flynn. Steve would not approve, not at all. But then,

Steve operated with certain fixed beliefs. Haugen wondered if, at some subliminal level, the Jesuit knew what they were doing—felt conscious discomfort and wondered what it was from.

I'll know more about things like that before the sun comes up again, he told himself. *Probably a lot more. That or nothing.*

In the cabin, Lois lay with her eyes closed, but she opened them when her husband came in. He went to the television and turned it on, then looked at the card and dialed to the local time and weather channel. The forecast hadn't changed. He turned it off again, and smiling, lay down beside Lois, putting out his arm as a pillow. She lay her head on it.

"Are you ready?" he asked softly.

She looked at him. "Yes," she said, and smiled. They'd talked about this years ago, discussed it months before on Maui, had made their plans then and gotten used to them. It felt comfortable to be here.

"Then I suppose we ought to get started."

Without saying more, they both got up, took wool sweaters from their bags, and waterproofs. Lois turned the TV back on while Arne went out and lugged the outboard motor to the boat, clamping it to the stern. Next he brought down the oars, which looked little used, and the can of outboard motor fuel.

Lois came out of the cabin and held up an envelope with "Sig" written on it. It held twenty one-hundred-dollars bills, and an explanatory note she'd written in advance. Handwriting too was difficult for Arne these days. The boat and motor were worth perhaps half the two thousand, in the money of the time, but the amount seemed appropriate.

They went back into the cabin, and while Arne was in the bathroom, Lois put the envelope on the table. Then they stood watching the local forecast one more time. After that, holding hands, waterproofs under their opposite arms, they walked down to the boat and got in. Arne started the motor and steered them down the current, past the gravel bar deposited by storm waves, and onto the lake. Now beach waves lifted and dropped the bow, splashing. There was no clear sign of the storm yet, but the wind was picking up a bit, out of the west.

Farther from shore, he steered on a heading of east southeast. A hundred or so miles that way lay the Upper Peninsula of Michigan. He looked at Lois; she smiled at him and he smiled back. It would be a joke on them if they got that far. But their gas wouldn't last, and the disease had stolen too much of his strength for him to row more than briefly. Though he'd give it his best, if the storm hadn't already swamped them.

He breathed deeply of the chill lake air. "We're on our way, Babe," he said.

She nodded. "We are. It's been a good trip all the way." Her look was fond. "I can't imagine it with anyone else."

He had nothing to add to that. His right hand on the tiller, he looked ahead, paying no attention to the shore diminishing behind them. It was time to change adventures, see what was on the other side.

EPILOGUE

The envelope in General Cromwell's basket had lettered on it: *For Jumper's Eyes Only,* and had been left unopened by his secretary. The return address on it bore no name. He was pretty sure the lettering was not Arne Haugen's, but the town was Duluth, Minnesota.

Cromwell snipped off an end, drew out the letter, and unfolded it. The letterhead was Arne's. He began to read.

Dear Jumper,
By the time you get this, Lois and I will have made the news again.
I want to thank you and Kevin Donnelly for the

most wonderful five months of my life. I came out of it loving my country and the rest of the world more than I'd ever known was possible. I hope Val comes out feeling the same way after two (or six?) years.

The media are going to call what Lois and I are doing suicide, and that's a reasonable evaluation. But we don't think of it that way. For a long time we've talked about going out on our terms, when the time came and if we had the chance. Her physical condition is well known, and mine should be too by now; my attorney was to release it. It's called Amyotrophic lateral sclerosis. So anyway, now is the time.

So what we're doing is challenging the sea and all odds, in a small boat with a storm due, and the water too cold to survive in for more than minutes. No sharks though, just salmon and lake trout.

Our last hoorah! Then we'll find out what comes next: heaven, hell, nothingness, universal one-ness, or recycling. Unless, of course, we pull off a miracle, in which case we've agreed to die in bed.

I'd appreciate your giving a copy of this to the media. People may want to know what went on with us that led up to this.

It's been good knowing you, Jumper.

Love,

Arne

and Lois

Here is an excerpt from the new collection "MEN HUNTING THINGS," edited by David Drake, coming in April 1988 from Baen Books:

IT'S A LOT LIKE WAR

A hunter and a soldier on a modern battlefield contrast in more ways than they're similar.

That wasn't always the case. Captain C.H. Stigand's 1913 book of reminiscences, HUNTING THE ELEPHANT IN AFRICA, contains a chapter entitled "Stalking the African" (between "Camp Hints" and "Hunting the Bongo"). It's a straightforward series of anecdotes involving the business for which Stigand was paid by his government—punitive expeditions against native races in the British African colonies.

Readers of modern sensibilities may be pleased to learn that Stigand died six years later with a Dinka spear through his ribs; but he was a man of his times, not an aberration. Richard Meinertzhagen wrote with great satisfaction of the unique "right and left" he made during a punitive expedition against the Irryeni in 1904: he shot a native with the right barrel of his elephant gun—and then dropped the lion which his first shot had startled into view.

It would be easy enough to say that the whites who served in Africa in the 19th century considered native races to be sub-human and therefore game to be hunted under a specialized set of rules. There's some justification for viewing the colonial overlords that way. The stringency of the attendant "hunting laws" varied from British and German possessions, whose administrators took their "civilizing mission" seriously, to the Congo Free State where Leopold, King of the Belgians, gave the dregs of all the world license to do as they pleased—so long as it made him a profit.

(For what it's worth, Leopold's butchers *didn't* bring him much profit. The Congo became a Belgian—rather than a personal—possession when Leopold defaulted on the loans his country had advanced him against the colony's security.)

But the unity of hunting and war went beyond racial attitudes. Meinertzhagen was seventy years old in 1948 when his cruise ship docked in Haifa during the Israeli War of Independence. He borrowed a rifle and 200 rounds—which he fired off during what he described as "a glorious day!", increasing his personal bag by perhaps twenty Arab gunmen.

Similarly, Frederick Courteney Selous—perhaps the most famous big-game hunter of them all—enlisted at the outbreak of World War One even though he *wasn't* a professional soldier. He was sixty-five years old when a German sniper blew his brains out in what is now Tanzania.

Hunters and soldiers were nearly identical for most of the millennia since human societies became organized enough to wage war. Why isn't that still true today?

In large measure, I think, the change is due to the advance of technology. In modern warfare, a soldier who is seen by the enemy is probably doomed. Indeed, most casualties are men who *weren't* seen by the enemy. They were simply caught by bombs, shells, or automatic gunfire sweeping an area.

A glance at casualties grouped by cause of wound from World War One onward suggests that indirect artillery fire is the only significant factor in battle. All other weapons—tanks included—serve only to provide targets for the howitzers to grind up; and the gunners lobbing their shells in high arcs almost never see a living enemy.

The reality isn't quite *that* simple; but I defy anybody who's spent time in a modern war zone to tell me that they felt personally in control of their environment.

Hunters can be killed or injured by their intended prey. Still, most of them die in bed. (The most likely human victim of a hungry leopard or a peckish rhinoceros has always been an unarmed native who was in the wrong place at the wrong time.) Very few soldiers become battle casualties either—but soldiers don't have the option that hunters have, to go home any time they please.

A modern war zone is a terrifying place, if you let yourself think about it; and even at its smallest scale, guerrilla warfare, it's utterly impersonal.

A guerrilla can never be sure that the infra-red trace of his stove hasn't been spotted by an aircraft in the silent darkness, or that his footsteps aren't being picked up by sensors disguised as pebbles along the trail down which he pads. Either way, a salvo of artillery shells may be the last thing he hears—unless they've blown him out of existence before the shriek of their supersonic passage reaches his ears.

But technology doesn't free his opponent from fear—or give him personal control of the battlefield, either. When the counter-insurgent moves, he's likely to put his foot or his vehicle on top of a mine. The blast will be the only warning he has that he's being maimed. Even men protected by the four-inch steel of a tank know the guerrillas may have buried a 500-pound bomb under *this* stretch of road. If that happens, his family will be sent a hundred and fifty pounds of sand—with instructions not to open the coffin.

At rest, the counter-insurgent wears his boots because he may be attacked at any instant. Then he'll shoot out into the night—but he'll have no target except the muzzle flashes of the guns trying to kill him, and there'll be no result to point to in the morning except perhaps a smear of blood or a weapon dropped somewhere along the tree line.

If a rocket screams across the darkness, the counter-insurgent can hunch down in his slit trench and pray that the glowing green ball with a sound like a steam locomotive will land on somebody else instead. Prayer probably won't help, any more than it'll stop the rain or make the mosquitos stop biting. But nothing else will help either.

So nowadays, a soldier doesn't have much in common with a hunter. That's not to say that warfare is no longer similar to hunting, however.

On the contrary: modern soldiers and hunted beasts have a great deal in common.

APRIL 1988 * 65399-7 * 288 pp * $2.95